# GHOST TOUR

### CLARYN VAILE

Published by:
D. X. Varos, Ltd
7665 E. Eastman Ave. #B101
Denver, CO 80231

Book cover design and layout by, Ellie Bockert Augsburger of
Creative Digital Studios.
www.CreativeDigitalStudios.com
Cover design features:
Gryphon Line art Logo Design Inspiration Vector By winner
creative / Adobe Stock
Close up of golden elevator By Richard/ Adobe Stock
Full Length Portrait of a Sexy Brunette Woman in
Fashion Dress b By Milles Studio / Adobe Stock

ISBN: 978-1-941072-76-9 (paperback)
ISBN: 978-1-941072-77-6 (ebook)

## Praise for *Ghost Tour*

"...starts off as a by-the-books haunted-hotel tale, but very quickly gets a lot better than that." – Jason Bettus, *Chicago Center for Literature and Photography*

"If you're looking for a great ghost story, look no further than Ghost Tour ... Colorado writer Claryn Vaile weaves a wonderful story of the paranormal within the walls of historic yesteryear." — Linda Wommack, Colorado historian and author of *Colorado's Landmark Hotels* and *Haunted Cripple Creek & Teller County*

"Claryn Vaile brings her characters to life as they share tales of ghosts, intertwining them in the plot as they try to save the historic hotel from modernization and certain "death" for the spirits inhabiting it." — Laura V. Keegan, author of *Haunting at Remington House*

"Suspense, fright, and fun abound on every page of Claryn Vaile's exciting novel *Ghost Tour*! A vivid, gripping work, *Ghost Tour* will keep you on the edge of your seat to the last page." – Dr. Derek R. Everett, Colorado historian and author

*To S. B. James*
*The light that helps me see in the dark.*

# CHAPTER 1

When her co-worker refused to venture up to the eighth floor after midnight, Momaday Benga responded to the page. Hotel security radioed in-room dining at 2:13 a.m. to report a cart with dirty dishes outside Room 864. Though she had no memory of a delivery to that suite, Momaday hurried to remove the clutter, upholding the Griffins Keep's reputation for impeccable service.

In-room dining was the only hotel outlet that never closed. The newer hires got the overnight shifts, and Momaday didn't mind. The Senegalese refugee was grateful to have found employment in her new country, especially a job that allowed her to take evening English classes. But in the wee hours, strange encounters were not uncommon.

As Momaday stepped from the service elevator into the eighth-floor space where intersecting hallways created an odd angle, she wondered if "Rosey" might appear tonight. Rosey was the name her colleagues had given a spirit that inhabited this floor of the hotel. Both staff and guests had occasionally reported the sounds of a child running and laughing, when no such thing was visible. The spirit liked to snatch the single roses from bud vases on room service trays and stick them in the filigreed railings of the staircase. Momaday herself had heard the sounds and thought of the elusive source as a playful ghost.

But no laughing spirit greeted her tonight. As Momaday turned the corner and started toward 864, an oppressive sense of dread enveloped her. The discovery of a red lacquered cigarette holder beside dirty china on the white linen cloth puzzled her. She knew what it was from 1930s American movies, but smoking was not permitted in any of The Keep guestrooms. No cigarettes were in evidence, only the long, tapered holder. Momaday picked it up and examined it. A snake, faintly etched in black, curled around it. She shuddered. Pushing open the door to the adjacent ice machine closet, she tossed it disdainfully into the trash.

"How *dare* you!"

Momaday could not be sure whether the hate-filled voice emanated from outside or from inside her head. From the far end of the hallway came the faint sound of a child screaming. The scream grew louder until Momaday could make out its repeated alarm.

"RUN!"

She turned, pulling the cart as she scurried backwards, retreating to the elevator, fleeing whatever was coming. The muffled scream trailed off down a hallway as the service elevator's "ding" indicated its arrival, and Momaday heard the doors slide open. She felt the predatory presence close in upon her.

"Filthy colored help. That was *mine*."

Frantically scanning the empty space in the direction of the malevolent spirit's approach, Momaday backed toward the open elevator and released the cart to grope the metal doorframe. Her next step was her last.

A sickening thud resounded from far below, then silence. The screams that had echoed through the eighth-floor halls were replaced by the sound of a child softly sobbing.


Momaday was not discovered until several hours later, when her broken body, splayed across the top of the car, prevented the elevator from aligning properly with the top floor.

Veteran hotel engineer Lochlan MacKenzie, the first to clock-in on the early shift, drew the grim task of calling the police and overseeing the removal of Momaday's remains. The coroner's staff zipped the corpse into a body bag and removed it from the hotel via basement freight elevator.

Lochlan had seen a lot during his 27 years toiling behind the scenes of the Griffins Keep. But he was still shaken when he arrived in managing director Conroe Beaumont's office later that morning to report the incident, omitting his own unsettling

2

suspicion as to the cause. Something, Lochlan feared, had violated The Keep's spiritual portal. Despite the Knights' sworn vigilance, a darkness had seeped in—a dangerous darkness that could affect the physical plane.

"Momaday was liked by everyone," Lochlan told the director. "Always smiling and positive. She loved working here and she loved life. Just welcomed a new grandbaby last month. It's a tragedy, an inexplicable tragedy."

Beaumont looked up from the papers he was studying only briefly. "Probably the result of employee carelessness," he said dispassionately. "Did you ask the coroner's office to check for drugs or alcohol in her system? Couldn't have been an elevator malfunction. Christ, they just finished a 6-month rebuild on that thing. You called the contractors, too, I trust."

Lochlan felt the color rise in his cheeks and collected himself before responding. "What do you plan to tell the staff?" he asked. "Some sort of memorial gathering would be appropriate."

Beaumont shrugged. "I hardly think that will be necessary. I mean, she was only here a couple months."

Lochlan's expression made his determination clear. "Eleven months," he corrected.

"Oh, all right," Beaumont conceded. "Lemme talk to Branson about how he wants to handle it. But this couldn't have come at a worse time. Until I get back to you, not a word to anyone. We're keeping this incident strictly under wraps for now. Understood?"

Lochlan understood. But news of Momaday's death had already spread among staff in horrified whispers. Had Beaumont grasped anything about back-of-the-house dynamics, he would have known that and addressed the development immediately. Instead, he informed Lochlan an hour later that the "All-Hands" staff meeting scheduled for 3:00 that afternoon would proceed as planned.

"Branson says he's got no time to waste on a freak accident and some easily replaced employee," Beaumont said. "His words, not mine," he added defensively, dropping his gaze. "Today's announcement is too important and takes absolute priority. There will be no mention of the unfortunate incident you reported earlier. I'll send out a blanket email tomorrow. Heartfelt sympathy to her family, that sort of thing. What was her name again?"

A curious congregation of history buffs and specter seekers began to coalesce outside the Treble Clef restaurant twenty minutes before the 1:00 tour start time that afternoon. They perched on marble benches or paced the stone floor. A mixture of visitors and Denver locals, some dressed up and others dressed down, they took in the elegant surroundings as they awaited the guide.

"This place always reminds me of Venice," a white-haired woman in a red sweatshirt said, "with the columns and the arches, the scrolled panels on the balconies, the stained-glass ceiling. It's like you step through the doors from a modern Western city into another place and time."

Her balding husband agreed. "A relic from the days when architecture added to the character and aesthetic of a community."

"It's sad to see the hotel showing her age. Some tarnish here, some chipped stone over there."

"But our vision blurs as we gaze upon a faded beauty as beloved as this one." The man bent to plant a kiss upon his seated wife's head, and she patted the hand he placed on her shoulder.

"You can almost feel the traces of all the travelers who have passed through before continuing on their journeys," she said. "If I were a ghost, I'd want to spend eternity here."

"You would not be alone." The elderly woman leaning on a walker had one drooping eyelid and a lopsided face. "There are countless ghosts here."

Her middle-aged daughter felt obliged to explain. "Ever since Mother's stroke, she claims that she's attuned to the spiritual world."

"I came so close to death that they reach across to me. I hear them all around us, right now," the stroke victim said. "They tell me they're happy to be here…most of them."

"I heard the hotel is for sale," a gentleman seated nearby remarked, changing the subject.

The white-haired woman clapped her hands in sudden inspiration, looking up at her spouse expectantly. "That's it! That's what you can buy me for our 50th anniversary. You'll do that for me, won't you, dear?"

"Were it within my budget, sweetheart, I'd tie it up in a giant ribbon and present it to you," her husband vowed. "But I read the hotel cost two million to build and furnish around the turn of last

4

century. Can't even imagine what the price tag would look like today."

"It's priceless, of course," his wife said, adjusting her fanny-pack. "If I can't have it, I just hope it's bought by people who understand how much the hotel means to the city."

The tour guide arrived precisely on time, smiling much too warmly for someone about to deliver tales of terror. "Is everyone here for our first public ghost tour of October? Terrific! If you'll follow me inside, we'll get this adventure underway."

At the restaurant host stand, she checked guests' names against her reservations list. She handed out clip-on badges to distinguish them from would-be tour crashers who might try to latch on as the group moved around the premises. Tendrils of silver-touched dark hair escaped here and there from beneath her costume top hat, bedecked with cobwebs and black velvet roses. Her blue eyes, bright as gas flames, shone below thick lashes and heavy shadow. She stood scarcely five-feet tall. Her voice sounded younger than she looked, and she exuded that perkiness so prevalent among those in the tour guiding profession.

"Welcome, everyone, to the Griffins Keep hotel. My name is Rebecca Bridger, and it is my privilege to serve as the official hotel historian. I'm only the third person to hold that title since the position was created in the 1970s. People stay in this job until it kills them."

She paused, deadpan for a split-second only before breaking into a mischievous grin.

"I'm kidding, of course. I've been here just five years, so if history is any indicator—and it always is—I look forward to many more ahead here at the hotel. I'm a Colorado native and a local historian, and these ghost tours are a fun way for me to share some of that knowledge with all of you. So let's get started.

"By a show of hands, how many of you are serious believers in ghosts—may have even experienced something ghostly yourselves?"

Of the thirty-some tour-takers, eight indicated their credulity. She was always amazed, but never surprised, by the number of people who willingly admitted to accepting such absurd fantasies. Rebecca did not believe in ghosts, any more than she believed in the church or its promises of a spiritual afterlife. She had believed in such things once and longed—more than ever as her later years encroached—for their assurances of immortality.

5

But tough truths and devastating betrayals had kicked the faith out of her long ago. Rebecca's personal disillusionment made conducting The Keep's ghost tours more onerous with each successive Halloween season. But she loved her job, and she knew how to put on a show.

"All right. How many of you are hardcore skeptics—you think the whole idea of ghosts is bogus and you can't believe you got talked into taking this tour?"

Half-a-dozen hands shot up.

"OK, good. It looks like most of you are open-minded, fence-straddlers. And that's perfect. Because the intent of this tour is not to convince you one way or another as to the existence of ghosts, but simply to share some stories of unexplained phenomena that have been reported here at the hotel.

"Now, while I can't vouch for the validity of any of the stories you'll hear today, I promise you that none of these reports is made up. All are actual accounts that have come to us from hotel employees and hotel guests over the years—witnesses who insisted their experiences were absolutely real. We invite you to make of them what you will."

Rebecca could tell the tour guests were beginning to warm up to her and settle in for the ride. No matter how many tours she led, she was always a little nervous at the beginning. She wanted them to like her. But even more than that, Rebecca wanted them to share her passion for the Griffins Keep.

"A little bit of background first, to give you some context for whatever ghosts may linger here. This grand hotel was considered one of the finest in the nation when it opened in 1890. Besides an architectural gem, the building was a technological wonder for its day, with its own electrical generating dynamos in the basement, hot and cold running water provided by the artesian well still used today. And it was one of the first fireproof hotels in the country. Our architect, Edward Brookings, was from Chicago, where they'd had a little trouble with fires in the 1800s."

The historically savvy among her guests enjoyed the understatement.

"So beneath the stone veneer of The Keep, the entire superstructure is iron, steel, and concrete—not a bit of wood. Even the floors and the interior walls are made of hollow terra cotta block, a type of ceramic. The Griffins Keep is, as they bragged on our letterhead for years, an 'Absolutely Fireproof Hotel,' which really appealed to people in the 1890s, when tall buildings could be deathtraps before the fire safety regulations in place today."

The tour-takers listened politely, absorbing the set-up.

"The Griffins Keep has hosted presidents and royalty, businessmen and politicians, celebrities and socialites. For decades, the hotel's motto was 'Best Rest in the West.' because it attracted the most discerning people—just as it does today."

Rebecca made a sweeping gesture encompassing the group of tour-takers to indicate that they, too, were among the privileged to enjoy the iconic landmark.

"Millions of souls have passed through this hotel, which closed only one day in more than thirteen decades. It's easy to imagine that some of those who had the time of their lives returned for the time of their afterlives."

Rebecca tilted her hat brim a bit lower on her forehead and drew a deep breath.

"Let's wade in with an incident that happened in this very space not long ago."

A few guests who had been ready to take off touring settled back in their chairs for the story.

"This restaurant has had several names and a long history of showcasing live music. That legacy figures into the experience of one of our housemen from a few years back. He was cleaning in the atrium lobby late one night when he heard the faint sound of music coming from the Treble Clef. When he went to investigate the source, he found the restaurant locked. But housemen have a magical master key that opens everything, so in he went.

"In the far corner of the room—right over there—he discovered four gentlemen, very formally dressed, playing beautiful music on their instruments. The houseman politely requested that they pack up and go home so that he could continue his cleaning."

Everyone glanced toward the corner she'd indicated.

"With that, according to the houseman, one of the musicians smiled at him and said, 'Don't mind us, Sonny. Our engagement here has been extended—indefinitely.' A moment later, as the strains of their music faded, so did the musicians—instruments and all—right in front of the astounded houseman's eyes."

And thus the historian dutifully delivered the first in a series of curious but comfortable tales that comprised the hotel's "ghost" tour. Rebecca characterized them as "Casper" stories—all friendly ghosts with PG ratings. Entertaining and innocuous, they intentionally omitted anything genuinely frightening or disturbing. These management-approved oldies had been passed down to her by the previous historian. The trick was in the telling, Rebecca had quickly learned. At their core, the stories were frankly lame.

The general manager of the Griffins Keep, Mr. Beaumont, insisted that the hotel was not haunted. He allowed the ghost tours because he recognized their public relations value. But he drew the line at paranormal investigators who sought permission to bring in electromagnetic meters or other ghost hunting devices. He would not have them disrupting the Keep's traditionally conservative, business-oriented clientele.

Rebecca understood the GM's reservations and respected his wishes. But it put her in a frustrating position. On the one hand, she appreciated the ghost tours as a way of foisting Colorado history on an unsuspecting public. But on the other, she was prevented from sharing unsettling tales that were just as much a part of the hotel's history as the Caspers.

She dared not, for example, tell the eager group before her about the terrible fire—the only fire in The Keep's long history—in the very venue in which they sat.

Or could she?

Today Rebecca reconsidered. Her niece and nephew, Hannah and Jacob, now in their 20s, were visiting from Colorado Springs. Aunt Becky's stories had always delighted them growing up—the scarier, the better. Seeing their disappointment at the ghost musician tale, Rebecca incautiously continued with the taboo postscript she'd never shared with guests.

"Now, in the 1930s, when this was the Aladdin Room, the restaurant was entirely draped in billowy silks, covering the walls and hanging from the ceiling to create the atmosphere of an exotic boudoir. One evening, a flicked cigarette ember set the fabric ablaze, enveloping diners and dancers in a suffocating canopy of dripping flame." She secretly savored the shocked expressions on her listeners' faces.

"Firefighters from a nearby station extinguished the blaze in less than twelve minutes after they arrived on the scene. But it was too late for the seven revelers who died agonizing deaths."

"Wait...Is this like the *Titanic* being 'unsinkable?'" a bespectacled guest in a bowtie sought to clarify. "I thought you said this place couldn't burn."

Rebecca explained. "The building is fireproof, yes. But not the contents. This restaurant space itself was undamaged. Only the decorative features, furniture and such, were destroyed."

"And the victims," a woman dressed for Afternoon Tea in a flowered dress said quietly. "Is anything known about them?"

Already regretting the beans she'd spilled, Rebecca knew there was no retrieving them. "The Keep's owners and management at the time wielded their considerable influence to bury the story," she confided. "But a small piece in the *Denver Times-Herald* reported that several victims of the tragedy were hotel orchestra members."

"Cool," Jacob whispered loudly to Hannah.

From behind Rebecca, an authoritative voice dissented. "There's no evidence that management ever tried to cover anything up," declared Mr. Beaumont. He glowered at Rebecca, who wished she could disappear into her top hat like a magician's rabbit. "If you want to continue conducting these so-called 'ghost' tours," he admonished her directly, heedless of her audience, "I suggest you stick to the script."

The flush that began with embarrassment deepened with outrage. Rebecca pulled herself together and continued the tour like the professional she was. But she was smarting still when she retreated to the basement to punch the timeclock after her shift. The service elevator she usually rode up to the archives had a hastily scrawled "Out of Order" sign stuck on the control panel.

Breakdowns and malfunctions were daily occurrences in the old building. To the casual visitor, the Griffins Keep was still impressive. But those who knew the hotel intimately understood that the façade was deceptive. As a "woman of a certain age," Rebecca could relate personally to the hotel's struggles with leaky plumbing, deteriorating appearance, and fluctuating internal temperature.

She was prepared to walk through the basement kitchens to the other service elevator when the out-of-order lift arrived unexpectedly, without a sound. The automatic doors slid open to reveal the floor of the car strewn with a dozen short-stemmed roses, weeping petals.

Finding the sight inexplicably disturbing, Rebecca hesitated as the doors closed slowly. She opted to take the service stairs instead.

# CHAPTER 2

Mr. Beaumont looked pleased later that afternoon as employees filtered into the Longs Peak meeting room and helped themselves to coffee and pastries from long tables just inside the entrance. Interdepartmental mingling was rare at these mandatory staff meetings. Housekeepers sat with housekeepers, accountants with accountants, cooks with other cooks. The whispered exchanges between co-workers seemed more solemn and urgent than usual.

"That must be why they called us together," Rebecca heard a room service staffer say. "They've got to say something about her. How can all the big-wigs look so happy?"

The back rows filled up first, as always. Only the hotel historian marched straight to the front so as to miss none of the presentation. Maintenance engineer Lochlan MacKenzie, who sometimes assisted Rebecca with the ghost tours, moved up to keep her company.

"Good afternoon, everyone," Mr. Beaumont began cheerily when all were settled.

"Good afternoon," a few associates replied less enthusiastically.

"I've called this All Hands meeting today to bring you all up to date on the new ownership of the hotel. As you may remember from our previous briefing, the more than 100 parties who expressed interest in the Griffins Keep had been narrowed down to three who submitted bids prior to the deadline date. After months of negotiations with the finalists, I have some excellent news that will affect you all."

The assembled associates braced themselves.

Mr. Beaumont pressed the clicker in his hand to bring up his first PowerPoint slide. "It is my pleasure to officially announce that the Griffins Keep Hotel and Spa has been acquired by Tagawa International Theaters, Hospitality, and Entertainment, Incorporated."

The big screen in the front of the room displayed the TITHE logo. Though entirely coincidental, the acronym was apt, as company founder Chad Tagawa was well known for contributing 10% of his corporation's profits to the Church of Scientology.

"Who is Chad Tagawa?" the next slide was headed, and Mr. Beaumont summarized the billionaire founder's rags-to-riches story. A third generation Japanese American, Tagawa had grown up in California, surfing, hang gliding, working at a sushi bar and taking the occasional community college business course. At the age of 23, Tagawa bought a microwave burrito and a lottery ticket. That ticket matched all the numbers in one of the biggest Powerball drawings of all time. A new American millionaire was born.

Chad's uncle Stan Tagawa was the financial genius who managed his young nephew's fortune, ambitiously acquiring one successful enterprise after another. Now 38, Chad Tagawa still enjoyed carefree bachelorhood, leisure sports, and microwave burritos—at his three palatial estates.

"What is TITHE?" the next slide asked. The corporation's bulleted list included a movie theatre chain, a film production company, amusement parks, casinos, cruise ships, and hotels around the globe. Subsequent slides highlighted examples of TITHE's signature properties: Wallaby Wunderland in Queensland, Australia, a wildlife park and family-friendly resort built on a repossessed sheep property, and Haunted Haggis Castle in the Scottish Highlands, a slickly refurbished seventeenth-century fortress that featured animatronic "ghosts" and full-moon "Druid Barbeques" in a circle of fake standing stones.

"What is TITHE's Corporate Vision?" As this slide appeared, Mr. Beaumont gestured for a young gentleman who had been standing to the side to come forward and take the clicker. "To answer that question, I'd like to introduce the future managing director of the Griffins Keep, Mr. Mickey Branson."

Rebecca supposed the blonde, brown-eyed Branson to be thirty-five, tops. Good looking, athletic, and confident, dressed California Corporate-style in polo shirt and khakis, Branson accepted the clicker and shook Beaumont's hand, beaming broadly. "Hey everybody, how're ya doin' this fine afternoon?" he began, energetically striding back and forth across the front of the room as the soon-to-be-unseated GM stepped aside.

"Wow, you all look so serious and worried. You'd think somebody had died or something." Several back-of-the-house employees cringed at this all-too-apt characterization.

"This is awesome news for you guys and The Keep," Branson insisted. "A brand new beginning! I'm excited. Are you excited? You will be by the time I finish this presentation, I guarantee it. Because TITHE is all about creating unique and entertaining experiences for our guests. It's about fun!"

*Lord help us,* Rebecca thought. *The Keep has fallen into the clutches of cheerleaders.*

Following Branson's whirlwind video overview of TITHE's successes worldwide, he explained that new management would be taking over The Keep in November. "And then," he rubbed his hands together, grinning, "we're gonna bring this old dinosaur back to life, just like in 'Jurassic Park.'"

"As I recall," Rebecca said to Lochlan after the All-Hands meeting, "Jurassic Park ended in disaster."

"Mmm," the engineer murmured, nodding agreement. "The dire consequences of manipulating natural processes without fully considering the ramifications. "

"All in the pursuit of popular entertainment and profit. Is TITHE missing a lesson here?"

"So it would seem," Lochlan said, "although in this case, they may be tinkering with *supernatural* processes."

*Here he goes again,* Rebecca thought. As much as she liked and respected the engineer, his theories about The Keep's "higher function" were a little too out-there for her. She knew Lochlan was dead serious about the building's mystical role in both Denver's development and the spiritual continuum. And she knew his commitment to preserving The Keep's magic was genuine—albeit delusional.

Rebecca's reasons for concern were more down-to-earth. Her personal and professional mission was preservation of the Griffins Keep's legacy. The hotel's history was inextricably intertwined

13

with the history of the city and the Rocky Mountain West. To understand The Keep's story was to understand Denver's distinctive character, the circumstances and choices that had shaped it. The past had value and connecting to it through a physical place that could be explored and experienced, like the Griffins Keep, provided a touchstone that deserved respect.

Like every other Keep associate, Rebecca was anxious about what to expect with the change of ownership. Though she had never been impressed by the current management group, it was a classic case of the devil-you-know vs. the devil-you-don't know. The hotel had not changed hands in more than thirty years, atypical in the hospitality industry. The owners had let things slide over the last few years with regards to maintenance and upkeep. Griffins Keep daily operations had become stagnant. Employees were overworked and underpaid. Standards slipped.

Devoted employees discovered that the more they struggled, the deeper their morale sank. They grasped the prospect of TITHE ownership like a low-hanging branch, hoping new capital and leadership might lift the hotel out of the quagmire of mediocrity into which it was sinking.

And then there was Rebecca's "manager." Director of Sales and Marketing Dick Plotz had never even taken her hotel tour. Only after she'd been on the job a year did she insist that they hold one of their one-on-one meetings in her "office," the hotel archives which he had never visited. He'd endured her showcasing of its treasures without interest or comment. From New Jersey, not Colorado, Plotz never quite got what the hotel meant to the city and to the West. He couldn't care less about The Keep's history because he couldn't see how it translated into direct profit.

While she preferred his hands-off style to micro-management any day, when Rebecca needed support or advocacy, Plotz rarely provided it. Acquisition by TITHE meant his days with The Keep were numbered. But Rebecca feared that the geniuses behind Haunted Haggis Castle would have even less regard for Griffins Keep legacy than Plotz had.

Not until the next day did Rebecca learn from Lochlan about Momaday's mysterious death. Usually out of the employee loop, she often felt like a snorkeler on the surface, observing but only partially immersed in the ecosystem that flourished below. The

14

other hotel associates existed in a world of which she was not really part. She floated on the interface between hotel staff and hotel guests, belonging with neither of them.

"No wonder the staff is so upset. But I don't understand," she said. "How could Momaday have fallen down an open elevator shaft? It makes no sense. Why would the doors open with no elevator there? Did she jump? Did she trip?" An even more disturbing possibility dawned upon Rebecca. "Was she pushed?"

"We may never know. It makes no logical sense, you're right," Lochlan agreed. "But you know as well as I do that some things that happen in The Keep have been known to defy logic." As they approached the group gathered for today's tour, he reminded Rebecca, "It's exactly those logic-defying stories these folks are hungry for." He split off from Rebecca and headed toward the back of the Treble Clef, leaving her to handle the check-ins and awaiting his turn as co-tour guide.

Following the usual introduction and ghost musicians tale— without the fire postscript—Rebecca said, "Because our group is so large today, we're going to divide you into two as we begin exploring the hotel. Half of you will be escorted by my colleague, Lochlan MacKenzie—there in the back"

He waved to identify himself. A tall, fit man in his late 50s, he wore his once-dark long hair pulled back and looked unaccustomed to the tie he was obliged to wear when leading tours. He leaned casually against a support pillar. His white shirt's rolled-up sleeves revealed the forearms of a working man. His smile revealed quiet assurance.

"Lochlan has been here at Griffins Keep as a maintenance engineer for many years, so he literally knows the place inside and out. If you have a particular interest in our architecture, or in The Keep's Masonic and Knights Templar connections, you'll definitely want to be part of Lochlan's group."

"So, you know where all the bodies are buried?" a comedian called out.

"Sure," he replied good-naturedly.

The historian continued. "The rest of you are with me, and we'll be starting with the Kipling cigar bar, so prepare to hold your breath,"

"My group is heading for the Pirates Pub," Lochlan announced, "Step lively, maties!"

"Are we allowed to take photos?" a guest asked Rebecca.

"Oh, absolutely," Rebecca replied. "I should have mentioned that at the beginning. You're welcome to take photos anywhere on the tour."

"What about special lenses for capturing things not visible to the naked eye?" a young man in a brown sweater vest inquired.

Rebecca shook her head. "Our management frowns upon such things," she answered automatically. But she was still smarting from Mr. Beaumont's public rebuke and miffed by his inconsideration. The GM would be gone soon, anyway. *The hell with him.*

"On second thought," she amended, "as long as you're not disruptive, I'll never know the difference. Just promise you'll email me any spirit images you might capture."

Several guests smiled at the possibility.

The Kipling transported guests to an Edwardian gentlemen's library, with its mahogany paneling, sofas and wingback chairs upholstered in burgundy velvet or deep-brown leather. Bookshelves filled one wall, complete with copious leather-bound volumes and a library ladder on a rail. The curved bar was black walnut, as was the floor-to-ceiling glass-fronted humidor cabinet where elite club members stored their private cigar collections for a substantial fee. By this time of day, the aromas of a dozen different smokes were battling for dominance.

"This is the only place in downtown Denver with a special license that actually allows smoking indoors," Rebecca explained. "And that continues a longtime Keep tradition of wheeling and dealing over brandies and cigars."

"I'm sorry, but I'm going to wait outside," an elderly lady said, holding a lace-trimmed hanky over her nose and mouth and excusing herself.

"I completely understand," Rebecca said, "and for the rest of you, I'll be quick.

"Now, before this space became a bar, the wall on that far side, with the leaded glass windows and louvered shutters—That was the original Grand Entrance to the hotel. It's in the middle of the Grand Avenue side of the building, and if you get a chance to look at that side from across the street sometime, you'll see that it has a much more impressive appearance than either of the two entrances we use today. Here on the ground floor, just outside, there's a profile of our founder Harrison Griffin carved in the stone on one side and his initials in a medallion on the other.

"Harrison was on the scene here in Denver during the 1859 gold rush that gave Colorado its start. But he knew that the one thing even more precious than gold in the West was water. A gifted diviner, Harrison located a huge aquifer beneath the baby city and made his fortune with the Griffin Water and Drilling Company."

"So that's how he was able to finance this place," a guest concluded for her.

"Exactly," she confirmed. "But what they could never have imagined in the 1890s was twentieth-century automobile traffic on Grand, which grew heavier and faster until it finally made loading and unloading hotel guests on this side of the building too dangerous. They had to close this entrance in the 1930s, and this whole wall was added to create the bar."

The tour-takers struggled to imagine the former layout.

"I'm sure our architect, Edward Brookings, rolled over in his grave when they made the change, because now, when people enter on the Carson Street side, it's like coming in the back door. You can't even see the Front Desk—it's around the corner—and everyone tries to check in with the poor concierge."

Nods from some of her listeners indicated their familiarity with the confusion.

"I encourage you, as we're walking out, to pause for a moment in the doorway and take in the view of the atrium lobby as it was intended to unfold before you when you entered the hotel. I'm sure you'll agree it is much more impactful."

Brooking's masterful vision had placed the entrance in the center of the hypotenuse of the right-triangular building, facing the 90-degree corner of the soaring atrium. The power of the design and the delight of the details both energized and soothed all who entered,

Ghost story time.

"Now, when this was the Grand Entrance, Harrison Griffin's office was in the back part of this room. And strange goings-on in that space after hours make us wonder if Harrison's spirit is still around, trying to run things in his namesake hotel.

"My favorite report comes from about six years ago. The manager was working late one night, figuring out the day's receipts and doing the deposit, when all of a sudden the sound system came on, skipping from track to track and loud to soft. The manager walked over to deal with the problem and discovered that the sound system was not, in fact, turned on—it wasn't getting any

17

power. And yet the noise continued. In frustration, he blurted out, 'Harry, please—I'm trying to work!' And it stopped instantly."

Most of her tour guests enjoyed this story. But a few, hungry for truly frightening fare, simply shook their heads.

If spirits did haunt The Keep, Harrison Griffin's topped the list of likely suspects. Besides his considerable fortune, he'd poured his heart and soul into the place. Whatever else might be said of the irascible Harrison, he had to be credited with giving the city of Denver an architectural gem.

The fate of that gem was now in question. What would TITHE's takeover mean to the hotel operations? To its appearance? To Rebecca's future as historian? She couldn't think about it in the middle of her tour. But it lurked at the back of her mind like a dark shadow, just around the corner in a dangerous neighborhood.


During the lull between lunch and dinner, only a few tables in the Pirates Pub were occupied. Lochlan herded his tour to an out-of-the-way corner nevertheless, in consideration of the hardworking wait staff.

"How'd we get a Pirates Pub in the middle of landlocked Colorado?" he began. "I'm sure you've wondered what that's about. How many of you are familiar with the name Kuhrsfeld?"

About half of them indicated their recognition..

"Easy to tell which folks are local," Lochlan said. "We Coloradans still associate that name with high finance and philanthropy."

"Kuhrsfeld Opera House," someone offered.

"Kuhrsfeld scholarships," said another.

"And so on," Lochlan said. "Well, three generations of Kuhrsfelds owned this hotel, from 1918 through 1982. Now the middle generation, Rolph Joseph Kuhrsfeld—R.J. to his friends—was quite the collector. The man was fascinated by pirate lore of the Caribbean islands in the eighteenth century. At one point he'd collected so many pirate pistols and ship models and maps and flags and sextants that his wife Lilah lost patience with all the paraphernalia cluttering up her toney mansion. She diplomatically suggested that R.J. design the hotel's new post-Prohibition tavern in a buccaneer theme and relocate the whole kit-and-kaboodle to The Keep. Clever lady, Lilah, don't you think?"

A few veteran wives in the group concurred.

"So this Pub is also the scene of an infamous murder at the Griffins Keep," Lochlan said.

"People died here?"

"Of course," the guide said simply. "Many people have met their ends at the Griffins Keep in its decades of operation, just as people had been born here, romanced here, married here, feted here and ruined here. As for how many people might have been conceived in its guestrooms," he added, "there's really no telling. Any of you among them?" He grinned as his meaning sank in.

The murder story he proceeded to tell was the tale of a tawdry love affair from 1946. The triangle involving a prominent local businessman, his fickle young trophy wife, and a smitten—and drunken—WWII veteran determined to eliminate his rival.

"Ooo—I remember this story from the Colorado Historical Society's magazine a couple years ago!" an excited guest interjected.

Lochlan acknowledged her with a smile and went on with the story. "The gunman fired wildly around the bar, wounding two bystanders before another man, Jerome Marston, tried to wrest the revolver from him. The next bullet went directly into Marston's heart, killing him instantly."

"We've got a photo of the bloody body on the floor if you wanna see it," offered one of the Pub bartenders.

Lochlan continued. "Many people believe the ghost of Mr. Marston haunts the Pub. Often, with sudden or violent deaths, the spirit lingers long afterwards in confusion, unsure of what's happened, unaware that they're dead."

Several tour-takers nodded, buying into this theory.

"Sometimes people'll tell us they've seen a young man seated at the bar in the mirrors behind the bottles here," the bartender added. "But when they look at the bar itself, nobody there."

"Hello, Mr. Marston," Lochlan concluded. "Time to move on, folks. The ballroom and its haunted chandelier await."

As he led his group from the Pub, Lochlan waved to Rebecca, en route with her half-tour to their next stop. She smiled, somewhat wearily, it seemed to him, and waved back

How could someone so small bear the responsibility Lochlan suspected would soon be thrust upon her? But he'd seen the evidence. He knew. Rebecca's spirit had been adjudged equal to the task, decades before either of them was born.

# CHAPTER 3

"So why's this place called Griffins Keep?" a tour guest asked before Rebecca got to that point in her usual narrative. "Griffins keep *what?*"

She explained. "The term 'keep' comes from Europe in the Middle Ages. A keep is a fortified tower, the strongest and securest part of a medieval castle. Keeps were places of safety for the nobility, used as a refuge of last resort should the rest of the castle fall to an adversary."

She paused before adding her tried-and-true disclaimer. "Of course, we aim to make *our* Keep the first choice for travelers, not their last resort." *Rimshot, please.*

"All right, next we're riding the escalators to the mezzanine level, where I'd like you to look out the window at our neighbor, Pierce Tower, the highest building in Denver."

On the second floor, her tour-takers craned their necks to look to the top of the skyscraper. "It's 72 stories, about 750 feet high," she said. "The Griffins Keep's water source, our artesian well, is as deep as that building is high. That's why we have the best ice and the best tea in Denver." Her tour guests were always impressed with this visual aid. Rebecca never missed a chance to tout the hotel's unique features.

"Several psychics and mediums who have visited The Keep believe that when they dug down that far and tapped into the aquifer, they created some sort of otherworldly passageway that has made the hotel a way station, not only for travelers in this realm, but also for spirits on their way to the afterlife."

Rebecca always struggled to present this possibility as even remotely plausible.

"Now the well itself," she continued, "is sunk right below the Pirates Pub. And that corner of the hotel—all the way from the subbasement to the roof—has more reports of unexplained phenomena than any other part of the building. Coincidence? Maybe. Or maybe those psychics know something we don't."

Eyes widened as she built the suspense. "We're going next to the space directly above the Pub, the Silver Spoon Club. Stay with me—or wander at your own risk."

They followed at Rebecca's heels like her Westy, Willoughby, expecting a treat. She led them through the dark paneled entryway in semi-darkness. The space itself was lit by natural light filtered through stained glass windows featuring heraldic shield and crest designs. From the exposed timbers of the roof were suspended milk glass-shaped chandeliers.

"This unusual room occupies one of the 45-degree angles of our right-triangular building," Rebecca said when all had gathered around. "Originally guest rooms, it became an exclusive private gentlemen's and dining club for decades. Now it's devoted to event rentals. It's the perfect shape for a wedding or any sort of program. It's also considered the most 'haunted' space in the Griffins Keep."

"Now you're talking," a vaguely familiar-looking tour guest said.

"Stories from both hotel associates and guests recount lights that have gone on and off for no reason. Doors have opened and closed by themselves. Some people have felt this carpet crawl under their feet like something alive. Some employees refuse to come into this room alone."

Pointing to the bar in the back of the room, Rebecca continued. "Other reports tell of a bartender who melts in and out of the wall over there."

"Does he mix drinks first?" a guest wondered aloud.

"I certainly hope so," Rebecca replied.

An elderly lady on the tour commented with a wink, "You know, I often find that, right when I need them, bartenders disappear."

The group's amusement buoyed Rebecca. If there were any effective deterrent to evil spirits, surely it was laughter.

22

"One of our most persistent ghosts is occasionally reported here in the entryway or just outside of it," Rebecca continued after a suitable pause. She walked her tour guests over to a lit display case in the back of the dark hallway. "And some employees have a theory about who this entity might be.

"Over the years, he's been described as wearing a dark suit or a dark uniform and a hat, which several people have said looks like an old-fashioned railroad conductor's cap. When people have tried to approach this spirit or speak to him, he always drifts down to the lobby level of the hotel and into the wall of our 90-degree angle corner."

Rebecca glanced around at the skeptical faces, empathizing completely, and plunged on.

"Now, when the Griffins Keep first opened, the entire ground floor was encircled by retail shops and businesses. And in that 90-degree corner was the Union Pacific Railroad ticket office."

"So this ghost is still trying to sell tickets to who-knows-who to who-knows-where," a guest speculated.

"That," the guide said, "or he's conducting spirits to the next station on their journey."

A middle-aged man in a herringbone sport coat boldly stepped up to Rebecca at the front of the tour group and announced, "I saw that ghost when I was here last year."

Momentarily caught off guard, Rebecca quickly retrieved the memory. "I thought you looked familiar," she said. "Mr. Everett, right? You were with that extended family group on an evening private tour." She turned to the group. "It was the only time anyone on one of my ghost tours actually saw a ghost. Do you want to tell them the story?"

"Uh, sure. OK."

Rebecca led the group to the entrance where the incident had happened, remembering that evening clearly. She'd gone up to preview the Club before the tour. All the lights had been blazing and the doors were locked, so she'd called Security, requesting that they turn off most of the lights to make it spookier. When Rebecca had come by the Club entrance a few minutes later, security guard Salma was in the process of unlocking the doors. She was peering through the crack between them into the entryway.

"Oh!" she'd said to the historian, apparently surprised by what she'd seen inside. "Curtis is here this evening."

23

"Excuse me?"

"Curtis," Salma repeated. "He's the spirit who haunts this space. I haven't seen him a quite a while, and I'm getting the feeling he doesn't want you going in there tonight."

"Stop teasing," Rebecca had said, always amused by these so-called "sightings." She'd gone on her way and brought Mr. Everett's group up about twenty minutes later. The doors to the Club had been still—or once again—locked.

When Salma returned to let them in, she'd muttered to Rebecca, "Told you you weren't welcome."

Rebecca had said nothing to her tour group that evening about Salma's warning, but it did provide an interesting preface to what had happened next.

Mr. Everett began, "So it was night and they'd turned off almost all the lights in here, and it was really dark. Rebecca told us a couple ghost stories, and as we were all leaving, I was bringing up the rear. As soon as we were outside in the hallway, I asked her and the rest of my family, 'Was that guy coming out of the restroom a hotel employee?'"

Rebecca jumped in. "We all stared at him. No one else had seen a man, and the restroom inside this entrance is a ladies room."

"I freaked out," the man admitted. "I saw his face, heard his footsteps on the floor. I saw a ghost! I saw an honest-to-god ghost!'"

Rebecca added, "The kids in his group began to scream, and even I felt a cold prickle on the back of my neck and down my arms. This gentleman was so convinced that he had witnessed something supernatural that I almost believed it, too. And this is the very restroom his ghost came out of," she concluded, pointing to it on her left.

Mr. Everett looked at her, puzzled, and shook his head. "He didn't come out of that restroom," he corrected. "He came out of the door here." He reached over to the opposite side of the entryway and touched the wood-paneled wall with his hand. No restroom. No door. A chill ran through them both. Several of the tour guests instinctively eased away from that side.

*What used to be there?* Rebecca wondered, desperate to make sense of it. The next day in the archives, she pulled out the blueprint showing the original layout of the second floor. Much had changed over the decades. But there had never been a room—

or a doorway—in the place Mr. Everett had indicated. Instead, a circle within an equilateral triangular shape on the floorplan appeared to indicate something inside the wall. Could this be the spiritual portal those psychics had sensed?

Lochlan would know what to make of it.


"Tell me about this new historian of Griffins Keep. Where are you from? Are you married? Children? And more importantly, what brings you here?" Lochlan MacKenzie had probed upon first meeting Rebecca five years earlier, taking her measure.

"I'm one of those rare Colorado natives," Rebecca had answered. "Grew up in Colorado Springs. Survived Christian boarding school in Texas, though my faith in the Church did not. Got my undergrad degree in Education, with a Theater minor."

"That explains why you're so good at leading tours," Lochlan said. "They combine both teaching and performance, when you think about it."

"Thank you," Rebecca said, appreciating the compliment before continuing her abbreviated bio. "Married once. Pretty disastrous, actually. No children, thank goodness. That might have required me to keep in some sort of contact with my ex. As it is, I haven't seen or heard from him in... well, twenty-five years, at least. Kept his last name, though. I'd never be innocent little Becky Holcomb again."

Lochlan had done a strange double-take at this revelation, Rebecca remembered. He'd looked at her as if peering through different lenses.

"Holcomb was your maiden name?" he repeated. "Rebecca Holcomb?"

"That's right. Why? Do you know a Holcomb? I have lots of family around."

Lochlan had shaken his head, made light of it. "No, it's nothing. Just saw the name somewhere, that's all. Go on, please."

"What brought me here? Hmmm..." Rebecca had taken a moment to consider her answer to this part of his questions. "Not the generous pay, that's for sure. I don't know, it's just... this is the Griffins Keep, you know? The most iconic, most elegant and most historic hotel in Denver. How could I resist, loving Colorado history as I do? What about you? Same questions."

"Edinburgh-born, a Baby-Boomer, like you. Denver-raised since the age of ten," Lochlan had replied.

"Honorary native, then."

"I like to think so. Never been married, no children. I'm not gay, by the way," he had added, assuming she might jump to the conclusion which had not, in fact, occurred to her. "Just never found the right woman, I guess." Lochlan had smiled a little self-consciously. "Friends tease that I'm married to The Keep."

"And how long have you two been together?"

"Started in my late 20s, way back. Always liked it, so I've stayed. An incredible building, an incredible history—an incredible challenge. I really consider it a privilege to care for the old girl. I also believe everyone at The Keep is here for a reason," he said. "Especially you."

"Why me especially?"

Lochlan shrugged. "Not sure. I just sense that your connection to the hotel's past is unique. Significant."

"I suppose you've seen a lot of changes over that many years, know all the nooks and crannies."

"Comes along with years of repairs, renovations, remodels. Some for the better, some not so much. It never ends. Surprising things turn up when you start tearing into these walls and floors."

"Really? Like what?"

Lochlan lifted his eyebrows, piquing her curiosity before he answered. "Oh, you know—things people have secretly stashed over the years and left behind, either intentionally or unavoidably. The Keep's like a huge honeycomb, with all the hollow terra cotta blocks that make up the fireproof floors and interior walls.

"I've uncovered lots of old liquor bottles, mostly bootleg from the Prohibition years. Naughty French postcards. Old newspapers, letters, receipts, photographs. Occasionally we find money—minor stashes only, dammit."

"Nothing beats the real-life mysteries," Rebecca said. "That's the best part of studying history, when research is like detective work. One clue leads to another and another, if you're lucky."

It had taken only a brief conversation with Lochlan to discover that his interest in The Keep's past veered well beyond strictly factual accounts. His personal friends were the psychics who had sensed the hotel well's spiritual dimension.

Rebecca encountered him often on the tenth floor of the nine-story Keep. The carpentry shop, paint shop, upholstery and

26

furniture repair shops in which Lochlan worked all shared the roof with the archives and her workspace. The next time he stopped in for a visit, she asked him about her latest mystery.

"You've told me of people who believe that The Keep's well is some sort of portal for spirits in the hotel," she began.

Lochlan nodded. "Spirits of the dead have long been associated with subterranean water. The River Styx in Greek mythology, for instance. Artesian wells spring from particularly powerful underground aquifers, sufficiently pressurized by associated geological formations to rise to the surface naturally when tapped. Spirits are thought to be attracted by the energy in such aquifers."

"Why is that, exactly?"

"Entities manifest themselves through energy. The greater the energy, the stronger the manifestation," the engineer explained simply. "That's how dousers—diviners like Harrison Griffin—detect underground water sources, by picking up on that energy subconsciously."

"But how would that work? Do the spirits come flowing out of the hotel water faucets, swirling into the toilet bowls, or what?"

Lochlan laughed. "Sounds like a tight squeeze. And a bit undignified, don't you think?" Then sensing her earnestness, he said, "I'm no expert in such things. But my friends, who seem to intuitively understand the workings of the spiritual realm, might not be so quick to dismiss such possibilities. Come to think of it, some of our best 'ghost' stories happened in or around our restrooms."

"I know," Rebecca replied, and her story of Mr. Everett came out in a rush. "But the ghost he thought he saw didn't emerge from the Silver Spoon ladies room after all. It came out of the blank wall by the china display case at the entry. Do you know what's inside that wall?"

"As a matter of fact, I do. It's a weird triangular shaft surrounding the old sub-basement boiler steam pipe. Intersects every floor and goes all the way up above the roof. Runs right alongside your archives here, as it happens."

Lochlan reached out and knocked on the wall to the right of her door. The hollow sound was tinged with a dull metallic ring. "No reason you would have noticed it. Hasn't been functional in decades. But it's still in there."

Rebecca had to sit down. The engineer perched on the vinyl upholstered footrest across from her. "Lochlan, do you think that smokestack could have been—could still be—a conduit for spirits?"

He stroked his graying beard, pondering the question as seriously as she had posed it. At length he said, "It could be. Absolutely could be. The steam pipe is in a direct line with the old boiler and its artesian source. It's a straight shot from the aquifer, intersecting every floor, and ultimately opening out into the heavens.

"Not sure what spirits look for in an inter-dimensional passageway," he confessed, "but in my estimation, that steam pipe seems a natural route from realms below to realms above—and beyond."

# CHAPTER 4

For the first half-hour of every tour, Rebecca skirted the atrium lobby, shepherding her group from one side to another, building up to the breathtaking architectural centerpiece as to the crescendo of a symphony. They stepped up now to the balcony railing on the mezzanine level, overlooking the majestic lobby in all its glory.

The hotel's striking Romanesque façade only hinted at The Keep's interior splendor. Amber-hued and warm, sunlight infused the soaring lobby with a golden glow, drawing the eyes up and up and up. A magnificent stained glass skylight topped the eighth floor, 100 feet above. Intricate filigreed wrought-iron panels decorated six tiers of open balconies encircling the floors below it. Stone columns rose from the lobby to the mezzanine level, supporting Florentine arches lit by starburst bulbs. On one side of the stunning space, the Grand Staircase wove in and out between guestroom floors.

First time visitors to the hotel marveled unabashedly at the atrium splendor, and through their eyes, Rebecca appreciated anew the beauty to which she had become almost inured in five years of exposure. Even experienced world travelers confessed they had not seen its like anywhere outside of Europe.

Near the center, a circular stone fountain burbled soothingly. Fed by the artesian well, the fountain was the atrium lobby's focal point, one of the few features unadulterated since The Keep's opening day. Water spilled out over the lip of a large Grecian urn and cascaded over its rim with a musical gurgle into a circular pool of golden onyx.

Flanking the urn on two sides were copper griffins, as big as Rottweilers, verdigris-green with age. Their bronze swords still shone in the light filtered through the stained-glass ceiling. The mythological creatures on opposite sides of the pool faced outwards from the center, at right angles to the original Grand Entrance. Each stood balanced on one foot atop a crown. With their other feet lifted and swords raised at attention by their sides, they appeared ready to battle anyone who approached. The tips of their wings touched above the urn, framing it.

"I think you'll agree this atrium is the most impressive part of the Griffins Keep. All this beautiful stone is not marble, as many people guess, but golden onyx. You generally think of onyx as black, but it does occur very rarely in other colors. Have any of you visited our State Capitol building? It features a unique rose onyx in the wainscoting. This golden onyx was found in a quarry in Old Mexico. More than 1400 surface feet of the stone was used in The Keep, depleting that quarry entirely. So you won't see onyx of this unique color anyplace else."

"Why did they go all the way to Mexico for stone when there's so much nearby in the Colorado mountains?" a guest asked.

Rebecca had wondered that herself. "It does seem like a lot of unnecessary transportation expense, doesn't it? There must have been something special about this particular stone that greatly appealed to the builders. Besides the unusual shade, natural variations within the stone create interesting patterns when cut and polished like this."

"Are there pictures in your stone?" a guest asked. "Like at the Capitol, our guide pointed out one pattern that looked like a butterfly and another that looked sorta like George Washington, if you used your imagination."

"Only one 'picture' that I know of," Rebecca said, pointing toward the Grand Staircase. "On the wall to the left of the stairs, just about four feet up—Can you see what might be taken for an open eye?"

Some guests nodded. Others shook their heads. *Moving on...*

"As I'm sure many of you know, ancient Roman villas were often built around an open center courtyard called an atrium. Our architect just took that idea eight stories high."

The visitors looked up with appreciation and amazement.

"Of course, you see open lobbies in hotels all over the place nowadays. But in 1890, this was an unprecedented innovation called 'daylighting' the interior space. The stained glass skylight is original, created and installed by a local glass company that's still in business with a fourth generation of the same family."

All leaned over the railing to take in the intricate ceiling, aglow with jewel tones regardless of outside weather conditions.

"Wouldn't it be awful if that glass cracked and fell!" a young woman on the tour gasped.

"Little chance of that," the historian assured them all. "The skylight is suspended between our eighth and ninth floors. Then, on the roof itself, there's a translucent protective structure with sloping sides that catches snow, hail, dead birds—anything that might damage the stained glass. So it's quite safe up there. It's not on the roof, but it's all natural light that filters through it."

The transcendent heart of the Griffins Keep never failed to impress.

"As you can see, today and most days, from noon until 4:00, our atrium lobby is the setting for Afternoon Tea, a formal but delightful affair with three-tiered trays of tiny sandwiches, tiny petit fours, and scones with clotted cream."

Pianists performing throughout the afternoon sometimes made it difficult for the tour guests to hear Rebecca. But live music accompanying Tea was a beloved tradition she wouldn't think of changing.

Directing their attention next to the far side of the lobby, Rebecca continued, "Have a look at the entrance to The Spa across the way. Our spa is one of our more recent additions. But as you look at that stunning onyx entrance, can you imagine a fireplace? A big, big, fireplace? Because that's what it was in the hotel's early years. Over that huge mantel, there used to be a third griffin, just like the two in our fountain. I think they should bring him back, don't you?"

The group murmured mixed opinions on the prospect.

"What's the deal with the griffins, anyway? They seem to be all around the hotel—in The Keep logo, the wallpaper, the elevator doors, the stained glass windows—like a combination lion and eagle," a guest observed.

"Well, besides the obvious connection with our founder's name, mythological griffins were the guardians of mountain gold treasures. And of course, there was a lot of gold being mined in the

31

Colorado Rockies at the time the hotel was built. Many of our earliest patrons built their fortunes on the output of those mines."

Hesitating a moment before venturing into the realm of sheer speculation, Rebecca continued, "There are those who claim that, when The Keep was being constructed, a huge treasure of mountain gold was buried somewhere below the foundation, and that these griffins have been guarding it ever since." People always enjoyed this idea.

"I choose to believe that," Rebecca invariably felt compelled to add, "based on nothing but legend. Please don't come back with picks and shovels and start tearing up the lobby floor in search of it."

"Are you going to tell us about the upside-down railing?" Someone had actually read the *Art and Architecture of the Griffins Keep* brochure in their guest room. Those who hadn't cast Rebecca puzzled glances.

"It's not the railing, per se," she corrected the enquirer. "These decorative panels surrounding all the atrium balconies are another feature of Italian Renaissance architecture. As you look at a single one of these panels, you can see that there's a definite top and bottom to the filigree design."

The tour takers took note.

"For some unknown reason, out of 740 of these panels installed in the atrium, one was installed upside down. It's almost impossible to spot if you don't know where to look. But we can see it from where we're standing. Everybody ready to follow along?"

She had their attention.

"Look straight across the lobby to the mezzanine level, center section. Then count up above the arch to the seventh floor, the highest open floor below the skylight. Find the post on the right-hand side of that center section, and count three panels in, toward the left. Do you see it?"

Results varied. Some guests took longer than others. Some needed the directions repeated, others required help from friends or family.

"But why is it upside down?"

"Ah, the million-dollar question," Rebecca said. "Why indeed. Some people think it was installed by a disgruntled workman. But if that were the case, they would have adjusted it when it was discovered, right? Others speculate that the reasoning comes from various artistic traditions that consider it blasphemous to try to create something perfect, which only the Deity can do. So the artist puts an intentional flaw, or error, in every work of art. Some think that panel may be The Keep's intentional flaw."

"What do you think?"

Rebecca shared Lochlan's theory only on the ghost tours. "Are any of you familiar with the Knights Templar?"

Most nodded tentatively.

"The Knights are a sort of subset of the Freemasons, an ancient and secretive fraternal order. The Knights arose during the medieval Crusades, when they protected pilgrims on their journeys to the Holy Land."

"Da Vinci Code stuff!" a guest contributed.

"Indiana Jones and the Holy Grail," another said.

"Exactly. Well, the Keep's architect, Edward Brookings, attained a very high ranking, or degree, as a Master Builder within the Freemasons. And for centuries, Freemasons have designed geometrical and numerological codes and powers into their important buildings. As a perfect right triangle, the hotel seems tailor-made for such secrets."

Some of the tour guests indicated their tentative acceptance of this possibility.

"OK, so stay with me. You all know the superstition surrounding Friday the Thirteenth, right? It's long been considered unlucky. Many trace that superstition back to Friday, October 13, 1307, when French King Phillip IV used false accusations of heresy to arrest all of the Knights Templar in France and to confiscate their sizeable treasury. The Knights were tortured, some were burned at the stake. It was several centuries before the Templars recovered from that blow."

At this point, the historian took a breath.

"Now here comes the intriguing part. Look back up to the upside-down panel. When you count the panels from the left-hand corner column to the upside-down panel, you get ten. When you count from the right-hand side to the upside-down panel, you'll find it's in position number thirteen. Put them together and you have the sequence 10–13–07, the 07 for the seventh floor: October 13, 1307—the date that lives in Knights Templar infamy."

A few raised eyebrows greeted this revelation.

"It's probably just coincidence," Rebecca granted. "But the order still exists. In fact, 300 of them attended the Griffins Keep's opening banquet. The Templars actually dedicated the building in 1890, and there are those who believe their spirits continue to watch over the hotel. As always, make of it what you will."


On a Lochlan MacKenzie ghost tour, the Knights Templar theory of the upside-down panel provided a springboard for diving into all the Keep's Masonic and KT connections he found endlessly fascinating. MacKenzies had been Freemasons for generations, and Lochlan had explored the possibility of joining as a young man. But he had been disappointed to discover that the organization in modern times seemed little more than a philanthropic fraternal order with myriad rituals to memorize. The deeper mysteries of the original order, hinted at in accounts he had read, seemed to have been lost or abandoned over time.

Having studied the order for several decades, Lochlan knew more about Masonic history and traditions than many who counted themselves among its members. Legend traced the order's origins to builders of the ancient Temple of Solomon in Jerusalem around 1000 B.C.E. Lochlan was intrigued by the parallels between that building and the Griffins Keep.

The Temple, like the Keep, featured a balcony walkway with many lodging rooms surrounding a central interior atrium. The Temple walls were faced with gold, the Keep's walls with golden onyx. The wingtips of the two angels in the Temple's Holy of Holies touched above the Arc of the Covenant they guarded, as did the wings of the two griffins flanking the urn in the hotel's atrium fountain.

The Temple, like the Keep, had three doorways. Its main entrance faced east, just as the hotel's original Grand Entrance had. The Temple entry was positioned to frame the rays of the sun rising on the vernal and autumnal equinoxes. Lochlan firmly believed that The Keep's entrance was identically positioned. It was blocked now from any sunrise by the tall buildings across Grand Avenue. But he had plotted the seasonal solar progression and cross-referenced it with the Keep's footprint, using a special program on his PC. In the resulting model, the equinox sunrises lined up perfectly with the original hotel entrance.

"The building itself is a sort of cosmic synchrometer," he told Rebecca on one of her visits to the rooftop upholstery shop.

"Like a giant sundial?"

"If you prefer," Lochlan granted, "but that analogy doesn't express its function quite as accurately. I believe the Griffins Keep is laid out to correspond with key positions of the sun throughout the seasons. The main entrance, as I've said, aligned with the equinoxes. The northeast corner marks the farthest point of the sun's path at the summer solstice, and the southeast corner corresponds with the sun's position at winter solstice."

"Why would the builders go to the trouble of positioning the building like that?"

"To demonstrate, in the tradition of Freemasonry, what they knew to be true about the predictable movement of the sun. Freemasons' structures were physical models that conveyed fundamental principles of celestial mechanics in nonverbal lessons."

"Like what?'

At this, Lochlan dropped into a chair awaiting reupholstering and motioned for Rebecca to take the wobbly-legged seat opposite his. "You'll want to sit down for the Big One," he advised.

Gingerly she complied, praying the broken chair would not collapse beneath her, "Ready," she announced.

Lochlan glanced stealthily to his right, then to his left. He leaned forward, cupped a hand to one side of his mouth, and whispered. "The Earth is not the center of the universe."

"Get out!" Rebecca exclaimed, feigning shock.

Lochlan leaned back and smiled. "It seems so obvious to us now that it's impossible to imagine what a volatile truth that simple fact was in the Dark and Middle Ages. But the very suggestion that our world revolved around the sun, rather than the other way around, was for centuries the height of heresy. Men were executed for such blasphemy. It cast doubt upon the teachings of the church, and that could not be tolerated. The Bible states that God created the Earth before He created the Heavens, clearly implying the world of man to be at the center of everything. Beginning around 100 BCE, geocentricity became accepted church dogma for the next seventeen centuries."

"So Masonic structures were like physical testimony to their knowledge of how the universe actually worked when it was too dangerous to come right out and state it."

Lochlan nodded. "Essentially, yes. But there's much more to Masonic architecture than that. They used principles of sacred geometry to maximize both physical and metaphysical energies."

Rebecca was skeptical. "The Keep's alignment is totally coincidental," she said, reciting the facts as they had been told to her. "Its right-triangular lot resulted from the random intersection of two early Denver street grids, one aligned with Cherry Creek and the other aligned with the cardinal directions—true north, south, east and west. I can't believe there was some Masonic plot determining its shape or positioning." But she wasn't as sure as she sounded.

Lochlan continued, oblivious to her argument. "Far from primitive, the Mesopotamian architects of Solomon's Temple times knew more about the natural world and the nature of the cosmos than many subsequent civilizations. They deduced from geometric calculations that the Earth was a sphere, and even had a good idea of how large it was. The Freemasons' forbidden knowledge included macrocosmic truths they understood long before others were ready to accept them."

"How do we know that they knew all this?"

Lochlan assessed her critically, sensing polite curiosity. "Look, there are no simple, sound-bite answers to questions like that. I've studied these things for most of my life. If you're genuinely interested, I can recommend books, websites, whole series of tapes."

Rebecca dropped her gaze, somewhat ashamed that she was not credulous enough to make the effort. "Maybe another time."

But after hearing Lochlan's far-fetched theory about the Grand Avenue entrance being perfectly synced with the equinox sunrise, she pulled out city maps of downtown Denver and analyzed them with new eyes. Clearly, one set of streets ran along the compass points, while another from the older part of town ran at an angle to them. Intersection, triangle, end of story. Or was it? More careful examination revealed easily overlooked but unmistakable anomalies in the pattern around the Griffins Keep. A tiny jog in the street to the west, a slightly tighter angle of the intersection to the northeast. Why had she never noticed these before?

Rebecca set out on foot to confirm what she'd seen on the map. Sure enough, a block away, Sixteenth Street veered a few feet from its otherwise straight course. Ditto with Grand Avenue where it crossed over Carson. Why the minor variances? Had the hotel's orientation really been intentionally tweaked, as Lochlan contended?

36

# CHAPTER 5

Momaday's death was more than a week ago. Rebecca could not pass the service elevator on the eighth floor without thinking of the congenial server and her tragic end. For three days, professionals had examined and tested the lift's mechanical and electrical systems. Finding everything in perfect working order, they concluded that what had happened could not possibly have happened. Management—both current and incoming—had swept the matter under the rug and apparently had no intention of acknowledging it—or Momaday.

Rebecca had read enough ghost stories to know that many told of spirits who could not rest until their tales were told, their plights recognized by those still living. Unfinished business shackled them to the corporeal realm, prevented them from moving on in their afterlife journey. Would Momaday be doomed to haunt the Griffins Keep as an unhappy ghost? Rebecca didn't believe in any of that, but she knew many of her fellow employees did. Momaday should not have to pass without respectful memorialization. It offended Rebecca's sense of justice. But what could she do? What influence could she wield? How could she give Momaday's story voice?

An email from Human Resources Director Angelina Mariposa that morning reminded Rebecca of the deadline for her contribution to this month's employee newsletter. It always included a feature on some aspect of The Keep's long history, researched and written by the hotel historian herself.

Rebecca's emailed submission brought a delayed response from Angie. "This is perfect. But dangerous. Please come by my office to discuss."

She reported to Angie's office in HR immediately. The attractive young Latina was invariably as composed and as compassionate as she was professional. She invited Rebecca to sit and closed the door.

"You're taking a chance with this piece, I'm sure you know," she said, "and I've decided to take it with you. This is important to our associates' morale. It must be addressed, and it's the right thing to do. I've decided to run it, but I want to be sure you understand the risk. We're going to ruffle some powerful feathers, and there may be repercussions."

"I understand," Rebecca said, "and I admire your courage in supporting my effort. Thank you, Angie," she added sincerely, "from me and from Momaday."

The next day, the latest issue of the *Griffin Gazette* caused quite a stir from top to bottom of the in-house strata. The historian had chosen to write about the contributions of immigrant associates throughout The Keep's long operation. Beginning with Italian, German, Scandinavian, and Irish immigrants of the late 1800s, the story chronicled the early twentieth-century influx of Central and Eastern Europeans, and Hispanic and Latino workers beginning in the 1950s.

"They served The Keep in housekeeping, maintenance, the kitchens and the laundry. They were wait staff and doormen, stewards and musicians. Though we know very few of their names, we know their hard work and dedication to excellence built the impressive reputation the Griffins Keep enjoys today."

The full-page feature concluded with a long list of the nations represented within the current staff: Ethiopia, Nigeria, India, Russia, China, Jamaica, Guatemala, Venezuela.

And Senegal.

Rebecca's piece was accompanied with a sidebar featuring a photo of Momaday holding her newborn grandson. It included an invitation.

"We welcome you to celebrate the life of Momaday Benga this Wednesday at 5:00 in the Silver Spoon Club. Momaday cared deeply for the Griffins Keep. Let us demonstrate that we cared for her, as well."

More than fifty associates accepted the invitation. Both Mr. Beaumont and Mr. Branson recognized their duty to attend, now that Momaday's death had been brought into the light.

"We are here as a community," said another African employee, "to comfort, encourage, and heal those who are hurting. Life and personality do not end with death. It is a path by which we join our ancestors in a realm on the other side of a deep river, a place of rest and safety."

The kitchens prepared traditional Senegalese dishes using lamb and beef, goats and oxen being unavailable. Drummers, flute players, and male singers performed traditional African dances, intended to provide the deceased with "light feet" for her journey.

Two photographs of Momaday, one in Senegalese garb and the other in her Keep uniform was projected on a large screen, underscored with the African saying, "When an elder dies, a library closes."

The future TITHE general manager made a point to take Rebecca aside midway through the memorial. They had never been introduced, but Mickey Branson wasted no time on courtesy.

"You and Ms. Mariposa acted without upper-management authorization in arranging this event, Ms. Bridger," he said. "If I was in charge, you'd both be facing serious consequences. Lucky for you, this thing seems to be turning out OK. Looks like it might even have been a good idea. But let me be clear. This sort of loose-cannon crap will not be tolerated when TITHE takes over next month. I'm not about to let you use the hotel's history to advance your personal agenda."

"Agenda?' Rebecca echoed, unintimidated by the bullying young executive.

"You know exactly what I mean," he said. "I'll be reviewing everything that's published in that newsletter from now on. You may or may not be allowed to contribute."

The adversarial dynamic between them was quickly and solidly established. But Rebecca knew that Great-Aunt Frankie would have been proud of her.

Frances Beryl Chase had been a pioneering female journalist, a reporter for the *Denver Mountain Herald* beginning in the 1920s. Frankie Chase was never afraid to take on the rich and powerful when she knew her cause to be just. Rebecca had always admired her father's younger sister.

At the conclusion of the hour, Momaday's family members were presented with money collected to pay the funeral expenses, and every guest was given a kola nut, associated with all important life events in Senegalese culture.

Closure. The primal yearning had been satisfied for all who took part. Momaday's daughter thanked Rebecca with a smile as warm as her late mother's.

"Now she can begin her deeper connection with all of creation," she said. "My mother is not ended. She is transformed."


When Rebecca encountered an unfamiliar young lady the next morning, perched on a stool overlooking the lobby from the Mezzanine and sketching on her drawing pad, she sensed that the artist was there on assignment. She'd seen Mickey Branson showing her around the day before

"Hello," she said in her cheeriest voice as she approached the young lady. "May I ask what you're working on?"

"Oh, hi," the girl replied, looking up. "You work here, right?" she deduced upon seeing the silver name badge.

"I'm the hotel historian, Rebecca. Always curious about new developments."

"Of course. Nice to meet you, Rebecca. I'm Kinsey, a designer with TITHE's production company in LA. Just brainstorming some ideas for this lobby area."

"May I see?"

"Sure," Kinsey said, passing the sketch pad to her. "I'm starting with the griffin theme and creating a sorta Harry Potter-Hogwarts thing around it. See, here in the corner I think we could put an inflatable kid-scaled castle. You know, a bouncy part on the bottom, maybe a slide from the turret on top. And from the skylight, we can suspend some actual griffins—papier mache, probably—three or four of them at different heights. Maybe one perched on the seventh-floor balcony railing."

Rebecca nodded, momentarily incapable of comment as she examined Kinsey's fanciful renditions.

"The fountain is cool," the designer granted. "But it's boring. Blup, blop, blup, blop—it's monotonous. We could get that guy who did the Bellagio fountains in Vegas to animate it—program a cyclical choreography of streams and jets and spurts, add some colored lights. Really make it pop."

"The Bellagio guy. Right."

"And you know that upside-down panel on the balcony? People love that, trying to spot it. I think we should have one on every level. Even change where they are every six months or so to keep regular visitors guessing."

"Your ideas are very creative," Rebecca said. "The new owners asked you to do this?"

"Oh yeah. I did all the guestrooms at Haggis Castle and the Dolphin Delights playground on the Bahamas cruise ship."

"You must be very proud."

"Yeah, sure I am," Kinsey said, looking away dreamily, reappraising the soaring atrium and laying her pencil aside. "But this place is different somehow. I don't know. I sorta don't feel right—like I'm messing with something that's always been exactly like it should be."

Rebecca smiled and touched her gently on the shoulder. "You're a very perceptive young lady," she said. "Tell your employers exactly that, and you'll have the eternal gratitude of all who love The Keep."


"From here we're going to head upstairs," Rebecca announced about two-thirds of the way through each tour. "And I urge you to brace yourselves for a little time travel. Because on these first seven floors, you're surrounded with decorative touches from the era of the hotel's opening—sort of late Victoriana, turn-of-the-last-century sort of thing. When the elevator doors open up on nine, you're going to be confronted with a completely different era."

With that teaser, the tour headed for the lifts. Rebecca rode up with the final elevator load of ghost tourers, and as she stepped out onto the top floor, she exclaimed rather belatedly, "Surprise!"

The most immediately striking difference on the ninth floor was that the center atrium was completely enclosed by glass brick. Gone were the Victorian touches, and in their place were streamlined, unfussy elements.

"It's like another hotel up here, isn't it? When you see these Art Deco details—terrazzo floors, rounded corners, these light fixtures and, my favorite thing, the numbers on the doors—what decade or decades do you associate this look with? Think old movies..."

41

Guesses were all over the twentieth-century map. But the history-savvy among the group generally pegged it as the 1930s.

"Can't you just see Greta Garbo coming out of this door?" Rebecca prompted. "These changes date to 1935, the middle of the Great Depression. Before that time, much of the Keep's eighth floor below us was two stories high. In one of the 45-degree-angle corners was the two-story Grand Ballroom. And in the other acute corner was a two-story room called the Ladies Ordinary—a combination ladies lounge and changing room. If you came for dinner in the hotel and you weren't staying here, there was actually staff to help you change into your evening wear back in those elegant days."

"Like 'Downton Abbey,'" an older lady contributed.

"The eighth floor also housed the dining rooms and the kitchen. But you know, during the Depression, so many grand hotels—all around the country—began downhill slides from which many of them never rebounded. They fell into disrepair and disrepute and eventually became the victims of what I call Urban Removal in the 1960s and 70s."

"Like the Ashford Arms that used to be across Grand," a longtime resident remembered.

"And the Knickerbocker at the end of Seventeenth," another guest said.

"I think the Griffins Keep's survival was due to the owners during those years, the business-savvy Kuhrsfelds. During the Depression, they realized that there was not going to be much call for big formal balls and private dinner parties. And they also recognized that many of Denver's wealthiest citizens—their friends—were being forced by the economy to downsize their living arrangements."

"Been there," a tour taker muttered to his wife.

"So the hotel owner at the time, R.J. Kuhrsfeld, decided to convert these top two floors into private residential apartments. They were called the Parapet Apartments, and it was a very prestigious, very pricey address. The steady income from those permanent residents allowed the hotel part of The Keep to continue operating, without sacrificing any elegance or excellence, throughout the Great Depression, World War II, and beyond—an early successful experiment with what we're now calling 'mixed use' and thinking we just invented."

"Do people still live up here?" someone asked.

Rebecca shook her head. "In the late 70s, early 80s, these gradually transitioned into our executive accommodations, the Keep-Sake Suites. And obviously, we've redecorated many times since the 1930s. But every time, they've chosen to keep a few of these Art Deco touches. The glass brick around the atrium was installed at the time of the apartments for privacy and quiet, and some guests still appreciate that. You notice we can barely hear the lobby piano from up here."

"What about ghosts?"

"Well, because many people lived in the Parapet apartments for years and years, and several people died in them, these top two floors are among the more likely places for spiritual activity." Rebecca's narrative varied somewhat from this point on, depending upon which suite she was able to show. Regardless, she drew from the well of stock ghost stories again and again.

"Are we going to see the haunted room?" a guest asked anxiously. The best known of all the Griffins Keep "ghost" stories referenced Room 940 and one of the earliest Parapet Apartment residents. As luck would have it, Rebecca had been able to reserve that room for show today. Her tour guests were thrilled.

The historian tapped the key card on the lock scanner. It had worked fine when she'd previewed the suite less than an hour earlier. Now it refused to open.

"Don't be difficult, Sybil," Rebecca said quietly, speaking, it appeared, to the door. She tapped the key to the pad again. Success.

As the historian ushered her tour inside, she explained, "As you can see, these Keep-Sake suites are decorated in an updated deco style, with the rounded furniture, the mauve tones—but still flat screen TVs and Keurig coffee makers. Some of them even have elliptical trainers or treadmills. Have a quick look around and then find a seat here in the front room."

When they were all settled in for story time, Rebecca began the narrative she had perfected long ago.

"Mrs. Dawson Thorne—Sybil Thorne—was the queen of Denver high society around the turn of last century. She moved from Savannah to Denver, determined to marry money, and managed to snag railroad heir Dawson Thorne. Sybil made it her personal mission to establish and oversee the social Who's Who of Denver. She was an unapologetic snob, but she was also very

43

beautiful. In her late 50s, she took a young man in his 20s as her lover—a 'cougar' before we coined the term."

She paused for the predictable bemused reaction here.

"Barkley Heath was a dashing daredevil aerial balloonist, as well as an investment manager with Kuhrsfeld & Company. Sybil was thoroughly smitten and not a bit discreet about their affair. She went so far as to hang a full-length portrait of Barkley in the foyer of her Capitol Hill mansion, right along with her husband Dawson's."

"Makes you wonder about Dawson," a guest commented.

"Anyway, when Dawson died, Barkley asked Sybil to marry him. It promised to be the social event of the year. Sybil outdid herself planning every lavish detail of the ceremony and the reception here at The Keep.

"But the day of the wedding came, and Barkley was a no show. He telephoned Sybil the next day to inform her that he'd married a younger woman."

She paused as a few listeners shook their heads or rolled their eyes, anticipating the fallout.

"Sybil was humiliated, heartbroken. She did not take rejection lightly. She had made Barkley successful by persuading all of her wealthy friend to invest with him, and now she vowed to break him. She knew the men who could ruin him financially, and she saw to it that that happened. Destitute and despondent, Barkley ended up putting a bullet through his brain," Rebecca said, pointing a finger gun at her own temple for effect.

"Talk about blowback," a leather-jacketed young man said.

"Less than a week later, when someone asked Sybil at a party what had happened to the dashing Mr. Heath, she casually replied that she hadn't the slightest idea."

Rebecca acknowledged the looks of disgust on her listeners' faces before summarizing, "So this is the sort of heartless you-know-what I'm talking about. Sybil spent the last 25 years of her life right here in Parapet Apartment 940, now our Room 940. She grew progressively senile and progressively reclusive until she died of pneumonia in this room at the age of 91 in 1955."

The historian paused and took a breath. "Our story now fast-forwards to the year 2000, when my predecessor in this historian position, Gloria Vanelli, began offering special themed tours that we still present throughout the month of February in honor of Valentine's Day, called 'Romance and Scandal.'" Rebecca's sensationalized exaggeration of the word "scandal" always brought smiles.

"Of course, Gloria had to include the story of Mrs. Dawson Thorne's scandalous romance as part of the tour. And when she started to give these tours, at the exact time she was leading them, our main switchboard began to get phone calls from Room 940. The operators who picked up these calls would invariably hear only static on the line. But every time Gloria was conducting a 'Romance' tour, the calls came from 940.

"Well, Gloria put two and two together and concluded that Sybil did not want her dirty laundry aired for the entertainment of the general public. So she dropped Sybil's story from the tour, and the phone calls immediately ceased."

At this point, her audience was usually intrigued but skeptical. *Time for the zinger.*

"Now the reason this is especially mysterious is that, at the same time all this was going on, the hotel was undertaking a major redecoration of these top two floors. And every single room on our eighth and ninth floors was completely stripped—not only of furniture, carpeting, and light fixtures, but definitely of telephones.

"There wasn't a phone to be found on the ninth floor when the switchboard got those persistent calls from Room 940."

Without warning, a loud voice from behind her startled Rebecca and her tour guests.

"We're offering these genuine cultured pearl earrings for the next thirty minutes only at the incredible price of just $29.95," the voice blared. The flat-screen TV had come on all by itself. Rebecca could clearly see the remote on the coffee table. No one had touched it.

"Pick up your phone and call now..."

The historian snatched up the remote and clicked off the Shopping Network. "Weird electrical glitches like this happen in old buildings all the time," she said, trying to minimize her guests' agitation.

"But the TV said, 'Call now.' That can't be a coincidence," a woman pointed out, speaking for everyone on the tour. Rebecca decided to roll with it.

"Well, I suggest we all thank Sybil politely as we leave. Apparently she is someone you piss off at your peril."

45

"I still don't believe in ghosts," an elderly lady with a cane told the guide as they hurried out of 940. "But I definitely believe in Mrs. Dawson Thorne."

"Do you tell people if they're staying in a haunted room?" a teenaged girl on the tour asked.

The historian smiled slyly and replied, "No. We let them tell *us*."

# CHAPTER 6

"While we're waiting to ride back down to the lobby," Rebecca began, pausing at the public elevators for her tour takers' attention, "notice the Mail Drop over there. We're on the top floor, and that cast-iron chute goes all the way down to One. The postman still empties it daily."

When the elevator arrived with a light and a ding, off stepped Mr. Beaumont with two Japanese-American businessmen. The visitors smiled at Rebecca before following the GM, who scarcely acknowledged her presence. TITHE reps, Rebecca assumed. She occasionally encountered them around the hotel, always accompanied by current managers and poking around critically.

"So these top two floors look completely different because they were added on top of the building in the 1940s," Mr. Beaumont told the visitors, as they walked off toward a showroom.

The tour guests looked to Rebecca, confused. "That's not what you told us about these floors," one of them said.

"That's because it's balderdash," the historian said, employing her favorite archaic word for bullshit and utterly careless of whether Beaumont heard her or not. Nothing irked Rebecca more than misinformation.

"I'm sure you've also noticed these wonderful 1930s rotary telephones on every floor opposite the elevators," she continued, returning her attention to her guests. "They're functional house phones that still work. Sometimes, when I have young children on tours," she said, "they ask what these old phones are. They can't figure out how they work or why they're attached to the wall. They make me feel positively historical."

Several in the group obviously recognized that feeling. As they stepped aboard the elevator, she suggested, "If you ever want to feel really old, try listing things, like rotary phones, that have become obsolete in your lifetime."

"Typewriters!" one woman contributed.

"Clotheslines," said another.

"Trash incinerators."

"Slide rulers."

"Eight-track tapes."

"Customer service."

"Common courtesy."

The elevator landed and the doors opened.

"Thank god!" a gentleman said, relieved. "Had that depressing exercise gone on much longer, I'd have had to drink heavily."

The historian invariably concluded her one-hour ghost tours in the ground floor elevator lobby. "So this last story is an experience of my own. I save it for the end when we're done riding the elevators."

People especially loved the personal accounts. The incident Rebecca shared had really happened, but it had puzzled more than scared her.

"About ten months ago, I was waiting for the elevator on the eighth floor with a hotel guest. And in a nearby room we could hear a crying baby. It wasn't a sad cry, but an angry cry or a frightened cry. I turned to the guest and commented, 'Sounds like somebody is not happy about staying here at the Griffins Keep.' The elevator arrived, we climbed aboard, the doors closed. And we fully expected the sound of that crying to get quieter. It didn't. In fact, as we started to descend, it grew louder and louder. Then at the third floor, it sounded as if that crying baby whooshed by the outside of the elevator doors—and stopped instantly."

She snapped her fingers to demonstrate how quickly the sound had ceased. "I was glad I was with someone else, because we looked at each other and said, 'Did you hear that?' 'Did you...?' And our mutual astonishment confirmed that we had both perceived the same strange phenomenon."

A mousy young woman who had hovered on the fringes throughout the tour asked seriously, "Were there always elevators here?"

Rebecca studied the woman's pale grey eyes for a moment before answering. "No," she said, "there weren't. These elevators date to the 1930s, the same time the top two floors were converted to apartments. Before that, a second grand staircase occupied this space. It was called the Ladies Staircase because it went up to the Ladies Ordinary I told you about on 8."

The young woman turned to the elevators and looked up, eyes wide. She seemed shaken.

"He was dropped," she whispered.

Rebecca wondered if she'd heard correctly. "What did you say? Who was dropped?"

"The baby you heard," the woman said. "His nursemaid... she couldn't stand the crying any longer. She dropped him from the railing of the eighth floor staircase. His crying stopped when he struck the landing."

The tour guests stared at the young woman, then at their speechless guide. Rebecca had to say something, anything. "Well.... I suppose that's an interesting possibility," she managed, "though I've never come across such a story in all my research."

*Good. That was good.* Surely she sounded more rational than she felt. But her blood ran cold. It was as if this stranger had supplied the missing video of a soundtrack Rebecca had somehow tuned into, and she instantly recognized the truth of it. How could the young woman have known what had happened? And how could the echoes of that awful incident have been replayed so many decades later?

Stone tape theory. Psychics and mediums had referenced it for years. In essence, the theory advanced the notion that the mineral content and crystalline structure of certain types of stone could somehow capture and preserve the sounds of events that occurred within walls constructed of—or faced with—those stones. Rebecca had first heard of it on one of those "ghost hunter" shows on cable TV. The paranormal investigators insisted they were able to tap these "recordings" and hear actual echoes of the past. In a cavernous old train station where a 1920s gangland shooting had taken place, they claimed to capture the sound of gunshots with their special spirit-sensing equipment. Shouts. A woman's scream. Their earnest credulity had amused her at the time.

But the young woman's chilling interpretation of the baby's cries on the elevator now caused Rebecca to reconsider her initial dismissal of stone tape theory. At the time of construction, the Griffins Keep incorporated more onyx than any other single building of its day. The semi-precious stone, similar in appearance to marble, was actually a variety of quartz. *Aren't quartz crystals used in radios and other transmitting devices?*

There was, of course, no stone on the elevators. But she knew from an article in the archives that the contractors had recycled and reshaped the rare golden onyx that had faced the old staircase in the new art-deco-styled elevator lobby. Might some of that onyx still reverberate with the final cries of a terrified infant?

"Our tour has come to an end," the historian said, eager to wrap up, "but the stories of Griffins Keep ghosts continue to unfold. When your time comes, we invite you each to join whatever spirits may linger here in the hotel. But we sincerely hope to see you again before then."

Today the guests applauded, as they often did. A well-dressed older gentleman smiled and thanked her as he slipped her a tightly folded $20 bill; other guests followed suite with smaller denominations.

The rest of the guests had dispersed when a man with dirty gray hair and a beat-up denim jacket held out his hand to shake hers.

"Hey, whoa... So you really are Becky Bridger! The Rebecca thing threw me off for a minute. It's Gary Floyd... 'Pink' Floyd. Remember me from Steamboat?"

She remembered him. She wished she didn't. There was always the chance on public tours of running into people from her painful past.

"Shit, it's been like what—thirty years or something? You look just the same, except classier. You're not still with Bryce, are you?" Gary asked.

"Not for a long time."

"That's good, man. Glad to hear it, I really am. No way he was good for you. Hey—we have to catch up. You free for a beer or something?"

"No thank you, Gary, I'm not."

"That's cool. I get it. It's really great to see you, though. So wow, you're good at this stuff. A big fancy historian now, huh? Who woulda guessed it way back when you were waiting tables at

50

The Cellar? Whatever happened to Bryce, do you know? Last I heard he was gonna be a big famous actor or director or something in L.A."

"No idea. Lost touch."

"Back in the day, he sorta pimped you, didn't he?"

Rebecca had never attached the ugly word to her ex-husband's machinations, but she realized as she heard it from someone else how apt the characterization was.

"I guess you could say that." *But you didn't have to.*

"I mean, I know it was the '70s and 'free love' and all that. But I think he got off on giving you to other guys for dope and drugs and shit. It was pretty sick, his own wife. Lots of us thought so. Did you really like it, or did you just go along because he asked you?"

"I wanted to do whatever made him happy." *I thought that was what love meant.*

"Oh man, don't know about him, but I reckon you made plenty of other guys happy."

"I think we're done here…"

"No wait. Don't be mad, Beck. Hey, I just hafta ask, compared to all the guys you did it with, I was pretty good, wasn't I? I mean, one of the best, right? 'Cause you sure acted like you enjoyed it, if you know what I mean…"

Acted. That was it exactly. To emotionally escape the sordid scenes staged by her ex-husband, she'd tried to imagine the other men he set her up with to be Bryce himself. Or tried to imagine herself as someone else. None of it was real. Pretending she was playing a role in a drama was the coping mechanism to which she had clung.

"Good-bye, Gary," she said. "Please don't come back here for another tour. Please."

"Hey, it's cool. Don't wanna be reminded of that shit now you're all respectable. I get it. You don't have to take it out on me. Geez."


The door to Sales Director Dick Plotz's office was open. Rebecca rapped on the metal frame and poked her head around the corner. "Knock, knock."

"Oh," Plotz said, scarcely looking away from his PC monitor. "You. We have a meeting, right?" As he peered at her over the rims of his square-framed glasses, Rebecca imagined the perverse

51

stylist who had convinced him his poorly dyed hair would look cool with bangs.

*It's been three months. Time for our "regular" bi-weekly.* Rebecca kept her sarcasm to herself. "We need to talk about the ghost tour packages."

"Yeah, right."

*Have a seat,* Rebecca invited herself when Plotz did not. "Dawn's joining us, isn't she?"

"Wasn't she out there?" Plotz asked, finally getting up from his desk. "She needs to be here."

His ever-cheerful admin assistant appeared in the doorway as if on cue, notebook in hand. "Rebecca! Great to see you," she said. "The memorial for Momaday was wonderful. I've got some mail for you to pick up when we're finished."

The three gathered around the circular table displaying Plotz's many sales awards under its glass top. He leaned back in his leather upholstered chair, laced his fingers behind his head, and exhaled impatiently. "So?"

"When we met a few months ago you mentioned planning a 'Haunted Happy Hour' package again this year. Do you have a date or dates in mind for that?" Plotz seemed to brighten suddenly. "Oh yeah. Halloween's on a Tuesday this year. Sucks. So I think we'll do the overnight package the Friday before."

He leaned forward in his chair. "I've got an awesome idea for a new twist. With everything here at the hotel about to change, and with the massive popularity of all these ghost hunter shows on TV, we should do something for the wackos who buy into this crap. Invite them to bring all their ghost-hunting gear—special lenses, magnetic meters, 'spirit' recorders—all of it. Hell, we can advertise for psychics and mediums to come and see what they can 'sense' in the old place. Charge them up the ass for this unprecedented opportunity."

Dawn and Rebecca exchanged wary glances.

"It would be popular all right," Rebecca began. "We often get requests from paranormal investigation groups to set up their equipment, spend the night in one of our 'haunted' rooms. But we always decline, because Mr. Beaumont doesn't want them disrupting business and insists that The Keep is *not* a haunted hotel. Have you talked to him about this idea?"

Undeterred, Plotz continued as though he were dictating copy. "One night only. For the first time in its long history, Griffins

52

Keep opens its doors to paranormal investigation. What has the hotel been hiding? What will scientific methods and extra-sensory explorations reveal? It'll be huge."

"But Mr. Beaumont..."

The sales manager waved his hand dismissively. "Don't worry about him. I'll get him on board. He's a lame duck now anyway, with the TITHE takeover"

Dawn rolled her eyes at Rebecca when Plotz looked away, foreseeing a massive clash of egos over this proposed bit of sensationalism.

For now, they went along. Rebecca said. "How do you see this event? Drinks in the Silver Spoon Club, my introductory 'Ghost' PowerPoint, then just set them loose in the hotel?"

"No, no. Can't let them run around by themselves. You'll have to take them around on the tour but let them do their thing as you go."

"I'd like to draw the line at audio and video-recording then," Rebecca insisted. "After all, it's the stories we're selling. If recorded versions of the tour were available everywhere, who would come to the hotel to pay for it?"

Plotz considered this for a moment, then nodded agreement. "OK, no recording the tour stories. They can take pictures, walk around with their thermometers looking for cold spots—whatever the hell these guys do. The media will be all over it."

"No question about that," Rebecca agreed, glancing again at the equally leery Dawn. "No question at all."

After the meeting, Rebecca followed Dawn to her desk to collect the mail she'd mentioned. "I'll look through my old emails for some of these ghost-hunting groups I've turned down in the past," she said. "But I'm not contacting any of them until we hear Mr. Beaumont's approved of all this."

Dawn nodded. "If we really do offer it, everybody's going to want to spend the night in the 'haunted' room, 940. And you know they'll be up at all hours, wandering the halls in their bunny slippers, setting up equipment around the hotel, desperate to 'capture' something. It'll be a nightmare for Security. It'll be a nightmare—Period."

Although TITHE management was not due to take over until November, their outsourced market researchers had already been at work for months, analyzing The Keep's clientele and hospitality niche. When they presented their findings to the sales team, Dick Plotz insisted that Rebecca be present. Typically left out of the marketing strategizing, the historian was wary of the invitation. Why was Plotz so keen on including her now?

Riesen-Shyne was an audacious L.A. marketing firm, all about "positioning" and "rebranding." Their presenter this morning, Marcus Riesen himself, delved right in with PowerPoint pie charts, probing for plums with a dispassionate thumb.

"To get a feel for the hotel and your customers, we conducted several focus groups, and I'd like to share the results with all of you." His hand-held clicker brought up the first graph. "The initial focus groups were drawn from regular and frequent Griffins Keep patrons. When asked why they chose The Keep over other Denver luxury hotels, their responses consistently mentioned two things: history and elegance. As you can see here, a combined 76% indicated those two factors as influencing their choice."

*Yes!* Rebecca wanted to cheer. Here was proof of what she'd been trying to tell Plotz all along. Surely now the marketing focus would reflect these results.

But Riesen-Shyne's interpretation of the data took none of this into account. Apparently they did not hear—or did not care— what current clientele valued about the hotel.

Mr. Riesen brought up the next pie chart. "The second round of focus groups was comprised of people who had never been to The Keep but who were considered desirable customers. When these folks were asked why they did *not* choose the Griffins Keep, time and again they responded with variations of 'I heard it was old,' or 'I heard it was snobby'—or exclusive or expensive. Here again, you can see the results charted."

And on those misperceptions, Riesen-Shyne chose to base their new approach to marketing the hotel.

"So, how are we going to appeal to this affluent, mostly younger, demographic?" Mr. Riesen asked before presenting his solution. "Are you ready for the Griffins Keep's first-ever TV commercial? Run the video."

Ready or not, here it came. An in-your-face blast of techno-pop music, quick-take images of young people posing around the hotel, and the tagline; "Griffins Keep: Trending Away from Traditional." Dick Plotz and the sales staff applauded and hooted.

"This is just a taste of the branding strategy and breakthrough tactics Riesen-Shyne is known for. We're gonna make the Griffins Keep the chic and contemporary hotel of choice for a whole new generation of consumers."

From that moment on, history would become a dirty word in the world of Griffins Keep marketing, determined to ignore what made The Keep distinctive.

"Why do we want to be like every other hotel?" Rebecca dared to ask when Mr. Riesen took questions. "There are plenty of places in Denver for people looking for trendy and modern. The Keep is the last place they'll come for that sort of thing. This should be the one hotel where they can find the warmth and the charm of another era."

Fully intending to harsh the Riesen buzz, she plunged on,

"And you're wrong about young people dismissing the past. Kids into steampunk have their own creative take on old tech and old styles. Many of them love historical fiction, historical architecture, historical fashions. And millennials get hooked on the cable TV period dramas as much as older viewers."

The young marketing guru glowered at Rebecca, saw his grandmother, and discounted her as hopelessly out of touch. "Surveys don't lie, ma'am," he replied, pissing her off further with his disingenuous courtesy. "No one wants to turn back the clock except those who can't keep up with the times."


So numerous and varied were reports of unexplained phenomena at the Griffins Keep that Rebecca often told different stories to different tour groups. She tried to gauge the particular interests of her audience and tailored her selections accordingly.

"How many of you are familiar with the phenomena known as 'orbs?'" she asked the guests on today's tour. Nearly everyone in the group was, some enthusiastically so. For the uninitiated Rebecca explained, "Orbs are relatively new players on the paranormal scene. When people began using digital cameras in the 1990s, they were occasionally surprised to find in their photos these glowing, iridescent bubbles—though they had seen nothing of the sort when they snapped the pictures. Theories of what these orbs might be range from motes of dust or specks of moisture to spirits of the dead or beings from another plane of reality.

Whatever they are, The Keep seems to attract them like flies to honey."

At the tour stop overlooking the lobby from the mezzanine balcony, she cited an example. "Last year, one of our bellmen was taking pictures of the Griffins Fountain below us here, and when he got his photos developed, he discovered quite a mystery in three of them.

"He was shooting from the Grand Staircase side, so in the background was the front desk, which is where it's always been. In the first photo, there's no one behind the desk, but there's an orb clearly hovering over one side of it. In the second photo—taken, he claims, less than minute later—the orb is gone, and behind the desk stands a man that no one recognizes. And in the third photo—again, less than a minute later—the man is gone, and there's an orb hovering over the other side of the front desk."

"Have you seen the actual pictures?" a skeptic asked.

"I have."

"Can we see them?"

Rebecca shook her head. "Sorry. Our managing director won't allow us to share any of the 'ghost' images we've collected. He's a non-believer, convinced they're all trick photos created with Photoshop or something like that." *Note to self,* Rebecca thought. *Screw Beaumont and bring the pictures along next tour.*

"I think the orbs are angels," declared a 60-ish woman in a periwinkle blue polyester pantsuit, taking pictures with her phone in hopes of capturing her own phenomena. "They're spirits of the dead, but only the *good* dead."

"Oh yeah?" said an irreverent young man in the group, apparently no acquaintance. "Then what happens to the spirits of the bad dead? If they're not orbs—or angels—what are they after they die?"

Unfazed by his challenge, the woman replied bluntly. "Nothing. Total, absolutely nothing. Death is the end. Evil souls don't get eternal life. Not in any form. They're just suspended, forever and ever, in a terrible black void."

Rebecca hoped no one saw her shudder. She believed she had experienced that fathomless oblivion in recurring nightmares, decades ago. She remembered the terror as if it were yesterday.

The woman turned to Rebecca and asked directly, "Do you believe in angels?"

"Me? Um, sure. Why not?" But Rebecca couldn't take the whole idea of angels seriously. Wings and robes, harps and halos? She believed in them about as much she did Santa Claus now. It was all part of the anachronistic Christian doctrine with which she was raised, but which she had finally come to see for what it was. Its dogma ranked alongside fairytales and legends, moralistic fables from a less sophisticated age. Rebecca considered herself more intelligent than the unquestioning faithful who swallowed its mythology. She had not counted herself among them in a long, long time.

# CHAPTER 7

If the guests on her ghost tour looked to be a hardy lot, Rebecca often escorted them down the Grand Staircase from floors eight or nine to the seventh floor, the highest open floor encircling the atrium. "The view of our skylight from that level is spectacular," she'd promise, "as is the view of the lobby."

They were never disappointed; though a few were disturbed by the dizzying height and chose to stand considerably back from the railing. Guests going to and from their rooms and staff in the performance of their duties were visible on six floors of balconies ringing the atrium.

"So here we've returned to the Victorian era, décor-wise. You can clearly see the intricate detail of the stained glass just above us. Most of the year," she continued, directing their attention to the void before them, "this eight-story atrium space is completely empty, as it is today. But from the Monday before Thanksgiving until after New Year's, our huge holiday chandelier, suspended from the center of this steel support structure below the skylight, hangs from about the fifth floor to the second floor."

Guests looked up and then down, trying to imagine the atrium decoration. Then, before she could herd them back to the elevators and down to the ground floor, someone asked, "Has anybody ever fallen or jumped from up here?"

The question was almost inevitable. Gazing down over the edge at the dollhouse-sized lobby furniture far below, one couldn't help but wonder about the possibility. But the hotel tour guides were not to discuss such things. Mr. Beaumont was intractable on this point. Didn't want anyone getting ideas—as if the accident/suicide potential of the space weren't obvious. So Rebecca, when faced with this question, gave the answer their managing director had officially sanctioned.

"The only instance we know of that happening was back in 1911," she began. "A youngster named Millie was walking on this seventh-floor railing, trying to balance, when she fell all the way to the lobby floor."

She paused for the predictable gasps of horror.

"Of course, she was knocked out cold for several hours. A doctor was called, and he finally managed to revive her. Astonishingly, after a few wobbly steps, Millie actually walked away from the fall, apparently unhurt."

At this, brows knit and skepticism abounded. Then, with the timing of a consummate storyteller, Rebecca added innocently, "Did I remember to mention that Millie was the hotel cat?"

Even with that key detail belatedly revealed, the story was astonishing. It usually satisfied the fall-curious, as the guide moved swiftly on. But of course people had fallen from the balconies into the open atrium on several occasions over the decades. And people had jumped.

Rebecca never shared with tour guests the tragic suicide tale of Dolores Cruz from just a few years earlier.

At 9:18 that January morning, the lobby of the Griffins Keep hotel had been quiet and nearly empty. Few witnessed Dolores's final act. The heavy thud had startled a gentleman checking out at the front desk and had caused a young lady setting tables for afternoon tea to drop her tray of china cups. It took several moments for the reality of the incident to register with those present.

Intending to minimize the mess when her body struck the lobby floor seven stories below, veteran hotel housekeeper Dolores had wrapped herself in a sheet before she jumped. Tidiness was her hallmark.

What she had failed to reckon into her grim preparations was the ricochet. Her falling form hit the ledge protruding from the third-floor balcony with such force that her shoes flew off in different directions.

Hotel management later explained that Dolores had been undergoing cancer treatments for several months. The prognosis was bleak. Her job performance suffered. The morning of Dolores's suicide, her supervisor had ordered an indefinite medical leave of absence—without pay. After 23 years of service, the dedicated employee had been devastated by the decision.

"The hotel was Dolores's whole life," a co-worker quoted in the newspaper recalled afterwards. "She told me she would never leave The Keep. Not ever."

Rebecca knew the story from Lochlan, one of the few unfortunate eyewitnesses to the plunge.

"Of course she haunts the place," he'd told the historian. "Sometimes when I step around—never over—the spot where she hit, I'll look up and speak to her in my head. *Your work here is done, Dolores,* I try to tell her. *You've earned your rest.* Maybe one day, she'll accept her death and move on."


The street vendor peddling "Brains-on-a-Stick" waved a sample in her face. A sunken-eyed bride in shredded gown staggered alongside an eviscerated clown. Denver's annual Zombie Crawl pervaded the Sixteenth Street Mall with walking-dead wannabees.

A sore thumb in Victorian period costume, Rebecca approached an official crossing guard at the nearest intersection. The last thing she needed after a long day of leading tours was this plague of pseudo-corpses complicating her commute.

"Excuse me, sir. Weren't the mall shuttles supposed to resume operations at 6:30?"

"Yeah, they were," the guard confirmed as he held up traffic with one gloved hand and beckoned the horde across with the other. "But time is lost on these guys."

Spawned years earlier, the Crawl had morphed into tonight's malignant mass of fifteen-thousand. It spread slowly southward toward Civic Center Park and a pointless conclusion, clogging the city's heart.

Rebecca should have checked her moon-phase calendar, should have had a contingency plan. She had relied upon public transportation almost exclusively since the self-destructive drinking binges surrounding her divorce had resulted in a near-fatal car collision with a child on a bike. The child had recovered. But more than thirty years later, the scare still haunted Rebecca. Most of the time, her old Volvo sat in the garage, gathering dust.

61

Not even the pedi-cabs ventured out this evening. No option. She would have to buck the zombie tide to connect to her bus home at Union Station, fifteen blocks away. The journey had never seemed so endless. At last Rebecca pushed through the heavy doors of the recently renovated train depot into light and life. The vaulted space vibrated anew with arrivals and departures, just as it had more than a century ago.

Sanctuary.

Rebecca breathed easier as she traversed the Great Hall and collapsed on a high-backed wooden bench. Her arthritic feet ached. She unlaced her vintage boots and hobbled out through the back doors in stocking feet. She inhaled the chill air and plopped ungracefully onto the lip of a concrete planter to await her bus. The cheeky moon flirted through peek-a-boo clouds. A whirlwind stirred some dry leaves into a rising funnel, many yards away. As she watched, the funnel swirled nearer, gathering debris as it progressed across the plaza. A moment later it surrounded her, shooting higher into the air before instantly dissipating overhead, showering her with autumnal confetti.

Rebecca couldn't help but smile as she brushed herself off. Magic still had its moments, even in a zombie-obsessed world.

Rebecca discounted ghosts, had lost faith in the church, and had written off the myth of "true love." But she still believed in magic and knew it was not something to trifle with.

When she was twelve years old, her father had been fired from his job. As a child, she was not privy to the reason for his dismissal. It didn't matter. She knew with certainty that her father was in the right and that his boss, Harold Proctor, was unjustified in his action.

Young Becky had recently seen or read something about voodoo practices. She decided to employ the cult's mystical powers to get even with Mr. Proctor for the wrong he had done her father. She crafted a voodoo doll of geometrical styrofoam shapes joined by toothpicks. She hollowed out the torso with a paring knife and stuffed it with a work glove she had snatched from Proctor's yard, which she passed every day on her way to and from school. She knew a personal article incorporated into the doll was essential to its sympathetic magic.

By the light of the next full moon, she cursed the doll by reciting Proctor's name thirteen times, then chanting "Die, die, die!" and stabbing a steak knife into its head with each recitation. She poured all her vengeance into the act.

The next day, her father announced that Harold Proctor had succumbed to a massive stroke. He had died, died, died.

*I did it,* Rebecca had believed. *I killed him with my magic.* She panicked. The power of life and death was far beyond anything she was ready for. *Never again,* she'd vowed in fearful contrition. *Never again will I call upon magical powers for personal reasons.*

As it turned out, Mr. Beaumont went out of town, looking for new employment, the last two weeks of October. Plotz waited until the last minute to publicize the special paranormal package on social media, but it didn't deter attendance in the least. Word of this unique opportunity to investigate the Griffins Keep spread fast among the supernaturally-inclined. Within two days, reservations surpassed the 80-person limit Rebecca had wanted to set, and another sixty people were waitlisted. Plotz was thrilled. Everyone else was worried.

Rebecca had watched the usual "ghost adventure" shows on TV and expected all sorts of paranormal investigative equipment on site that night. EMS—electro-magnetic sensors—purportedly detected the bio-energy of spirits, the electro-magnetism that makes hair stand on end. Full-spectrum cameras picked up light beyond the visible, including ultra-violet and infra-red. Night vision cameras and thermal imaging cameras, originally developed for the military, had been adopted by serious ghost hunters to detect and capture things lurking in the dark.

Parabolic microphones picked up subsonic frequencies at levels below the human capacity to hear. Used with so-called "spirit boxes," the special mics were believed to capture phrases or whole conversations uttered by spirits, which were then displayed on the boxes as written words onscreen. The ever-expanding arsenal of high-tech ghost detection devices sought, paradoxically, to prove scientifically the existence of things beyond the explanation of science.

It was going to be quite an evening.

The Banquets and Catering staff outdid themselves in decorating the Silver Spoon. Beyond the entrance dripping with

63

cobwebs and skeletons, corpses with glowing red eyes lounged in the foyer chairs. Dry ice and fans created a swirling mist. Bats dangled from the chandeliers. Rats peeped from the eyeholes of skulls set around the room. The window ledges along one wall of the triangular room displayed nearly twenty entries from The Keep's interdepartmental jack-o-lantern carving contest.

An open mini-coffin served up ghoulish appetizers. After dark, only city light through the stained glass windows lit the room. Candles glowed in the center of each round table.

Spirits aplenty poured forth from the bar as The Keeps' special guests arrived. The "Mile-High Haunt Hunters" wore matching T-shirts. So did the buxom believers who called themselves the "Ghost Busties." More than one witch had taken her costuming cue from Stevie Nicks. Several wizards flitted about in tall pointed hats, one with a Gandolph staff. The Mountain West Paranormal Investigators identified themselves with MWPI logos emblazoned on the backs of leather jackets. The eclectic crowd included people of all ages and approaches who shared but one thing in common: a determination to believe.

This was not, Rebecca recognized immediately, an audience that would settle for Casper stories. As the cocktail reception cranked up, a few of the curious visited the "gypsy" palm reader and crystal-ball gazer hired for the occasion. But kitschy Halloween trappings were not what they'd come for.

These hunters were loaded for game. *Bring on the phenomena!* they seemed to demand.

The plan was for a 45-minute abbreviated cocktail hour before Rebecca presented a PowerPoint with the backstories of several potential Keep specters. What the plan failed to take into account was that eager ghost hunters with a few drinks in them had little patience for a presentation. Sensing their restlessness, Rebecca foreshortened her spiel and got right to the business of organizing the guests into four roughly equal groups and launching them, under the guidance of her three associate historians, into the allegedly "spiritually active" spaces of the Griffins Keep.

"I'm told by several of the mediums among us this evening that The Keep's spirits are excited to finally be recognized," she said. "Apparently they are eager to share their stories."

The logistics of routing multiple groups was tricky. "It's imperative you move along to your next stop after no more than ten minutes," Rebecca emphasized to the other guides before the event, "because the next group will be right behind you. If your guests balk, remind them that they'll have the rest of the night to return to any of the sites on their own for further—and longer— investigation. Remember, this is just an overview—a little history, a couple stories, then off. We should all re-convene in the Silver Spoon by 9:00."

Rebecca's quarter of the guests remained in the Club after the others had departed. "You're lucky to be starting in the hotel space considered by many to be the spookiest part of the building," Rebecca began. "You heard the stories of the ghostly bartender and the railroad conductor in my presentation. You've got about five minutes now to see what your tech gear or your ESP can detect here before we have to move on."

Camera shutters clicked. Ghost meters flashed and beeped like Geiger counters. Guests hovered around the bar seeking spirits, alcoholic and ethereal. All busied themselves contently except for one woman dressed all in black, her face barely visible behind the dark veil of a vintage mourning bonnet.

"The spirits in this space are most unhappy," she informed Rebecca somberly. "They think these decorations are disrespectful, and they're upset by the whole spectacle. I doubt you'll contact any presences under these circus-like conditions."

The historian took her point and saw no reason to defend the arrangement her boss had orchestrated. "I think I would probably feel the same way if I were a ghost," she said. "Hopefully the spirits will be more receptive later this evening, when most of this has died down." But even as she said it, Rebecca knew the majority of the investigators would likely settle into the Silver Spoon till all hours. Intimate spiritual encounters seemed unlikely.

Precisely ten minutes later, the historian announced, "OK, you can bring your equipment and bring your drinks. But we have to vacate this space for another group and head for our next stop." Amid grumbles, the ghost hunters reluctantly complied and followed her to the mezzanine railing overlooking the atrium lobby.

"Oh my god!" a Ghost Bustie leaning against the balcony railing directly in front of Rebecca cried. "Look at all the orbs I got in this picture!"

Her compatriots clustered around excitedly. "Here's one, two, three..."

"I'm sensing several distinct entities in this space," an older woman announced. "One is definitely a male presence, very dominate, very strong. And at least two feminine entities, much weaker, smelling faintly of flowers or perfume." Several sniffed the air for traces of sweetness. "I sense that the big one controls the other two. Their aura is subservient, even fearful. But for some reason, they can't get away from him."

"I'm not getting any of that," said a pink-caped wizard with dark-framed glasses. "I'm sensing joy and warmth. Like a reunion with loved ones, or coming home after a long absence. It's a sort of effervescent happiness."

Rebecca hoped the woman who had expressed concern about the unhappy spirits in the Silver Spoon had caught that last observation. But she scanned her twenty faces for the mourning bonnet in vain. The guest must have decided to pass on the tour and returned to her room.

The dynamic among these paranormal enthusiasts was extraordinary. Some erupted with insights, prompting others to either enjoin or dispute their impressions. Some bent silently over their gauges and meters, praying for recordable, measurable data to validate their intuitive perceptions. Some were disappointed when nothing jumped out at them.

The scream from the seventh floor balcony on the opposite side of the atrium startled, but did not surprise, the assembled ghost hunters— or the staff. The hyper-sensitivity charging the hotel atmosphere on this bizarre occasion made such an outburst inevitable.

Security rushed to the scene to find a woman crumpled on the floor.

"It was horrible, horrible," she said feebly. "More than she could bear. So hopeless, so defeated. She jumped—from right here. Oh god...I saw it...her falling so far...something fluttering...white, stocking feet....and then the sound—the sickening, heavy thud as she hit the floor—dead." Wracked with sobs, the woman struggled to her feet with help. "Get me away from here. Far, far away from here. Please god."

Rebecca continued touring her group, only later learning details of the commotion above. The tenor of the event turned from light-hearted to anxious.

From the atrium, Rebecca's group moved to the Grand Salon (disappointingly inert, according to an intuitive with them), then

66

down the Grand Staircase to the delightfully dark Treble Clef. Regrettably, no ghost musicians deigned to appear. Rebecca led her safari through the kitchen and down the service elevator to the part for which they had all been waiting: The Keep's sub-basement.

The fact that the Griffins Keep sub-basement was rarely seen by outsiders made the usually forbidden space especially tantalizing.

"I'm sure you've all heard stories of a tunnel said to have once run under Carson Street, connecting the hotel to the Silken Rose, a notorious brothel. We have here the evidence that such a passageway did, in fact, exist at some time in the past." For a moment, she feared one of the Busties was going to wet her pants as she squealed with excitement. With cameras and sensors at the ready, they all looked where Rebecca pointed.

"You can see how these manufactured bricks appear quite different—and newer—than the stone around them. This bank of electrical boxes obscures most of the blocked off entrance to the former tunnel, but we've outlined it in chalk to make it easier for you." The glow-in-the-dark sidewalk chalk had been Plotz's idea.

"We believe the tunnel was used for coal cars between the buildings' furnaces back in the day. A set of tracks at the other end in the Silken Rose basement, where their furnace used to be, seems to confirm this theory. But we can easily imagine the passage was used for other dirty transport before it was blocked up, probably in the 1950s."

"Shit!" a Haunt Hunter exclaimed, turning his camera's viewscreen around for all to see. "Check out all the orbs leaking through here where the bricks have been moved."

"I hear laughter, very faint, inside the wall," another contributed.

A parabolic mic crackled, and the young man holding it translated. "It said 'pay me.'"

"No, it said 'maybe'," his colleague insisted.

"I distinctly heard 'Sadie'," reported another.

A guest in a MWPI leather jacket shook his head and whispered confidentially to Rebecca, "Spirit voice interpretation is an inexact science, at best."

"Can we come back down here later tonight?"

"You may." Rebecca said. "That's why you signed liability release forms. But you'll need to go through Security and get

67

someone to accompany you." Kevin, security supervisor, had scheduled extra staff throughout the night for exactly that purpose.

"I heard there was another tunnel from here to the Capitol," a wizard said.

"We've never found any evidence of one down here," Rebecca reported.

She drew their attention next to a circular platform nearby. "The water source for the boiler, which used to sit on this brick foundation, and for the entire hotel, is in this corner. There are actually two artesian wells here below the Pirates Pub. This one with the heavy blue steel cover currently supplies all our water. It taps an aquifer more than 700-feet below us. But the original well is just behind it here—this hole in the old wooden cover. Hasn't been used since the 1930s, when the aquifer it tapped at about 480 feet was exhausted."

The real deal was an anti-climax for many of the investigators who'd expected great things from the fabled Griffins Keep well. Neither one of the bores was much to see. "You can look down the open hole if you've got flashlights," Rebecca offered, "but you can't see the bottom."

"The bio-energy here is palpable," declared a woman in wiccanesque garb. "This old well may be disused, but spirits are still streaming through it into the hotel. Does anyone else feel that?"

"I do," affirmed a thin, dark-skinned woman who had been silent until now. She gingerly touched the wooden cover around the old well opening and trembled. "The rush of souls emanating from here... It's too much...." she said breathlessly before swooning to the cold concrete floor.

"Sweet Jesus!" gasped her companion, dropping to his knees beside her. Prepared for such an eventuality, Rebecca unclipped the radio from her waistband and called Security. "We've got a fainter here by the well, Salma. Over."

"She's so faking it," one Ghost Bustie whispered to another, "just to get attention."

Salma was there within a minute and easily brought the woman around with an ammonia capsule. "Are you okay now, ma'am?" she asked when the swooner sat up. "Take my arm and we'll go get you some fresh air outside."

68

Ghost meters went crazy around the well mouths, but the tour guide insisted it was time to move on. Nearby sounds of the next tour group approaching indicated their basement time was up. "Okay, if you'll follow me to the service elevator over by the laundry, we're going next to the ballroom."

The rest of the paranormal event unfolded virtually without incident. Every group but one returned to the Silver Spoon Club more-or-less on schedule, and Grace's guests wandered in about fifteen minutes later. While the psychics and mediums and ghosthunters and magic folk enjoyed coffee and Halloween treats, Dick Plotz, delighted by the evening's success, burst into much-too-loud laughter at the most inappropriate times. He passed around a microphone and invited participants to share any experiences or impressions they cared to from the tours.

Plotz dismissed Rebecca and her exhausted associate historians around 11:00. Many of the guests stayed up all night—camping out in notoriously haunted spaces, prowling the property with their various recording and detection devices, or settling into their hotel rooms. But no significant disruptions occurred.

"I attribute tonight's relatively smooth achievement to the Power of Preventive Worrying," Rebecca confided to Dawn as they exited through the employee door into the chilly night. "My mother always maintained that worrying hard enough about something keeps it from happening."

"Maybe that was it," Dawn said, "Or maybe The Keep's spirits themselves made sure that positive energies prevailed tonight. A lady in my group claimed she actually saw the ghost of Harrison Griffin on the mezzanine balcony. And she said he was smiling."

# CHAPTER 8

"Call It what you will. Assign a gender, if you must. Ascribe a motive, if you can," Maureen said to her housemate Rebecca the next evening as they polished off a pitcher of margaritas. "but Somebody Up There hates older women. Ask anyone who bunches the bedding on and off all night as she feels her youth burn away, or who wakes herself with gasping snorts, though she never snored before in her life. Ask anyone who gazes with trepidation into the morning mirror, only to see her aging mother—or worse, her father - gazing back."

Rebecca agreed wholeheartedly. Menopause sucked. No two ways about it. No more periods, the obnoxious optimists would point out. Big whoop. The minor monthly mess had been a way to periodically shed water-weight bloat. Rebecca sometimes missed the regular "visitor." The baggage that came along with the uninvited end of ovulation was odious by comparison.

For a while in her early 50s, Rebecca had imagined that she might be the only woman in history to miraculously escape the inevitable. But Nature was disinclined to make an exception in her case, and menopause, though relatively late in arriving, waltzed right in without knocking. It wasted no time rearranging things to suit itself.

Gradually, insidiously, facial hair grew faster and coarser. Head hair grew thinner and drier. Rebecca swore she was shrinking. Compacting, actually. Hips spread and bosoms slipped. Flesh rolled out from over and under her bra like bread dough.

She was spared daytime "hot flashes"—at least so far. But the equally uncomfortable "night sweats" made restful sleep impossible.

It wasn't called "The Change" for nothing. Like a reverse adolescence, hormonal shifts were transforming the body she scarcely recognized as her own. A glance in the mirror reflected her clothes hung on the frame of an unfamiliar middle-aged woman.

Failing eyesight was a blessing. Rebecca kept the lights dim in the bathroom to soften the ugly details. She could live with the lines at the corners of her eyes, across her forehead and around her mouth. It was the sags that made her want to hide. Cheeks that had once shone like apples were slowly descending. When she held a compact mirror to her chin line, her grandmother's features appeared. Her hands, too, were becoming grandmother hands, with bulging veins and age spots. She didn't feel on the inside like she looked on the outside. Unfair! Where was a ref to stop the clock?

On bad days, it was hard to see anything positive in growing older. "It beats the alternative," her life-insurance agent cheerily observed in his annual birthday greeting card. Sometimes Rebecca wasn't at all sure about that.

Puberty had been painful, with its plumpings, eruptions and oozings. The difference at this end of the hormonal spectrum was that, over the years, she had become a master of disguise. Hair color, chemical peels, firming lotions, depilatory, fade cream and make-up were trusty allies in the daily battle to hold back time. But all the pricey products in the world were merely fingers in a dyke whose cracks spread with alarming speed. At her core, Rebecca knew it was only a matter of time until age swept away all her puny attempts to keep it at bay.

How lucky, Rebecca mused, that she was alone at this stage of life. A man, practically any man, would probably be repulsed by the physical changes wrought by menopause. Rebecca's ex, J. Bryce Bridger, certainly would have been. No wonder so many middle-aged men left their wives for younger "trophy" models. That heartbreak, at least, was already behind her.

Never underestimate the importance of a handy restroom to a menopausal woman. The little-known, rarely frequented 10th floor ladies room right outside the archives almost made up for Rebecca's abominable salary.

When Nature called, Nature insisted. What did she expect with a breakfast of oatmeal, yogurt and coffee? Her private tour was just ten minutes away, but first things first. Rebecca wiped off the seat with a wad of toilet paper as she always did, and sat, relieving herself, as the euphemism went. A sharp knock on the door startled her.

"It's occupied," she called out to the impatient next customer. Rebecca peered through the downward-facing slats in the bottom third of the door to see the feet of whoever aimed to rush her. She saw nothing but the floor. The pushy pest must be standing well to the side.

Finished, Rebecca stood and flushed. The knock came again, this time louder and more insistent.

"Just a minute." She ran the hot and cold faucets until she got the mix just right and washed her hands. As she dried them on paper towels, she turned and glanced again through the slats in the door. Pant-legs this time, pinstriped, the rubber tip of a cane. And two-toned, black and white wingtip shoes. A gentleman's wingtip shoes.

What was a man doing, rapping on the ladies room door? No way she was opening up. Rebecca took her time, wiping down the counter, washing out the sink, fooling with her hair, tucking in her blouse. When she looked through the slats again, the feet were gone.

"Still out there?" she called. No answer. No movement of any kind. She opened the door cautiously and scanned the area. Apparently all alone, she bolted toward the service stairway and down to her waiting tour.

The private ghost tour scheduled on that Thursday afternoon was for just two people. The older woman, about Rebecca's age, had long, white-blonde hair that fell almost to her waist. In flowing sleeves, ankle-length paneled skirt, and vintage high-heeled lace-up boots, she looked like an exotic fortune-teller.

"I'm Rosslyn," she said, reaching out to take Rebecca's hand. "I have something of a psychic gift."

*Of course you do,* Rebecca thought. *Psychics, mediums, sensitives. If I had a nickel...*

"I've known it since my first spirit communication when I was nine years old."

73

"Nine. Really? I'll be interested to hear your impressions as we explore the hotel today."

"I've been to The Keep many times with a friend who works here," Rosslyn began, "But I felt it the very first time I walked in. This place is so alive with spiritual presences that it blew me away at first. I've been sitting in your beautiful lobby for about half an hour, growing accustomed to it, sifting through the spiritual cacophony."

The younger woman was obviously her daughter. "This is Miranda." Miranda smiled shyly and said nothing as she shook Rebecca's hand.

Unexpectedly, Rosslyn retreated several feet and appraised their guide from head to toe with wide eyes. "You know you're a magnet, right?"

"So I've been told."

The woman meant a spiritual magnet, of course. It was not the first time an extra-sensitive observer had noticed and commented upon the way Rebecca seemed to attract paranormal presences. Most recently, in photos a tour guest had taken in the Silver Spoon, they had been amazed to discover almost a dozen "orbs" collected around the guide.

"They seem to be drawn to you, like a kindred spirit—no pun intended," Rosslyn noted. Maybe it was because Rebecca was so immersed in the past, coming into contact with historic documents and artifacts almost every day. Maybe the ghosts related to her period costumes. But the historian knew it was something more.

Rebecca could trace the odd "magnetism" to an episode in her late-30s. The two-month archaeological dig on the Balearic island of Majorca was one of several lifelong dreams made possible by Great-Aunt Frankie's bequest. During the excavations, Rebecca had apparently unearthed more than she bargained for.

The site had been a Bronze Age village, nestled into the face of a seaside cliff under a protective stone arch. Around 600 B.C.E., the overhang had unexpectedly collapsed, killing and burying most of the inhabitants. For nearly a century after that, the site had been used as a mass grave.

Rebecca and the other "volun-tourists" dug and sifted through human skeletal remains, many preserved in layers of quicklime, for two weeks. Morning after morning, the Mediterranean sun beat down as they dumped sediment onto

74

screen frames and gently agitated them to separate dirt from the bones and burial relics. The skulls were the most disturbing finds, though mercifully most were smashed to pieces.

Rebecca would never forget the day she made her discovery: a *myotragus Balearicus* horn. The small goat-like creature, once plentiful on the islands but hunted to extinction in ancient times, had a single horn in the center of its forehead. Like a unicorn.

The horn Rebecca uncovered, porous and rough on its surface, was completely intact, about 3½ inches long. A small center hole drilled through the end opposite the point indicated that it had been worn on a cord as talisman. She never understood herself why she chose to pocket the artifact before anyone else on the team got a chance to see it.

*It's not stealing. It's mine.*

She'd wrapped it carefully in soft cloth torn from the hem of a T-shirt. By day, she tucked it into her bra between her breasts. By night, she kept it under her pillow. The feral village cats no longer congregated on her bunk bed. The nightmares that had plagued her since they'd started digging up human bones ceased.

For too many nights in a row, Rebecca had dreamt of a fathomless black void, depriving every sense. Nothing visible, no sound, no scents. Nothing to touch, to hold onto or to push against. Drifting. Falling. No bearings. Excruciating emptiness. She feared that awful oblivion more than anything. The horn had made those nightmares go away

Once home, Rebecca had threaded a wire loop through the hole in the horn and suspended it from a thin gold chain. She wore it only rarely, but always on Halloween, when she used to dress as a gypsy. Dangled amongst her many costume jewelry ropes of beads, bells and coins, the horn pendant made her feel strangely powerful.

Her housemate Maureen, a reluctant but talented intuitive herself, confirmed, but could not define, the relic's magic. Possessing it had changed Rebecca in such a profound way that she needn't wear it to radiate its spiritual magnetism. Safely stashed away for years in a jewelry box in the attic, the talisman's attraction somehow pervaded her being still.

"Extraordinary," the psychic Rosslyn said now. "I've never encountered anything like your supernal drawing power. How do you cope in a place as rife with spirits as this hotel?"

Rebecca shrugged. "Truthfully, I don't even notice. Whatever spirits may be drawn to me seem disinclined to interact. They don't really communicate or touch me or anything. Apparently, they just like being near."

The historian hastened to redirect the conversation. "But you're not here to hear about me, Let's begin your tour."

As they moved from stop to stop around the hotel, Rosslyn contributed her impressions. Her daughter, looking a bit overwhelmed and confused, remained quiet. Her demeanor changed dramatically, however, as they approached the door to Room 864.

"There's the ghost of a little girl up here," Miranda said, smiling at the empty hallway to their right. "She's telling me her name is Hennie. Her happiest times were spent on this floor, and she found her way back"

Miranda paused as if listening, then nodded solemnly. "We'll be careful," she said to the air. Turning to her mother, she explained. "Hennie is warning us about some bad spirit nearby. 'Protect yourselves,' she says.'

The young woman looked directly at Rebecca then. "The bad spirit doesn't like you," she said. "She wants to hurt you. And Hennie says she can."

Rosslyn was as taken aback by Miranda's statement as was Rebecca. "Miranda!" she admonished sharply, "We don't blurt out everything we perceive without considering others' feelings. What have I told you about filtering? I think you owe Ms. Bridger an apology."

Miranda instinctively bristled, then hung her head. "Sorry," she muttered, again retreating inside herself.

Her mother added softly, "She has a gift, but she's very young and inexperienced. Please find it in your heart to excuse her."

"Of course," Rebecca said graciously. "I'd be excited, too, if a spirit actually spoke to me."

The public elevator whisked them back down to the mezzanine level, where their tour concluded in one of Rebecca's favorite spaces.

"This beautiful room is the Keep's Grand Salon," Rebecca explained, holding the tall, heavy door open for her tour guests. The space was the single largest in the historic hotel, with a 20-foot high ceiling. "In the hotel's early years, it was a formal sitting room, especially for lady travelers. All this stone is white onyx from the same Mexican quarry as the golden onyx in our lobby. The Grand Salon sits directly above the original Grand Entrance, which is why it has this large bay window in the center. Huge fireplaces once flanked the window, and this ceiling fresco featured vigilant angels on high. In the early 1930s, the fresco was nearly ruined by a plumbing leak. But with the help of a local artist, it was fully restored."

"It's awesome," Miranda said, craning her neck to inspect the work.

"Within the oval, the artist depicted the seven archangels. The smaller four were believed to be the overseers of politics, military matters, commerce and trade—not coincidentally the purview of The Keep's traditionally successful and powerful patrons. The two larger angels flanking the center figure are known as the Powers, warrior angels who are also the keepers of conscience and of history. My personal favorites, for obvious reasons," Rebecca confided.

"The impressive winged figure in the center of the fresco is an even higher caste of heavenly being, a Dominion. You can tell them apart from other angels by the orbs of light fastened to the heads of their scepters or on the pommel of their swords."

"Orbs of light?" the psychic echoed, peering up at the fresco with piqued fascination.

"In this case, the artist chose to depict the orb atop the Dominion's scepter, since the Powers were already wielding swords."

"How on earth did he get it to glow like that? Is there a light hidden above the painting?"

"Looks like it, doesn't it?" Rebecca said. "I'm told he mixed his paint with mother-of-pearl and seven types of metallic leaf to achieve the effect."

"And the swords of the Powers—are they gilded with real gold?"

"Twenty-four carat. A tissue-thin veneer applied in delicate sheets, just like on the dome of our State Capitol. You can see why this room is so popular for weddings, receptions, and all sorts of special gatherings."

Rebecca paused, allowing her guests to take it all in. "Curiously, we don't know of any ghost stories in this space. Do you sense anything, Rosslyn?"

77

The woman slowly scanned the room before answering. "Absolutely nothing. I think this may be the most spiritually silent space I've ever experienced. It's unnatural...as if it's been sanitized. All the decades of human experience that transpired here, and not a trace remains. Some sort of potent spiritual cleansing took place here. It drove everything out, both positive and negative energies. This goes way beyond smudging, even beyond exorcism."

Rosslyn paced around the vast space slowly, pausing briefly here and there, looking up, then down, then up again. At several points, she laid her hands on the onyx, as if trying to absorb the room's secrets.

"There must have been some terribly powerful, terribly dangerous activity in this room at some point in the past," she concluded. "The psychic residue it left was apparently so toxic, so vile, that the space had to be purged completely. I can't even imagine what could have compelled such drastic cleansing—or how it might have been accomplished."

# CHAPTER 9

The lanky frame still moved with a masculine grace. The long, wavy hair, tied back when he worked, was salt-and-peppered now. Graying brows, graying beard and mustache. A furrowed forehead; a long, prominent nose. Dauntingly deep dark eyes that shone with searching wonder, undimmed by age. Rebecca sometimes tried to imagine Lochlan as a younger man. The image matched a vague memory, on the tip of her brain. When it finally clicked, she was almost afraid to ask.

"Did you used to play in a band?"

"I did, many years ago."

"Skye Span?"

Lochlan nodded and smiled. The Celtic-Rock band had enjoyed a spate of popularity in the 1970s.

"I loved your music," Rebecca almost gushed. "You played the violin and sang lead vocals."

"Guilty as charged."

"I saw you perform at Snowmass one summer. It was magical. Really magical. And then afterwards, we met the band backstage, my husband and I. Went to your condo, and ..."

She stopped abruptly. The memory from this point on grew painful. Scarcely daring to look at him, she glanced up and knew that Lochlan knew. He had made the connection long ago, soon after she started at The Keep. He'd never said a word.

"The poker game."

He nodded. "I won."

She swallowed hard. "We slept together."

"That we did."

"No, I mean, we really just *slept*," she insisted earnestly as the memory unfolded completely. "You didn't...take advantage of me, as they used to say."

"Some would call me fool. I prefer the term gentleman."

"What you must think of me..."

"It was your husband I thought badly of. He 'traded' you to our drummer Ian for a bag of cocaine."

Bryce had left with his coke and a giggling groupie and abandoned Rebecca, with no way home. It had not been the first time, nor would it be the last. Each desertion cut a little deeper. And she'd swabbed her wounds with alcohol.

"Ian would not have let you sleep," Lochlan said. "You were so messed up, had way too much to drink. It wasn't right. So I bet against him, with you as the 'pot.' Beat him with a straight flush, I'll never forget."

"You didn't think I was pathetic or... immoral?"

He shook his head. "I thought you were hurting and vulnerable. I didn't judge. Your only transgression was valuing yourself too cheaply."

Rebecca's eyes blurred with tears. "Thank you," she said softly, "for banishing at least one of my many ghosts."

Rebecca shouldn't have picked up the call. Should have let it go to voicemail. It was only ten minutes until she was scheduled to present a luncheon hotel history program. But she was expecting a call from a lady interested in scheduling a private tour for her Red Hat Ladies group.

"This is Rebecca. Can I help you?"

"Hello? Who...?"

"This is Rebecca, the hotel historian. Is this Betty?"

"Betty? No. This is Deanna. Who are you?"

"I'm the hotel historian. Can I help you?"

"I don't know if you can help me. I just told the operator I needed to talk to someone about some weird things that happened to us in our room at the hotel last week."

"Some weird things?" Rebecca repeated. "Like unexplained things? I do our hotel ghost tours, and I'm always interested to hear new stories." *If you can cover it in five minutes...*

"Well, OK. It's been a week now and I can't stop thinking about what happened. It really bothers me, and I have to tell somebody there."

"All right," the historian prompted. "What happened?"

"It was last Tuesday night. We were celebrating our 25th wedding anniversary and we were in Room 864. It's a beautiful suite, really big and open."

"I know the room."

"Well, that night we were just sitting on the sofa having champagne and chocolate-dipped strawberries. But then we began to hear sounds coming from the other side of those double doors opposite the sofa. Voices and laughing—lots of people—and music, like a party.

"We didn't know what was through those doors, so I stepped outside our room and a few feet down the hall to see what was next door. I saw the 'Kuhrsfeld Board Room' sign, and I peeked around the corner. The doors were partly open, and I could see the conference table and some of the high-backed chairs around it. But it was completely dark. There was no one inside."

"Yes, the board room adjoins the suite you were in. Often, if companies are using the room for several days of meetings, their president or CEO stays in 864. What time was this in the evening?"

"Oh, it wasn't evening anymore. It was 10:30 or 11:00 at night."

Nothing would have been scheduled in the board room at that late hour.

"We were getting really weird feelings by then. My husband swore he heard scratching inside the wall. We watched some TV in the bedroom to try and shake it. Then we finally went to bed around 12:30.

"You know that big ottoman in the bedroom? Up against the wall? We both left our cell phones in their chargers in the middle of the ottoman when we went to bed.

"At 4:07 in the morning—I know because I looked at the digital clock on the nightstand—a loud sound woke us both so suddenly that we sat straight up in bed and grabbed each other. Seconds later, another loud noise, like a firecracker, came from the direction of the ottoman, and my cellphone flew out of its

81

charger and across the room at the foot of the bed. The charger pulled right out of the wall. We were both so scared, we could hardly move or talk. We just sat there holding each other, with hearts pounding, holding our breath."

"I can imagine."

"Of course, we couldn't go back to sleep. We were so upset. After about ten minutes, when nothing else happened, we got up. I never packed so fast in my life. I was too afraid to go pick up my phone, but my husband said when he touched it, he felt a chill run up his spine.

"We checked out of the hotel at 4:30 without a word about the occurrences. But like I said, it's been bothering me more and more ever since then."

"I can completely understand why all this would upset you," Rebecca said, amazed as always by the power of imagination. "And I'd like to talk with you more about your experience, all the details. But I'm very sorry I can't do it right now. I'm late for a presentation. Can I get your contact information and I'll call you..."?

"Have you heard about anything else like this in the hotel? Or am I crazy? I'm not crazy. My husband heard and saw everything I did."

"I haven't heard anything quite like your story before. But can I call you back tomorrow and talk some more? I'm really sorry, I have to go."

"All right. I'm not usually like this. Please understand."

"I understand. Can I get your phone number, please, Deanna?" The distraught caller finally gave her number but continued to fret for another few minutes before Rebecca seized upon a break to end their exchange without seeming rude.

Intrigued though she was, Rebecca did not call Deanna back the next day. Nor the next. The luncheon speech, combined with the sudden onset of a wicked cold, completely robbed the historian of her voice. Rebecca conducted the following day's three tours in hoarse, raspy whispers—all the creepier for the tour guests, she hoped. When she finally regained her power of speech and contacted Deanna, the woman answered calmly and cordially. But her angst quickly resurfaced. If anything, she seemed even more overwrought than three days earlier.

"I've always believed in spirits. But my husband...well, he's very skeptical and logical. The fact that he can't explain what

82

happened to us makes him angry because I know he was freaked out, too."

"Of course he was."

"I want to know what happened in that room. The bellman told us all those top rooms used to be apartments in the Depression. I want to know who lived there. And what was in that space before then?"

"I'll do what I can to find answers," Rebecca assured the haunted recent guest. "We have original blueprints of the 8th floor. And partial lists of residents of the Parapet Apartments. And I promise I'll get back to you next week with whatever I may find out. Is there an email address where I might send the information?"

On the other end of the line, the woman drew a deep breath. "Thank you," she said. "I'll look forward to hearing from you."

Rebecca's work was laid out for her. She cleared a large space atop the archives island worktable and carefully withdrew the unwieldy original blueprint of the 8th floor. She had examined the floor plan many times before, but never with the scrutiny she now brought to the task. She took note of the relative positions of the stairs, the elevator, and the hallway angles as they related to the current Room 864. Excitedly, she hurried down to the 8th floor to confirm her calculations. It was just as she'd thought.

The wall between Room 864 and the boardroom exactly corresponded to the original division between the serving area of the kitchen and the far end of the ballroom itself.

Had Deanna and her husband somehow eavesdropped on a long-ago soiree?

The former resident piece of the Room 864 puzzle was trickier. Documents in the archives Parapet Apartment files included a few random reminiscences of permanent residents of the top two floors, supplied by relatives and former employees. The only other resource providing clues to the residents' identities was a series of typed "Christmas Poinsettias" lists from the 1940s and 50s, noting all those slated to receive plants from the hotel management for the holidays, along with their apartment numbers.

None of the lists included 864. Rebecca could only assume that the space currently so numbered had previously been subsumed into another, larger apartment to one side or the other.

Had there been a full moon on the night in question? No, the historian-detective remembered. The Zombie Crawl had coincided with the official October full moon three nights earlier—a so-called "Blood Moon."

The term was new to Rebecca. The first full moon following the autumnal equinox, she learned online, had been known since ancient times as the Blood Moon. The magic of the Blood Moon is that its full-night light shines for multiple successive nights. For this reason, pagan cultures planned their nocturnal activities and rituals for the unusual series of bright nights around the Blood Moon. It was a moon of spirituality that marked a powerful time for divination and for energizing crystals.

Spirituality. Divination. Dusk-to-dawn lunar illumination. No wonder the October moon had long been considered the harbinger of extraordinary events. Who could be sure the nocturnal rituals attuned to that phenomenon were relegated to the distant past?


"You know I'm uncomfortable with this," Maureen grumbled as her friend tapped a magnetic key on the lock pad of Room 864.

"Of course I know, Mo," Rebecca said, depressing the latch handle to open the suite. "And I'm sorry. But this room is the source of our latest report of unexplained phenomena. I've got to know what you make of it, while it's still 'fresh.'"

Maureen was a talented intuitive. Though she rarely spoke of or tapped into her psychic ability, unexplainable perceptions had convinced Rebecca over the years that her friend's gift was the real deal.

"Thanks for not telling me what supposedly happened here," Mo said. "Makes it easier to form my own impressions—untainted, as it were, by whatever others think they may have experienced. Gawd, I hate this Art Deco stuff."

"That's beside the point. Tell me something I don't know."

Maureen paused in the front room and breathed deeply. She turned and glanced toward the double doors in the wall opposite the sofa, then proceeded into the bedroom. Before continuing into the master bath, she stopped.

"Whoo boy," she said. "Here she is. This must be the spirit that's been stirring things up. She was in that far corner by the bed, but now she's moving back and forth between here and the

84

bathroom—super-snooty, very haughty. And she's angry. She doesn't want us here."

Maureen reached around the corner to switch on the light in the dressing room. It fizzled and popped as the bulb burned out. "Oh, she really, really doesn't want us here. She's telling me we're not good enough for this place. None of the people you've been bringing in here on tours are good enough for the Griffins Keep. She seems particularly incensed by women wearing pants. And— oh wow—tattoos. She's appalled by people with tattoos."

Mo turned suddenly and looked over her shoulder. "She touched me! And now she's actually waving us away, dismissing us from her space."

"'Nuff said," Rebecca noted, as the two women headed for the door and beat their retreat. At the threshold the historian turned back toward the bedroom "I'll be back," she said to the spirit. "You don't live here anymore."


Maureen Wischmeyer had visited the Griffins Keep on several occasions. The first time she strode unsuspectingly into the atrium lobby, she was bowled over by the crowd of spirits swarming the hotel. In all her world travels, the only other place she had encountered such an array of spirits was the Muse d'Orsay, a former grand railway depot in Paris. Maureen sensed, as most psychics did, that some of The Keep's spiritual sojourners belonged there, but that many others were simply passing through.

Once, while waiting for Rebecca in the lobby, she'd had a delightful internal conversation with the spirit of a young woman from Wyoming whose husband was in town on business. The friendly ghost communicated to Mo that she was awaiting a carriage to take her to the opera, and she was certain the year was 1874. Of course, on a logical level, this did not compute. The Keep had only existed since 1890, and before that time the triangular lot had been a cow pasture. But in conversing with spirits, logic rarely comes into play.

Maureen and Rebecca had bonded in college on a student production of "The Prime of Miss Jean Brodie." Mo played Mary; Rebecca played Sandy. And J. Bryce Bridger was the lecherous married art teacher, Teddy Lloyd. The young women became fast

85

friends, just like their characters. And like their characters, Rebecca and Bryce became lovers.

Bryce Bridger had always reminded Maureen of young Michael Landon in TV's old "Bonanza" and "Little House on the Prairie." He had the same easy-going charm, the same gorgeous wavy hair and disarming smile. But Bryce never had quite the acting talent of Landon.

She couldn't tell Rebecca that, of course. As far as Becky had been concerned, the sun rose and set on Bryce. Mo knew that her friend felt flattered by the handsome aspiring actor's attention. Becky had never had a boyfriend before Bryce. She'd never felt the way he made her feel. She would do anything for him, she'd told her roomie. Anything he asked of her.

So Bryce had taken Becky's virginity, willingly given. He'd taken her innocence, belatedly abandoned. And he'd taken her as his wife because he wanted to live with her. Preacher's kids like Bryce just didn't do that sort of thing without the prerequisite of matrimony in those days.

Maureen had all but lost touch for several years when Bryce and Becky moved to Steamboat Springs, where he pursued an acting career—and other women.

At about the same time that Becky's marriage fell apart—and Becky with it—the love of Maureen's life, Victor, was killed in a climbing accident in Boulder Canyon. The former roommates reconnected and found mutual support in their friendship. And when Rebecca's great-aunt left her a charming old Tudor-style "cottage" in Denver's Botanic Gardens neighborhood, the two had moved in together once again.

Chubby as a child, Maureen still struggled with that now-inaccurate self-image. Her shoulder-length hair remained thick and believably auburn. She dressed like a lady, walked like a hiker, and laughed like a champagne overflow.

Some people mistook the two for sisters. Maureen suspected that she and Rebecca had shared other lives together, in other relationship dynamics. She never discussed this with her friend, but Mo knew Rebecca sensed it, too. They were as comfortable together as an old married couple. And just as adept at unspoken communication.

"Do you ever miss having a man in your life?" Lochlan casually asked the divorced historian one day at lunch. "I mean, to have steady male companionship for years and then not—is it hard?"

Rebecca shrugged. "My male companion was never what I'd call steady. I'm much happier living without a man than I ever was living with one."

"What about, you know, intimate relations? Ever miss that?"

"You mean sex," she clarified. "I had more than enough of that with more than enough men when I was supposedly married. Swore off it long ago. You're single. I shouldn't have to tell you that's why god made hand-held shower massagers." She smiled mischievously, enjoying his blush. "Seriously. They're always ready when you are. Climax and clean-up in one easy step. And no agonizing relationship complications afterwards. A boon to singles everywhere."

Almost regretting his prying, Lochlan persisted, nonetheless. "I know you had some terrible experiences with empty—or deceitful—sex in the past. But it doesn't have to be like that," he said earnestly. "The need for intimate connection is a basic physical craving, like hunger. It can be sated in a wide range of ways, from a drive-thru meal to a dining experience. The difference is the way the elements complement each other to become more deeply fulfilling on a higher level. It's simple sustenance elevated to artistic expression."

"A sort of sensual symphony," she said, dramatically flourishing a forkful of meatball like a conductor's baton.

"When it all comes together perfectly, yes. Gourmet lovemaking, if you will, nourishes not just the body, but also the soul."

"Sounds delicious," she granted. "But it costs so much more."

"Without question. And there are no guarantees of satisfaction. But some experiences are beyond price."

"I do remember tasting it," Rebecca said, suddenly serious, "But someone always snatched my plate away before I finished."

"New restaurants open all the time," he pointed out. "Tastes change. I'm simply suggesting that you take a chance and sample something new every now and then."

# CHAPTER 10

Pete Jeffries boarded the Griffins Keep public elevator on the fifth floor.

"Going up?" Rebecca asked.

"Sure. What the hell. Doesn't matter." Taking off his wire-rimmed glasses, the sandy-bearded front desk assistant manager wiped his other hand across his forehead. The usually cheerful and cordial 30-something Keep associate looked thoroughly defeated.

"Rough morning?"

"Angry guests. Berserk guests. Too few employees trying to handle too many crises."

"Wanna hide out in the archives for a while?"

"God, yes." Pete jumped at the chance.

"You've been up there, before, haven't you?"

"Just that once when I helped you carry up some stuff you'd had out for people to see."

"So you know it's the hotel 'attic' where all the treasures are hidden," she said, pushing through an inconspicuous door in the ninth floor wall that led to the service staircase. "Look at the intricate iron scrollwork on these railings. They've always been behind the scenes, but the builders took pains to embellish them nonetheless." The railings must have been beautiful before someone thoughtlessly spray-painted them silver. Now they looked as tacky as the surrounding walls of peeling plaster painted public-pool turquoise.

"A sad reminder of a time long past when pride in the details mattered here," Pete said as they climbed to the rooftop repository

On the tenth floor of the nine-story building, the historian unlocked the door with a peephole installed by request at her eye-level. "Can you believe that when I started here, this door had a sign broadcasting 'Hotel Archives?' They might as well have just added 'Welcome Thieves!'" Getting rid of that sign had been Rebecca's first order of business as historian.

Gesturing toward the vinyl covered footrest, she offered Pete a seat. "This room, the old upholstery shop next door, and the area where the restrooms are now, was all the Executive Housekeeper's 'penthouse' apartment in the 1940s and 50s."

She pulled a folder from the file cabinets and handed Pete a large black-and-white glossy photograph. "This is what this space looked like when she lived here. She had almost as many shelves for her own collections as the archives has now. And here's a photo of her from sometime in the 1940s. Marjory Crispin. Doesn't she have a smile that could sell toothpaste?"

Pete studied the pictures appreciatively. "These are cool. She looks nice."

Rebecca lifted the light-blocking Roman shade in the corner for a look outside. "Check out this old screen door. It opened out onto the rooftop patio where Marjory threw private parties for friends on full-moon summer nights. She had potted trees and flowers all around her lawn furniture. Must have been quite the view before all the HVAC stuff cluttered up the roof."

"And before all the skyscrapers surrounded the place," Pete added, peering out. "Yeah, I totally know that screen door. I started out in Engineering when I first worked here. Sometimes I'd go out there and sit on the roof ledge. Nobody can see it from the street, so nobody would think I was going to jump or anything. Just a good place to get away for a break and a smoke." A thought occurred to him, and he turned to Rebecca. "It must have been her who closed the door!"

"Marjory?"

"Must have been. One time when I went out on the roof here, I came back to find this screen door closed and latched. And that door doesn't close by itself. In fact, it's really hard to close. Sticks open, like it is now. The hinges are rusted stiff. But somebody—or something—shut me out there. I swear I heard a woman's voice in

90

my ear saying, 'Back to work' and the door opened—all by itself. Had to be that housekeeper. Makes sense."

Rebecca hesitantly considered his theory. "Maybe Marjory's spirit is still up here," she said, surprised at herself. "On several occasions, when I've gone to use the ladies room, I've pushed on the door to go in and, from inside the empty bathroom, someone's pushed back. Pushed back hard. It's unmistakable."

The two of them looked at each other and smiled slyly, like children sharing a secret.

"Probably just a weird air pressure thing," Rebecca offered sensibly.

"Yeah, probably," Pete said, "Unless it's not."

"It's not scary or anything," Rebecca hastened to add. "Just unexpected and—I don't know—unexplainable."

Pete agreed. "I find myself wishing whatever spirits are here would show themselves. It would be awesome to actually see them."

Rebecca screwed up her mouth and shook her head. "Mixed feelings on that," she said. "But I like to imagine Marjory is a guardian spirit of this place. She'd definitely be a good ghost. I'm not sure all of them are."

"How could they be? If ghosts are the spirits of people, and obviously people come in good and bad," Pete reasoned. "But the general aura—I think that's the right word—of The Keep is very positive—almost like magic sometimes. Things that shouldn't work out somehow *do* work out. Potential disasters are mysteriously averted. I think anyone who's worked here for a while has a story like that. It's weird but wonderful."

"Lochlan has an astrologer friend who did The Keep's horoscope. She says it has always attracted good fortune," Rebecca said. "But she also predicted that the last part of this year will begin a time of major upheaval for the hotel."

"No surprise there, what with TITHE taking over. Who knows what the new owners will do to the place. Could be change for the better."

"Could be," Rebecca tried to sound optimistic. "But you were in that TITHE marketing meeting. Saw that commercial. Doesn't bode well, if you ask me."

"You're preaching to the choir," Pete said. "That crap made it so obvious these new guys don't get what makes The Keep special.

If I ever run into that Chad Tagawa, I'm gonna ask him 'Why'd you buy this hotel when you obviously hate history?'"

"The astrologer says the stars indicate some sort of terrible imbalance ahead. Sometimes lately, I almost think I feel that coming. Crazy, huh?"

"You feel it, too?" Pete was serious. "I've had that sense for about three months now. Vaguely disturbing..."

The ensuing moment of pensive silence was broken by Rebecca. "Wanna see the most amazing treasure of the archives?"

She hurried over to the wooden cupboard opposite a bank of filing cabinets and withdrew the topmost container from a stack of identical plastic storage tubs. Setting it on the vinyl footrest, she unsealed the lid and lifted it off, leaning it against the cupboard. Carefully, she parted the folds of a hotel towel lining the tub and lifted out a tissue wrapped object, about a foot long. From another sheet of tissue, she unwrapped a small fur hat with a purple plume.

Rebecca gingerly removed the tissue from the object and stood it on the island worktable. She placed the hat on its head and stepped back, appraising it with a sad smile.

"It's...it's a doll," Pete said, moving closer to inspect it. "A soldier, with a trumpet."

"A coronet, to be exact. Isn't he gorgeous? He's just one of a 14-piece military band, handcrafted by a French dollmaker while he was imprisoned during the Revolution. His uniform is made from actual uniform scraps of the time, as is his fur hat. Each bandsman holds a different instrument," Rebecca said. "But the most amazing thing is that each face was carved to look like one of his fellow prisoners."

"Whoa. You can totally see his personality. Looks like a mischievous young man trying hard to be serious," Pete said, slowly turning the figure on its square wooden base to admire the button and braid details. "How'd these come to be at The Keep, anyway?

"Kuhrsfelds acquired them on their world travels, along with the other French Revolutionary knick-knacks to decorate their new restaurant. The entire band was displayed for years in one of the glass cases in the Versailles Room. They're one of a kind, more than 200 years old."

"Why have I never seen these before?"

Rebecca pointed to the figure and directed, "Look closely. They haven't been cared for properly. Decades of exposure to light and dust. No temperature or humidity control. This one's boots are flaking. His scabbard is shredding. His hat is splitting. His uniform is pocked with insect damage. And he's in better shape than most of them. Every time I open these tubs, I can smell faint decay."

"Can they be saved?"

The historian began to gently rewrap the bandsman in acid-free tissue. "They could be stabilized, even restored by professional conservationists," she said. "I had the complete set of figures assessed about a year ago. Gave the report with the estimates to Mr. Beaumont. He sent it right back to me with a sticky note: 'Take good care of these until our profits improve.'"

Reverently, she laid the artifact in his towel-lined coffin and resealed the lid. "It's the same story for so many things here in the archives—the blueprints, the guest registers, the scrapbooks. They're fragile, perishable, steadily degrading, in desperate need of professional rehab. But they're completely off the radar when the owners and managers set the annual budget. It breaks my historian heart."

Pete empathized. "Everybody who works here ought to see this stuff," he said. "Guests, too."

Rebecca couldn't agree more. "These are the things that give The Keep its resonance. This," she concluded, encompassing the archives in a grand sweeping gesture, "all this is what makes the Griffins Keep unlike any other hotel in Denver. Maybe any other anywhere. And when people who work here and people who visit here understand that, they begin to understand its deeply rooted significance, its contribution to the city's character."

Pete glanced at his watch. "I've gotta go." He gave the historian an impulsive hug before turning for the door. "Thank you, Rebecca," he said sincerely, "for putting the little day-to-day hassles in perspective. And thank you, Marjory, for keeping an eye on things."

Raising a triumphant fist in the air, he proclaimed, "The Keep endures! Long live The Keep." He poked his head through the gap before closing the archives door. "And heaven help her beleaguered staff."


Rebecca dreaded the 4:00 private tour scheduled on Halloween itself. Ghost tours for groups of children presented special

93

challenges. They couldn't care less about the history of the Griffins Keep. A waste of time, the hotel's backstory simply made them fidget. They wanted to be scared. They wanted to giggle and cling to each other or startle each other. They pretended to see things, to hear things as Rebecca led them around the property. Sometimes they listened to her stories. Sometimes they told their own.

Today's group was part of a local rec center's afterschool program for kids. The sugar-charged children running around the lobby had apparently already dived into the Halloween candy. So be it. The historian smiled and determined to have fun with it.

"I was recently possessed by a spirit," a boy of about nine announced earnestly to her and the group at the outset. "I actually saw it leave my body. And I've been able to see ghosts ever since."

"Really?" Rebecca tried not to sound patronizing. "Wow."

The problem with this group was that at every stop on the tour, half-a-dozen little hands shot up.

"I just saw two black eyes right over there on the wall," announced one young girl, hurrying across the Club room to point out the spot.

"I can see the shadow of a dead lady lying on the floor," claimed another, tracing the imagined silhouette in the carpet.

"I just saw a white flash like lightning over there," said a boy, pointing to a fifth-floor corner of the atrium.

"I felt something brush my arm!"

"Did you hear that whispering sound?"

"I saw blood on that wallpaper, and then it disappeared!"

"Let's raise our hands ONLY if we have a question, guys."

Rebecca silently blessed their leader for his belated attempt to rein-in their imaginations. But the titillated hysteria continued to rise, despite the best calming efforts of the adults. When it came time to take them to an upper floor, a cluster of mini-drama queens crowded so close to Rebecca that she could scarcely make her way to the elevator.

The historian had insisted that the description of the ghost tour on the website add the note: "These tours are primarily historical and not intended for children." For all the good that did. *Might as well don a big red nose and floppy shoes*, Rebecca thought before biting the bullet. *Such a rewarding application of my graduate studies in history.*

94

"You have a question?" Rebecca asked when an obnoxious child waved her raised hand incessantly. The historian was in no mood for precociousness.

"Yeah. So is that all your own hair?"

Totally unexpected. The artificial clip-on fastened atop Rebecca's upswept Victorian do was a close match, but not, apparently, perfect. "You're very astute." *And very rude.*

"I'm a what?"

"Astute. It means you're clever. You're unusually observant."

"Oh yeah!" the pudgy girl exalted, fist bumping her friend. "I so rock!"

"Actually, no one's ever asked me that before." *And you're going to regret being the first.* "As a matter of fact, this is *not* all my own hair. This piece," she said, slowly fingering the add-on, "came from the head of the original hotel historian, Charlotte Woods—right before they buried her last month."

Rebecca was surprised to find that she derived a perverse pleasure from the shock on their young faces.

"Eeew!"

"Nuh-uh!"

Rebecca nodded solemnly. "It was her final wish that I rip it from her dead scalp and make it into a hairpiece."

"Gross, dude!"

"No way. Why would you?"

"Because it's bewitched. When I put it on, the roots grow into my skull and clear into my brain and inject all her knowledge about the hotel's history." Dramatic pause. "It hurts like crazy when I pull it off at the end of the day, but it's worth it."

"Get out! You lie."

"Do I? Are you sure?" She inclined the top of her head toward them and advanced a step. "Touch it if you dare. But I can't promise her hair won't start to penetrate your skin, too."

"I think that's quite enough," the group leader interjected.

"I certainly hope so," Rebecca agreed. "You all know I'm just having a little fun with you, right, kids?"

But for the duration of the tour, no one asked another question.

On Labor Day weekend, Charlotte Woods had passed into the Colorado history about which she had always been so passionate.

Rebecca got news of The Keep's first historian's death in an email blast from the Colorado History Museum's volunteer coordinator. It was sad, of course. But the 89-year-old's mind had drifted into other realms months ago. Her body finally let her go.

Charlotte and her husband had no children. She had devoted herself entirely to the hotel, its history and its archives. Rebecca was her heir in that regard, and she felt the obligation keenly.

"So much of her spirit is already here," Lochlan had observed as they sat in the archives the day after Charlotte's memorial service, remembering the late hotel historian. "We should invite her formally."

In response to Rebecca's puzzled look, he'd explained. "There's an ancient Kabbalah ritual that helps searching spirits find their way, welcomes their spiritual light. Be honest. Would you be comfortable with Charlotte here?"

Wary and skeptical, Rebecca had finally nodded.

"My psychic friend told me how to do this." Lochlan proceeded to write Hebrew symbols and their phonetic pronunciation on sheet of paper, folded it in half, and reverently placed the newspaper clipping with Charlotte's obituary inside.

"Repeat these words whenever you think of her for the next several days," he'd instructed. "It opens a spiritual door and invites her in. If this is where she wants to spend eternity—even a little bit of it—she'll know she can come here."

They practiced saying the strange words aloud several times, like a chant, before Lochlan had to get back to fixing a leaky toilet. *What could it hurt?* Rebecca asked herself.

The next morning, she'd entered the archives, surprised to find her PC screen glowing with the start prompt screen. She always turned it off when she left for the day; just must not have shut it down properly last night. But the next day, though she was certain she had shut it down completely, she found the start prompt up again. Pure chance, of course, that this coincided with the Kabbalah "invitation" to Charlotte's spirit. Nevertheless, she wondered.

That evening, Rebecca deliberately sat through the entire shut down until there was no question the machine was off

"If you're really here, Charlotte, turn the PC on once more tonight," she'd said aloud, feeling silly. The following day, she had unlocked the archives and, before flipping on the lights, she discovered the PC screen glowing again in the dark.

"Oh yeah," Dawn, the Sales admin assistant, said casually when Rebecca mentioned the odd occurrence. "That's happened to me a couple times. It's some freak thing in the local network. A 'wake on LAN' I think they call it. For some reason it sends a signal that kicks on a bunch of the connected computers for no reason."

It sounded plausible to Rebecca, with her limited understanding of networking mysteries. But why had it never happened in the archives before? And why two days in a row?

Before Rebecca left that afternoon, after her PC had shut down completely, she crawled under the desk and unplugged the machine from the dusty power strip on the floor.

Drawing a deep breath the next morning, she turned the key in the archives lock, opened the door, and looked toward her desk in the corner. The computer she was certain she had disconnected incandesced impossibly. The chill that ran up her spine slowly melted with astonishment and understanding.

Rebecca glanced at the Kabala packet on the archive island and smiled uncertainly. "Good morning, Charlotte," she said softly as she closed the door behind her. "Welcome home."

# CHAPTER 11

The day after Halloween was a dreary, windy Wednesday.

"It's *Día de los Muertos*," Salma announced when she encountered Rebecca at the time clock that morning. "The day when the veil between the worlds of the living and the dead is thinnest. The day those who have passed can come through to our side. Move with extra care around The Keep today."

Requests for ghost tours diminished but did not stop with the end of October. Today's 1:00 private tour finally appeared at 1:55. The organizer had apprised Rebecca when making their reservation that his charges were brain-damaged patients, and they might run unavoidably late.

The amiable woman in a wheelchair pointed and grinned at every turn, exclaiming, "Pretty!" The gentleman piloting her chuckled at the oddest times. The woman with the white cane feared to move without a guiding hand, and the timorous black girl refused to go anywhere until Rebecca explained what was going to happen next. And next. And after that.

How much did they get out of her simplified versions of the standard ghost stories, Rebecca wondered as they toured the lower floors of the hotel. She knew it didn't matter. It was all about the journey. New surroundings, sensory stimulation, the soothing cadence of storytelling. The two caregivers seemed to enjoy themselves, and Rebecca imagined they appreciated the diversion.

Outbursts were minimal, eyes were wide, and the tour went as well as could be expected—until the showroom stop: Room 864.

Rebecca invited everyone to sit after exploring the suite. But a young girl twisted and wracked by cerebral palsy suddenly fell to the floor and began to crawl around the room on her hands and knees, despite her caregiver's urging to stand up.

"I don't get it. She's never done this before."

The girl shook her head back and forth and declared, "She push me. She push me down."

Rebecca stared with rising horror. *She doesn't want us here,* Mo had said of the haughty spirit she'd sensed in the suite just a few days before. *She's telling me we're not good enough.*

"Who pushed you? Nobody pushed you. Come sit by me," the caregiver beckoned the girl on the floor, patting the sofa cushion beside her.

Rebecca gamely launched into the story of the party sounds beyond the double doors, as if everything were normal.

"Get out!" the woman in the wheelchair blurted.

"Hush, Olivia,' admonished the other aide. Then to Rebecca, "Sorry. I don't know what's got into her."

*"Get out!"* Olivia ordered more loudly when the historian attempted to resume her narrative.

A long-haired patient who had lurked on the fringes of the group, silent until now, covered his ears and howled. The caregivers exchanged anxious glances as the situation unraveled.

"Get out Get out *GET OUT!"*

Rebecca bolted toward the door of the suite, opened it, and quickly guided the blind woman out, motioning for the others to follow. No one needed urging.

As they headed back to the elevators, Olivia quieted and whimpered softly. The young girl, helped from her knees by a caregiver, stood and wavered, clinging to her arm. The howler stopped and lapsed behind, silent again as they distanced themselves from the suite and its spiritual hysteria.

"What's coming next?" the reticent girl asked Rebecca in a whisper, suddenly afraid to proceed.

Unnerved, the historian found herself for the first time fearful of that uncertainty. "I wish I knew," she said, taking the girl's hand. "But we have to move on."


By early November, Beaumont, Plotz, and the rest of the former management team had drifted happily out of the picture on golden parachutes, and TITHE brought in their own people to fill the top positions. Rebecca's new immediate supervisor was a woman. A young woman. They all seemed young. LaTishia Jordan clearly considered Rebecca a relic and made no attempt to hide the fact. "You're about to retire, aren't you?" she asked when they met.

"Wasn't planning on it," Rebecca said, though it was a day-to-day decision since the TITHE takeover.

"I heard you had money, don't really need to work."

"I don't believe that's any of your business, one way or another," Rebecca replied evenly, glowering at Ms. Jordan's impudence. "I've been here five years because I enjoy it. As long as I continue to enjoy it, I intend to stick around."

Despite her apparent lack of collegial courtesy, Ms. Jordan was The Keep's new Public Relations Director, and Rebecca was glad to see the PR function brought back in-house. The outsourced firm had never really understood what made The Keep special, because they experienced it only superficially. Rebecca hoped that by immersing herself in the hotel's daily life, Ms. Jordan would absorb at least some sense of its magic and proud heritage. That, of course, remained to be seen.

"So I see from this job description that you lead tours and answer people's questions about history. Is that all you do? Doesn't seem like that would take thirty hours a week."

Rebecca tried not to sound defensive. "You'd be surprised," she said. "I hope you can visit the archives soon so I can show you all the things that need to be sorted and filed, all the email and telephone inquiries I get that require research, and all the tour requests I process in a typical week. I also change out the historical display cases across from the Front Desk in the lobby every month or so, and an outside window along Carson Street. I do a history piece for new employee orientation and write for the newsletter. And of course, there are media requests from time to time."

"Oh yeah, I heard from the old PR team that you were pretty good with interviews. I'll probably handle most of those from now on. I'll let you know if I need historical info."

"There are two excellent books on Griffins Keep history you should read..." Rebecca began, but Ms. Jordan stopped her with a raised hand and shake of her head.

"Like I said, when—if—anybody cares about that stuff, I'll get it from you." She cleared her throat and glanced at her agenda. "Now, I want to change the way we're doing hotel history tours.

101

These online reservations and requests are too inefficient, and people can't always get the dates and times that work for them. I want you to record your script. We'll mark the stops with little numbered plaques around the hotel, and we'll make it available as a self-guided audio tour people can pick up from the concierge whenever. I don't want you wasting time returning calls for these private tour requests anymore. It's a hassle for Sales and for Accounting. There's no point."

Blindsided, Rebecca practically spluttered. "But...but people like the personal touch. They like be able to ask questions. The tours are an important component of our hospitality, an important part of our public relations..."

Ms. Jordan shrugged. "You said it yourself. There are books they can read if they have questions about things the recording doesn't cover. People want their entertainment on demand. These days they insist on it. Have your complete script ready for me to edit by next Wednesday. I'll get the website people working on changing the Hotel Tours page, and I'll do a press release about the new audio tour as soon as you can record it."

She looked directly at Rebecca for the first time since raising the subject. She seemed surprised to see something like horror in the historian's expression. "What?" she asked, genuinely puzzled. "I'd think you'd be glad to finally cut back on leading the tours in person. What did I see in your stats for last year—something like 300 of them? Five years of that? Aren't you sick of it? You must sound like a tape recording half the time already."

*Ouch.* That hurt, because it was true. Rebecca often caught herself saying the exact same thing in the exact same way, tour after tour. It was impossible not to fall into a sort of routine rap after so many repetitions. But she always made an effort to mix it up a bit, to tailor the stories to each group and their interests. To keep it fresh and lively. Most of the time she managed it. But the ruts were getting deeper all the time.

After consideration, Rebecca said, "I think the audio tour would be a great option for some people. But I encourage you not to abandon expert-led tours altogether. At least not until you shadow me on one and see firsthand how it engages and involves our guests in a way no tape recording could."

"We'll see," Ms. Jordan said. "You'll of course honor the tours already on the calendar. I was actually shocked to see how many are booked in the coming months. And we'll still have the

102

personally-guided option for special groups. But you need to be open to change," she admonished Rebecca. "The old ways are all being re-examined, and many are being drastically revised to bring this business into the twenty-first century. Personal tours are quaint, I'm sure. But are they really necessary? Think about it."


The new owners embarked immediately upon reshaping the hotel in their own image. Rebecca arrived one morning to discover several papier mache griffins dangling from the stained-glass skylight support lattice, and an inflated bouncy castle occupying a corner of the atrium lobby, just as the designer had envisioned. The Griffin fountain was so far unadulterated. Apparently the Bellagio fountain guy wanted no part of the project.

TITHE replaced all of the managers with its own people, outsiders who knew nothing about the Griffins Keep's place in Denver's history or in Denver's heart. They didn't know how things had been done in the past, and they didn't care. Never mind that The Keep was unlike any other property they had ever managed. They quickly imposed their generic template on everything. Not only managers were let go, but also general staff. With the drastic cuts, personnel was reduced by more than a third. Many who had worked at The Keep for years or even decades had quit, uncomfortable with the new slapdash paradigm. No one who left was replaced. The level of service for which the hotel had always been renowned suffered noticeably.

TITHE's new logo for The Keep, unveiled with great fanfare at a media event, was everywhere evident. It featured a cartoon griffin with huge eyes and chipmunk cheeks.

"Where are my display cases?" Rebecca demanded of the new front desk manager. "They've always been right here, where guests checking in or out can see them. Every month or so, I switch out the displays to highlight different aspects of Keep history."

The cocksure young man shook his head. "Not anymore, lady," he said. "Every trace of history is outta here, per Mr. Branson's instructions."

Rebecca's absence of surprise did nothing to blunt her outrage. "What about the cases themselves? They're beautiful antiques."

103

"Forget about 'em," the new manager advised. "They've already been shipped off to our furniture liquidators in California."

An Us-and-Them dynamic soon prevailed among staff. Arrogant TITHE associates strutted throughout the premises, dictating new policies and procedures and soliciting no input from longtime staff.

"I feel like I'm walking on shifting ground," Dawn commented when Rebecca encountered her on the service elevator one morning.

"Or on eggshells," the historian said.

"It doesn't feel right. All out of whack and unbalanced—like everything could fall apart at any moment."

Rebecca tried to inject a positive note. "Probably just growing pains. A rocky period of adjustment that will pass soon."

"I hope you're right," the usually optimistic admin assistant said, attempting a smile. "But I'm updating my resume, just in case."


The middle-aged women who appeared on a bright late autumn Thursday were casual but genial acquaintances. "We studied under the same master medium," they explained to Rebecca at the start of their private tour. "I'm Margaret and this is Molly. Of course we want to hear about the hotel history, but we hope you won't mind if we wander a little or linger a bit here and there to tune into whatever impressions and messages entities from the hotel's past might convey to us."

Rebecca assured them she had no objections. Here was a perfect example of why Ms. Jordan's cookie-cutter recorded tour wouldn't work for everyone. The women had begun receiving extra-sensory perceptions even before the historian arrived.

"The level of paranormal activity in here is amazing" Margaret said.

Molly concurred. "This throng of spirits would be frightening if they weren't so overwhelmingly benevolent. I'm sensing that most of them are delighted to be here. The place is awash in warm, contented auras."

"While we were waiting for you, I saw a very distinguished gentleman descend the Grand Staircase," Margaret said. "He nodded acknowledgement to a couple of ghost guests in the lobby

104

and drifted on out the Carson-side doors. The guests whispered among themselves after he passed, 'That was Mr. Kuhrsfeld himself. That was Rolph Joseph, Sr., the old man.'"

"Are you sure it wasn't Harrison Griffin?" Rebecca asked. "Seems he would be more likely to continue overseeing his hotel."

"Oh no," insisted Margaret. "It was Mr. Kuhrsfeld, all right. Another one of the guests whispered that he kept a beautiful mistress in an apartment upstairs, next to his own. Do you know anything about that?"

Rebecca shook her head. "But the Kuhrsfeld patriarch did live—and die—in an apartment here in the hotel after he left his wife Nellie in the 1920s."

Except for seeing and hearing things that weren't there, the two women seemed quite rational and intelligent. Smartly dressed, they appeared to be business professionals on a break from work. Margaret was a large woman, tall but not heavy, almost regal in bearing, with an expressive round face and golden hair pulled back into a neat French twist. Her hazel eyes sparkled one moment, flashed the next. Molly's strawberry blonde hair was short and wavy. The blue-gray eyes magnified by her glasses seemed to hold a serene secret wisdom. She fairly glowed with an inner warmth. The ladies' earnestness and genuine wonder was infectious.

"There's a handsome young man up on the third floor balcony directly across from us," Margaret declared as they stood where the original Grand Entrance had opened onto the lobby. "He's a bellman, and he's watching everyone who enters the hotel, especially the women. He's quite the charmer—and a jewel thief! The rich old ladies love him and invite him into their rooms. Even when he robs them blind, they scarcely seem to mind."

"I see a little girl in a long Victorian nightgown on the fifth-floor balcony," Molly said. "She's pushing a doll carriage with her little dog in it, around and around the atrium."

"I can always tell when you're 'reading' spirits," Margaret told her fellow medium, "because you get those red streaks on your neck."

"Red streaks?" Rebecca sought explanation.

"Oh yes," Margaret said. "Whenever the spirits communicate with us, we get a flush of heat. With Molly, it's more obvious than most."

105

"Sounds like a hot flash," Rebecca observed without thinking that her comment might offend.

"Well, yes, actually, it is sort of like that," Molly replied. "But it's more than that, too. It's like the spirits take your air. It's hard to breath, and a lot of times they crowd your personal space. It can be very uncomfortable."

Both women sensed an almost endless parade of spirits through the lobby. "Ladies promenading gracefully with rustling crinoline petticoats, hoping to be seen and admired. Gentlemen strutting, puffing on cigars, doffing bowler hats, feeling very superior and sure of themselves."

The two women played off one another's perceptions. "There was a gunfight here in the lobby," began Molly, "A big argument. One of them stole something from the other. Very heated."

"I'm getting it, too. An angry fight. Lots of shouting," Margaret confirmed. "Are they fighting over a woman?"

"A woman? No. I think it was over...a cow!" The mediums laughed, then turned to the historian for validation. "Could that really have happened?"

"A gunfight over a cow? Seems unlikely," Rebecca began. "Then again...The Keep was always the hotel of choice for wealthy stockmen. Maybe the argument wasn't over a cow, but a bull— prize breeding stock, you know? Anything's possible."

As the three walked the hotel, floor by floor, Rebecca was surprised to find herself re-energized by the sensitives' perspective. She'd become burned out on The Keep's oft-repeated ghost stories after five Halloween seasons. But the things the women seemed to see and hear and smell throughout the place were somehow opening her eyes anew.

"So much positive energy!" they effused over and over. "And so many secrets. This is such a place of power. People could be made or broken here."

One smelled cigar smoke and saw playing cards and stacks of poker chips on an invisible table in the Silver Spoon space. The other claimed to actually feel the agony of a cook who was badly burned in the old club kitchen space. "Hot grease, all up and down this arm," she said, shuddering. "I only felt it for a moment, but now my whole arm is tingling. That poor boy."

They continued their exploration.

"Oh my!" Margaret exclaimed when the elevator doors opened on 8. "This is the party floor."

106

Molly nodded and smiled. "Laughing, dancing...drinking! It didn't always look like this, did it?"

"Not at all. Before these top two floors were converted into apartments in the 1930s, this floor had private dining rooms and the two-story Ballroom and Banquet Hall in one of the 45-degree corners."

"Lovely! Let's head that way, can we?"

"Young ladies giggling. Young men teasing. A band playing—up there," Margaret said glancing up as they rounded the corner to the Grand Staircase.

Then, looking as if the floor had fallen out from under them, the women's cheerful demeanors suddenly transformed. Margaret stepped back so quickly she almost stumbled, raising an arm as if to shield herself. Molly stopped in her tracks, transfixed and trembling.

"Oh Jesus. This is bad. Something really, really tragic happened here."

"I'm sensing a man...very violent, very cruel...."

"And a woman...terrified, desperate. She's some sort of servant or maid."

"He's choking her, strangling her—she can't cry out, can't breathe."

The mediums looked at each other with wide eyes, struggling to interpret their strong perceptions.

"What was here?" Margaret asked, pointing to the glass blocks that had enclosed the atrium since the Parapet Apartment days.

Rebecca swallowed. "It was open to the atrium, with a filigreed railing—just like floors Two through Seven. You would have been able to see the lobby, far, far below."

"I can't stay here," announced Margaret weakly, suddenly mobilized. "It's unbearable."

# CHAPTER 12

Disturbed by the turn the tour with Margaret and Molly had taken, Rebecca hesitated to continue. "I was going to show you our most famous 'haunted' room next. But if you'd rather not..."

"We're fine, dear," Margaret hastened to assure her, "Aren't we, Molly?" The other medium nodded. "We both put on protections before we came today—just in case. You never know what you might encounter in a place this active. Let's go pay a visit to Sybil."

The two mediums were obviously well acquainted with the life—and afterlife --story of Mrs. Dawson Thorne. Rebecca was relieved not to have to tell it again. They climbed the stairs to 940. Rebecca knocked on the door before tapping the key card on the pad. For once, it worked on the first try. The historian had intentionally left off all but a few of the lights in the suite when she'd previewed it before the tour. They closed the door gently behind them.

"I smell soup," Molly said. "Someone's making soup over there."

Margaret was quiet, gazing around the sitting room, taking it all in. "I'm drawn to this corner," she said, walking slowly to the far side of the room. "I sense Sybil sitting here for hours on end, not even looking out the windows. She's sad, so very sad— remembering the social life she no longer enjoys and just wanting to disappear. It's like she's collapsing inside of herself, imploding..." Margaret's eyes filled with tears and her voice was choked. "I smell medicine, but she doesn't want to take it. Doesn't care if she dies. She feels ugly and abandoned. Her sons don't even come to see her. And her nurses are cruel to her. So lonely, so sad..."

"I see a very old woman restrained in a wheelchair in this bedroom," Molly said from the doorway. "She's slumped over, would probably slip out of the chair without the straps. She feels like a prisoner... She doesn't want anyone to see her like this."

"During Mrs. Thorne's years in this apartment, they say she grew increasingly reclusive and increasingly senile," Rebecca confirmed.

"She's very insecure, pitiful and helpless—not at all the haughty person you always hear she was in her social heyday," Margaret said, still visibly affected by the grief she sensed.

Sans segue, the medium turned to the historian. "Sybil has message for you," she said, regarding Rebecca sternly, "Stop saying she was 'heartless' on your tours. She wants you to know she had a heart—a generous, trusting heart—and it was broken by her young man. He was the true love of her life. Her husband Dawson was never emotionally available. I'm getting that he liked men—boys, actually..."

She had Rebecca's riveted attention.

"Sybil wants you to know that she never intended to destroy the man who betrayed her," Margaret continued, "Never meant to drive him to suicide. The news of his death devastated her.

"And she asks that you never speak her lover's name. On tours in this room, when you tell her story, don't say his name. It hurts her something awful to hear it and remember how he deserted and humiliated her."

Taken aback, Rebecca promised never to mention the name of Barkley Heath in the suite again. Sybil Thorne had been a flesh-and-blood person, the admonishment from Beyond reminded the historian—not just a character. If her spirit did indeed haunt this suite, the sensitivity and vulnerability the woman had in life would linger, as well.

Caught up in the surreal moment, Rebecca wondered aloud. "If Mrs. Thorne was so unhappy during her years at The Keep, why is she still here? I would think she'd haunt her old Capitol Hill mansion, where she could relive all the elaborate parties of her happier glory days."

The mediums seemed to ponder her question for several moments.

"I don't know why she's here," Margaret said at last. "But I suspect she's punishing herself. I wish we could set her spirit free and let her rest in peace. Even if she wasn't always the nicest person during her lifetime, surely she doesn't deserve to endure this sort of torment for eternity."

"Be careful, Margaret," her fellow medium cautioned. "That's not our call to make."

Margaret glanced at her wristwatch then, and the mundane intervened. "Gracious, my parking meter ran out half-an-hour ago! The time just flew by, didn't it?"

Molly agreed and said that she had to move on, as well. "But it's killing me. We're just beginning to scratch the surface of The Keep's many layers."

Rebecca considered her proposal carefully as they rode the elevator back to the lobby. "This has been fascinating for me, too. Would you ladies consider returning next week as my guests? I'd love to show you the hotel archives and hear more of your impressions of the place."

The mediums grinned at each other with delight. "Would we?! That would be a dream come true. You have our emails. Just let us know when. The sooner the better. Thank you!"


"The Keep spirits support you, you know," Margaret said as they explored the archives together the following week. "They appreciate your passion and all you do to protect the artifacts. You have two guardians in this space—both female, both very proprietary. They want to be sure you know these things are not yours, but only yours to care for."

"Yes, of course."

"One of them says, 'Bring back the book.' Does that mean anything to you?" Molly asked.

*Representative Women of Colorado.* She'd taken the rare 1911 book home from the archives months ago for research. "Yes," Rebecca replied. "I understand the message. Please excuse me, Charlotte," she added sheepishly, glancing toward the ceiling.

Rebecca randomly withdrew an old 1898 guest register from the storage slots on one side of the center island cabinet and opened it on the desktop podium for the mediums' inspection.

Molly lightly traced the signatures with her finger, almost reverently. "I can feel their personalities in their handwriting," she marveled. "This is wonderful!"

The original blueprint of the ground floor that Rebecca next laid out for the mediums' inspection evoked a strong reaction from Molly.

"The architect has so much pride in this design, so much satisfaction in this accomplishment. But something's not quite right..." Molly followed the outline of the floor plan with her open hand, palm down, hovering just above the rendering. "This was his masterpiece, his perfect creation. But someone made him change something at the last minute. An adjustment—minor, I think, but more than he wanted to make. Something about a capstone—I'm getting that word 'capstone'—and 'blood.'" He had to make the change against his will, and he had to make it...in the dark?"

Rebecca shrugged. "I've never heard about any last-minute adjustments, unless..." She remembered Lochlan's assertion that the Keep was intentionally positioned to correspond to the cosmic cycles. "Could the building footprint have been slightly tweaked to align the entrance with the equinox?"

Molly's eyes turned from the blueprint and flashed at the historian. It was as if the medium had momentarily receded and something else had surfaced. "You're not supposed to know that," her menacing voice accused.

Rebecca instinctively recoiled from the intensity of the reaction. Molly blinked and laughed uneasily. "So sorry," she said. "I don't know where that came from. Don't let it bother you. Just a blip from Beyond. All good now."

Later, as they circumnavigated the fourth floor balcony, Margaret fell behind.

"Come stand here," she called, beckoning Molly back to a spot they had passed. "Now look up there." She pointed to the northeast corner of the stained glass skylight, high above the concierge desk. "Do you sense anything?"

Molly drew a deep breath, closed her eyes, then opened them again and directed her gaze to the space her fellow psychic indicated. "Oh my!" she said, startled. "It's bright! Terribly bright. Like something burning. Like the sun...but the sun's somewhere over here." She glanced in a generally southwestern direction, then back to the high corner opposite. "What ...what is it?"

112

"I don't know," Margaret confessed. "But I'm sensing great power...protective power. Whatever it is...whatever *they* are...they're the reason the hotel has closed only once, the reason things that seem hopeless work out inside this building. They're guardians...more than one, but I can't tell how many..."

"Are they ghosts?" Rebecca asked for clarification.

"Oh no, not ghosts. They were never human."

"They're something else entirely," Molly said, "They emanate from the building somehow, and yet they've always been here."

"I'm sensing wings," Margaret said. "Huge wings."

"Griffins!" Rebecca concluded with satisfaction. "We've always said griffins guarded The Keep."

Margaret was unconvinced. "I don't think so. Griffins wouldn't...*blaze* like this. Such intense light! They're hard to describe. Part elemental, part ego, part engine..."

"I'd call it The Keep's essence," Molly declared.

When Rebecca later shared their perception with Lochlan, he was not surprised that the mediums had identified some sort of guardians in that particular part of The Keep. "In Freemasonry, all journeys begin in the east and end in the north, he said, "So the northeast corner of a structure is very symbolic, very important. That's why Masonic cornerstones are laid there. So these guardians—whatever they are—the fact that they inhabit that ceiling space in the northeast of the atrium makes sense."

"But what *are* they?" Rebecca asked.

Lochlan frowned at her as though she were being intentionally dense. "You know what they are."

The historian shrugged helplessly. "Well, they sound like angels."

"Not just angels—a special 'class', if you will, of celestial beings. It's obvious to me they're Dominions, like the one in the Salon fresco."

"The residual presence of the Freemasons in this place is strong," Margaret told Rebecca on her third visit with fellow medium Molly. "I've brought some Masonic things of my father's I discovered after his death to try to draw out their spirits."

She handed the historian several small scraps of paper. One was labeled "The Tree of Life," a strange depiction resembling a block print, with leaves that looked nothing like leaves and a trunk that looked more like a spinal cord. Another was a drawing of a triangle with a sort of backwards "s" shape inside of it. The handwritten caption read "Signet—Sign of 32nd Degree Scottish Rite Mason—Prince of the Royal Secret." Below this on the same small slip of paper were a series of words in some language unknown to Rebecca,

"Kabbalah," Margaret explained. The same language Lochlan had used to invite Charlotte's spirit into the archives. An even smaller scrap had another Kabbalah phrase, labeled "Word of the Master Mason—Given in the manner in which it is received—toe-to-toe knee-to-knee breast-to-breast hand-to-back ear-to-cheek." On the reverse of this typed note were several handwritten scribbles, difficult to make out. Rebecca squinted and guessed: "'11333 perfect number...Moses Burning Bush...Secret name Ya-weigh...Lady of Perfection.' Weird. Do you have any idea what these mean?"

Margaret shook her head. "No. But *they* do—the builders of The Keep. I hoped bringing these secret things into the light would get a reaction out of them. And it has."

"The Masonic spirits are very upset that she's exposing these esoteric words and symbols without the knowledge that goes with them," Molly said. "They're actually cursing at her. They're telling her to put them back where she found them."

"And I'm telling them that I will—IF they share some secret of the building with us. These are my bargaining chips," Margaret explained. "And I sensed the strangest revelation from the Masons a few minutes after I arrived. Something about bones. They told me there are bones in each corner of The Keep. Inside the structure itself."

"Bones? What kind of bones? Animal? Not human bones, surely." Rebecca found the message both bizarre and disturbing. "Why are the bones there?"

Margaret raised her hands in surrender. "That's all they'll tell me. I'm sorry."

"I'm getting something else." Molly cocked her head like a dog hearing a whistle inaudible to humans. "'How dare you judge us?' they're demanding. They're angry. 'You don't know what this city was like. Chaotic. Cruel. Uncivilized. We did what was necessary. Made sacrifices, took care --- in the ancient traditions—to ensure success. To ensure continuance.'"

114

"We always love to come to this blessed place," an elderly Hispanic woman told Rebecca one afternoon when she stopped to compliment the woman's hat at Lobby Tea between tours. "Our Lord left his mark of favor on this hotel."

"I'm not sure I know what you mean," Rebecca replied hesitantly.

"The image of Our Lady on the wall," the old woman said, "right over there by the doorway."

Rebecca's blank look prompted the woman to rise from her chair with some difficulty and take the historian's arm. "Come with me. I'll show you."

The woman's tea companions, probably her daughter and granddaughter, just smiled tolerantly and motioned for Rebecca to go along. Her guide steered her slowly across the lobby toward the Spa. The Mexican onyx that originally framed the massive lobby fireplace now provided an imposing entryway. To the right of one of the 3,000-pound flanking columns, the old woman pointed to a pattern in the stone.

"You can see her, the Blessed Virgin, here," she said, tracing it with her finger. "Here is her head, covered and bowed. And here," she continued, reverently touching another dark blemish, slightly lower on the stone, "is her Sacred Heart."

She looked at Rebecca with deep satisfaction. "This is a sign that Our Lord watches over the hotel. We always feel safe and protected here."

*Signs and wonders,* Rebecca thought. *Everyone sees what they want to see—maybe need to see—be it sacred images, mystic secrets, or ghosts.*

Rebecca squeezed the old woman's hand. "Thank you for showing me this," she said sincerely. In sharing her miracle, the devout woman had bestowed a blessing of her own upon a skeptic too blind to have seen it herself.


Like most urban centers, Denver was essentially two cities, widely disparate realities for the Haves and Have-Nots. The Griffins Keep catered to the privileged and prosperous, while her neighbor, Pinnacle Church, welcomed the less fortunate. Every Tuesday, Thursday, and Saturday, their soup kitchen served more than 200

115

hot meals to the homeless. Keep associates volunteered once a month to help set-up, serve, and clean up after the free lunch. It was during one such shift that Rebecca met Charles, a gracious elderly gentleman member of the congregation who offered to give her and other interested volunteers a behind-the-scenes tour of the church.

The hotel historian was joined by Dawn from Sales, Amy, admin assistant for the Engineering department, and Luke, the charming bellman who sometimes led historical tours of the Keep in Rebecca's absence. Charles was slow but nimble, they quickly discovered as he led them down a wooden ladder into Pinnacle's unfinished basement.

"In the early years, we were tapped into the same aquifer as the Griffins Keep," he explained, pointing in the general direction of their old well. "In fact, our pipe organ pump was hydraulically powered by pressure from an artesian well, just like your elevators." He showed then the huge leather bellows that breathed life into the massive 4,275-pipe organ. "Wasn't until the 1930s that we got this electric blower. Can you believe this beauty is more than ninety years old and still going strong? Won't be long before they can say the same of me!"

"When did Pinnacle cap its well?" Amy asked.

"That would be 1917," their guide reported. "The aquifer at the 480-foot level dried up with so many Denver homes and businesses tapped into it. Most everybody switched over to city water around that time. Except for The Keep, of course, which decided to drill down to a deeper source."

Back up the ladder and into the sanctuary, the little group continued their exploration. "Every window in the sanctuary is stained glass—all original and made by the same outfit that did your stained glass skylight," Charles said. "Our two buildings have lots of things in common. Of course, Denver was a pretty small town back then. Most new buildings used the same contractors and artisans."

"What about Masonic connections?" Luke had been talking with Lochlan, obviously.

"A great many of our founding members were Freemasons," Charles said. "They were among the most prominent and influential men in the city."

"What about you, Charles? Are you a Freemason?"

116

Their guide smiled enigmatically. "Let's just say I can keep secrets," he replied before continuing. "Pinnacle's cornerstone was laid by one of the local Masonic lodges. Over the decades, its inscriptions were obscured by coal soot residue and weathering, and for a while, it was completely forgotten. It wasn't until we undertook exterior restoration that the foundation stone was rediscovered. We opened it about ten years ago on the 130th anniversary of our first service. Found all sorts of wonderful things left for us by our forebears. Newspapers, letters, photographs, church programs and bulletins, a hymnal, a membership list. And the symbolic golden trowel used to spread the first mortar on the foundation stone."

"Cool. Where's the Griffins Keep's cornerstone?" Amy asked. They all turned to the hotel historian.

"I've asked Lochlan that same question," Rebecca said, "and he tells me that Masonic cornerstones were always laid in the northeast corner of their structures."

"That would be the Pirates' Pub corner, right? I've never noticed anything there."

"Apparently there isn't. Lochlan thinks the stone might have been moved—or removed—by the Kuhrsfelds when they remodeled that whole corner in the '30s. But the hotel may never have had a cornerstone. Freemasons traditionally dedicated them only in public or religious buildings, not commercial."

"Sounds like a mystery we'll just have to live with," Dawn concluded.

Knowing that one of Pinnacle's many highly prosperous members had ordered an imposing $30,000 pipe organ, the church architect had designed the sanctuary as a concert hall.

"The acoustics are sublime," their guide declared. "I believe Isaac, our organ master, is coming in a little later this afternoon. If we're lucky, we may hear him practice. But before that, let's go crawl around the pipes, shall we? Watch your heads," he cautioned as he directed them through a small wall panel he'd pried open. The organ pipes rose in graduated forests. Some metal. Some wood. "The largest is 42-feet high. The smallest, thinner and shorter than a pencil. The newer bank over there was added later to produce the sound of brass horns."

They took turns posing among the pipes for cellphone photos.

Back in the sanctuary, Charles pointed out the impressive pulpit. Adjacent to that, the baptismal font featured a white marble Madonna and Child.

"Now, I have to take back what I said earlier about every window in the sanctuary being stained glass," their guide said after identifying the tranquil sculpture's artist and donor. "Have a look over on the south wall, way up above the balcony near the ceiling. See that small, square opening? Some of our Masonic members added that window when the baptismal statue was installed. From December 21 through Christmas Day every year, the sunlight streams through that window directly onto the Madonna."

"How magical!" Amy said, looking up and imagining it.

Rebecca wondered if she'd heard right. Building elements aligned by Freemasons to key positions of the sun? December 21- - the winter solstice. Here, it seemed, was an example of exactly what Lochlan had suggested regarding The Keep's orientation in relation to the annual solar trajectory. Maybe his theory wasn't so farfetched after all.

The high point of their tour—literally—was Pinnacle's bell tower. Though it appeared from the street to be part of the church structure, the tower and its soaring spire were completely freestanding. Made entirely of stone, the steeple pointed 183 feet heavenward, like a divine antenna for spiritual transmissions.

"Does the steeple have a lightning rod?" Rebecca asked.

"Not really necessary now, with all the skyscrapers in the neighborhood," Charles told her.

"But what about in the early years? It had to have been higher than anything else around. And topped with a metal cross, seems like it would naturally attract strikes. Has it ever been hit by lightening?"

"Only once, I'm told," Charles said. "A freak occurrence, as I understand it, back in 1917. Perfectly sunny day, not a cloud in the sky. They were doing some sort of work at the Griffins Keep, and there was an accident. You know, the hotel still generated its own electricity back then. Direct current from the basement dynamos, prone to—irregularities. An electrical bolt shot from the flagpole atop the Keep to the cross on our steeple.

"Guess they were never sure what happened exactly. But they say the shock wave of the thing shook the whole neighborhood."

118

# CHAPTER 13

*Denver Mountain Herald*, June 21, 1917:

The Griffins Keep Hotel closed today for the first time in its twenty-seven-year history when workmen drilling onsite for a new water source apparently struck a pocket of natural gas and set off an explosion, causing moderate damage to the northeast corner of the building. Guests occupying the effected rooms reported bright flashes and a rush of chill air around 11:40 am. Eyewitnesses outside the hotel described a 'shimmering shaft of blue-white light' erupting from the rooftop and glancing across the intersection to the Pinnacle Church steeple tip, where it dissipated instantly.

Several windows and light fixtures in The Keep shattered. The hotel's main electrical circuits inexplicably overloaded. No one was injured in the incident, but an unidentified woman, last seen reading in the Ladies Ordinary on the eighth floor of the hotel, was reported missing. Investigators determined that she must have fled in the commotion and chosen not to return.

According to management, the Griffins Keep's guests are being accommodated by neighboring hotels until repairs can be completed and the site is certified safe. The hotel hopes to reopen no later than tomorrow evening."

The historical newspaper clipping Rebecca pulled from the archives files raised more questions than it answered. A rush of chill air—with a gas explosion? It didn't fit. Electrical overload and a shaft of light that shot across to the church steeple? That sounded more like a power surge than an explosion. And what about the "unidentified woman" who went missing at the same time? Was she ever actually located, or merely forgotten?

Rebecca couldn't help but muse that had Great-Aunt Frankie been reporting for the *Herald* at the time, the anomaly might not have been so summarily dismissed.

Frankie Chase was the quintessential plucky female journalist, a whip-smart "muckraker" ala Nellie Bly. Fearless, forthright, and sometimes fanatical, she was a force to be reckoned with on the Denver newspaper scene for half-a-century. She smoked. She drank. She swore. And she lived life on her own terms.

Frankie Chase delighted in pushing boundaries. Widow-and-orphan sob stories were not for her. Frankie covered the politics, crime, and social issues of the day. Tireless and talented, she championed many a progressive cause in the early twentieth century. Denver's adult public education, juvenile justice system, family planning, and even civic Christmas lighting were due, in large part, to her crusading and persuasive columns. No one could tug the collective heartstrings and shape public opinion like Frankie Chase.

The *Herald* later lured the intrepid reporter away from the *Times* with buckets of money and the promise of carte blanche to cover any stories that appealed to her. Soon after, Frankie had married to avoid the stigma of spinsterhood and regretted it almost immediately.

"I suppose I thought I could transform myself into the passive, obedient creature my husband—and most men back then—wanted in a wife," she once explained to Becky. "I expected more of myself than he did." Divorced quietly by mutual consent after less than three years, Frankie thereafter invested all her passion in her career. In retrospect, Rebecca speculated that had she followed Aunt Frankie's example during her own marriage,

120

rather than her mother's long-suffering model, she might have saved herself years of pain.

After more than forty years with the *Herald*, Frankie was fired at the age of 71 for an "altercation in the newsroom" (according to a rival paper).

"That damned new editor was always criticizing my writing style. Hell, it was plenty good enough before he came along in the 60s. 'Too flowery,' he said. 'Not objective,' he groused. When he demanded I write an apology for my criticism of some asinine state legislators, I let him have it—and I don't mean the apology."

At the age of 76, Frankie went back to her hometown of Cripple Creek, where she bought and ran the local paper for many more years. A heavy smoker all her life, she finally succumbed to lung cancer at the age of 82.

"I always thought it was so sad that Frances was childless," Rebecca's mother had commented on several occasions. But it seemed to Rebecca that her great-aunt had no regrets in that regard.

For her part, Rebecca had always considered herself "child-free"—a term which sounded much less pathetic than "childless." The timing and circumstances had never been right for motherhood in Rebecca's childbearing years, and she was grateful to live in an era of reproductive choice.

"But who will take care of you when you get old?" her younger sister Ruthie, the mother of seven, sometimes fretted.

"I'm not going to get old," Rebecca would reply simply. She had seen enough of old age to know it wasn't for her. The Golden Years were not for the faint of heart, she knew, with the physical failings and escalating indignities. She would pass, thank you very much. Rebecca had no intention of outliving her useful body. With luck, some sort of accident would take her out, long before she would even consider leaning on anyone else for support.

Content without children—except occasionally for a few days around Christmas—Rebecca nevertheless loved the role of aunt. She enjoyed her nieces and nephews, spoiled them, then sent them home to their parents when they got too whiney or tiresome. It seemed to her the perfect arrangement.

Rebecca and her niece Hannah had a special relationship, just as she had had with Great-Aunt Frankie. Hannah was born on Rebecca's 30th birthday. Soulmates, they shared mutual admiration and affection. Rebecca had hooked Hannah on

121

Colorado history early with the same Bancroft Booklets that influenced her own affinity for the subject in her youth.

The little paperbacks, which sold for 25 cents in the 1940s and 50s, were aimed at the Colorado tourist and transplant audience. Author Caroline Bancroft's stories of the "Unsinkable Molly" Brown and "Silver Queen" Baby Doe Tabor captured both the drama and the melodrama of the state's boom-and–bust backstory. Before becoming a historian, Bancroft had written for popular "true romance" magazines. By her own admission, she made-up key details, developments, and dialogues to enhance her narratives. But for many, Bancroft's creative writing brought history to life for the first time. Rebecca aimed to do the same for tour guests of The Keep, albeit with more allegiance to accuracy.

When Frankie Chase died 25 years ago, she left everything to her beloved great-niece Rebecca: a healthy bank account, a substantial financial portfolio, the Denver Tudor house, and the Cripple Creek newspaper office building which sold for an exorbitant sum to a large casino company when Colorado legalized small stakes gaming just a few months later.

The windfall had transformed Rebecca's life and priorities. She didn't consider herself wealthy, but money was no longer a concern. She had been able to pursue her passions rather than a paycheck ever since. She'd traveled extensively, volunteered on archaeological digs, earned her Master's in history, and landed inevitably at the Griffins Keep.

The dozen relatives of perennial Parapet Apartment denizen Collier Hendricks had scheduled their private tour months ago to coincide with the one time of year when they all got together. They'd understood when they'd booked the tour that the chance of actually seeing "Uncle Collier's" old apartment was entirely dependent upon the hotel's occupancy. With Suite 901 un-available, they seemed content in a neighboring room.

As far as Rebecca could determine, Hendricks held the record for longest resident guest of Griffins Keep. From 1937 until his death 41 years later, the eccentric bachelor was a fixture of the hotel, familiar to—if not beloved by—both staff and other Parapet residents.

"We haven't very much information on any of the Parapet residents," Rebecca told the relatives. "But there was a funny little reminiscence from a longtime housekeeper in Hendricks' file. She recalled that whenever she went to clean his suite or change his linens, he was notorious for tormenting her—pinching and grabbing and such. Apparently housekeepers had to put up with a lot of that in pre-feminism decades. For years after he died in his apartment, this employee reported that she was frequently pestered by a horsefly buzzing around 901, which she believed to be the reincarnation of Hendricks himself."

"Wouldn't surprise me a bit," muttered the elderly matriarch of the family.

"Sounds about right," her husband concurred.

An adult niece had brought along several scanned photographs and documents recovered from basement boxes which she handed the hotel historian. "Thought you might want to add these to Uncle Collier's file."

In the first photo, two fair-haired children with shoulder-length curls, posed for their studio portrait in ruffled Little Lord Fauntleroy suits and looking for all the world like girls, were identified as Collier and his younger brother Lawrence, circa 1895. Other pictures showed a smiling Collier at Harvard Law School, Collier surrounded by his fellow army interpreters in World War I France, and Collier proudly posing with his new Pierce Arrow motorcar in front of Griffins Keep's grand entrance.

"He always loved this hotel and couldn't wait to move in when they opened the apartments."

"So he was a lawyer?" Rebecca asked.

The older gentleman, Lawrence Hendricks' son, clarified. "He had a law degree. But he liked to boast that he'd worked only one day in his life, and that was for the Kuhrsfeld Investment Company."

"Then what did he *do*? How did he live?"

The old lady explained. "Trust fund took care of everything. His father made millions in Cripple Creek gold. Collier was the quintessential dilettante. Man About Town, *bon vivant*. Walked to the University Club almost every day and lunched with friends for hours. A patron of the arts. A connoisseur of fine wine. An impeccable dresser, as you can see in that later picture."

An older, still dapper Collier lounged on a park bench in the photo she indicated. Straw boater shading his eyes, pin-striped suit, walking stick topped with a brass hound's head.

"Love the two-toned wingtips," Rebecca said as a vague recognition struggled to surface. Where else had she seen black and white wingtips? Not long ago...

"After the pictures you'll find a letter that totally corroborates your housekeeper's memory of Uncle Collier," the niece prompted.

The reproduced correspondence typed on old Griffins Keep stationary was dated June 13, 1948. From Executive Housekeeper Marjory Crispin, it warned Mr. Kendricks that if his harassment of female housekeepers did not cease immediately, he would be assigned a male housekeeper at a substantially higher monthly rate.

"Whoa!" one of the younger family members exclaimed. "You tell 'im, Marjory!"

"Why did the men housekeepers make more money than the women?" another youngster wondered.

In Rebecca's subconscious, synapses suddenly sparked. Connections crackled. The 10th floor ladies room—Marjory's old bathroom—the sharp knock—a glimpse of feet and pin-striped trouser cuffs through the slats of the door. Black and white wingtips.

*It couldn't be. It had to be.* Rebecca smiled to herself.

"Do you think Collier Hendricks might haunt the hotel?" the niece's husband asked the historian, noticing the sudden change in her expression.

"Sure. Why not?" Rebecca replied, surprising herself. "What else has he got to do?"


On Saturday morning, Rebecca discovered Lochlan in the archives with two visitors. He was showing the Brookings blueprints to a willowy woman, about their age. Her long, straight, white-blond hair hung in curtains around her face as she bent over the drawings in serious scrutiny. When she looked up at Rebecca's entrance, her green eyes shone with excitement. She reached out to take the historian's hand.

Lochlan smiled. "Rebecca, I'd like you to meet my old and dear friend, Rosslyn MacKay, astrologer, psychic, and medium extraordinaire."

The woman frowned at Lochlan. "I'm not that much older then you, thank you very much," she sniffed, pretending insult, then smiled warmly. "Rebecca and I have met. She took us on an amazing tour a month or so ago. So wonderful to see you again, Rebecca! Lochlan's talked about you for years. You remember my daughter, Miranda."

"Rosslyn, of course," Rebecca said. "I never made the connection between you and Lochlan."

"That was on purpose," she confessed. "I wanted to check you out for myself, sort of spy on you to take your measure before you knew anything about me."

"Roz is a Scot, too," Lochlan said. "Clan MacKay has spawned Freemasons for countless generations. We met when we were both working at a bar in Five Points in our 20s," Lochlan said, "Roz as a waitress and me in the band. Been soulmates ever since. Even if we go a year or more without connecting, when we get back together we just click as if no time has passed at all."

"And what do you do these days?" Rebecca asked her.

"I work in hospice care."

"She uses her special gifts to ease people's transition from this realm of existence to the next," Lochlan said. "Makes the final days of life less frightening for the dying and their loved ones."

"Doesn't pay beans," Rosslyn said. "But I hope I'm racking up some points in the karmic ledger, you know?"

Rebecca nodded. "So what do you make of our Keep blueprints?"

"Oh, they're marvelous! I can feel Edward Brookings's spirit just radiating from every one of them. The Griffins Keep truly was a Master Builder's masterwork." She turned back to her inspection of the original ground floor plan. "With this building, Brookings conceived, positioned, designed, aligned and manifested a physical representation of the higher esoteric principles the Freemasons are all about."

"I'm sure Lochlan has discussed this with you already, but we wonder if the building has—or had—a cornerstone, and where it might have been laid," Rebecca said.

"Seems to make the most design sense that it would be in the 90-degree-angled corner at Seventeenth and Carson," Lochlan said. "But I've always suspected the corner where the Pirates Pub is today—the northeast corner of the structure, where Freemasons traditionally laid their foundation stones. Nothing evident there today, of course. Could be below street level, hidden by all sorts of later mechanical equipment in the basement. Or maybe the

Kuhrsfelds found and removed it when they were doing all their 1930s remodeling."

The psychic swept her open palm back and forth across the blueprint, just as Molly had done on her visit, her hand hovering just above its surface, deep in concentration. The puzzled look on her face suddenly brightened with a Eureka.

"Wow," she almost whispered. "I'm getting that the *whole building* is a cornerstone! A cornerstone for the city itself."

Positioned as it was at the intersection of the financial and political districts of Denver, the Griffins Keep's keystone location had anchored the community since its debut. Rosslyn's revelation rang true.

"I'd like to get some of those old "birds-eye" maps of the city from 1890 and plot the lines radiating from the two sides of the Keep's right angle corner," she said excitedly. "I'm pretty sure the resulting diagram will border and encompass every significant building around that time."

Something else had been nagging at the historian ever since Margaret brought her father's Masonic secret items to the hotel. "Another medium told me that the spirits of the Freemasons involved with the construction of the hotel revealed to her that there were bones incorporated into each corner of the building. Does that make any sense to either of you?"

Lochlan and Rosslyn exchanged knowing glances. The engineer explained. "In ancient times, stone masons were known to put the bones from sacrifices inside the foundation stones of their buildings. The bones were thought to impart structural and spiritual strength."

"What kind of bones?"

"Animal, usually. Cats, lambs, even bulls were among the animals typically sacrificed. Some cathedrals and monasteries were said to have religious relics sealed inside their foundation stones."

"You mean, like the bones of saints?"

"Or a piece of the True Cross, a vial of the Virgin's tears, a scrap of Christ's shroud. Anything that would infuse the building with religious significance and power."

"By the same token, ancient builders often smeared sacrificial blood on the top of the foundation stone or capstone— like an altar," Rosslyn added. "I've even read that for extremely important structures, the Master Builder would sacrifice his own spouse and sanctify the foundation stone with her blood and bones."

"Jesus," Rebecca swore without thinking. "Sounds like I'd better do some research on the circumstances of Mrs. Edward Brookings' death." She was only half joking.

Lochlan cautioned, "Remember, these were ancient practices. I've never heard of builders, even Freemasons, incorporating sacrifices or relics in historically recent times."

Miranda, who had hovered in a corner and said nothing until now, trembled. "I feel the bones in this place," she said quietly. "And blood. At the roots. They feed the building life. They're vital to its function."

"Its function?" Rebecca sought to clarify, remembering Lochlan's earlier assertion. "What do you mean by that?"

Rosslyn moved to the corner and put a comforting arm about her daughter's shoulders. "Many of us sense that the Griffins Keep is much more than a hotel," she told the historian. "The Keep is a waystation in a vastly larger sense. Lochlan and I have talked about this a lot. I believe this building serves as a portal between realms of reality, between the worlds of the living and the dead.

"I know it sounds wild, but over the course of many visits and many years, I've come to understand The Keep as a sort of processing center for souls on their spiritual journey," the psychic continued. "The spaces surfaced with onyx are like huge amulets, imparting the healing and centering magic properties of the stone to all inside. Onyx has long been associated with the cycle of life, death, and rebirth. It's believed to aid psychic contact with the dead, as well as between-lives progression."

Glancing up at Rebecca's face as he carefully slid the blueprints back into their drawer, Lochlan smiled knowingly but said nothing.

"This building is a sanctuary for contemplation, for acceptance and for furtherance. A gateway to enlightenment," Rosslyn concluded.

Lochlan offered his own take. "The artesian water, the central sunlight, the structural geometry—they're all integral to The Keep's mystical purpose."

"Think of it as a sort of halfway house *en route* to the next level and, ultimately, to The Light, the source of all things," the psychic said.

"You make it sound like a church."

127

"A temple," Lochlan corrected. "Not unlike the temple built for Solomon by the first Freemasons. It's what I've been trying to tell you all along."

Acknowledging the skepticism in her eyes, he took Rebecca's hand and patted it affectionately. "It's a lot to take in. I understand. It's OK to doubt."

"The Keep's truth will reveal itself to you when you're ready," Rosslyn assured her. "I revisited the building's star chart last week, and it looks like the developments around the winter solstice are going to be even more profound than it appeared at first."

"Is that a good thing, or a bad?"

The astrologer took a moment to frame her forecast clearly. "A challenging thing," she declared. "It's like The Keep is going to undergo a major identity crisis. Many changes will be imposed upon her by outsiders. It's going to be a very difficult period for the hotel and, I have to assume, for those who love her."

She looked from Lochlan to Rebecca and back. "If my predictions are right, you two will need to hold onto each other for balance and strength in the coming months."

# CHAPTER 14

"You'll be happy to hear we plan to incorporate all sorts of historical elements in the reimagined Griffins Keep experience," Jason Nguyen assured Rebecca as she sat at the big board room table surrounded by members of the new marketing and sales teams.

"Like a bouncy castle in the lobby?"

Jason chuckled amiably. "No, no. That's a family-friendly addition, nothing really to do with history, obviously."

"Obviously."

"Let me give you an example of what I mean. We read in one of the hotel histories that the Army's 10th Mountain Division—guys training to fight in the Italian mountains—practiced repelling from balcony to balcony in the atrium during WWII."

"Actually, it was one drunk soldier on one unauthorized occasion," Rebecca corrected.

"Really? Well that doesn't matter. We want to recreate unique experiences for our guests, set up bungee jumping from the balconies. Hey, we could have rock climbing on the outside of the building, too. It'll be *way* cooler than those fake climbing walls people are used to. We can have one side for repelling down the building, another for tech climbing up it. And we can still do the atrium balcony thing, right guys?"

"We could riff on the Depression when dudes who lost all their money in the crash or whatever jumped to their deaths from the seventh floor. Except we'll spin it in a black comedy direction.

Call it the "Stock Market Ups and Downs Bungee Leap" or something like that."

"Awesome concept, Brendan!" Jason said enthusiastically. "Madison, tell Rebecca what you've been working on."

"Well, I'm basing it on The Keep's historic tradition of High Tea. But this will be an updated take on that, capitalizing on Colorado's legalization of recreational marijuana."

Rebecca waited for it, nausea rising.

"So instead of a cigar lounge, we can turn the Kipling into the 'Pot Party Pad.' Don't know about the licensing issues yet. But can't you picture it? I see '60s hippie-style décor. Beanbag chairs, black light posters, wait staff in super-wide bellbottoms and beads. And bongs. But here's the historical part. To go along with The Keep's rep for elegance, they'll be like fine china or porcelain bongs, with a custom Keep griffin logo. And we can sell them as souvenirs, too."

"Yeah, it'll be like really 'high' tea. Get it? And the '60s are history, right?" Jason said, eagerly soliciting Rebecca's buy-in.

Rebecca slowly got to her feet and scanned the faces of the MBA whiz kids around the table.

"Stop," she said as calmly as she could. "Just stop. What you're envisioning has nothing to do with Griffins Keep history or Griffins Keep tradition. Call me when you're ready to get serious about respecting and celebrating the hotel's past. But I will not be party to the sort of carnival crap you're pitching here."

As Rebecca hit the double-doors and fled the asylum, she heard Madison stage-whisper, "She's probably just pissed because she actually remembers the '60s."


"Gotta get out of here for a while," she explained when Maureen asked why she was packing a bag so hastily. Rebecca felt the situation at the Keep spinning out of control as its new management began to impose their tawdry vision on the hotel's future. She'd made enemies already, she knew, with what they surely perceived as her fuddy-duddy intractability. Menopausal meltdown, they probably said behind her back. *Resistant to change? Hell yes. Unreasonably uncooperative. Damn straight.* But was her knee-jerk recalcitrance helping anything? Influencing anyone?

"Where are you going?"

130

"Someplace where history can envelope me," she declared. "I'm off to D.C."

"Fine choice," Mo said. "though I've always been partial to Baltimore. Any idea how long you'll be gone?"

"As long as it takes me to regain perspective. Could be weeks. They won't miss me at work."

Mo picked up Willoughby, who had been fretting at her heels, fully aware of what a suitcase prefaced. "Well, we'll miss you," she said sincerely. "Just hope it helps. I really do, Beck."

As her plane lifted off from DIA, Rebecca could almost feel the stress of the last few weeks slip from her shoulders and flutter to the quickly receding ground. Nothing like flight to remind one of just how small earthbound concerns are in respect to the Big Picture.

Checking into the Willard Hotel near the Mall was like stepping back in time. Beloved and respected by both locals and travelers, the hostelry was a historic gem in the heart of the nation's capital. Rebecca had stayed there several times since starting at the Griffins Keep.

"Ms. Bridger," the front desk manager greeted her warmly. "A pleasure, as always, to see you again. You'll be staying in the Tabor Suite as usual, of course."

"Hello, Alistair," she said, smiling somewhat sadly. "You know me so well. I'm suddenly starved for history."

"We've heard, of course, about the recent unfortunate developments at your hotel," Alistair said, "and you have our most sincere condolences. But as far as we are concerned, The Keep will always be a distinguished historical hospitality colleague. And it is our great pleasure to accommodate you in classic style."

*Bless him,* Rebecca thought as she tapped her card key on the lock scanner. Her suite was named for one of Colorado's most famous "Silver Kings," Horace Tabor, who had married his controversial second wife at the Willard while serving as U.S. Senator for one month in 1883. Elegant yet comfortable, spacious yet intimate, the Tabor Suite felt like home—only better. A bottle of chilled champagne in a sterling ice bucket on the foyer table welcomed her in style. The note from Alistair on the silver tray said simply, "Welcome back to the Willard, where history still matters."

Rebecca peeled off the foil, removed the metal crown cap, and eased the cork from the champagne bottle. She poured herself a

131

glass filled almost to the rim and opened the window to breathe in the melancholy scents of early winter.

Slowly sipping her drink, she mentally replayed the marketing session at The Keep. Madison was right. She did remember the Sixties. But she'd been a schoolgirl, no more involved with the dope-smoking hippie culture than wholesome Sally Field in *The Flying Nun* TV series popular at the time. Might as well have been a nun herself, cloistered at an all-girls Christian boarding school in Plano, Texas. The wildest thing she recalled from those years was playing "The Chipmunks Sing the Beatles Hits" afterhours in the boarders' dorm and inciting several other girls to jump on their beds and rock-out to Alvin and the contraband tune-age. Busted for that shocking bit of rebelliousness, she'd had to spend three consecutive Saturdays knitting potholders for charity.

Looking back, Rebecca could trace the roots of her disillusionment with the church to those school years. The U.S. was becoming more deeply mired in the war in Vietnam. Her older brothers Joseph and Micah were both called during the draft lottery. Joseph, who heeded "Thou Shalt not Kill" over "My Country, Right or Wrong," had fled to Canada rather than serve in what he considered an unjust and unwinnable war. The church and all their family friends had shunned and vilified him. Their father had disowned Joseph and never forgiven him. Their mother, ashamed, rarely spoke of her eldest son, even decades later.

Micah had served in the Southeast Asian conflict for eighteen months. The Micah who left was not the Micah who returned and who overdosed on drugs soon thereafter. Both tragedies broke Rebecca's heart and hardened her outlook.

Adults—church adults, including her own parents—didn't know everything and they weren't always right. Adolescent Rebecca recognized their hypocrisy in espousing Christian beliefs while supporting the war. The realization had rocked her young world and spawned years of critical questioning that led her away from her religious upbringing.

Rebecca closed the window of her Willard suite against the suddenly cold air and finished a second glass of champagne before drawing a bath. She slipped into the warm, scented water and relaxed utterly for the first time in weeks.

132

The Willard Hotel, the "Queen of Pennsylvania Avenue," reigned just two blocks from the White House and two blocks from the National Mall. The institution traced its roots back more than 150 years, though the current building had debuted ten years after the Griffins Keep. The Willard had not been "absolutely fireproof."

The Edwardian lobby décor bespoke what the Willard website described as a "unique blend of contemporary luxury, historic charm and sustainable hospitality that subtly reflects the spirit of the city." A small hotel history museum on the ground floor honored its Washington lineage and legacy. Why couldn't The Keep incorporate something similar?

One evening in the Willard's iconic Round Robin & Scotch Bar, Rebecca chanced to encounter a former Secretary of State who had stayed at the Griffins Keep on multiple occasions and who still remembered the historian's program at a fundraising luncheon there. They chatted briefly before the subject of TITHE's takeover came up.

"I was so sorry to hear from a colleague about the changes they're making to my favorite Denver hotel," the prominent lady lamented. "I've always said The Keep was the most gracious, most restorative place I've ever stayed. But from what I can gather about its new emphasis on entertainment and the decline in service, I doubt I'll be returning."

The Smithsonian Museums, the Capitol building, and the Library of Congress were heady tonics for Rebecca. The eight-day regimen of concentrated history was all it took to restore her to fighting shape. Validated and invigorated, she returned to Denver, optimistically determined to persuade the new Keep management of the cultural—and yes, commercial—value of connections to the past.

She'd propose an onsite hotel museum and gift shop. Griffins Keep guests and visitors were always asking for a gift shop, and the hotel had none. With a few logo items in the Coffee Shop, a few more in the Spa, there was no single source for affordable but tasteful mementos of a visit to the venerable Denver hotel. Rebecca would bring both museum and retail experience to the venture. Surely with all the remodeling currently planned, a place could be found for such an important addition.

The getaway to D.C. had refreshed Rebecca's perspective and re-newed her resolve. It felt good to be back. On the tenth floor, she found the archives door slightly ajar. She pushed it open—and stopped dead.

The center island—gone. The wall of shelves—gone. File cabinets, cupboards, even the window shades—all gone. Rebecca took in the fresh paint and new carpet and feared she was going to be sick. Nothing remained of her work corner but a charred spot just above the baseboard. It was as if the archives had never been there.

Two ladies in tight-skirted dark suits with TITHE name badges arrived on the service elevator and excused themselves as they pushed past the stricken historian.

"Oh, this is a great space!" the taller one said to her associate. "Windows with a rooftop view. And a ladies' room right outside—did you see it? The competition for this place is going to be cutthroat. Bet on it."

Competition for this place? Rebecca couldn't believe her ears. She felt dizzy, disoriented. It was obvious, if only she could bring herself to accept it.

The Griffins Keep archives were no more.

This was exactly how management did things, she knew from similar examples. Decisions made and implemented immediately, without notification of—let alone consultation with—the affected staff. One evening a smiling Director of Restaurants would be greeting Versailles Room diners; the next morning he was dismissed, informed that his duties had been redistributed and his position eliminated. Thank you for your eighteen years of dedicated service. Don't let the Employee Entrance door hit you on the way out.

Rebecca had known the new management placed no value on the hotel's history. Why hadn't she seen this coming? She had to find Lochlan. He could tell her what had happened. He would understand her shock and despair as no one else. She turned and stumbled toward the paint and carpentry shop, desperately hoping he'd be there, putting things back together as he always did.

"Lochlan!" she cried breathlessly when she found him refinishing a nightstand. "It can't be true. Where has everything gone?"

The engineer strode calmly toward her. "Sit first," he ordered, leading her to a chair awaiting reupholstering. "Breathe."

She tried to follow his directions, inhaling deeply. The familiar scene ceased swimming before her eyes.

"They packed up everything and moved it into the sub-basement for now. I heard they're considering donating it all to the Colorado Historical Society," Lochlan explained, and added, "They'll be able to take proper care of it there—temperature and humidity control like we never had. You know we always talked about that. It's probably for the best. We just have to accept this. We have no choice."

Rebecca looked into his eyes and saw that he felt the loss as keenly as she. She caught his hand and squeezed it. "I shouldn't be surprised. It was just so fast. I'm reeling. I should never have left for so long...."

"Wouldn't have made any difference to their plans," Ian said. "This way you were spared watching it all go down."

Rebecca wondered if that scenario would actually have been more painful. And another question occurred to her.

"Am I still historian, do you think? Do I still have a job here?"

Lochlan replied honestly. "Doesn't look good. I imagine HR will want to talk with you."

"I'm in shock," she said as her eyes welled with angry tears. "It's the history that makes The Keep so special. The guest registers, the blueprints—they belong here. This is their origin. Their presence gives the place its meaning, I can't believe they'd just pack it off like that...they could have talked to me first...I could have organized things better before they took it all away..." She planted elbows on her knees and leaned her forehead on her clenched fists.

At length, she looked up, sniffled, and wiped her eyes on her cuff. She shook her head in hopeless surrender. "So much for Charlotte and Marjory being guardian spirits of the archives. I almost believed in them after Charlotte's death." She felt betrayed, abandoned, and foolish.

Lochlan surprised her then by smiling at this. "Our ladies put up a fight, make no mistake," he said. He pulled up a stool and perched conspiratorially beside her.

"Seems the historian key ring disappeared the first day they started moving things. They had a spare key for the archives, but

135

not for the cupboards and cabinets. Had to break into those to get the stuff out.

"And toward the end, when all the artifacts were gone and they disconnected your computer, the outlet sparked into a fire. If it weren't for the extinguisher you kept in there, the whole room could have been razed in no time, dry as it is." He smiled again as he recounted it. "A shame you missed all that. I think our guardians expressed their dismay at the pillaging of the archives quite clearly."


"Of *course* you still have a job here," Brenda, the woman who had replaced Angelica in HR assured Rebecca. "After all, you haven't done anything wrong. But with the elimination of the hotel archives, we've naturally eliminated the historian position, as well. You'll be moving into the Sales office, and they're just thrilled about it. Ms. Jordan's been wanting to make Dawn her personal assistant, so you can step right in as the new receptionist. The timing is perfect, and the move'll actually mean a slight pay rate increase for you. I'm sure it will work out for everyone."

"You'll still be the corporate memory," Dawn said as she cleaned a few personal items out of her desk and made way for Rebecca. "And LaTishia says she still wants you to do a few private tours. Mostly site tours for sales prospects, of course, so you'll have to learn all the packages and pricing stuff."

Like Rebecca's previous supervisor, LaTishia Jordan had never bothered to shadow one of her historical tours. Public tours of the hotel were no longer offered, replaced by the audio tours available from the concierge desk. But Ms. Jordan did acquiesce to the occasional special request from large meeting or conference groups who wanted a private historical or ghost tour or presentation.

"I also want your help with some of our social media outreach," Ms. Jordan said when next they met. "I realize you don't know anything about Twitter or blogs. Are you even on Facebook? But we'll take care of the tech part. Just need you to write a bunch of little hotel history factoids we can tweet. An occasional short piece for our blog whenever we're short of important things to post. Heavy on the ghost stories, of course. That's the only history our target demographic of young people care to hear about. You can even make some stories up, if you need to."

The former historian sat silently across the desk.

"Look, I'm going to be straight with you, Rebecca. It's about your attitude. I know sales receptionist is not what you signed on for, but if you don't like it, you are welcome to leave. Marketing is all about positivity and aggressive promotion. There's no room on our team for anyone who isn't totally onboard with what TITHE is doing with The Keep."

Rebecca cast the younger woman what she hoped was a withering glance. "I'll keep that in mind," she said, suddenly realizing she was now in a perfect position for subtle subterfuge.

# CHAPTER 15

To: Brittany Johnson
Subject: Meeting Request

Good morning, Brittany –

I would like to meet with Mr. Branson a.s.a.p. to discuss the contents of the hotel archives. Please let me know when I might speak with him today or tomorrow.

Cordially,
Rebecca Bridger

The reply to her email was anything but cordial.

Rebecca –

The hotel archives have been eliminated. The objects previously collected therein will be dealt with in whatever manner Mr. Branson sees fit. They are no longer your concern.

Brittany

*Stay calm,* Rebecca told herself. *Maintain professionalism.*

Brittany –

I would appreciate the opportunity to discuss options for the dispensation of the various hotel artifacts with Mr. Branson before he settles upon a course of action. I still consider stewardship of the hotel's history my responsibility and have several recommendations I wish to propose. In the spirit of the "open door" policy Mr. Branson espouses, please advise me of the earliest appointment time you can arrange.

Rebecca

A communication lapse of several hours ensued. At last, Brittany responded curtly:

Next Monday from 1:30 to 1:50p in the Executive Office.

Round One to the Historian.


Rebecca had already gathered information on the process for and advantages of donating archival items to History Colorado and the Denver Public Library Western History department in preparation for this eventuality. The griffin girded for battle as she rode the service elevator to the new executive offices the next day.

The familiar 10th floor landing was familiar no more. Mr. Branson had commandeered the former upholstery shop for his Managing Director office. The light-speed remodeling had transformed the empty archives into his executive assistant's office. The plain wooden door with its peephole at Rebecca's eyelevel was replaced by a heavy glass door etched with the TITHE logo. Puce-upholstered scoop pedestal chairs coddled their sitters like eggs. Chrome accent tables casually usurped the space so recently occupied by bookshelves and file cabinets. A huge photo of Chad Tagawa hung on the wall formerly graced by Hamilton Griffin's portrait. Assaulted by this complete obliteration of her beloved workspace, Rebecca's bravado shriveled.

Brittany's reception was about as warm as the chic décor. "Mr. Branson is on an important conference call," she informed the historian. "It may be some time before he can fit you in."

Annoyance began to restoke Rebecca's determination.

"I'll wait," she said, sinking into one of the ultra-contemporary chairs. She withdrew the documentation she'd brought along, taking the opportunity to crib once more before their meeting. Fifteen minutes passed. Thirty minutes. Brittany focused exclusively on her PC and the occasional phone call, making no attempt at polite conversation.

"Pretty great having a restroom right outside your door up here, isn't it?" Rebecca ventured after forty minutes. Brittany looked up, almost startled, as though she'd forgotten there was someone else in the room.

"Mmm, I suppose so," she replied, returning to her computer screen. "It's broken half the time, though. The plumbing in this old building sucks."

Before Rebecca had the chance to respond with the rude counterpoint she had in mind, Mr. Branson appeared.

"Oh, Rebecca," he said, somewhat at a loss. "We had a meeting, didn't we? Come in, come in," he beckoned. "So sorry to have kept you waiting."

He ushered her through the door that had replaced one of the archives windows and connected, via a build-out, to his office. Marjory's patio screen door was gone.

"Good to see you," he began, indicating the seat she should take. The furnishings in his office were black and taupe. The walls were covered with oversized photos of showcase TITHE properties, including, of course, Wallaby Wunderland and Haunted Haggis Castle. Rebecca clenched inwardly. "What can I do for you today?"

"I'm here to talk about the hotel archives," she began bravely, "or rather, the items that used to be housed in the hotel archives."

Mickey Branson assumed his position of authority, enthroned behind the big black desk in a high-backed leather chair. "Oh, that," he said, looking only mildly uncomfortable. "Must have come as something of a shock to you, I suppose. But you took all those days of vacation, and once I decided to establish my office up here, there was no time to waste. Hated Beaumont's old office. Had to move those things out to get the remodeling started. You understand."

She understood. She seethed.

"These new executive offices are beautiful," she lied. "Put you right where you should be—on top of things."

Mickey chuckled appreciatively at her faux fawning. "We like it," he said. Rebecca wasn't sure if he was speaking of himself and his assistant, or in the royal plural.

"So, I understand all the documents and artifacts are currently in locked storage in the sub-basement. And I wanted to discuss your plans for them."

"Of course," he said, stalling. "Of course you do. I'm assuming you have some thoughts."

"I do, yes, thank you," she began. "I think, in a way, dissolving the hotel archives was the right thing to do. So many of the irreplaceable artifacts have never been properly cared for. I'd like permission to select some of the most important pieces to conserve and feature in a small onsite hotel museum and gift shop. The planned remodel of the Mezzanine level provides the perfect opportunity to set aside a space for that. Then, were the hotel to donate the remaining items to the historical society or the public library, not only would they be stored properly, but also they would be available to researchers."

Brabson smiled tolerantly and shook his head. "I get what you're saying, Rebecca," he said, "But we can't pay the bills with the gratitude of history nerds, can we?"

She stared at him, not wanting to comprehend his meaning. "I beg your pardon?" When he didn't respond, she pulled out the papers she'd brought. "I've prepared these executive summaries to overview my museum proposal and the simple process for donating to the local historical repositories. Please look them over and let me know if you have any questions."

Branson refused to take the papers, waving them away. "No, no point. Chad—Mr. Tagawa—has another idea for the stuff that will bring in some great PR, as well as some cash."

Fighting to quell her rising dread. Rebecca echoed, "Cash?"

"We've got one of those 'Antiques Road Show' guys, lives in Denver now, coming in Saturday to scope out the whole collection, do some cataloging and appraising. You don't happen to have a complete inventory of all the archives stuff, do you?"

Rebecca managed to shake her head. "None of the historians has ever had time or resources for such an undertaking."

"Didn't think so. Anyway, we'll need you to work with this guy to explain some of the things to him. Just give him a general idea what he's looking at. Decide which stuff is valuable and which isn't really worth anything."

"Toward what end?" She had to hear it to believe it.

"An auction, of course. Chad's awesome idea. Give all these people who love the Griffins Keep so much a chance to bid on their own little piece of its past. At first he thought about putting the main stuff on eBay. But then he thought, Live event! How cool is that? It's gonna attract mega-attention. And some of that junk is probably worth a bunch, right?"

Rebecca found she that could not speak, horrified by Branson's enthusiasm. If he saw it in her eyes, he didn't care.

"Look, I get how you could imagine all this hotel history stuff falls under your personal purview. But it isn't yours. It belongs to the Griffins Keep, and The Keep belongs to TITHE. The decision is not up for discussion. As a hotel employee, your job is to perform whatever duties management assigns. I'll expect you Saturday morning at 7:00 to meet the appraiser—Mr. Duncan, I think—and offer him any assistance or expertise he requires."

*Go to hell*, Rebecca thought. "I'll do whatever I can to help," she said. *To help save the artifacts from being scattered like chaff on the wind.*

A ray of hope shone at the end of the archives dismantlement tunnel. Other than Rebecca and previous historian Gloria, no one knew exactly what comprised the collection. Lochlan had a good idea, but not even he could list the specific guest registers included, the precise number of silver pieces, china pieces, historic menus, or scrapbooks. The art appraiser who had inventoried display items in the hotel's public spaces a few years ago had evidenced little interest in the archival contents. As Rebecca had told Mickey Branson, no comprehensive inventory existed.

If no one knew what was supposed to be there, neither would they know if any of the artifacts went missing. Rebecca vowed that, before the antiques appraiser got his hands on them five days hence, the most significant treasures would disappear. But how?

"Unacceptable," Lochlan said when Rebecca told him about the imminent auction. "Ownership shouldn't give them the right to loot and pillage The Keep's past. I know what you're thinking, and I'm with you all the way. This'll take a good bit of planning."

"There's not much time," she reminded him. "The 'Road Show' guy will be here first thing Saturday morning."

Trying to manage her expectations, he cautioned, "We won't be able to save much. You'll have to give careful thought to what's most important, most irreplaceable. We can start tonight. Pick a few of the old registers with VIP signatures—Thomas Edison, Henry Ford, Queen Marie. No security cameras in the sub-basement where they dumped everything. And we should be able to smuggle out a few things at a time via the abandoned auto elevator that used to go down to the underground garage. Hasn't been used since the 60s. I can park right around the corner at ground level."

"If we're caught, we'll lose our jobs," Rebecca said.

"If we're caught," Lochlan amended soberly, "we could go to jail."


The meandering subterranean space of The Keep's sub-basement was pungently musty from decades of periodic flooding. Parts of the uneven concrete floor were still damp. Lights were few and far between. The sub-basement's shelves and cages held heaps of discarded construction materials, buckets of unused paint, and countless wooden pallets. Cartons of discarded glassware, silverware, and china. Broken chairs and tables of all sorts and sizes. Retired bureaus, nightstands and desks. Lamp bases, lamp shades. Framed mirrors and framed artwork. Stacks of old wastebaskets featuring The Keep logo, custom-made for the hotel's centennial and now obsolete. This was where old Keep supplies and adornments came to die.

The plastic recipe box with file cards painstakingly compiled by Charlotte Woods, listing the register numbers containing notable guest signatures, had been gathered up with all the other archive contents. Except for the few she had memorized, Rebecca had no idea which books she should try to rescue. As it turned out, it didn't matter. Assessing the disheveled mess in the sub-basement storage area by the dim light of a single bare bulb, the historian realized that the registers, and most of the hotel artifacts, were hopelessly disordered. How was she ever going to find anything? She bit her lip and fought back tears.

Lochlan put his arm around her shoulders. "It's going to be OK," he whispered. "The spirits of The Keep will lead us to the things that matter. This means as much to them as it does to us. Be still and open to their guidance."

It seemed they had no choice. The engineer produced a key to the padlock on the metal cage doors and opened them. Rebecca sank to her knees on the cold cement floor in utter discouragement. How to begin?

On a lower shelf, Lochlan spied the hotel blueprints. "At least they kept them flat," he said. "We can't take them all, of course. I'd say the ground floor, the eighth and ninth-floor plans. They're the most changed over the years, the only record of the original layouts."

Rebecca concurred. Her co-conspirator gently, loosely bent the 38" by 46" plans in half to carry them. "Pick a couple registers," he instructed, "and let's get the hell outta here." Rebecca stared at the fragile and crumbling ledgers, carelessly stacked in tipsy piles on the concrete. The indignity of their treatment broke her heart.

Register number 64. Right in front of her. How many times had she opened it on the worktable in the archives to show a visitor Thomas Edison's 1903 registration signature? She picked it up and reached for another. Register #37. And #82. She had no idea what famous names might be listed on their pages. She prayed Lochlan was right about the spirits guiding them.

It was 1:15 AM, Tuesday morning. The bowels of the hotel were as quiet as a mausoleum. Lochlan replaced the padlock, and they moved quickly in the direction of the old parking elevator. Rebecca didn't remember it being so far away.

"Hello?" called a voice from behind them and around a corner. "Who's here?" A woman's voice. Salma. She was making her nightshift security rounds. She'd heard them. Rebecca and Lochlan froze.

She spoke into her radio "Salma to Security. Over... Hey, Brian. Thought I heard something down here. Probably nothing, but I'm checking around. Over." Moments later she rounded the corner and caught her breath. There was no point in running. She'd seen the thieves clearly. Their crime-in-progress was obvious.

Rebecca and Lochlan stood silently. The historian's wide eyes beseeched Salma's understanding. The security guard hesitated a moment, considering what to do. A sly smile crept across her features. She gave them a knowing thumbs up, then turned and casually walked back the way she'd come.

"Salma to Security. Over... No sign of anybody here. Brian. Everything's good. Just a couple ghosts. See ya soon. Over and out."

Rebecca and Lochlan dared to breathe again.

"Too close," Lochlan whispered. "Salma's cool, but we got lucky. This was a warning. The Keep isn't down with our plan, doesn't want us taking these things to hide at my place."

Rebecca nodded. "I think we both sense it's not the thing to do. Despite our good intentions, it's stealing. And it puts you at such personal risk. But we can't sacrifice these artifacts to auction. What else can we do?"

"I don't know. But for now, let's stash these elsewhere down here until we think of something better. I know just the place. Come on."


Unlike the artifact cabinets which had been emptied, their contents tossed into cartons without rhyme or reason, the filing cabinets had been moved down to storage intact and unrifled. With the aid of an Excel spreadsheet she'd created when first acquainting herself with their contents, Rebecca could quickly locate particularly valuable files with relative ease. On her next wee-hours foray into the sub-basement with Lochlan, she planned to do exactly that.

The first hotel publication, an 1890 hardcover booklet produced in-house describing the hotel's features to guests in flowery phraseology and color lithographic prints, topped her list of file cabinet treasures to be rescued. She would take only one of the two copies in the drawer. The printed menu from the lavish seven-course banquet prepared for the Triennial Conclave of the Knights Templar, the inaugural event held on the Keep's opening day; another menu from the banquet feting President Teddy Roosevelt, and a third from the visit of young Queen Elizabeth in 1954 were essential to preserve. An ostrich-feather and ivory fan carried at the Keep's Grand Opening and donated by the history-conscious ladies of the Aspen Thrift Shop; exquisite promotional pamphlets from the 1890s, printed on silk and bound with satin ties; photographs and etchings of the hotel and interior spaces, changed beyond recognition in subsequent decades; historical wine lists and chef's recipe books. The historian scarcely slept,

146

obsessed with compiling her wish list of items to retrieve from the displaced files before time ran out.

She had become griffin, gathering bits for a nest on the craggy cliff face to fiercely defend from pillagers.

Just after midnight Wednesday morning, the two-person artifact rescue team ventured once again into the sub-basement storage area. This time their objectives were clearly defined. Rebecca went straight to the filing cabinets. She used her locator guide to pull pre-determined items from the drawers and stow them in a canvas tote bag she'd brought from home. Lochlan shone his flashlight on framed photographs stacked against the wall, flipping through them and extracting only the best images of former Keep owners, management, and staff. Into a small duffle bag, he carefully slipped select custom Reed & Barton silver pieces from the hotel's early years.

In less than fifteen minutes, they were hustling their priceless retrievals up a dimly lit flight of stairs to the obscure basement corner which already concealed the blueprints and registers removed the night before. Over them all, Lochlan tossed an opaque plastic tarp he'd snatched from the paint shop. It was the best they could do for now.


The next step in Operation Archives Retrieval required neither Lochlan nor stealth. Approaching the Security office Thursday morning, Rebecca prayed silently that Salma would be on duty. To her dismay, the hulking Max Barnes filled the window this morning..

The big man, long past retirement age, had disliked the new historian at first. Max thought the job should have gone to him, with his decades of first-hand Keep knowledge as a Pub server and room service waiter. For the first year, he'd quizzed Rebecca at every opportunity, trying to gauge her level of local historical competence. Finally convinced that she knew almost as much as he about Keep history, and possibly even more about Denver and the West, he'd lightened up. Occasionally he brought in a historical photo or artifact to share with Rebecca: old Denver Tramway tokens, poker chips from the Silken Rose, a Pirates Pub paper napkin autographed by John Wayne. Once Max pulled out a photograph of Arapaho Chief Little Raven posing with several other Indians at a treaty negotiation. "My high school graduating class," he had declared deadpan.

"Good morning, Max," Rebecca said brightly. "I need someone to take me to wherever they moved the archives things and unlock it so that I can get a few personal items they moved along with the hotel stuff."

Max peered at her suspiciously. "Why'd ya have stuff of yer own with the hotel things?"

"Well, you know they cleared it all out while I was gone. Didn't give me any chance to go through it. Along with the artifacts, they moved all the items I used for the changing lobby display cases. Some of those things were my own from home. A miniature tea set, an old stereopticon, my grandmother's opera glasses..."

"How do we know they're yours?"

"Because I wouldn't lie about that. I'm trustworthy."

"Hmmf," Max snorted. "Sure ya are."

At that moment, Salma walked into the Security office. "Hey, Max. Hey, Rebecca," she said. "Anything I can help you with?"

Max began the slow process of rising from his chair. "Yeah," he said. "You can man the fort while I take her down to sub-basement storage. Don't wait up."

"OK, Max. Take your time." Salma winked at Rebecca as the old man shambled out ahead of her. "Don't ask, don't tell," she whispered. "Don't worry."

"So where'd they put this archives stuff?" Max asked as they started down the stairs.

"How should I know?," Rebecca replied innocently. "I'm a rooftop dweller—*was* a rooftop dweller," she corrected herself. "I'm counting on you to know the basement layout."

"Yeah, OK. Should be over this way." The big man moved slowly and deliberately through the maze of sub-basement corridors until they came at last to the locked storage cage imprisoning the archival treasures. Max fumbled overlong with the key and unlocked the padlock. "It's all yers." he said.

Rebecca flashed back to the uncomfortable exchange with Mickey Branson just a few days earlier. *The hotel history stuff...It isn't yours. It belongs to the Keep, and the Keep belongs to TITHE.*

"Not all mine," Rebecca corrected. "Only a few things. Hopefully they're all together in one of these boxes." Scanning the shelves, she spied a distinctive lidded box that held many of the display items, and a large paper shopping bag stuffed with more of them. She found her miniature tea set, the opera glasses, a pair of elbow-length gloves, a heart-shaped antique porcelain box, some old Colorado scenic postcards, the stereopticon.

"That stereo-viewer thing your grandma's, too?" Max asked.

"No. It belonged to my husband's grandparents."

"You don't have a husband," the security staffer said suspiciously, looking unsubtly at her bare ring finger.

"I don't," Rebecca confirmed, "but did once. We found these in a trunk in the barn on their Nebraska farm after his grandpa passed."

"That everything, then?"

"That's it. But I didn't bring anything to carry it in. Think I could use this lidded box and set the other items in it on a shelf?"

"Don't see why not." With that accomplished, the historian exited the storage cage and Max snapped the padlock shut. He paused for a moment, seemingly pondering the displaced archival contents. Still perusing the shelves, he asked Rebecca, "Ever think of smuggling any of this Keep stuff home with you?"

"Of course not. That would be unethical."

"Yeah, and illegal. Lots of things have disappeared from here over the years, though, you know. Pretty easy to get away with. Can't watch every inch of the place every minute of the day and night. Lots of spaces without security cameras"

Max turned and looked her in the eye with unnerving directness. "Ever think of hiding some of it? You know, to keep it from being lost to folks who don't give a damn about the hotel history?"

Caught off-guard by the frank interrogation, the historian returned his unflinching gaze. Did Max know what Lochlan and she had been up to? Suspect their plan? It almost seemed as if he were offering a suggestion.

Rebecca hesitated before replying cautiously, "I suppose some might consider that justifiable—if it were the only way to preserve The Keep's treasures, make sure they'd still be around for future employees and guests to enjoy and learn from."

"Hmmf," Max snorted once again. Beneath his gruffness, Rebecca sensed that her answer had somehow satisfied him. "Got somethin' to show you," he said, starting off across the sub-

149

basement in the opposite direction from which they'd come. "Leave yer box here, just on the floor. We'll be back."


The padlocked room Max led Rebecca into housed banks and banks of electrical panels.

"What do all these panels control?" Rebecca asked.

"Dunno," Max said. "Stuff in the hotel. Doesn't matter. Follow me over here."

They came at length to the far side of the electrical room. Whitewashed stone blocks comprised the wall. A wooden doorframe set flush in the stone outlined cement bricks, also whitewashed, that appeared to block off a former entrance.

"Was this a doorway leading somewhere?"

"Of course it was," Max said impatiently. "Opens into a tunnel. They closed it up sometime in the '40s. But a little person can still get into it through this vent." He pointed to a nearby opening in the wall, about three feet off the floor and 3½ feet square, framed in aluminum and covered with a metal grate. "Here, use this to pry it off." He pulled out a pocketknife and handed it to her.

The grate seemed stuck in several spots, but Rebecca persevered and managed at last to loosen it and pull it off. She leaned the metal piece against the wall on the concrete floor.

"Now what?"

"Now ya crawl in there," Max directed, handing her the flashlight.

"You're kidding."

"Hell no, I'm not kidding. I used to be able to do it. It's small, sure, but so are you. Ya crawl in there about ten feet and you'll see an opening on the side into the blocked off tunnel. Follow that about fifteen yards and see what you find. Go on. Be adventurous. You're gonna thank me."

# CHAPTER 16

Rebecca paused to consider who was crazier—the old man who gave insane instructions for crawling into a dark hole or the historian who followed them. Into the shaft which lay beyond the grate hole, she shone the flashlight beam.

"There's something in there," she said uneasily. "What is that thing?"

"Something in there?" Max repeated, momentarily confounded. "Oh, that. Yeah, that's some Denver Power electrical transformers. High voltage. Be careful. You should turn off into the tunnel right before them. I think..."

Rebecca tried to hand back the flashlight. "Don't think so," she said, moving to pick up the grate and replace it in the opening.

"Hold it, hold it," Max said, refusing the flashlight. "I wouldn't've brought you here if it wasn't important. Important to The Keep's history. You care about that, right?"

"You know I do."

"Then get yer fanny in that hole and don't be a baby."

The historian drew a deep breath, stood on tiptoe and put a knee into the opening in the sub-basement wall as Max directed. She leaned in and pulled up her other knee. She could hear the high voltage hum of the transformers further down the passageway, like angry bees swarming.

Keeping low, she was able to crawl along the dirt-floored shaft slowly, carefully. Her boney knees ached. Then there it was, on her right—another passage, veering off at a ninety-degree angle. She slipped out of the shaft and into the tunnel. Here she could stand. She brushed loose dirt from her black pants and beamed the flashlight all around. The walls of the tunnel were lined with stone. Limestone, she guessed. Guiding herself with a hand along one wall, she ventured into the chilly passageway she would never have dared to navigate without a compatriot watching her back. She shivered.

The series of wall-mounted lanterns spaced at 8-foot intervals surprised her. Probably kerosene-lit at some point in the past, the dead, dark sentinels marked her progress with reassuring regularity. Judging by the cobwebs, there must be spiders everywhere. Could there be rats? What the hell was she doing?

Then up ahead, on the right-hand side of the tunnel which continued further into the fathomless dark, her beam illuminated a rough-hewn wooden door. Did she dare open it? She felt like a lab mouse in a maze. Was Max trying to trap her? To scare her? Had she been a fool to trust him?

She'd come this far. She couldn't resist the mystery. The splintery door had a cast iron handle and hinges, but no visible latch or lock. It opened at her push, and Rebecca beheld a large room, about the size of a three-car garage with a 9-foot ceiling. Aiming the flashlight into the space, Rebecca could scarcely believe her eyes.

The collection of objects cluttering wooden shelves that reached floor to ceiling dwarfed the displaced archives. The beam splashed over ten times the china and crystal pieces formerly housed in the rooftop depository. Other shelves held gilded antique clocks, ornate table lamps with fringed shades, silver coffee pots and pitchers. Against the opposite stone wall leaned a dozen filigree panels like those that ringed the atrium balconies. Beside them, rows of stained glass windows with fruit and flower designs—from the demolished eighth-floor ballroom?

Remnants of decorative stone trim from the building's exterior lay on the concrete floor to one side. A strangely fringed chandelier and faded red, white and blue bunting hung from wooden beams crisscrossing the ceiling. From one dark corner, the dead glass eyes of a stuffed trophy elk shone back at her in the flashlight beam. An old barber chair. A billiard table with ornately carved legs was laden with cake stands, multi-tiered trays, assorted serving pieces, and folded linens. Large trunks and wooden boxes stacked against the back wall could contain almost anything. Could that really be a music stand from the old Aladdin Room orchestra?

Who assembled all this? When? And why? It was too much to process. Max had led her here. Max would know.

Rebecca hurried back through the tunnel to the transformer shaft and scooted back through the opening into the electrical room where Max, seated on an old wooden cable spool, awaited her return.

"It's...it's amazing!" she said breathlessly. "How do you know about this place, that room? Was it you who collected and hid all those Griffins Keep artifacts? Does anyone else know about them?" The questions tumbled out on top of each other in a rush. She looked at Max and shook her head in astonishment. "I'm sorry. I'm just...flabbergasted!"

At this the old man smiled. He put a finger to his lips, warning her to keep her voice down, though they seemed to be quite alone. "Pretty great, isn't it?" he said. "I know everybody around here thinks I'm just a crazy old coot, full of bullshit. But I sure as hell can keep a secret—when it's important."

"Why is that tunnel even here?" Rebecca pressed him. "Where did it go?"

"From here to the Capitol," he said, "sub-basement level all the way. Guess it's gotta be about three, four blocks long. Feels longer when you're in it. Other end's been caved in since before I came to The Keep. But I'm told it handled traffic right up into the 1940s. Big wigs and politicians and special interests, all that."

"What about the room with all the old stuff?"

"They used to store liquor in there before—and during— Prohibition. When they moved that elsewhere, the little museum you saw was born in that space."

"Who started it? Why? And how?"

"It was during the Kuhrsfeld years, when they were changing everything, making it 'modern.' Kinda like now. Some longtime employees were sick about them removing so much original stuff, selling it or just pitching it—like it was nothing. Made it their mission, I guess you could say, to save some of it, tuck it away where it wouldn't be found. Only a couple guys knew about it. And when they left, they passed the secret on to a colleague they trusted."

"And eventually, you became that colleague."

153

Max nodded. "About thirty years ago, right before he retired, my old Pub boss, Ernst Huber, brought me down here, just like I brought you. Every now and then I'd find a way to add something to the collection. Things that shouldn't be lost."

"But all those big things—the barber chair and the elk—they never would have fit through this little vent. And the room's not even locked!"

"Course it's not locked," Max said impatiently. "Who's gonna go in there? But you can bet it was locked before the tunnel was closed off, back when all the big stuff was stashed there."

He paused for a moment and looked up at her earnestly. "So now you know about it. In case you ever need to hide anything for a while. But you gotta promise to keep this place secret. Wouldn't wanna hafta kill ya."


"This is so *fun*!" Rebecca whispered as she and Lochlan dug through the treasures hidden in the sub-basement secret room the following night. Impulsively, she wrapped herself in a gold damask drapery panel. Lochlan reverently placed an inverted sterling silver ice bucket upon her head and proclaimed, "Her Royal Highness, Queen of The Keep."

For the first time in ages, Rebecca felt beautiful—and young.

As she continued to scan the space with her mini-flashlight, its beam glinted off something half concealed under another folded drape. Withdrawing it from the cover, she caught her breath. "It's a sword!" she exclaimed as she examined it more closely. "In fact, I think it's the bronze sword of the long-lost Third Griffin, the one that once guarded the lobby fireplace. God bless whoever managed to snatch it from the Kuhrsfelds when they pilfered the griffin itself for their private garden!"

She raised the bronze implement triumphantly and turned to her crusading cohort. "Kneel, Sir Knight."

Solemnly, Lochlan obeyed and bowed his head before her. She touched the sword first to one shoulder, then the other.

"I dub thee Sir Lochlan of Griffin, defender of The Keep and guardian of her secrets."

He lifted his gaze and gently kissed the tip of the blade without taking his eyes from hers. "The Power of the Past compels me to pledge my troth to this castle and to her Queen," he vowed.

154

The vaguely remembered sensation was as unmistakable as it was unexpected. Thrilling, heady, ravenous. The flush that rose in Rebecca's cheeks and radiated throughout her body was menopausal by no means. A furtive glance, as Lochlan slowly stood, revealed her temperature was not the only thing that was rising.

A sweep of their arms, an avalanche of folded linens, and half the billiard table was cleared.

Rebecca cast aside her weapon and surrendered utterly.

"Your mimosa," Rebecca announced, handing her housemate the frothy drink in a stemmed goblet. "Fruit salad in that bowl. Hash-browned potatoes in the skillet. I'm just about to whip up the blender Hollandaise for Eggs Benedict. Would you like one English muffin half or two? I'm having three myself."

Maureen took a sip, then set down the glass and tied her robe around herself. "You're up awfully bright and early for someone who didn't get in until after 1:00."

"Yes, Mother." Rebecca couldn't stop smiling. "If you must know, I was with Mr. MacKenzie in that secret sub-basement room I told you about."

"Doing what, may I ask?"

Rebecca turned away, slowly pouring hot melted butter into the blender. "Oh, you know. Going through rescued hotel artifacts, playing on the billiard table."

"Must have been strenuous," Mo observed. "You seem to have built up quite an appetite."

"I'm famished. Haven't eaten since yesterday lunch," Rebecca admitted, switching on the blender. When it finished, she dipped her little finger into the sauce, licked it and beamed with satisfaction. "But I did have quite the gourmet experience last night."

The afternoon before the archives auction, all the artifacts up for bids were displayed on long tables around the lobby for public inspection. Rebecca cringed as curious potential buyers pawed through historic banquet menus, leafed through crumbling scrapbooks, and perused the pages of guest registers with splintered spines.

155

Among the preview shoppers, she noticed an obviously wealthy man with his daughter. Spying the military band figures, the girl tugged her father's sleeve.

"Look, Daddy! These dolls could be boyfriends for my Barbies."

Inspecting them briefly and noting the starting bid, her father disagreed. "No sweetheart, they're old and dirty. Look, there are little holes in their jackets, their hats and boots are coming apart. Their arms and legs don't even move."

"I don't care. I want them. They're just Barbie's size and they're handsome. Puhleeeze, Daddy? Pretty please?"

"We'll see, Vanessa. Now put that one down."

"I can't watch anymore," Rebecca whispered to Dawn. "You take over guard duty for a while. I'm begging you." She had been directed by Ms. Jordan to be on hand to answer any questions about the items. Rebecca had had enough. She went in search of a place to disappear.

*Some of the things are safe,* she reminded herself. *Some of them are safe—Thanks to Max.* How was she ever going to make it through tomorrow's auction when she would be expected to supply historical context for The Keep's treasures and to watch without comment as they were carried from the building that gave them meaning, likely never to return?

As she fled the lobby, Rebecca stopped at the far side of the Front Desk and looked up to the seventh-floor atrium corner where the mediums had reported sensing powerful entities that oversaw the hotel in some mystical fashion. She folded her hands together, as if in prayer, and whispered, "Help."


No bolts from above. No divine intervention. No paranormal prevention. Despite Rebecca's desperate plea, The Keep's guardians, whatever they might be, did nothing to stop the public auction of hotel artifacts the following evening. More than 200 invited guests took their seats in the Grand Salon. Champagne was served, hors d'oeuvres were passed. Denny, one of the hotel's five talented pianists, entertained before the proceedings got underway.

"Despite the festive face they're trying so hard to put on this travesty, it's a sad, sad day for the Griffins Keep," Denny confided

156

quietly to Rebecca when he finished playing. "I'm so sorry you have to go through this."

Rebecca had to excuse herself after the first half-hour, claiming she was ill. She was.

"I know you're in no mood to hear more about the auction," Lochlan said the next morning, touching her gently on the shoulder, "but after you left last night, there were a few positive developments."

When Rebecca said nothing, he continued. "The Colorado Historical Society bought the old registers in one lot. And the set of blueprints—the remaining blueprints," he added with a conspiratorial wink, "went to the Western History department of the Denver Public Library. Great news for researchers, right? And they'll be digitally scanned and preserved professionally, just as they should have been all along. Oh, and Denny outbid everyone for those old record albums by the Griffins Strings."

"Could be worse, I guess," the historian conceded sullenly. "I'm almost afraid to ask...What about the military bandsmen? Did that little girl get them for her Barbies' beaus?"

"No...wait, what?" Lochlan said, confused. "I don't know about any little girl. But I can tell you for sure that the bandsmen weren't auctioned off after all."

"What are you talking about? They were expected to draw the highest bids of anything from the archives."

"That they were. But apparently someone with very deep pockets made such a generous offer before the event that management agreed to sell them outright, without even putting them on the block, so to speak."

Rebecca tilted her head quizzically. "That seems very weird. Who would want them that badly? They must have had some sway with the management, as well as ample funds."

"It's a mystery, to be sure. But I have to believe they've found a loving home, and that's what really matters, right?"

Rebecca smiled despite herself. "You make them sound like rescue dogs."

"When you think about it, they *are* like pound pups, in a way. Saved from an uncertain fate, adopted by someone who can obviously afford the professional care they deserve."

At that, Rebecca managed a slight smile. "I hope they live happily ever after, wherever they've gone."

157

Lochlan gave her a reassuring squeeze and seconded her sentiment. "To the lads!" he said, raising his coffee mug. "We shall never see their like in the Griffins Keep again."

His premature conclusion was, as it turned out, wrong.


Once again, the beast emerged from hibernation—just in time for the holidays. The decorating team wrangled the holiday chandelier in the center of the lobby. Drifts of glitter scattered across the floor evidenced their struggle. A sturdy cable attached to its crown suspended it from a winch in the center of the steel support frame below the skylight, eight stories above. Six ropes restraining its uppermost arms spread out across the space in a hexagonal web as the team endeavored to keep it level. Other workers festooned its appendages with dangling lantern-like fixtures, gigantic red balls and bows. Only when balance had been achieved was the LED light fixture raised a few more feet for the next round of assembly.

Rebecca documented each step of the installation with photos snapped from multiple angles over several hours. Lochlan offered to take a few views looking down from the skylight as he worked the winch in the center of the steel support grid beneath the stained glass. He cranked it up incrementally over the course of the full-day process. Guests often asked how the behemoth was put up, and the pictures would be worth the proverbial thousand words.

The chandelier was a joint venture of The Keep and the Denver Symphony Snow Ball committee. Since 1950, the Snow Ball had been the biggest annual event hosted by the hotel. Because it was traditionally held right before Christmas, the committee dictated the decorations and colors. They were not known for moderation, as the chandelier demonstrated. Its glitter alone weighed more than 500 pounds. Dripping with LED lights and suspended directly above the hotel's 20-foot crystal Christmas tree next to the Griffin Fountain, it evoked a stalactite-stalagmite effect.

"It looks like a giant squid," Rebecca declared to Lochlan.

"Some people say a spider," he said, studying the completed contraption hoisted into its final position between the third- and fifth-floor levels of the atrium. "I imagine it as a sort of carnival ride."

158

Every Keep associate had his or her own opinion of the holiday focal point.

"Absolutely beautiful."

"Gaud-awful."

"Something out of a fairytale."

"Tacky as hell."

"Magical!"

"An insult to the architecture."

Revered or reviled, the chandelier dominated the heart of the hotel throughout the holidays. TITHE management loved the thing, and even temporarily removed the lobby papier mache griffins to maximize its impact.

"I still say it looks like it should be hovering over Devil's Tower," Mo declared the next time she visited Rebecca at The Keep, alluding to the alien Mother Ship in *Close Encounters*.


The holidays found the new management in over their heads. Because they knew nothing of Griffins Keep traditions and the hotel's role in the larger Denver community, they were caught completely off guard by the huge demand for Thanksgiving dinners, holiday teas and holiday parties. Temporary staff on loan from other TITHE properties had no idea what they were doing. The "alien overlords"—so dubbed by the few remaining veteran Keep employees—had yet to realize that the Griffins Keep was unlike any other hotel.

The Snow Ball was a debacle. TITHE, with no concept of the privileged patrons' expectations for the event, disappointed and dismayed the entitled elite at every turn. Insufficient staffing. AV equipment malfunctions. Mediocre food on chipped china. The society scions, who had always demanded perfection in every detail, discovered that under a TITHE regime, perfection was no longer anywhere to be found. Ball organizers and guests alike vowed never to return to the Griffins Keep and resolved to take their lucrative soiree elsewhere in future.

Management shrugged off the failure as if it were nothing. "We've got the Extreme Skateboarding Con coming next month," Branson bragged. "Who needs Denver's 'old money'?"

Margaret and Molly the mediums met Rebecca in the lobby when they came for Holiday Tea the first Saturday in December. They were both stunning in fabulous hats, but Margaret was livid.

"We made these reservations last January," she said, "And now we're told they've run out of scones and tea sandwiches and are discontinuing service for the rest of the day—and it's not even 2:30!"

Molly shook her head and added, "They offered us a beer and fish-and-chips in the Pirates Pub as a consolation. I ask you, do we look dressed for fish-and-chips?"

"It's not so bad for us," Margaret relented, surveying the disconcerted queue, "We're flexible. But look at all these disappointed little girls in their fancy Christmas dresses. Look at the older ladies with their walkers and their wheelchairs, who've probably come here with family or friends every year for decades. We're all just out of luck today."

Rebecca was not about to defend the mismanagement, but she tried to make the ladies feel better. "Shutting down Tea early is a terrible shame. I've never heard of it happening before. Confidentially though, you might have been unimpressed if you had been served. All The Keep's pastry chefs have been let go. The fresh-baked scones, pastries, cakes, and breads for which the hotel has always been renowned have been replaced by day-old goods from outside cut-rate vendors. We've gotten lots of complaints."

The mediums looked at each other, then back at Rebecca. "No wonder the old spirits are so distraught," Molly said.

"We sensed it right away when we came in," Margaret explained. "Harrison Griffin, Edward Brookings, and countless spirits from the hotel's uncompromising early years—employees and guests—are terribly upset by recent developments. I keep hearing the phrase 'erosion of excellence.'"

"The spirits aren't alone in their concern," Rebecca told them sadly. "The special, thoughtful touches that have always defined the Griffins Keep as exceptional are disappearing at an alarming rate. And, not surprisingly, so are a great many longtime devoted patrons, sometimes angered and sometimes broken-hearted by the changes TITHE cuts had wrought."

"The spiritual and the corporeal planes co-exist closely in this place," Molly reminded her. "The distress you and your fellow employees are feeling is reflected in the hotel's spiritual realm, and vice versa. This is very worrisome. A shortage of tea items only hints at the larger dilemmas soon to unfold." She glanced up at the seventh-floor corner above the concierge desk, "The Keep's

160

essence is in very real jeopardy, and The Keep's ghosts are preparing to push back."

The Monday morning announcement from Mickey Branson was chillingly officious:

> Please be informed that effective tomorrow, Surf's Up Safety and Security Services will assume all of the hotel's security functions.

> By outsourcing our security efforts, we will be able to enhance guest and associate safety, accountability and emergency response through state-of-the-art technology from a trusted firm long associated with the TITHE family of companies.

> The hotel is grateful for the service the current security team has provided to our community.

By the time Rebecca saw the email blast, the changeover was already a *fete accompli*. "Did you have any warning that this was coming?" she asked Amy when she encountered her in the coffee shop.

The engineering assistant shook her head. "None. The Security layoffs blindsided everybody."

"So Salma's gone? Chuck? Franklin?"

"Kevin was the only one kept on."

"What about Max?"

"That was the worst," Amy confided. "Max looked like they'd just unplugged his life support. He was actually crying when the new guys escorted him out. The Keep has been everything to him for 54 years—especially since his wife passed away. His job here is the only reason he has to get out of bed in the morning. It was so sad. I can't imagine what he'll do now."

"You'd think they could find *something* for him to do here, just part time," said the barista. "He's like a living history of this place."

"You're right about that. Could I get his home contact info from you?" Rebecca asked Amy. "I could invite him to come visit me to share his Keep memories and stories. Do you think that might make him feel better? Knowing he's leaving a sort of legacy?"

"I think it's a really nice idea. I'll email you his home number as soon as I get back to my desk. I just hope he's going to be OK."

Max Barnes sounded okay when he finally responded to Rebecca's three voice messages five days later.

"Punk kids marched me outta there like some kinda criminal. Company's got a helluva way of showing their great 'appreciation' to long-time loyal staff." His tone, more bitter than sad, reassured the historian that Max was still full of vinegar.

"It was a rotten way to break the news to you," she said, "and I'm so sorry it was such a rude surprise. Like when they took over the archives. I think I understand, at least a little, how you must feel."

"Yeah, maybe you'll get it after you've been there 54 years."

Rebecca hurried on. "Max, you know how we talked before about my doing a sort of oral history interview with you, so we could record all the things you remember for future Keep histories? I'm really hoping you'll still consider that. Nobody else has all your personal knowledge about the old days at the hotel."

After a pregnant pause, Max said, "Yeah, well, maybe I could do that, if you think what I have to say is worth anything."

"Oh, absolutely!" Rebecca assured him, then couldn't help but tease, "Of course, I'll be using my bullshit detector on your more colorful recollections, as always."

She could almost hear him smile on the other end of the phone. "All right. Sure. So when do you want me to come do this thing?"

The historian had already given the question some thought. It was bound to be awkward if he returned to The Keep too soon. "Let's wait a few weeks and then talk again about a good time. Things are really hectic in the hotel right now with Chad Tagawa and all the TITHE big wigs hanging around and stressing everybody out."

"Tagawa's there, huh?"

"Through next Friday, I think."

"Hmmph. Branson, too?"

"Of course. They always seem to be in meetings, cooking up something, along with Chad's uncle and the other TITHE guys."

"Next Friday," Max repeated before falling silent for several moments.

"So I'll call you again in a couple weeks," Rebecca said. "We'll figure out an interview date then. Thanks so much for agreeing to let me pick your brain. I'm sure you have a lot of valuable info and insider insights to share for posterity."

"Yeah, OK. Whatever you say. Hey, promise you'll guard our secret stash in the tunnel, no matter what."

"Of course I promise. Max. Talk to you soon, and take care." Rebecca hung up with the self-satisfaction that she had set something good in motion.


The huge man shambled into the busy Pirates Pub at 12:37 PM the following Friday. He plucked a napkin from a table and draped it over one crooked arm, old-fashioned waiter style, as he headed directly for the corner spot occupied by the hotel owner and the managing director. With a sweeping gesture of his other arm, he bowed grandly before them.

"Messrs. Tagawa and Branson," he pronounced loudly and clearly. "Damn you, gentlemen. Damn you both to hell."

All conversation ceased.

"Should I call Security?" the hostess whispered to a server, who simply shrugged.

"I was serving this hotel before either of you was born, and I will not be dismissed," he declared calmly. "I'm gonna haunt you sonsabitches to the enda time."

Before anyone could react, he withdrew the small revolver from inside his jacket and raised it to his temple. With a squeeze of the trigger, Max Barnes went down in Griffins Keep history.

# CHAPTER 17

"I blame myself," Rebecca confessed to Lochlan the morning after Max's suicide. "If I hadn't told him Tagawa and Branson were going to be here together, if I hadn't made him feel like his story was over..."

"Don't be absurd," Lochlan said, gently but sternly. "You sound like the characters on a soap opera who all think their actions alone led to the Tragedy. It's pointless to dwell on 'what-ifs.' Max is gone. The people truly culpable for his drama were those to whom he played his final scene. Safe to say it will be some time before either of those gentlemen dine in the Pub again, let alone get a good night's sleep."

They sat together outside on a capstone atop the Grand Avenue side of the hotel roof edge, trying to put the unspeakable incident in perspective. The December air was cold and the wind was raw. Lochlan had found a blanket that he wrapped around them both. Rebecca shivered still.

"All the news reported was that a former employee took his own life. Didn't say he'd been fired from the job that meant everything to him. Didn't say he cursed the Keep owner and manager with his last breath."

"That's why it's so important for the hotel historian to record and preserve his story—the whole story—in The Keep's secret sub-basement archives," Lochlan said. "Someday, maybe decades from now, a hotel employee or a local researcher will come across the true tale of Max Barnes, his selfless efforts to preserve and protect artifacts of The Keep's past, and his decision to make an unforgettable statement with his exit.'"

Rebecca nodded. "And then, at last, he may be able to rest in peace."


Pinnacle Church, true to the Protestant work ethic, offered no fewer than six Christmas Eve services, spaced two hours apart, from 1:00 'til 11:00 on December 24. Rebecca opted for the first, crossing the street from The Keep right after lunch. Except for weddings and funerals, she had not attended a church service in more than thirty years.

A kind elderly gentleman in a red vest escorted her to a door on the north side of the church and, finding it still locked at 12:30, produced a key to let her in.

"Am I too early?" she asked.

"Oh, no. There are others already here. Welcome, and Merry Christmas to you."

Not a member of this church, nor of any church in memory, Rebecca felt like an intruder, a stranger to those who greeted her at the sanctuary entrance with a program and a white candle, skirted by a paper drip-guard. Yet it was all so familiar, a ghost from numberless Christmases Past. She settled herself at the end of a center pew, about a dozen rows from the front.

Colossal organ pipes dominated the east wall before her. The familiar chords of Christmas carols conspired to evoke all the nostalgia and all the memories of Christmases growing up in the church. Something buried deep in her subconscious began to flicker. Something tender and hopeful, long suppressed, began to stir. Her eyes welled with tears. What subliminal message, implanted by her religious upbringing, now threatened her composure?

The organ swelled with ancient songs by which she was inexplicably overcome, weeping for no apparent reason. Seeing her red-rimmed eyes, the strangers around her would probably think she'd suffered some recent loss or crisis. The tragic death of Max Barnes was fresh, of course. But was she also crying for her own loss of faith?

Raised in a Christian fundamentalist family, Rebecca had left the church decades ago. After her divorce, she was mad at God for a very long time. Prayer had been futile. In pain and despair, she

166

had turned to His house for refuge and comfort. Instead she found the loving forgiveness espoused by church people often masked judgmental censure, and the Lord Himself, it had seemed, was never home. She didn't miss the mindless ritual and the thinly veiled hypocrisy of organized religion, she told herself. Why then, was this Christmas service bringing her to tears?

She dabbed at her eyes with a blouse cuff and tried to focus on the preacher stepping up to the pulpit. At that moment, the sun emerged from the clouds outside. Its rays shone through the south-facing little window near the vaulted ceiling, which Charles had pointed out on their tour the month before. Like a blessing from Heaven itself, the beam fell upon the face of the Madonna gracing the baptismal font.

The assembled worshippers seemed to catch their breath as one. Amy had been right. It was magical. Even miraculous, if one chose to interpret it as such.

Rebecca thought of the Freemasons whose knowledge of astronomy and geometry had enabled them to position the high window so perfectly. Their combination of science and belief in a Divine Power was something she could embrace. The Freemasons accepted both knowledge and mystery in a cosmic symbiosis. Rebecca gazed upon the statue's sunlit features and found she could smile.

The woman further down along the pew rose to come nearer and tipped her lit candle to light the visitor's. As Rebecca looked around the sanctuary at all the individual flickering lights and joined in the singing of "Silent Night," a strange and surreal peace enveloped her. Rebecca Holcomb Bridger, prodigal daughter of the church, breathed in the wonder of a living, joyous spiritual galaxy that filled the sacred space—and her heart. In that moment, in that place, The Lord truly dwelled.


J. Bryce Bridger was dead. Rebecca's mother phoned with the news on New Year's Day. Her prelude had been ominous. "I'm afraid I have some very sad news," she'd begun after pleasantries about how they'd spent their respective New Year's eves. "I'm sorry to have to be the one to tell you, because it's not a very pleasant way to start the year."

Rebecca had been worried that the news would be something terrible about her mother's health, or a bad turn of events for one

167

of her siblings. The grim pronouncement of Bryce's demise came as an unexpected relief. But her mother's tone had been so earnest that Rebecca had dared not confess how little she cared about the development.

It came as a shock nonetheless. Rebecca hadn't heard from or heard of her ex-husband in decades. He had been only a year older than she. What happened?

"Bernie said it was something about his heart," her mother explained, referring to the local mortician who had been a family friend forever. "That's all I know. His obituary is on page thirteen, section E of yesterday's *Gazette*. It says there's a memorial service for him the day after tomorrow at his late father's church here in the Springs," her mother concluded.

Torn, Rebecca stalled responding to her mother's unspoken question. "I'll have to think about whether I want to attend or not. It's all pretty sudden."

"Well, I'm going to get another volunteer to work my shift at the hospital that afternoon. I just feel like someone from our family should be there."

Her mother had always been charmed by Bryce, having no clue about the way he treated her daughter in private. Those days seemed completely unreal now.

"I'll think about it," Rebecca repeated. "I'll let you know tomorrow what I decide to do."

She hung up the phone and scooped the anxiously attentive Willoughby into her arms. "I guess I should feel sad, shouldn't I?" she asked the terrier. But taking stock of her post-news emotions, she found only disassociated interest.

Bryce's dreams of becoming a professional actor had never quite worked out. The last she'd heard, he'd been eking-out a living in dinner theatre productions, tending bar, and making TV commercials for local auto dealerships and furniture warehouse showrooms.

Fifteen years earlier, her parents had encountered Bryce at his mother's funeral. "He was fat with long frizzy hair and wore dark glasses the whole time," Rebecca's mother had reported. "He looked like an aging drug dealer."

He was an aging drug dealer

In the end, it was curiosity that made Rebecca decide to attend Bryce's memorial service that Friday afternoon. Who were the people in his life all these years after their marriage ended?

What would they say about him and how would they remember him?

Feeling like a hostile witness, Rebecca realized that her recollections of the man being eulogized were very different from those of the mourners surrounding her. If pressed to relate a happy memory of her time with Bryce, she found she could not come up with one. Not a single positive recollection. Odd. She'd known him for ten years, had loved him enough to pledge her life to him at one time. Surely they'd shared countless joyous moments. Why else would the divorce have hurt so much? Over the years, repression of the good memories had been essential for her emotional recovery. Remembering the precious times, the passionate emotions, crippled and cut. Only now did she realize how thoroughly she'd sublimated them.

Sitting in the same sanctuary where she and Bryce had been married was surreal. The dais was still decorated for Christmas, with three lit trees of graduated heights behind the pulpit. Large screens one either side of the central stationary cross displayed twin images of a Christmas star throughout the service. Rebecca had been hoping for a video retrospective. Couldn't at least one of Bryce's filmmaker friends have put one together? She wanted to see what he looked like in his later years. But there were no videos or even photos.

As the mourners formally filed out after the service, pew by pew, she continued to search for familiar faces.

"Do you want to go to the reception?" her mother asked in her overly solicitous tone.

"Not sure," Rebecca said, drifting to the back of the foyer. "Let's just wait here a few minutes."

She still recognized no one, but someone recognized her.

"Becky? Scott Dickerson," he reminded her. "Bryce's bud from high school."

Rebecca found herself smiling and clasping his hand. She'd always liked Scott.

"Great to see you. Really great. You look terrific," he said warmly. "So how about that eulogy? Great work of fiction, eh? Since when did Bryce become valedictorian of his class? Obviously this preacher didn't know him at all. Bryce would have gotten a good laugh at that. He would have thought most of this was really bizarre."

169

"Except for the music, it didn't seem much like him at all," Rebecca agreed.

"Probably his sister Pam's doing. She was always a bit clueless. Can you believe her get-up? She still seems to think she's Cher or a flower child or something."

Rebecca relaxed, loving the ease of reconnection with someone from the past who didn't make her uncomfortable. She could go into the reception with Scott. It would be fine.

"I think I'd like to mingle a little bit after all, Mom," she said, "but you go on. I'll come by the condo afterwards and we'll visit." Before her mother had a chance to respond, Rebecca was off to the fellowship hall on Scott's arm.

She regretted the decision almost immediately. Everyone was so somber and glum. Tables arrayed with casseroles and Jell-O salads and a huge silver coffee percolator brought back memories of her own church upbringing.

"Don't miss them brownies," a ponytailed man, who looked like he'd been in the mountains way too long, whispered conspiratorially to Scott. "They've got a little somethin' special, if you know what I mean."

"Would you like to meet Marsha?" Scott asked, referring to the woman Bryce's obituary had called his "life partner." Rebecca let herself be led along and was soon facing a woman about ten years younger than herself, with runny mascara-rimmed eyes. They looked at each other quizzically and attempted polite smiles.

"Marsha, this is Becky Bridger—or are you Holcomb again? She was Bryce's wife."

"Oh," Marsha said, obviously taken aback. "Yeah, Bryce talked about you sometimes. Always remembered your birthday. Said you were really smart and had a good sense of humor."

"That was nice of him." Rebecca didn't quite know how else to respond. "I really don't know what he was like after our divorce."

"He was wonderful," Marsha said, dabbing her eyes with a wadded-up Kleenex. Scott put a sympathetic arm around her and she blew her nose. "How could you ever have left him?"

Scott cast Rebecca an apologetic glance, knowing the real story and understanding how touchy the topic was.

"I guess we just had different opinions about what it meant to be husband and wife," she said. "Bryce liked the idea—and the

170

practice—of 'open marriage' a lot more than I did. It just didn't work out."

Marsha stared at her, uncomprehending at first, then nodded slowly as if she understood. "Well, thank you for coming. Weird how shit turns out, isn't it?"

And that was enough. More than enough. Rebecca excused herself and retreated to her trusty but rarely driven Volvo in the parking lot. On the drive home, she thought about Lochlan, how very different love was with him than with Bryce. She could trust him, relax with him, delight in him without fear. He had emboldened her to be vulnerable again.

That night, working in the hotel archives, Rebecca was mildly surprised to see a man come through the bookcase wall. With shoulder-length wavy hair, he wore a chamois shirt and faded jeans. His blue eyes were alight, his arms outstretched. She flew easily into his embrace, recognizing him, but not recognizing him. Enfolded against the soft fabric and pressed close to his chest, she was suddenly overcome. A warm wave of tenderness and contentment engulfed her. Endearment, elation, enchantment—all comingled in an inexplicable rush.

She sensed that this man had been special to her for a long time, but his features were unfamiliar as he smiled benevolently and said nothing.

"Who are you?" she asked, struggling to understand.

"You know who I am," he replied softly, releasing her and gradually fading back into the wall.

Rebecca awoke to the sharp barks of Willoughby, startled by the morning trash truck. The warm, ecstatic feeling lingered, as did her question from the dream. *You know who I am.* Tears filled her eyes for the first and only time since the news of her ex-husband's death.

He had come to say good-bye. He'd left her with assurance that he had always cared, in his own way.

Their closure was complete. J. Bryce Bridger would haunt her no more.

The demand for ghost tours of the hotel diminished greatly after the holidays, though never completely disappeared. When Rebecca previewed Room 864 in preparation for yet another private ghost tour in late January, she dropped the shades and

171

doused the lights in the front room for spooky effect. Remembering the brain-damaged patients' incident and Mo's detection of a haughty resident spirit, she couldn't bring herself to go into the dimly lit bedroom.

The four young women on the private tour were excited at the prospect of encountering hotel ghosts. When they reached the showroom, Rebecca related the odd occurrences of October and the spirit "a talented local medium" had perceived in the suite.

"Apparently this spirit doesn't think any of today's guests are good enough for the Keep's high standards. She is increasingly angry at being disturbed by the visitors I've brought into her room. So I keep showing it intentionally, daring her to do something about it."

"Yeah, she's dead. We're not. Get over yourself, ghost!" one of the young women declared to the empty space.

When it came time to move on, one of the guests wanted to stop and take a few photos of the bedroom space. She stepped into the doorway and aimed her camera-phone toward the supposedly haunted corner in hopes of capturing an orb. Then she turned to the space directly in front of her and snapped another flash photo.

They all saw it. A flash within the flash. Brighter, more intense, and more instantaneous than the artificial illumination. Unmistakable. Bone chilling.

"Ohmigod..." the young women exclaimed as one. "What *was* that?!"

The photographer shot again. Again. This time the bright streak shot across the flashed space ike horizontal lightning.

A jolt surged through Rebecca as her knees gave out and she crumpled to the floor. In that fraction of a second, the entity imprinted itself on her mind. A woman, with wild hair flying in all directions. Flesh dripping from her face. Eyes like havoc - hateful, vengeful, dark with rage. Black holes sucking her in. The vision took her breath away.

"Oh god, Rebecca! Are you OK?" one of the girls asked, offering a hand up and helping her back to her feet.

"Did you see it?" the historian almost whispered, stricken and wobbly.

"Yeah, we saw the flash—whatever it was. I'm shaking."

"But did you see the woman?"

The tour guests shook their heads, startled and confused. "I didn't have to see her to know she's really pissed," the photographer declared. "She wants us outta here."

Rebecca practically shoved her awestruck tour guests from the suite. Flesh goose-bumped up and down her arms, long after they'd slammed the door and scurried down the hallway to the elevators. The ghost tourers were thrilled, chattering noisily in titillation.

"That was NOT a friendly ghost," one girl declared, laughing nervously.

"We just saw a real spirit on our ghost tour!" the girl with the camera announced to a bemused co-passenger when the group boarded the elevator.

"She even saw it!" another young lady said, turning to indicate Rebecca. "And she's the hotel historian!"

"Really?" the passenger asked Rebecca directly, as if her confirmation would lend official credibility to the claim.

Rebecca nodded. "I'm afraid so," she admitted, employing exactly the right word to describe her reaction.

She couldn't process it yet. Had to wrap up the tour, get away by herself and calm down. Easier intended than done. The young women were so amped up that they could scarcely keep still.

"That was so awesome!"

"OMG—Cammie is gonna die for not coming with us."

"Thank you, thank you, *thank you* for showing us that room! Now you have a new story for your ghost tour."

Rebecca had much more than that, she realized as she finally bid them good-bye and reboarded the public elevator. Sharing the lift this time was a woman with frizzy dark hair and round glasses. She had just had her toenails painted in the Spa—purple—and was carrying her boots until the polish dried. She smiled at Rebecca as though she sensed her revelation.

"I think I just saw an actual spirit here in the hotel," Rebecca confessed to the stranger.

At this, the woman's smile became a beam. "I'm so happy for you!" she said.

"Happy?" Rebecca repeated. "I don't think happy is one of the emotions I'm feeling right now."

"It will be, when you get a chance to reflect upon what you just experienced. Embrace it, hon, don't fear it. You've been given an opportunity for true wonder."

The elevator stopped at the fifth floor and the barefoot woman departed with boots in one hand and a cheery wave. "Isn't the unknown wonderful? Keeps us from getting too cocky, imagining we understand it all. Mystery is marvelous!"

Back at her desk after an extended bathroom break, Rebecca snatched the slip of paper with the protection blessing Mo had given her and read it out loud, three times in rapid succession. "'Almighty God, cleanse my body, mind and spirit and surround me with the white light of Your Love.'"

She wasn't sure she believed in the protection, but its recitation calmed her. The horripilation on her arms and neck subsided at last, and she collapsed in her office chair. Something other-worldly had been in the bedroom of 864. Rebecca had no doubt of it as she mentally replayed the incident and the horrible vision over and over. Only upon reflection did she realize that what she had seen had not been a whole woman, but only the head and torso from the waist up, hovering in midair.

Though Rebecca had always been open-minded about the existence of spirits, today's personal encounter took previously detached speculation to a new level. Rocked to the core by this fundamental shift in perception, skeptical underpinnings came unpinned. Accepting the possibility was one thing. Witnessing it firsthand—quite another.

# CHAPTER 18

"How do you take it so calmly, seeing spirits like you do?" she asked Maureen at home that night after describing her sighting. "It's so... not normal."

"And hence the term *para*normal," Mo teased gently. "You've glimpsed beyond the veil."

For the first time, Rebecca felt as though she had peeked into a hidden realm. More than a revelation, she gradually began to accept this new vision as the affirmation of an alternate reality she had always suspected, deep down.

"Listen, you have to remember I've been able to see this stuff since I was little," Mo reminded her. "It's never seemed that unusual to me. But I figured out pretty early that most other people were oblivious to the supernatural. Thought I was some kind of freak for a long time. But my grandmother understood. She assured me that my weird ability was nothing to be ashamed or afraid of. But when I told her about visitors or messages from the spirit world, she'd always whisper, 'I believe you, darling. But let's just keep these things to ourselves.'"

The old friends shared a smile. "I get that," Rebecca said. "Not sure I want to confess my new perception with anyone at work. I have a rational rep to maintain there."

"You'll tell—eventually. A select few, at least. Lochlan, for sure. Those mediums you've been spending time with. This is too big to keep entirely to yourself."

They sipped their chamomile tea in companionable silence for several minutes, listening to windblown sleet on the kitchen windowpane.

"The weirdest part is that I knew—I *knew* —beyond all reason or understanding, that whatever that entity was, it was malevolent. It intended harm. And for a split second, when we saw it streaking across the doorway—it shot right through me, right into me. The energy, the emotion, like a personal violation. I wish I could describe it better. I'm shivering again just remembering the sensation...and that horrible woman. My hairs really did stand on end."

"Wait—What? You felt like it was inside you?"

Rebecca nodded.

"OK, so that's significant. I've never experienced anything like that with spirits."

"Stop trying to freak me out, Mo. I'm already feeling creepy enough."

"Sorry, but I'm totally serious," her friend insisted. "Obviously the ghost hunters and psychics prowling around The Keep lately have stirred up some sort of dormant phenomena. It may be time to dig out that ancient talisman of yours.

"The *myotragus Balearicus* horn? I don't even know where it is anymore."

"Find it. I mean it. Now that you've encountered one spirit at The Keep, I predict that you're going to start seeing more of them. Some sort of door has been opened at the hotel with all the recent activity. There are spirits—a few unhappy spirits—who don't like the attention and light shining on them, for whatever reason. And it might be a good idea to keep that little artifact with you from now on."


Jackhammers erupted on the mezzanine level, where former offices were being converted to meeting space. Rebecca had sometimes tried to imagine how disruptive the major remodel of the top two floors must have been in the 1930s. She had to imagine no more. The construction began at 9:00 every day and proceeded until 7:00. The Keep's legendary ambiance was blasted by the sounds of power tools.

Outside, the sandstone façade was being stripped of its last remaining decorative trim. The work was justified as "stabilization" to the landmark commission that approved the alterations to protect the public from falling bits of stone, rendered unstable by decades of freeze-and-thaw cycles. The work rattled windows and coated everything with fine dust.

Assaults on the building were relentless, from without and within. Complaints spiked. Tensions rose. And the sanctuary-like atmosphere, for which the hotel had been so long renowned, dissipated. No one at The Keep was resting in peace these days.

Rebecca arrived one morning to find one of the service elevators down.

"Damnedest thing," the repairmen explained. "Whole load of bedding tossed down the laundry chute somehow got tangled in the elevator mechanisms. These shafts have paralleled each other since the 30s. Never had a problem. But some kinda gap opened up between 'em. Have a look."

Rebecca leaned in and peered up the elevator shaft from the ground floor. Slashed white sheets, as high as she could see, dangled from the cables above like a mass lynching of ghosts.

"But how...?"

The repairman shrugged. "All I know is it's gonna take months to fix this mess—*if* we can even find parts for this dinosaur."

Remodeling workmen soon encountered unforeseen complications. Structural anomalies, electrical and plumbing problems caused delays and occasional minor disasters. Floors buckled. Pipes burst. Messiest of the malfunctions flooded the entire basement late one morning. Hotel associates had to slosh through several inches of water to clock in or out.

HR threw together an emergency pizza "party" in the mezz-level Grand Salon when the employee dining room turned estuary. The chief maintenance engineer never could provide an explanation for the high tide, which subsided as mysteriously as it had swelled a few hours earlier. But Lochlan had no doubt about the cause.

"The spirits of The Keep's past are conveying their anger," he said. Rebecca had confided to him her unsettling encounter with the spirit in Room 864 and had been a little disappointed at his lack of astonishment. It had seemed the most natural thing in the world to Lochlan that a spirit had not only appeared to but had essentially shot through Rebecca.

"Rosslyn predicted the spirits would make their displeasure with these alterations known," he reminded Rebecca as they ate their pizza. "And so it begins."


While preparing to leave for work a few days later, Rebecca sneezed—and swore.

"Leakage?" Mo empathized knowingly.

Her roommate grimaced. "Another lovely curse of later middle age. Incontinence."

"Thank you, Poise pads."

"It seems to me that if we have to undergo this monstrous metamorphosis of menopause, we should at least come out of the process with some sort of reward."

"Reward? Like what?"

"I don't know. Like magical powers or something."

"Doesn't work that way. We didn't get any magical power for going through the agony of puberty."

"Oh, but we did," Rebecca insisted. "Maybe the greatest magical power of all. After puberty, women have the power to conceive life."

"Never really thought of it that way. Probably because I never chose to use that particular magic. But I suppose it is sort of the payoff for putting up with monthly periods—if you want to reproduce."

"So what do we get for enduring menopause?"

"Hey, you've seen 'Menopause: The Musical.' In the last act, they're all self-confident and powerful."

"And resigned to living out their remaining days in decaying bodies. Heartwarming stuff."

"Hold on, now. Maybe there is some magic associated with 'the change.' I mean, think about all the mediums and sensitives you've encountered at The Keep. How many of them have been menopausal women?"

"Nearly all of them. So what?"

"Maybe there's a basis for the long cultural association of so-called 'crones' and witchcraft. You know, crone used to be a respectful term applied to old wise women. When women lose their procreative powers, perhaps they gain another sort of potentiality. An aptitude for tapping into the next level of existence, to pierce the veil, bridge the gap between the earthly

178

realm and the spiritual plane. Not all old women embrace the gift, obviously. But then, not all younger women have a talent—nor an inclination—for motherhood. In both cases, it may be a matter of choice, as well as capability."

"You're really reaching now," Rebecca said, buttoning her blouse.

"Maybe. But come to think of it, you yourself may be a case in point. How many encounters with unexplained phenomena have you had since you started menopause?"

"More than I'll admit to you—or anyone. But that's just because of all the time I spend at The Keep, not my hormonal imbalance."

"I propose that's it's the combination of the two factors—the unusual level of paranormal activity at the hotel, plus sensitivity due to physiological changes, equals a receptive dynamic previously unknown to you."

"Your imaginative talents are wasted in university administration, you know," Rebecca said, slipping on shoes. "Helluva try. But what about people like you who've had psychic abilities since childhood?"

"The exception that makes the rule."

"What about male psychics?"

"Oh, stop being difficult. You wanted a reward for menopause and I gave you a possibility. I give up."


By early March, Rebecca was fed up with playing Sales receptionist, a complete waste of her talents and training. Her new awareness of The Keep's spiritual dimension made functioning on the mundane plane more difficult and ludicrous every day. She missed her rooftop archives retreat. Missed her autonomy. Missed being surrounded by echoes and traces of The Keep's past and especially missed long talks with Lochlan. She watched the younger sales reps engrossed in their social media, pandering to potential clients, turning to her only to order their office supplies or make copies. She was grateful for the upcoming private tour, booked many months earlier, which gave her a reason to get out of the office.

The overhead lights were off when Rebecca walked in to preview the Silver Spoon Club. She'd been oblivious to the storm raging outside until she entered the empty corner space. Only paparazzi flashes of lightning, unusual this early in Spring, lit the dim triangular room through the stained-glass windows.

Between events, the space was in disarray, with chairs stacked here and there, a rolling cart laden with plastic bus tubs of dirty dishes. Table skirts and used linens lay crumpled or mounded on the floor and atop a few tables against the back wall. She used the house phone behind the bar to call for a quick straightening up before she showed the place to guests.

Thunder shook the room. The sound of china falling from a bus tub compelled her to glance back at one of the tables. Its linen cloth had slipped to the floor, revealing the prone figure of a thin, pale woman in a crimson gown.

Rebecca froze.

One bare arm dangled limply off the edge of the table. Lightning flashed again. The head turned slowly, unnaturally toward her. Lifeless eyes opened. White lips parted.

"See me."

Clear as glass, the words hung like ice crystals in the air as their source blurred and dissolved before her disbelieving eyes.

*Now that you've encountered one spirit at the Keep.... you're going to start seeing more of them,* Mo had predicted.

The historian told no one of the episode and swept it neatly under the rug of rationality. But the image haunted her subconscious thereafter like a Poe story. Suddenly Mo's suggestion to keep the horn talisman with her seemed like a very good idea.


Yesterday's listing of Griffins Keep VIP guests revealed that Mrs. Stan Tagawa had checked in for a week-long stay—Portia Kuhrsfeld-Tagawa.

Rebecca remembered coming across the 1964 gossip column years earlier in one of the scrapbooks kept by a Keep employee: "Debutante Portia Kuhrsfeld Weds Family Gardener." The story detailed her parents' shock and disapproval of eighteen-year-old Portia's elopement with their Hawaiian estate's young groundskeeper, Mr. Stanley Tagawa.

"We are sorely disappointed by Portia's rash and ill-considered decision to marry without our knowledge or consent," R. Joseph Kuhrsfeld III had told the columnist. "Her stepmother and I are frankly concerned about her future with a young man so clearly beneath our family's social and economic standing."

Rebecca had applauded Portia's leap of independence. But the name Tagawa had meant nothing to her at the time. This personal history explained TITHE's determination to acquire the Griffins Keep. Chad Tagawa's uncle Stan must have long coveted the ultimate symbol of his father-in-law's power and prestige.

From a historical viewpoint, Rebecca was eager to record Mrs. Kuhrsfeld-Tagawa's memories. If nothing else, she could store them in the secret sub-basement room indefinitely. She knew just the hotel associate to arrange an introduction.

"As you can imagine, the family was scandalized when she eloped. And with a Japanese American!" veteran banquets and catering manager Holly Merriweather dished confidentially when Rebecca sought her assistance. "Her father practically disowned her at first. Would have nothing to do with his new son-in-law. But Portia was always the apple of Joe's eye, and apparently, when his first grandchild was born, he lightened up and welcomed his darling daughter back into the bosom of the family. Gradually, Joe Kuhrsfeld not only accepted his former groundskeeper as kin, but actually took Stan under his wing and mentored him in the various Kuhrsfeld enterprises."

"And just how do you know so much about this soap opera?" Rebecca asked

"Hey, you can't coordinate the Snow Ball for 34 years without getting the dirt on all of Denver's elite families. Portia Kuhrsfeld-Tagawa actually chaired the ball many years ago. She was a delight to work with. Very down-to-earth, not a bit snobby. But also somehow very sad, it seemed to me. She hasn't been back to Denver in years—until now."

"So you don't think she'll mind talking with me about her memories of The Keep?"

"Are you kidding? She'll love it. And she must have loads to share. High time she sat down with a local historian for a proper interview. Come on. I'll introduce you!"

They knocked on the door of Room 523 and were greeted by a slender, well-dressed woman in her early 70s. Portia Kuhrsfeld looked casual but chic in a pale blue silk blouse and knife-pleated gray wool slacks. Her chin-length white hair was tucked behind her ears and dark brown eyes peaked over tortoise-shell readers.

Her subtly regal air made one feel privileged to be in her presence. She smiled when she saw her old friend.

"Holly!" she exclaimed warmly, reaching out to embrace her. "You haven't aged a day. So good to see you. Yours is just about the only face I recognize around here from the old days. Come in, come in. Please, sit," she directed, indicating the sofa behind the coffee table in the corner suite's front room. "And you must be the hotel historian Holly's talked so much about."

"Portia, this is Rebecca Bridger. Been with us for about five years now, and we're very fortunate to have someone so knowledgeable and passionate about Denver history sharing our stories with Griffins Keep visitors."

Mrs. Kuhrsfeld-Tagawa extended her hand. "A pleasure, Rebecca. What a wonderful—and unusual—job you have! How on earth did you get the position?"

Rebecca took the grand lady's hand and dropped her gaze modestly. "It was really just a combination of the right timing and the right skill set. I knew the last historian, and she knew that my education and experience were a good fit for the job requirements. She graciously recommended me to management when she moved back home."

"And the rest is history, as they say," Portia concluded.

"Well, yes and no," Rebecca felt compelled to clarify. "The hotel historian position was recently eliminated, along with the archives. Now I'm pretty much just a sales receptionist."

"Oh yes, I remember hearing about that. Got some TITHE email announcement about them auctioning off most of the hotel's historical treasures. An attachment showcased some of the most valuable pieces and invited board members to pre-bid on them. Unconscionable," the older woman sympathized. "No doubt a bit of TITHE reorganization, am I right?"

Rebecca nodded without comment.

"Nevertheless, Holly tells me that you'd like to record some of my memories of the Griffins Keep for posterity, as it were. Not sure I like the idea of being considered living history, but I guess there's no point in denying it. The hotel I remember from my childhood was so different from the way it is today. I hardly know where to begin."

"I think I can help with that," Rebecca said, withdrawing several loose sheets of paper from the portfolio she'd brought along. "I've taken the liberty of suggesting a few questions

182

intended to start your recollections flowing. Don't feel obligated to answer them all, of course. Ideally, they'll get you thinking about other aspects of Keep history that I haven't even mentioned. They're just a starting point, a basis for our discussion. I thought I'd leave them with you and give you a few days to jot down notes before we start any serious interviewing. What do you think?"

Portia pushed her readers into place and leafed through the pages, scanning the questions. Frown lines creased her forehead. "Gracious,' she said with a sigh, "This is a lot. Not sure I want to get into all of it, or even that I can tell you anything about some of these topics. But I appreciate all your forethought, and I'll see what I can offer. I'm flying home to Hawaii on Sunday. Could we plan an hour or so tomorrow afternoon?"

"Absolutely. Thank you so much for fitting me in. Whenever works for you, I'll be there."

"Two o'clock then. Here in my suite. I don't mind if you take notes, but please don't bring a tape recorder or record it on your phone or anything. That would make me too nervous."

Surprised to hear that anything might fluster the impressively composed Mrs. Kuhrsfeld-Tagawa, Rebecca easily agreed. "I can't tell you how much I'm looking forward to our conversation."

# CHAPTER 19

"'How have the Keep's surroundings changed during your lifetime?'" Portia Kuhrsfeld-Tagawa read from the questions Rebecca had supplied the day before. "I guess we can thank DURA—the Denver Urban Renewal Authority—for obliterating most of the Keep's neighbors in the 60s and 70s. Their mission statement in those days must have been 'If it's old, it goes.' Multiple city blocks were razed, gorgeous old gems demolished throughout downtown. I'm sure you've seen photos of the Tabor Grand Opera House, the Mining Exchange building, the Republic Building, the magnificent old department stores. We shudder at those heartbreaking losses today, but in those years, few people realized how much the old buildings contributed to the character of Denver.

"Thank goodness last-minute local landmark designations saved Pinnacle Church, the Silken Rose, and The Keep. Before all these skyscrapers surrounded the place, there were various small businesses, and several other hotels in the neighborhood. None to compare to the Keep, mind you. But several fine hotels for less affluent travelers. All knocked down, imploded, vanished without a trace. Hard now to remember when The Keep was the one of the tallest buildings in downtown. Can you imagine the views of the front range, the eastern plains, Capitol Hill and the Civic Center that used to be visible from the hotel's upper floors?"

Rebecca could. "It must have been amazing."

"Guess you can tell I'm not a great fan of 'progress' as far as the Denver cityscape goes. Next question: 'What aspects of the hotel's interior have changed?'

"The front desk used to have cages, like teller cages in a bank. There was a newsstand where the concierge desk is now, a flower shop in the lobby, a beauty parlor and a gift shop on the mezzanine level. For years, a photography studio occupied the space where the spa reception area is today and where the old Grand Fireplace once stood. There used to be a third griffin, like the two in the fountain, mounted above that fireplace."

"I've seen a picture of it in one of the old scrapbooks. The griffin was turned sideways, with its sword pointing toward the right. Do you know what might have happened to it?"

"My grandfather took it to our estate on Oahu, where it still stands guard in the back garden. Lost its sword somewhere along the line, though. I have no idea where that ended up."

Rebecca knew exactly where it was.

"I'm sure you know about all the drastic changes my grandfather made in the '30s. Moving the main entrance from the Grand Avenue side to the Carson Street side. Replacing the original public elevators with new ones and demolishing the second grand staircase in the process. And most heinous of all, the conversion of the top two floors into those dreadful deco apartments."

"The Parapet Apartments," Rebecca said.

"I never saw what the eighth floor looked like before that remodel, but my Aunty Gretchen did. She used to tell me about the two-story Grand Ballroom and Banquet Hall—the beautiful onyx wainscoting, the magnificent chandeliers, the stained glass in the ninth-floor windows. I've only seen a couple photos of it."

"A couple is all we have, I'm sorry to say."

Portia shook her head sadly. "Aunty Gretchen's favorite childhood memory of the space was the vast polished dance floor. She remembered sliding across it in stocking feet, laughing and pretending she were ice skating or waltzing with her best friend, Henrietta, Harrison Griffin's grand-daughter. Poor Hennie died of scarlet fever while still a girl—right here in a quarantine eighth-floor room of the hotel. So tragic."

The name pricked something in Rebecca's memory. Henrietta...Hennie? Could she be the ghost Miranda had

186

encountered near 864, the one who had warned of a 'bad' spirit nearby?

"No wonder my aunt never forgave Grandfather for destroying that magnificent ballroom."

"What do you remember about your Grandfather Kuhrsfeld?" Rebecca asked.

At the question, Portia appeared pained. "He was a very intense person, a very cold person—even to his own grandchildren. My sister Patricia and I were terrified of him. He had no tolerance for playful children or for anyone who did not fall in line with his dictates. I guess that's what made him such a successful businessman."

She looked down at the floor before adding, "It probably won't shock you to learn that he was a Nazi sympathizer and a founding member of the Colorado Klan, along with my great-grandfather."

Rebecca had made both discoveries about R. J. Kuhrsfeld about a year earlier. "I know the twentieth-century KKK started with a meeting right here in the Griffins Keep in 1920. Not surprising, since the hotel had always been a bastion for wealthy, exclusively white clientele. Management characterized The Keep as offering 'no accommodations for Coloreds' until Civil Rights legislation of the 1960s forced them to abandon that policy. One of the less illustrious aspects of our past," Rebecca noted, "invariably omitted from glowing Keep histories."

"Grandmother Kuhrsfeld was no better," Portia continued, referring to Lilah. "I don't think she loved anything but money and status. We hated going to their house. Had to dress in our Sunday best, sit quietly, even call our grandparents 'sir' and 'ma'am.' I often wondered what my father's childhood in that atmosphere must have been like."

"What do you remember about your father's involvement with the hotel?" Rebecca asked.

Portia pondered the question for a long moment before replying. "As you probably know, after Grandfather's death in the late 50s, hotel ownership was transferred not to my father personally, but to the Kuhrsfeld Foundation. And though Father was chairman of the foundation board, he really had little interest in the management of The Keep, left it to others. We lived here, on and off throughout my youth, in a big Parapet apartment on the

187

eighth floor. It was closer to our school than our Capitol Hill mansion, and that house held some bad memories for Father."

"Your mother's fatal accident?"

Portia nodded. "My stepmother Faye loved the prestige of living at The Keep, where she'd had a smaller apartment before she married Father."

"What was living here like?"

"Uncomfortable," Portia admitted candidly. "The hotel staff all treated us differently. Some of them became great friends as I got to know them over the years. But with others, I felt like I was somehow feared, even resented. It bothered me, especially in the self-conscious adolescent years. My stepmother, on the other hand, insisted upon their deference. She liked being Queen of the Parapet. Very imperious. Thought she was superior to everyone else, especially non-white staff. Used to wave her red lacquered cigarette holder around like a scepter."

"Which apartment did your family live in?"

"It was 865."

"There's no Room 865 today," Rebecca said. The eighth-floor configuration had changed quite a bit with the conversion to executive suites in the 1980s.

"Our apartment was in the center of the Grand Avenue side," Portia explained. "What's now the Kuhrsfeld Board Room was our living room, and we had rooms on both sides of it."

"864 and 866?"

"If you say so."

Pieces began to fall into place as Rebecca processed this new information. Of course the Joe Kuhrsfeld family would not have been included on the hotel's annual Christmas poinsettia gift list, the only source she had for Parapet Apartment residents. They were the hotel owners.

And the red lacquered cigarette holder rang a distant, nearly forgotten bell. Where had she encountered something like that before? Rebecca remembered an archives contribution from a houseman who found just such a holder in the trash, around the time of Momaday's death. How could that possibly tie in?

She had to ask the one-time resident. "Do you believe The Keep is haunted?"

A cautious smile transformed Portia's features. "I don't recall that question on your list. I imagine you get asked about it all the time."

Rebecca nodded. "So many people are obsessed with the subject. Most of them seem desperate to be convinced by some evidence of spirits. They've heard The Keep is haunted and they want it to be true."

"Of course they do. Of course. Because the existence of ghosts provides hope that death is not the end. But so many ghost stories are about unhappy spirits, trapped spirits, spirits with unresolved issues who can't move on to the next level of existence. Those are the ones that really scare us."

"You're avoiding my question," Rebecca persisted. "What do *you* believe?"

Reluctant to continue, Portia nevertheless sensed Rebecca's personal agenda on this particular subject and replied at length, "I'm no expert on existential matters. But I will tell you this—in strictest confidence, mind you. There's something very strange about that boardroom space, our former living room. On three separate occasions when I was growing up—all in October, right around Halloween—when Patty and I were alone in the apartment, we heard faint orchestra music. It seemed to be coming from directly above us on the ninth floor. And voices, as if several people were conversing at once. I suppose it could have been a phonograph or a television. But it was eerily wavering, louder, then softer, then louder again... a sort of oscillation. And there were voices, laughter. We weren't scared, just intrigued."

It was Deanna's anniversary night story all over again.

"The third time we heard the music, we crept outside to investigate the sounds. The muffled conversations could have come from any room down the hallway. But it was very late, two or three in the morning. It didn't make sense to us. We both got goosebumps and scooted back to our own apartment.

"Just outside our door, at the foot of the staircase between the eighth and ninth floors, stood a couple dressed in formal wear—he in a tailcoat, she in a long blue gown. He had his arm around her waist, and their backs were toward us. They were gazing straight ahead at the glass-brick wall of the atrium, as if they could see through it. The man was humming along to the music. And as we stared, transfixed, the pair grew more and more transparent, until they seemed to just melt away into thin air. The whole thing probably lasted only a few seconds. We both saw it, Patricia and I, but we never told anyone else about our experience."

189

"You doubted your own perceptions," Rebecca said.

The older woman studied her seriously for a long moment. "You've seen something yourself," she guessed. "Something you can't explain rationally. Then you understand. There are layers of parallel existence within this hotel we can only glimpse."

Rebecca nodded, grateful for the validation of her new awareness.

"Marvelous, isn't it? The most delicious secret. This calls for a toast," Portia announced, picking up the phone to call room service. "I'm ordering us a bottle of champagne."

"Thanks, but I can't, I'm just on lunch break..."

"And I'm treating. I'm a VIP guest, and I insist. I'm not tackling any more of your questions until we take a break."


Portia Kuhrsfeld-Tagawa did not ask Rebecca to share her personal experience with unexplained phenomena. But she did ask what the historian—deposed historian—intended to do with the notes she was taking of their interview.

Rebecca hesitated before confiding. "I set aside a few hotel artifacts, documents, photographs—without authorization or disclosure—in a safe place, away from the things to be auctioned off last November. I plan to add your memories to that cache."

"Good for you!" her new friend declared with a spontaneous thumbs-up. "I'm pleased to hear it. Your secret's safe with me. One day, when the hotel management's attitude returns to appreciation of The Keep's past, you'll be considered a hero for your small subterfuge."

The two women listened to classical music on the Bose radio as they sipped their champagne. Portia gazed out the window five stories above the intersection of Carson and Seventeenth. "I miss the view of the mountains," she said. "Before all these skyscrapers, you could see at least a hundred miles along the Front Range on a clear day from The Keep's upper floors. That's the price of progress, I guess."

Portia set her empty flute on the coffee table. "Better now," she announced. "Ready to continue our interview. Fire away."

"What is your favorite Griffins Keep memory?"

Portia smiled. "I've been thinking about this since I first read through your questions," she said. "There are so many to choose from. Stuffing Pop Tarts into the mail drop slots. Launching paper airplanes from the seventh floor into the atrium lobby.

"But I'd have to say my single most cherished memory is the Snow Ball when I debuted as one of the Ice Princesses. I don't want to tell you how long ago it was, but even by that time the tradition was anachronistic, the remnant of an earlier time when Denver society controlled everything and The Keep was a citadel of snobbery. Being a Princess still meant that you were presented as a candidate for marriage into an equally prosperous family. And although I recognized it for the elitist and sexist ritual it was—God help me—I loved the elegant white dress and elbow-length gloves. Descending the Grand Staircase, feeling beautiful with my elaborate up-do and my first diamond earrings, all eyes on me... It was the closest thing to a Cinderella experience in my entire life. Never had a formal wedding, so the Snow Ball meant even more to me than it might to others. It's shallow and vain, I know. But there it is, and I won't apologize."

"No reason you should."

"I realize the whole overblown affair is self-indulgent and self-congratulatory. But it's also elegant, gracious, timeless and genteel—qualities increasingly rare in today's world, it seems to me."

Rebecca realized as their conversation evolved that she liked Portia Kuhrsfeld-Tagawa. Liked her a lot. They seemed to see things in the same way.

"On to a question I hope you've had time to give some serious thought," the interviewer continued. "What do you think the Griffins Keep means to the people of Denver and Colorado?"

Portia cocked her head and studied Rebecca's face. "Are you from here, Rebecca?" she asked.

"From Denver? No. I grew up in Colorado Springs. But I came to Denver—to the Griffins Keep—every year at Christmastime with my Great-Aunt Frankie for Holiday Tea."

Portia nodded. "Then you know the answer to that question as well as I do. But I'll try to put it into words."

She poured herself another glass of champagne and refilled Rebecca's flute. They both took sips.

"From the beginning, the Griffins Keep has represented the very best that Denver has to offer. Both locals and visitors have found welcome here, rest here, haven here. The Keep is the setting

191

for celebration and accomplishment, secrets and scandals, joys and heartaches."

The woman who had practically grown up in The Keep sipped her champagne once again before continuing, and Rebecca tried to record her well-chosen words in notes.

"The Keep brings together all the elements that make a great city—finance, politics, commerce, philanthropy, culture and hospitality—under one soaring stained-glass ceiling. It is an oasis of elegance in the midst of the Great American Desert, a wellspring of refinement in the dust of the uncivilized Wild West. The Griffins Keep stands for uncompromising excellence, impeccable service, and quality in every detail."

It pained Rebecca to think about how all that was changing under TITHE ownership.

"I would say this hotel embodies what Coloradans have always strived for, what they value, and what they're proud to share with the rest of the world." Portia drew a deep breath and smiled at her own passionate summation. "How's that?"

Rebecca leaned back in her chair and clapped her hands together. "I wish I could write fast enough to have caught all that. Wow."

Portia smiled, and Rebecca sensed that she, too, felt a warm camaraderie blossoming between them. It made addressing the final topic somewhat easier.

"One last question, if I may, please," Rebecca ventured. "It's a two-parter. How do you feel about the hotel being back in your family's hands? And what do you think of the changes currently occurring under TITHE's auspices?"

"Ahhh... the BIG question," Portia began, hesitating. She set down her glass and peered over her readers into Rebecca's eyes. "May I tell you something off the record, completely in confidence?"

The historian laid her pen and paper on the table between them. "You can trust my discretion. I really want to know, for my own information."

Satisfied, Portia began. "Although the Tagawas—Stan and Chad—are technically my family, we haven't been close in many, many years. My husband began to change soon after my father decided to welcome him into the Kuhrsfeld empire. He taught Stan 'the ropes' as they had been taught to him by my grandfather. As you may have gathered, the Kuhrsfeld dynasty was successful,

192

but it was also ruthless. When I fell in love with Stan, in those early years, we were both young and idealistic. It was his simplicity, his sincerity and his honesty that attracted me. I guess you could say I was sort of a hippie back then—peace and love and flower power—all that stuff that seems so foolish now but seemed so revolutionary in the 60s. I believed The Beatles when they told me 'All You Need is Love,' and I truly believe that's what Stan and I had at first."

She smiled weakly, then dropped her gaze and fiddled with her rings. "I watched Stan harden under my father's mentorship, little by little, becoming the man I now scarcely know—and no longer love. It happens. It hurts. We stayed together for the children, and later just because it was easier than battling through lawyers over all the finances. When you have homes all over the world, it's not difficult to lead very separate lives. For all intents and purposes, our marriage ended long ago."

Rebecca related to the heartache, if not the contributing factors.

"When his nephew Chad won the lottery, helming TITHE left Stan no time for a personal life. We almost never see each other anymore. I'm here with him now—in separate suites, I'm sure everyone has noticed—only because of my past with The Keep. I had to see what he and the company were doing to the place."

"And what do you think of the changes so far, and the further changes planned?"

Portia's eyes flashed and her demeanor darkened. "I'm appalled. What TITHE is doing to the Griffins Keep may be even worse than what my grandfather did to the hotel in the 30s. They're turning a palace into a circus tent, a Grande Dame into a cheap whore. TITHE's so-called vision for Griffins Keep is a perversion. The company trivializes every property it touches, but it never mattered to me until now."

"Surely you're in a position to do something about it," Rebecca said hopefully. "Won't your husband listen to your concerns and opinions?"

Portia shook her head. "He hasn't listened to me in years. And I'm only a minority shareholder in the TITHE corporation. It breaks my heart to witness the tasteless transformation of a place so dear to me. But I'm helpless to stop it."

As her eyes began to brim with tears of frustration, Rebecca caught Portia's pale hand and squeezed it sympathetically. "Welcome to my world," she said sadly.

# CHAPTER 20

When she responded to his request to meet in the carpentry shop, Rebecca found a furtive Lochlan, apparently concealing something under his painter's coat.

"You're not going to believe this," he said, closing the door. "I found this yesterday in one of the walls we're dismantling to create new meeting room space on the mezz level." From inside his coat he withdrew, in brown paper wrapping, a book, about 5" x 8" and about a half-inch thick.

"What is it?" Rebecca asked, reaching to take it from him. "Some sort of ledger?"

Lochlan shook his head, handing it over. "A journal," he said, "from the late 1920s, early 1930s."

The mauve-colored cover was made of a soft suede-like material. The pages inside were notebook-lined. When Rebecca opened the journal, a handwritten note fluttered out of the inside cover. She carefully retrieved it from the floor and read aloud:

*April 10, 1931*
*To whomever may come upon this journal:*
*I cannot imagine how many years will pass before this notebook is found. I took the opportunity to conceal it within a wall of the proposed beauty salon as they run new wiring throughout the second floor of the hotel.*

*This journal chronicles the strange and troubling events I have personally witnessed or heard about from reliable sources during my tenure with the Griffins Keep as hotel stenographer. Were I to reveal them now, it would surely mean my job, as so many prominent and powerful people are involved with the incidents described herein. But I feel bound by my conscience to record what I know, even if it should remain hidden until long after I am gone.*

*Take care, Dear Future Reader, with whom you share my account. Regardless of how things have changed between my time and yours, I suspect that influential men will still be keeping secrets at the Griffins Keep, as they have since the beginning. May God forgive me my cowardice in not confronting the evil when I encountered it."*

The note was not signed.

"Helluva preface," Rebecca said. "Have you read the journal itself?"

"What do you think, with an intro like that? Took it home last night and was up 'til midnight with it. Your turn now."

"Her penmanship is lovely," Rebecca noted as she scanned the first few pages. "Hotel stenographer. I'd forgotten they had such a position."

"She mentions at some point in the journal that she learned her trade at the Opportunity School here in town, soon after her husband passed away. The school's employment bureau helped her get the Keep job as soon as she completed the course."

"So what's this 'evil' she speaks of in the note? Sounds ominous."

"Read her account for yourself. We'll talk first thing tomorrow."

Rebecca finished reading the journal by 8:00 that night. But she was up until 2:00 AM, unable to sleep after what she'd read. What it described was disturbing. What it implied was unthinkable.

Covering a period of about a year and a half, from 1929 -1931, the stenographer's journal entries were not daily, but random, written apparently when developments compelled her. Early entries reflected the excitement of her new position with the

196

prestigious Griffins Keep. Stationed at a small desk in the lobby, her services were available to any guest of the hotel. She took dictation and typed up correspondence, reports and proposals of all sorts. Her written communication skills were impressive and efficient.

Several entries reflected the writer's routine encounters with notables of the day. Attorney Clarence Darrow, nationally known for the so-called "Scopes Monkey Trial," actor Douglas Fairbanks, Sr., and aviator Charles Lindbergh all availed themselves of the hotel stenographer's services during their stays at The Keep. In one entry she remarked upon her brush with Eleanor Roosevelt, then the wife of the governor of New York, who hosted a fundraising dinner for Democratic women at the hotel. In the process of dictating several personal letters, she impressed the stenographer as radiating a compassionate intelligence. "Mrs. Roosevelt had a way of making you feel you were the most important person in the room," she wrote in her journal.

Even more crucial than speed and accuracy to a professional in the Keep stenographer's position was discretion. As scribe to its powerful and influential patrons, she was privy to a great deal of sensitive information. Potent information. Often volatile information. The stenographer fretted in her journal that she sometimes worried about matters which were none of her concern. A frequent guest, once noticing her furrowed brow, advised, "'Let the day's business go through your fingers, not through your head.'"

Having started just a few months before "Black Thursday" in 1929, the stenographer noted a dramatic shift in the demeanor of The Keep's wealthy clientele after the Stock Market Crash. "Gone is the brash confidence and swagger of previous days, and in its place, anxiety and desperation plague the hotel's stalwarts. I sense that these captains of business and politics would do almost anything to safeguard—or to restore—their fortunes."

The stenographer, it became apparent as Rebecca read on, was also at the beckon call of hotel owners R. J. and Lilah Kuhrsfeld. She transcribed insincere regrets and made-up "prior commitments" for RSVPs to parties Mrs. Kuhrsfeld elected not to attend. She typed-up heartfelt apologies and passionate promises from Mr. Kuhrsfeld to his mistress, a department store fashion model he kept in a suite at The Keep. The stenographer made it clear in her journal that she did not respect the Kuhrsfelds. Nor did she trust them.

By 1929, the eighth-floor site of the two-story Ladies Ordinary had been converted to a Convention Hall, where traveling salesmen were invited—for a substantial fee—to showcase their wares. Based upon the reports of colleagues in the banquets department, the stenographer speculated that the space regularly hosted more nefarious activities after hours.

> They have told me in confidence that every Friday night around 11:00, they deliver platters of food and contraband alcoholic beverages for 40 people to the Hall. As soon as the servers leave, the doors are locked. When the custodial staff are admitted around 5:00 AM, the chaos they are tasked with clearing gives every evidence of orgiastic depravity.
>
> My friend Malmud says he has personally witnessed loose women from the Silken Rose being smuggled through the coal tunnel under Carson Street and up the service elevator for these parties. Rumor has it that both the elder and the younger Mr. Kuhrsfelds host the weekly debaucheries with the eager collusion of the Rose's madam, Dolly Lacey.

The journal reported equally hush-hush meetings of local powerbrokers and business leaders taking place periodically in the Grand Salon late at night. Doors locked. Staff barred. But unlike the wild parties in the Convention Hall, these congregations left no trace whatsoever of their mysterious activities.

"The Salon is always spotless the next morning," a custodian told the stenographer. "They clean up after themselves and one would never know they were there, let alone what they were doing."

Further entries revealed that the stenographer counted many friends among her fellow Keep employees, acquaintances from their shared Opportunity School days. All were recent immigrants who had learned English and employable skills at the nation's first public school for adults. All were grateful for their positions with the hotel. But none of them was deaf or blind. They heard things, they saw things, and they confided to the stenographer discoveries that concerned them.

198

*This morning Sofia told me she had seen a live, bleating lamb brought into the basement butcher shop. When she asked the butcher about the unusual delivery, he waved her away, saying, "This is how we ensure the freshest meat."*

*Today Pavil reported one of the bags he'd carried up to a prominent guest's room fell open, spilling a hooded black robe embroidered with strange symbols."*

*Luca in stewarding was both impressed and disturbed by the array of long, gleaming knives he was directed to sharpen for a special guest of the Kuhrsfelds."*

*Bridget confessed tearfully this afternoon that she is quitting her job, though she needs the money desperately. "You would cringe at what I've seen in some of the hotel rooms," she said to me. "In that rich Romanian's suite on the sixth floor-- a child, a little colored girl, chained to the radiator, staring at me like she was drugged. To my shame, I was too frightened to help her. When I reported it to Mrs. Merchant, she told me that we must respect our guests' privacy above all, and that I should forget about the child if I knew what was good for me. I won't stay another minute in a place where such wickedness goes on."*

The suspicious entries did not appear all at once, but over a period of about two months in 1930 around Christmas time. Around the winter solstice.

"Coincidence?" Rebecca asked Lochlan when they met in the paint shop to discuss the journal the next morning. "I know you put great stock in the mystical energy of astronomical events."

"I do," he confirmed, "as do the Knights Templar, as do the Freemasons, and as do Satanists, for that matter. Momentous things are presaged by the movement of the planets and the stars. Their power can be tapped for good, or for evil."

"So what do you think was going on in those days at the Griffins Keep? Lambs and knives and black robes add up to ritual sacrifice in my book."

"And the little girl chained to the radiator?"

199

"Don't," Rebecca pleaded. "I can't even think about it."

"OK," Lochlan agreed, gently placing his hand on her forearm. "We won't go there."

*December 23 - The angels wept. Management claims the moisture on the Grand Salon ceiling fresco is due to leaky plumbing. But I am not the only one who has seen tears in the eyes of the archangels—as if they had witnessed something terrible.*

*This building has mystical powers, some say. My beloved James was a member of the local Scottish Rites Lodge. Just before he died, he confided to me that the Freemasons know many Griffins Keep's secrets. He said the structure channels spiritual energies intended for the good of the city, which was still struggling when the hotel opened.*

*I suspect that certain unscrupulous men have been attempting to pervert those energies to their own purposes in recent months. Dabbling in the occult, summoning diabolical forces to do their bidding. I'm frightened of what may come of their efforts.*

*March 9 -This afternoon Mr. Kuhrsfeld dictated an urgent letter to a Professor Ivan Kolov:*

*"It is my understanding that you assisted Mr. Nikola Tesla with his electro-magnetic experiments in Colorado Springs several years ago. I have also been given to understand from colleagues versed in spiritualism that you are experienced in harnessing electrical energies to purge spaces befouled by dangerous forces. I solicit your assistance with just such a matter.*

*'Money is no object. Electrical generation is no issue. As many as four Corliss engines will be at your disposal. Secrecy is imperative. I beseech you to come to Denver at once, as terrible entities, unwisely summoned, are beyond our control."*

The stenographer had added a postscript to this entry:

*Not knowing whether Mr. Tesla will be remembered, I should explain that he is considered a 'mad scientist' for his work with transmitting electrical energy through the earth without wires and for creating manmade lightning. It is also rumored that he has experimented with electro-magnetic connections to the spiritual realm. He has even invented a 'spirit radio' for communicating with the dead and claims to have received signals from other worlds.*

*Mr. Kuhrsfeld was drinking straight scotch as he dictated this correspondence. His hand trembled. He never looked me in the eye. He instructed me to bring the letter to him directly as soon as I had typed it up. 'I'll arrange for its delivery myself,' he said, still not meeting my eyes. I have often seen him tense, agitated, anxious. But never like this. Never terrified.*

*March 18 - Professor Kolov arrived today and immediately sequestered himself in the Grand Salon. The room has been designated off-limits to all until the professor completes his work. From the trunks which accompanied him were unloaded spools of wiring, metal rods, and all manner of coils and tubes, switches and meters. What on earth can he be planning?*

*March 21—It is a good thing that hotel occupancy was low last night. Apparently Professor Kolov's activities in the Grand Salon used so much power that the basement generators could scarcely meet his demands. Staff who worked the graveyard shift reported that the professor's equipment created such a tremendous charge that they could feel it coursing through them, as far away as the Front Desk office. The hotel detective claimed the light visible from beneath the locked Salon doors was so intense that he had to look away.*

*No one is quite sure what the professor was up to. But when he emerged from the room, witnesses swear, the hair on his head was completely frazzled and standing on end. The Salon itself, they said, smelled of sulfur and ashes.*

201

*"It is finished," he said in the letter to Mr. Kuhrsfeld he dictated to me the next morning. "The negative energy has been neutralized and dispersed. You will be troubled no more by the 'problem' you invited. I must warn you in the strongest possible terms to never, never tap into those forces again. You were very fortunate that polarity reversal worked this time. But if you call the trouble back into being, never contact me again."*

*March 30—Mr. Kuhrsfeld has been like a man possessed since Professor Kolov's visit. He seems determined to reshape The Keep for reasons he does not share. "I'll castrate this place if it takes my entire fortune," I heard him tell a close associate.*

*Work has already been undertaken to retouch the ceiling fresco in the Grand Salon where moisture streaked the archangels' faces. The carpet and draperies are being torn out and burned in the basement furnaces. I doubt we will ever know what actually happened in the Salon, either in the period before Professor Kolov's arrival or during his mysterious visit. But many of us employed at The Keep have the sense that the hotel and its inhabitants escaped disaster of dire proportions by the narrowest margin.*

Rosslyn handed the stenographer's journal back to Lochlan two days later. "This goes a long way toward explaining all the drastic changes made to the building during the Kuhrsfeld years," she said. "Somehow, R.J. loosed something horrific while trying to channel the Keep's powers to the ruthless advancement of himself and his cronies."

She shook her head in wonder. "Whatever it was, it scared the hell out of him. But refusing to accept blame for bringing the evil on himself, he blamed The Keep, along with the Freemasons who had empowered it. By altering its physical features, he must have believed he could undo its magic—magic the builders intended for enlightenment, but that he tried to use for dark purposes."

Lochlan agreed. "To some extent, he succeeded. By changing the main entrance from the Grand Avenue side to the Carson side, he redirected the orientation and the flow of the place. And I have to assume his demolition of the eighth-floor banquet hall was an intentional assault on the space in which the Knights Templar dedicated the building."

"He changed or eliminated so many of the potent architectural details—shut off the artesian-well elevator hydraulics, completely destroyed the second grand staircase, chiseled off the huge stone griffins that flanked the Seventeenth Street entrance, even removed the griffin above the lobby fireplace—all in his effort to diffuse the building's esoteric powers."

"Makes the current remodeling and redecoration look pretty insignificant by comparison," Rebecca realized.

"Were you able to find out anything about our journalist?" Rosslyn asked.

Rebecca reported some success. "I found an in-house publication from 1930 in one of the archives cartons we hid in the basement. It listed all the hotel guest services, including the floral shop, the barber shop, and the hotel stenographer, Dorothy Wright.

"I looked up her obituary at the DPL Western History department," the historian said. "Seems Dorothy didn't stay at The Keep for long after the journal entries stopped. Got a good job at the Colorado National Bank and taught evening classes in stenography at the Opportunity School until she retired. She passed away peacefully in her sleep at the age of 72, survived by her son and daughter and five grandchildren."

"Sounds like a happy ending," Lochlan said. "Wonder if she still visits the Keep?"

"What do you plan to do with her journal?"

"I believe I'll put it back where I found it. That particular wall is gone now, of course. But I'm sure I can find a space in the terra cotta block in the same general area to tuck it away for some future Keep engineer to uncover down the line. Share the thrill—and the shock—of its discovery with posterity, just as Mrs. Wright intended."


Rebecca was no stranger to the seduction of occultism.

A folded note discovered on her husband's bureau in the fifth year of their "open marriage" had led her to conjure sympathetic

203

magic a second time. On pale yellow paper, written in a feminine hand, she read the instructions, "Please proceed to the screening room to get your brains screwed out."

She'd stared at the message for a long time. Almost from the beginning of their marriage, she'd known that her husband was cheating on a regular basis, had known that he wanted her to do the same, in order to share the experiences for his perverse entertainment. But to hold the visceral proof of his betrayal in her hands brutally kicked the heart out of her.

Had he left it there intentionally for her to find? When confronted with the evidence, Bryce had admitted it was from Bianca, a fellow theatre student studying costume design. Their affair had been going on for more than a year.

"She inspires me to perform in ways you never could," he'd told Rebecca. He wanted a divorce. It was the beginning of their end.

Rebecca had blamed the seductress rather than the willing seductee. She had never felt such hatred, pouring the pain of all Bryce's betrayals onto Bianca and vowing revenge. Remembering the voodoo doll incident of her childhood, she set out to acquire some personal possession infused with Bianca's essence upon which to vent her anguish. A sympathetic friend who worked with the costumer had supplied the perfect object: a pin cushion.

"I saw Bianca prick her finger on a needle the other day before she reached for this," the accomplice had explained. "It must have absorbed a few drops of her blood. Will it work for your purposes?"

Rebecca had slit the cushion open on one side and stuffed the screening room note inside. Under a full moon two nights later, she'd intended to pierce the bundle with sewing shears. But on that bright, cold midnight, as she'd stood outside of Bianca's apartment to perform the curse, a saber-tooth icicle had broken loose from the roof gutter and fallen at her feet. With all the malice she could muster, she'd stabbed at the cushion with the icy dagger. When it snapped off without puncturing the dense packet, Rebecca feared she had failed in her vengeful ritual.

But one week later to the day, while hiking up to Bridal Veil Falls with a group of friends, Bianca had slipped from the trail on a patch of ice and fallen to her death on the rocks 60-feet below.

Ice. Coincidence? No one—including Rebecca—could prove otherwise. But she knew that she had summoned something primal to serve her bidding. The realization excited and terrified her. Sensing that she was wading too deeply into darkness, she'd pulled back once again from the dangerous brink.

# CHAPTER 21

The music was totally unexpected. With the scaling back of Lobby Tea, the longtime musicians had been let go. All one heard in the atrium anymore was Muzak.

But what was this Rebecca was hearing through the door of the mezzanine sales office?

A single violin. Live. Could it be?

Rebecca ignored the ringing phone and stepped out onto the second floor balcony. About twenty people were enjoying Tea in the lobby below. Seated on the old Victorian-style furniture that she thought TITHE had gotten rid of, they clustered around a single long table by the Griffin Fountain. At its head was a tiny, elderly lady in a spectacular purple hat and feather boa. The affectionate multi-generational group feting her could only be friends and family. A huge sheet cake set before the guest of honor featured more candles than Rebecca had ever seen at once.

But it was the musician who drew her attention. Long, wavy, gray-streaked hair fell to his shoulders. The formal jacket and white shirt that he wore were apparently borrowed from banquets staff. The kilt was his own—MacKenzie dress tartan, she had no doubt. Rebecca flashed back to that clan's motto, as recited by Lochlan soon after they met: "I shine, not burn."

And shine he did. Lochlan's violin gleamed in the stained-glass-filtered sunlight. Its song rose like passion to fill the open eight-story space with soaring sound. The spritely Celtic melody lilted throughout the atrium to be absorbed by the structure already resonant with thirteen decades of piano, harp, string quartet, jazz combo, and orchestra music.

Dawn came out to the balcony and joined Rebecca. "It's Imogene Lawbaugh's 100th birthday," she said. Every Griffins Keep staff member knew the name. Imogene had been coming to the hotel since she was a little girl. Her mother had been the hotel's seamstress. Her aunt and uncle had lived in one of the Parapet apartments for years. She celebrated the end of Prohibition in the Pirates Pub. She got engaged in the Versailles Room, married in the Silver Spoon Club, and honeymooned in one the Keepsake Suites. She hosted countless fundraisers for charitable causes at the hotel throughout her long and colorful life. Her annual birthday celebration had been held without fail at The Keep every year since she turned nine.

Rebecca had tried repeatedly to pin down Mrs. Lawbaugh for an oral history interview. Imogene was always willing but somehow never able. She'd driven until she was 92, when her vision failed and she had to give up the 1965 blue Cadillac DeVille she called the H.M.S. Griffin. She'd been wheelchair-bound for the past 8 years. It was hard for her to get around. Hard for her to remember little day-to-day details. But at turns, she recalled incidents from her youth as if they were yesterday.

"Honey, the stories I could tell you about the goings on in this hotel would curl your hair!" she once told Rebecca. But when the historian had called her the next day to arrange a chat, Imogene had had no idea who she was. Sadly, the old lady's memories were already as elusive as butterflies. It was too late now to catch them. Rebecca hoped she would never grow that old.

She gazed down upon the still-bright spirit of Imogene, whose perishable container was rapidly approaching its expiration date, and wondered. *Are the physical failings of old age Nature's way of making it easier for the spirit to abandon the body?* In countless acts of betrayal, the body which begins as a boon becomes a bother, and at last a burden. Rebecca's own arthritic feet ached after just one site tour, literally stopping her in her tracks, long before she was ready. Her aging body limited her in more and more ways. What would it be like to be free of it? What would it be like to move without feet, without flesh? Body-free. The prospect of release was seductive.

"Mrs. Lawbaugh's such a beloved fixture around here among the few remaining veteran staff that they did everything they could to make this milestone birthday perfect for her," Dawn said, "When Imogene mentioned her fond memory of a violinist who played in the atrium many years ago. I remembered that Lochlan used to perform professionally, and he kindly agreed to play for the occasion."

"He's wonderful, isn't he?" Rebecca marveled as Lochlan coaxed Vivaldi from his instrument. Transcendence could still be achieved by those attuned to the Griffins Keep's power to lift spirits and elevate the mundane. *As it was purposed, may it ever be,* Rebecca prayed silently, her faith its magic rekindled.

Ignoring more immediate and basic needs, TITHE was determined to modernize all the guestrooms on floors three through seven. The desecration had begun. Although she knew it was scheduled, Rebecca's first encounter with the dismantlement as she walked the sixth floor came as a rude shock.

"Excuse me, ma'am." She turned to face a middle-aged workman behind her who had spoken. "Did I not see you leading a tour up here last evening? It sounded like a ghost tour."

"Yes, yes you did. And yes, it was a private ghost tour. I'm the hotel historian. At least, I used to be, when The Keep had a hotel historian. Now I'm just the occasional tour guide. Rebecca Bridger."

"Very nice to meet you, Rebecca," he said, shaking her hand. "I am Manuel Otero. I am supervising all of this work," he said, indicating the redecoration with a sweep of his arm.

"No offense, Manuel. I'm sure your men do excellent work. But I hate what they're doing to these rooms. This horrible carpet doesn't belong in an Italian Renaissance hotel."

Manuel nodded. "I agree with you. But this is what the owners have selected."

"Well, they sure as hell don't have a clue about the traditions that should define this property. Pardon my language, but this makes me so angry!"

"I understand your displeasure. This is a beautiful hotel. Amazing architecture. I would very much like to talk with you sometime about the hotel's history, especially anything you know about its construction."

209

"I'd like that," Rebecca said, composing herself. "I'm sure with all this redecorating and remodeling, you're bound to lay bare a few secrets not even I know about."

Manuel cocked his head and inquired seriously, "Why do you mention 'secrets'?"

"No reason, really. Except that The Keep's architect was a member of the Order of Freemasons. And some people say that Masons designed geometrical and numerological secrets—even powers—into their structures."

"Is that so? Have you or others uncovered any such secrets in the Griffins Keep?"

Reluctant to mention the upside-down panel and Lochlan's endless theories, let alone anything about the hidden journal, Rebecca shook her head. "We can't even find a cornerstone, which Freemasons usually installed with much fanfare and ceremony in their important buildings."

"In the northeast corner."

"Then you know something of the Freemasons, too?"

Manuel glanced around the hallway, then gestured for her to follow him into one of the rooms being refurbished. "Come in here, please, Rebecca." He quietly closed the door behind them, though it had only a hole where the latching mechanism had been.

"You noticed nothing when I shook your hand," he began, his voice discretely lowered. "But had you been a Freemason yourself, you would have known, by the way I grasped your hand and positioned my thumb between your knuckles, that I was a brother. You would even have known that I have achieved the degree of Master Mason."

"Then we really must talk. How long will you be working here at The Keep?"

"It is a big job, five floors, nearly 200 rooms. My crew and I will be here for at least another three weeks." He handed the historian his business card. "Call me on my mobile. We can go someplace for coffee soon. We have much to discuss, I think."


"What do you know about the history of Freemasonry in Colorado?" Manuel asked as soon as they'd gotten their coffees and found a relatively secluded corner at the Tattered Cover bookstore the next day.

"Very little, I'm afraid," Rebecca admitted. "I know that the lodge here in downtown Denver was one of the first established in Colorado."

"According to the brothers I have talked to, the only thing that came before the first Masonic meeting in Denver was the first saloon. Freemasons were among the earliest settlers, who met and formed the lodge in November 1858—even before the gold rush that gave Denver its start the following spring."

"I do know that most of the men prominent in business and politics in the latter half of the 19th century were Freemasons, and that the organization was very powerful and influential well into the early 1900s."

"That is very true. Your first territorial governor, Mr. William Gilpin, and the territorial secretary who designed your state seal were among the earliest Freemasons in Colorado. I have been studying this, you see, since I met with my brothers of Colorado Lodge #5, who counted the Griffins Keep architect Edward Brookings among its members. Did you know that Brookings was also the architect of the Silken Rose building?"

"I did. When it opened as a boarding school, it was Brooking's third Denver building."

"Can you imagine the neighborhood around the hotel when it first opened? Three buildings only—the school, the church, and the hotel. One dedicated to education, one to faith, and the third to hospitality. The symbolism of threes is everywhere here, including the triangle shape of The Keep and the many Holy Trinity elements of the Pinnacle Church. In Freemasonry, as in ancient numerology, three is a very important number."

"Did the Denver lodge brothers tell you anything about Masonic connections to the Griffins Keep?"

Manuel lifted his coffee cup and drank, looking over its rim into her eyes. Then he leaned forward and placed his hand over Rebecca's. "They shared many secrets. But first I must learn something. Is there anything in the history of the hotel that speaks of a buried treasure?"

Rebecca proceeded with caution. "Well, you know about the griffins, right? In the fountain, in the wallpaper, the stained glass windows. Used to be two flanking the Seventeenth Street entrance, and another one above the Grand Fireplace. Griffins in mythology are the guardians of mountain gold treasure. And it has long been rumored that during the hotel's construction, a treasure of gold was buried beneath it, and that the griffins placed around The Keep continue to guard it. I love the story, but as far as I know, it has no basis in fact."

"What if I told you there is a basis?"

Rebecca spluttered in mid-sip. "You mean *after* I blew latte through my nose?"

Manuel handed her a napkin and awaited her recovery.

"I would be skeptical, but intrigued," she said quietly.

"What I am going to tell you now is in strictest confidence. Can I entrust you with a most significant secret?"

Rebecca nodded solemnly.

"My brother Masons of Denver tell me that Freemasons throughout the territory, and later the state, acquired a significant portion of the gold extracted from Colorado mines. In the early years, they didn't trust banks, so they hid caches of their mines' outputs in secret locations, many of them in and around Denver. They say the largest golden cache of all was hidden under the Griffins Keep, with Edward Brooking's full knowledge and cooperation."

"I've always wanted to believe that," the historian confessed. "But what proof have you?"

Manuel glanced around the space, making sure that no one might overhear what he said next. "The Freemasons have a document, written by Brookings in 1910. He entrusted it to the lodge with the stipulation that it not be unsealed for 100 years."

"Why 100?"

"Ten times ten, another powerful number in numerology. And he knew that no one living at the time would be around a century later. The Freemasons opened the Brookings document in 2010. It described a treasure of golden ingots, deposited deep within the ground beneath Denver as an offering to the Deity-- and as the mystical source of financial power for the new city."

The contractor continued. "Brooking's document also revealed the location of the buried golden treasure, but it is in a riddle. I wrote it down." He withdrew a folded piece of paper from his briefcase on the floor between them. Reverently, he read:

> *The stone Madonna's heart of gold*
> *O'rsees a cache of wealth untold.*

212

"Stone Madonna?" Rebecca echoed. "There's no stone Madonna in the Griffins Keep. Never has been. It must refer to Pinnacle Church's marble statue of the Virgin Mary with the baptismal font. Not The Keep."

"So it seemed to the Freemasons who opened the document," Manuel said. "So sure were they about the meaning of the clue that they requested permission from the church leaders to search the area beneath the Virgin's statue with a metal detecting ground scanner."

"Did they find anything?"

"They found the remains of an old tunnel and some tracks leading toward The Keep about three meters down. But the 3D scans detected nothing that appeared to be a treasure, even when they probed ten meters beneath the church."

"I don't understand. Did someone find the treasure before 2010 and remove it?"

Manuel shrugged helplessly. "No one knows. It seems strange that Brookings' riddle leads nowhere. The Freemasons were always convinced the treasure was beneath the Griffins Keep. But the clue seems to point elsewhere, and the Pinnacle statue theory is a dead end. I was hoping you would know something about the hotel and its history that might solve the mystery."

"I'm so sorry, Manuel," Rebecca said with genuine regret. "Like I said, I know of no stone Madonna—or 'heart of gold'—ever existing in The Keep, unless it was in someone's private room. Could it have been hidden inside one of the hollow terra cotta blocks of the floors and interior walls? I understand many unexpected things have been discovered there over the decades."

"It is possible. I have no other idea. I am looking always as we tear into the structure to remodel bathrooms. Perhaps the Madonna—and the treasure she oversees—will never be found. And perhaps that is exactly what Edward Brookings and the Freemasons intended."


"At least as a designated local landmark, The Keep will fare better than the Metropolitan Building across Grand Avenue," Lochlan said. The Keep's 1880s neighbor had weathered multiple incarnations over the decades, housing at various times law offices, an investment firm, a restaurant, a theatre—even a

213

Buddhist temple in the 1970s. It was about to become a parking lot.

"Have you heard when the demolition is scheduled?" Rebecca asked.

"Next week, we're told," Lochlan said. "They plan to implode it. The dust will coat the hotel, Pinnacle Church, everything for blocks around. "Not that the Metropolitan was ever an architectural standout. But I always hate to see tangible history destroyed."

The engineer paused, then brightened. "On the plus side, that building should be coming down just in time."

"Just in time—for what?"

"You'll see," he said, smiling mysteriously. "If my calculations are right, it's going to blow you away."

The seven-story Metropolitan Building did not go quietly. The collapse of tons of brick and stone so shook the ground that many watching the demolition from inside The Keep feared for the integrity of the stained-glass skylight. Its survival testified to the skill of the master builders who designed and erected the hotel.

The suddenly exposed air space above the neighboring lot gapped the line of buildings along Grand Avenue like a tooth extraction. For the first time in anyone's memory, sky was actually visible from east-facing rooms on the lower floors of The Keep. Lochlan was ecstatic.

"Thursday morning, the 20th, 7:03," he told Rebecca. "Be here, front and center, just outside the Grand Entrance."

"Seven o'clock in the morning," she wailed. "I am *not* a morning person. It'll be cold. The sun won't even be up yet."

Lochlan grinned. "That's exactly the point."

On the chilly morning of the vernal equinox, Rebecca snuggled up to her coffee mug and stood with several others who had accepted Lochlan's invitation to witness the sunrise. Kevin from Security was there, Amy and a couple of open-minded co-workers from Engineering, Manuel the contractor, Dawn from Sales, and Lochlan's psychic astrologer friend Rosslyn. Commuters who cruised past on Grand in the pre-dawn light paid no attention to the strange group staring expectantly at the empty Metropolitan space.

The horizon itself was still obscured by a low building to the east of the demolition scar. But as the rising sun peered over its roof, affirmation of Lochlan's prediction spread before them on

214

the hotel's facade. The original entrance to the Griffins Keep was precisely positioned to align with the rays of the equinox dawn.

"I'll be damned," Kevin marveled. "You nailed it, dude."

"Magnifico!" Manuel raised his arms high and wide, as if to embrace the former entryway.

"I think the carving of Harrison C. Griffin looks happy," Amy declared with a smile of her own. "This is so cool!"

Rosslyn touched the stone on one side of the entrance arch. "I sense the whole building is energized," she said. "For the first time in many, many years, it is once again attuned to the sun in its journey across the heavens, as it was always meant to be."

Rebecca processed the evidence silently. This could not be coincidence. Lochlan was right. His contention that Freemasons imitated the Temple of Solomon in the hotel's creation seemed solidly plausible.

Throughout the morning, as word of the amazing phenomenon spread, hotel associates sneaked outside to see for themselves. Those who grasped the significance returned to their tasks invigorated by apparent proof of The Keep's inherent magic.

Rosslyn walked the building for quite some time after the equinox sunrise, reading the vibrations of the stone, both outside and within the walls. Rebecca encountered her midmorning in the Grand Salon.

"I knew you'd come," the psychic said. "The sun should be striking this center bay window right about now." Each of them grabbed a long metal rod to pull the heavy draperies apart. The sun's rays streamed into the room and illuminated a patch of onyx on the opposite wall. "Fantastic! Just as in the Temple, the sun at equinox shines between the two pillars."

Rebecca remembered Lochlan explaining that the support columns in the Salon were extensions of two onyx pillars that once flanked the entrance on the ground floor. Before the Kuhrsfelds enclosed those columns within a wall to create the Kipling space, they certainly would have framed this morning's rising sun. Rebecca felt the last of her skepticism melting.

The two women stepped simultaneously, as if responding to a secret signal, into the patch of sunlight, blinking in the brightness but relishing the warmth. A low humming sound made them both look up.

There in the ceiling fresco, the orb on the top of the archangel's scepter began to glow. It was not the sunlight that

215

illuminated it; the angle was all wrong. The illumination came—impossibly—from within the painting.

"Do you see it, too?" Rosslyn asked in a whisper.

Rebecca nodded. "What...?"

Before she could frame her question, she felt it. A tingling, like touching her tongue to a battery. A bit shocking, but not unpleasant. Weird. She turned to tell Rosslyn about the odd sensation, and found the astrologer staring at her wide-eyed.

"I've never seen anything like this. Are you OK?"

Rebecca smiled uneasily. "Honestly? I feel sort of like a vibrator set on low. Or like a hive full of bees. What's happening?"

"Hold out your arm and see for yourself," Rosslyn instructed, struggling to remain calm.

Rebecca did as directed. Her arm, her whole body, was glowing like the archangel's scepter. From overhead, a stream of opalescent light dipped down from the fresco like a tornadic funnel cloud, drenching her in a layer of luminescence. Rosslyn, untouched by the light, watched in amazement as what looked like living energy coalesced around the historian.

The humming grew louder, the tingling sensation more widespread. Rebecca felt like a little girl. She giggled like a little girl. "It tickles!'"

When she tried to brush off the glow coating her skin and clothes, her hands went right through it. A sense of well-being infused her. She stretched out her arms for balance and began to twirl around in a dervish of delight.

"What's going on in here?" Hotel ops manager Vince Murano burst into the Grand Salon and assessed the scene in an instant, annoyed. "Is this part of this equinox idiocy I've been hearing about all morning? Why are those draperies wide open to the sun? Do you want to fade the carpet?" He strode across the large room and jerked the window coverings closed. At the same instant he shut out the sun, the glow around Rebecca ebbed back up into the ceiling and blinked out.

"What business have you in here?" he challenged Rebecca. "I know of no tours scheduled today. You should be at your desk in Sales. Where's your name badge? And who on earth are you?" he demanded, turning to Rosslyn and frowning at her hippie-era outfit.

Rebecca recovered herself and shot back. "This woman happens to be a V.I.P. Sales client who arranged to see the Salon

216

specifically in the sunshine. She is planning a huge wedding for her daughter in July, and the photographer insists upon natural lighting for the ceremony and posed portraits."

Murano bowed his head in apology. "I do beg your pardon, Madam," he said, backing out of the room. "I'm confident you'll find the Griffins Keep a perfect setting for the celebration of your daughter's nuptials. Please excuse my interruption."

# CHAPTER 22

"It tickled?" Lochlan said when Rebecca and Rosslyn told him of the episode in the Grand Salon. "Seriously?"

Rebecca shrugged. "I don't know how else to describe it."

"Whatever it was, it had this sort of electrical charge to it," Rosslyn tried to explain. "All the little hairs on my arms and the back of my neck were standing on end. It was like an aura...only something more than that. Like an aura of favor, a visible blessing."

"An aureole?" Lochlan speculated. "A sort of full-body halo. That has to be a good thing."

"A very good thing," Rosslyn confirmed. "Have to confess I was envious."

"But why me? I don't understand." Rebecca's confusion scarcely muted the euphoria that lingered still. For a few moments she'd felt carefree and childlike. No, not childlike exactly. Ageless. If she could bottle that sensation and market it to menopausal women, her fortune would be made.

Rosslyn considered the mystery. "From what I've just witnessed," she said at length, "I have to conclude that the hotel spirits have a special affinity for you, Rebecca. Maybe because you keep the past alive.by sharing the history. Maybe because you identify so strongly with the place. Whatever the reason, they like you. And I sense that they're counting on you to advocate for them somehow."

Lochlan fixed his gaze upon the historian, but he spoke to the astrologer. "Rebecca's connection to The Keep is like no one else's. I have faith that the role she's meant to play will be revealed very soon."

The remodeling of floors three through seven continued apace over the next month. Occasionally, when she was feeling masochistic, Rebecca would walk the level currently under destruction. The carpets were installed first, so for several weeks, the guestrooms absurdly combined that bold floorcovering with the Victorian-style furnishings.

"The design firm's notes claim this pattern compliments the filigreed design of The Keep's balcony railings," Lochlan said. "But it reminds me of something else...Can't quite place it yet."

On the rust-red and mustard-colored background, the black pattern featured two crossed barbed spears or spikes within an inverted triangle. Two sides of the triangle crossed and extended into curled ends, embellished with a dual wing-shaped accent centered between them. The hideous oversized design repeated again and again, crawling across the hallways and into the guestrooms.

"It reminds me of some cheap Vegas hotel," Rebecca declared.

The walls on all the lower floors were recovered in one night. Employees arrived that morning to find the flowered wallpaper completely obliterated by slick black lacquer. Stark, severe, and blank, the effect was beyond soulless. It was actually soul-sucking.

"The idea is to make the railing panels 'pop' when viewed from the lobby,'" Lochlan explained, parroting the designer's press release once again. "Gotta say it edges out the mirrors flanking the toilets in every guest room for Most Heinous Decorating Misfire. Who the hell thought guests would want to see themselves sitting on the john, endlessly reflected on both sides into infinity?"

Rebecca felt sick. "How can you make light of it?" she challenged him. The new look was many things. Funny was not one of them.

The room contents began to arrive—the FF&E in hospitality industry lingo: Furniture, Fixtures and Equipment. One March afternoon, when Rebecca took a tour group down the stairs from

220

eight to seven for the view, the doors to all the rooms on six gaped open. Their dark, curved bed headboards leaned against the hallway walls, surrounding the atrium space like tombstones. By the time the tour concluded and she grabbed her cellphone to photograph the ephemeral sight, the headboards were gone forever.

Days later, Rebecca steeled herself to inspect the New Look overtaking the first floors. From room to room she gamboled, peering inside, sometimes entering. The cumulative effect was about as cozy as a filing cabinet. Cold. Vapid. Zombie rooms.

"So, I saw you prowling around the sixth floor yesterday," Ms. Jordan said the next morning. "What's your take on our new décor?"

Rebecca hesitated. "Is that a polite inquiry, or do you really want my opinion?"

"I think I can handle honest feedback."

"OK. I hate it," the historian declared without apology.

Ms. Jordan smiled. "Good," she said.

"Good?"

"Yes, good. That's exactly what I wanted to hear. You see, Rebecca, you're not the demographic we're aiming for with the new look. Focus groups show it will appeal to the younger professionals and families—a whole new consumer base of millennials."

"Did those focus groups include any of our regular guests? Did they include any staff who interact with our guests on a daily basis and who understand what they value about this hotel? If you ask me, we're shooting ourselves in the foot. This 'trending' guestroom décor will be off-putting to guests seeking historic hotel ambiance, the heritage tourists, and people who have been coming to the Griffins Keep for decades."

"Heritage tourism is a fading fad. And people who've been coming here for decades are old," Ms. Jordan stated flatly.

"They're also affluent," Rebecca countered, "and discerning. They expect a certain level of excellence and elegance, and I don't see them embracing this generic 'refreshing.' At the same time, I seriously doubt that room décor will be enough to attract new clientele looking for an ultra-modern hotel experience. You can't change the classical architecture of the lobby." *Or could they?* Certainly R. J. Kuhrsfeld had done his best to reshape it in the

221

1930s. There was nothing to stop TITHE from implementing any alterations they chose.

"Yes, well, Rebecca, when you earn your MBA we'll continue this discussion. Until then, I expect you to get onboard with the changes and present them on your tours with unreserved enthusiasm. Do I make myself clear?"

"Clear as the plexiglass on the new nightstands," Rebecca replied.


Reports of unexplained phenomena throughout the hotel increased dramatically as remodeling efforts amped up over the next several weeks. A construction crew member told Manuel that he saw a sofa he had just installed in a suite collapse under an invisible weight. Two other workmen refused to return to a room where they saw a dark vaporous cloud escape from the hollow terra cotta blocks of a bathroom wall they had begun to demolish.

One guest saw indistinct figures reflected in the huge mirrors flanking the toilet in his redesigned room. Another was awoken by the crash of an oversized picture falling off the wall and a menacing male voice saying, "Leave it."

A housekeeper cleaning a recently remodeled room swore that she felt something brush past her shoulder right before the TV and radio came on simultaneously at full volume.

Moans from inside the walls. Strange shadows outside upper-story windows.

The most bizarre incident happened in the basement by the pantry service elevator. A prep cook reported that something yanked his pant leg hem so hard that it knocked him off his feet. "So I'm sprawled on the floor and I hear a voice right beside my ear say, 'Gotcha, Sparky.' That's what Max Barnes always used to call me."

When Kevin replayed the security tape from the time the cook indicated, a dark column moved into the picture just before his fall and then instantly disappeared.

"The spirits are even more unsettled than before," Margaret reported when Rebecca asked her and Molly to come by the hotel one rainy afternoon in May.

Molly agreed. "Very disturbed, unhappy. Out of balance and uncentered."

222

"Like everyone else here," Rebecca said. "But what can any of us do about it?"

Margaret looked up from their seats in the lobby and cast her gaze about the atrium balconies, then at Molly. Her fellow medium, perceiving similar messages, answered the question in her eyes with a nod.

"The good sir knights, the Knights Templar overseeing The Keep, are carefully watching these developments. They've set sentries at all the guestroom doors, keeping the benevolent spirits shut inside, preventing them from mingling with dangerous new forces arising within The Keep. These dark entities have been summoned by unconscionable men of power, living and dead, scheming together."

Margaret paused and took both Rebecca's hands in hers.

"The protective spirits have been waiting for you to ask what you can do. There is a role for you, Rebecca, a role no one else can play. I'm hearing that the Knights will be calling upon you when the time is near."

"The time for what?"

The medium released Rebecca's hands and shrugged helplessly. "That's all I got. I'm sorry. But I have the sense that it's very important. *You're* very important."

Later, as the mediums walked toward their parked cars, Molly said, "I'm glad you didn't tell her the rest of it."

"I couldn't," Margaret replied sadly. "What good would it do for her to know she may not survive the ordeal that lies ahead?"


"Hey yo, history lady—What's your name?" the visiting Chad Tagawa called out one day as she traversed the lobby.

"I'm Rebecca Bridger."

"Yeah, right. So Becks, we've never really talked, and I just wanted to say hey."

"Hey."

"Ya know, even though we don't really need all that history stuff anymore, I think you sorta represent the hotel to a lotta people."

"Thank you?" Rebecca said, not certain what he meant by the statement.

223

"Because you're sorta like from another time and old. And you probably used to be pretty good looking, but you could use some work, you know what I mean?"

She stared at him. "You're not very good with people, are you, Mr. Tagawa?"

He grinned. "Don't hafta be," he said, "when I've got more money than God." He backpedaled when she didn't smile. "Kidding! I'm totally kidding about the God thing."

Rebecca shook her head and started away. "Please don't feel obliged to speak to me again."

On the mezzanine level, she opened one of the tall, heavy doors to the Grand Salon and halted, aghast. In the center of the room, a huge tarp covered the floor. Three workmen on ladders were assaulting the ceiling fresco. Mickey Branson himself was directing the vandalism.

"Can't have religious-themed art harshing The Keep's new fam-fun vibe," he explained to the historian with a wave and a smile.

"But...but that painting dates back to the hotel's opening," she protested feebly.

"No duh. And it's totally depressing! Makes people think of church and shit. We're gonna replace it with a wizard or fairies— something more popular. Angels, gawd. Whoever thought they belonged in a hotel?"

She stood watching the casual obliteration of The Keep's celestial guardians with horror. "Does Stan Tagawa know about this?"

"Oh yeah, of course. His orders, actually. He and Chad hate this thing. Stan wants it gone by his visit Friday."

Two of the workmen slathered plaster around the perimeter of the painting, working their way inwards. Knowing the answer, Rebecca asked, nonetheless. "What's the guy with the scraper doing?"

"Trying to chip the gold off those swords before they cover it all up. Don't know what we can do with it, but it must be worth something."

Rebecca stared as one archangel after another disappeared beneath fresh ceiling plaster.

"Wait!" she cried, suddenly animated. Impulsively grasping Branson's upper arm, she pointed upward. "Don't let them cover up the orb on the Dominion's scepter."

224

Mickey glanced at her grip on his arm, then up at the fresco. "Why not?"

"Well, because," she began, releasing him and stepping back, "Because it's got kind of a magical quality, you know? It could probably be incorporated into the new design somehow, like a crystal ball or a fairy wand or something."

The managing director considered her suggestion. "A crystal ball? Yeah, maybe. It does have that cool glowy effect.

"Leave that weird ball thing in the center uncovered for now, you guys," he told the plasterers. "We'll let the artist have a look and see if she wants to use it."

Rebecca breathed a sigh of relief at her temporary victory. When she returned to the Salon later that day, nothing of the fresco remained but the Dominion's ethereal orb in the center. Even with the lights off, it radiated eerily. Rebecca smiled, recalling the sun's effect upon it on equinox morning. The orb's presence was important. Of that she was certain, without understanding why.


In a city which boasted 300+ days of sunshine a year, rain was a rare occurrence. Some people were oblivious to the weather, their moods unaffected by dreary skies and damp atmosphere. Not so for Rebecca. Like many lifelong Coloradans, she was spoiled by the high, dry climate.

This rainy May morning depressed her more than usual. She felt defeated, unanchored by all the physical disruptions at the Griffins Keep. She bemoaned the incremental wane of elegance. The historic hotel was not alone in its rush to mediocrity. With ongoing "urban infill," much of downtown Denver was keeping apace.

Members of the Past Timers, a loose association of local historians who had long lunched each Friday afternoon at the Wynkoop Brewery, lamented the transformation of the surrounding LoDo environs as its historic brick warehouse district was overshadowed by what some of them characterized as "Soviet Block architecture." The hastily erected square, featureless buildings were too dull to be called ugly. Architectural continuity, compliment, and balance were nowhere to be found in the cretinous conglomeration, evidencing not a penny nor an instant spent on aesthetic design or detail. No individuality. No character.

The Past-Timers included both amateur and professional historians. A few stalwarts constituted the core group—the retired judge, the city auditor, the ghost town photographer, the university press editor. Others drifted in by invitation upon occasion to talk about their history projects and to seek opinions or expertise. The dynamic assemblage was endlessly fascinating, and Rebecca joined in whenever she could. The beer never failed to stimulate lively discussion.

"Still working at The Keep?" the judge asked her as he drained his Railyard Ale that warm May afternoon. "I hear it was bought by Californians. Lord save us from parasitic real estate investors!" He raised his empty glass and clinked Rebecca's. "Waiter, another here, if you please!"

"Still there," Rebecca confirmed, "fighting to keep history from oblivion. What are you working on these days, Judge? Finish that book on Dwight Eisenhower's paintings?"

"At long last, yes. Put that one to bed about a month ago. I've moved on now to a biography of the flamboyant deco-era architect Baylor Templeton. Interesting character. Quite the *bon vivant* ladies' man in the 30s and 40s, it turns out. Never let marriages cramp his style. Actually came across a great story about Templeton and the Griffins Keep the other day that might interest you."

"I'd love to hear it. Didn't know there was a connection between the two."

"Oh, my yes. The hotel hosted most of Templeton's notorious wild parties—both during and after Prohibition. Apparently The Keep was the place to go if you had the money for premium liquor. Brought it in through ex-patriate friends of the hotel living in Europe and Canada, the Caribbean and South America. Templeton soirees were never 'dry'—nor dull. They say the most desirable women in the West graced his gatherings."

"Go on."

"Well, according to one of Templeton's stepchildren that I interviewed, in the midst of one of these Dionysian affairs, a female guest—probably a call girl—who apparently overindulged in alcohol or other substances, actually expired of heart failure in the middle of the party. Rather than put a damper on the festivities, Templeton ordered Keep banquet employees to move her body onto a table by the wall and cover it with a tablecloth. And the party continued unabated until dawn."

A chill ran across the back of Rebecca's neck. "They covered her body with a tablecloth?"

"So I'm told. Seems a bit callous, I must say. But that was Templeton's style."

"She wore a crimson gown," Rebecca said without thinking.

"Beg pardon?" The judge cupped a hand to his bad ear.

"Oh, nothing. Never mind. But I think I'll join you in a second ale."


Of course Rebecca had to tell Lochlan about her sighting in the Silver Spoon when the judge's revelation seemed to bring it full circle. But the story Lochlan shared in return was stranger by far.

"Rosslyn came in Sunday when I got off work. She senses the dangerous level of disturbance around here, even when she's miles away. Somehow The Keep called to her, she said. Thought maybe she could help to reassure the spirits, restore some balance. So she brought Miranda, and we prowled around awhile."

"Were they able to calm the ghosts?"

Lochlan dropped his gaze and shook his head. "If ghosts were all we encountered, it might have been fine" he said. "But this was something else altogether."

Rebecca had never seen him so distraught. He wrung his hands as he paced the floor of the empty Club and avoided looking her in the eyes.

"From the moment she saw it, Roz recognized this pattern in the new carpet as sigils."

"A what?"

"A sigil. It's a magical symbol which represents a fallen angel or demon. Sigils were used in the Middle Ages to conjure demons and to compel them to carry out the magician's will and desire."

"Sounds like what R. J. Kuhrsfeld attempted in the Grand Salon in the 1930s," Rebecca realized with rising horror.

The look in Lochlan's eyes as he glanced up confirmed her suspicion.

"And Stan Tagawa—"

"—as Joe Kuhrsfeld's ardent pupil, would have learned about R.J.'s forays into the realm of the occult," Lochlan concluded. "Ancient 'magick' was essentially the supernatural manipulation of reality and unseen powers to carry out your bidding, Stan Tagawa may believe he can succeed where R.J. failed."

227

"The guest rooms directly above the old Grand Entrance have been taken out of inventory since the remodeling began," Rebecca reported. "919, 921, 923, 925—all in the center of the Grand Avenue side. Front desk tells me they've been strictly off-limits for weeks now. Not even housekeepers are allowed in."

"Nor engineers. We're told the Tagawas have reserved that block of rooms for 'confidential gatherings' for which invited participants begin to arrive around midnight."

"God forbid you're right about what's going on up there," Rebecca almost whispered. "Could such things really go on in this day and age?"

Lochlan shook his head. "You were right to despise these new decorative features of The Keep, Rebecca. Through them, something very dark is eclipsing The Keep's positive light. And poor Miranda suffered its assault directly."

Rebecca remembered that Sunday had been a wildly stormy night. Sheets of wind-driven rain had lashed at her windows for hours.

"The overhead lights here in the Club were off, and the space was illuminated only by city light filtered through stained glass panes," Lochlan began. "Just as a gust of wind rattled the northside windows, Miranda cried out. Something had grabbed her and was pulling her down. Roz hurried to her side, and I managed to snap a flash picture on my cell phone.

"The girl was on her knees, her head straining sideways toward the floor as if she were being yanked by the hair, until she toppled over completely, one side of her face smashed into the carpet. Rosslyn grasped her shoulders with both hands and tried to pull her up. The two of them rolled one over another until they were several feet from the spot—right over there. Miranda shuddered as Roz got to her feet and backed even farther away from the invisible sinkhole. I rushed over to steady her, asked if she was OK, then went to Miranda. Curled up fetal-like on the floor, she nodded that she was unhurt, but she couldn't stop trembling."

Rebecca tried to imagine the bizarre scene. "Can we please get out of here?" she said, hastening toward the entry way. She followed Lochlan through a door into the service stairway space where they could continue in private.

"What on earth happened, do you think?"

228

"Nothing on earth," said Lochlan, clearly still mystified. "After several tense moments, Rosslyn drew a deep breath and said 'It's gone now. I've never felt anything like that. Huge. Dark. Primordial.'

"When I asked what she meant, she turned back and stared at the floor where her daughter had been pulled down. 'I felt it when I grabbed Miranda,' Roz said. 'Something primitive and terrifying.'

"That's when I remembered the picture I'd snapped," Lochlan said, withdrawing the phone from his pocket to show Rebecca. He searched for the shot he'd taken at the moment of Miranda's attack and handed the device to Rebecca with a warning glance.

She couldn't believe her eyes. Behind Miranda's shoulder, blurred but nonetheless unmistakable, a claw-like shadow, looming larger than the girl herself.

"Rosslyn begged me not to let Miranda see it," he said, gently taking back his phone and re-pocketing it, "and I never will. Only later was Roz able to speak of the terrible entity again.

"Whatever it was, she sensed that it predates Time itself," Lochlan continued. "It's been here since the land was covered by an ancient sea, before the mountains were pushed up. It came from a place even deeper than the source of The Keep's well."

"How could it reach the surface?" Rebecca almost whispered the question. "And why now?"

"Has to be connected with the alterations to the building and its contents," Lochlan replied, "and with whatever rituals Tagawa and co-horts are practicing on the ninth floor. Miranda seems to be the random element that drew it out."

# CHAPTER 23

The Denver Woman's Press Club was one of the oldest women's press clubs in the country. It was also Rebecca's favorite affiliation. Their mission since 1898, "To Drive Dull Care Away," said it all. Great-Aunt Frankie had been an active member, responsible for most of the fundraising that had allowed the DWPC to purchase their historic clubhouse. She'd often invited young Becky as her guest to special press club events and programs, and the ladies had sort of adopted her. Years later, when Rebecca sold Frankie's Cripple Creek newspaper office to the big casino company, she'd donated a large percentage of the proceeds to her great-aunt's beloved DWPC and their scholarship fund. And when her article on the history of Griffins Keep had been accepted by *Colorado Heritage* magazine, Rebecca had taken advantage of her new "published writer" status to officially join.

"Thank you for inviting me this evening to present 'Gentlewomen of the Griffins Keep,'" Rebecca began one mild spring night in early May. "I welcome this opportunity to examine that half of the population often overlooked in tales of Denver's days of old, and of the pioneering West in general. My presentation today profiles a dozen ladies with ties to the city's most elegant hotel. Taken together, their stories shed light on the changing personal, social, professional and political roles of women over the more than thirteen decades the Griffins Keep has reigned as the Great Lady of Denver hotels."

Her PowerPoint slides highlighted the feminine aspects of the hotel's early history, and prominent guests including Sara Bernhardt and Queen Marie of Romania. Mrs. Dawson Thorne and Mrs. R.J. Kuhrsfeld were featured, of course, as were obscure hotel employees, such as 1930s stenographer Mrs. Wright and executive housekeeper Marjory Crispin. Rebecca's program ended with her tribute to the first hotel historian, Charlotte Woods, "who unearthed the treasures I was privileged to mine for these wonderful stories." Charlotte, too, had belonged to the DWPC, and many remembered her fondly.

Rebecca always reserved time at the end of her program for questions and comments. Listeners often enjoyed sharing Keep stories of their own.

"Does the hotel still have lace curtains in all the windows?" a long-retired reporter asked.

"Lace curtains? Oh, no, I'm afraid they haven't had those in a long time. Everybody wants light-blocking shades these days."

"What's happening with The Keep under the new ownership?" another writer wanted to know.

Rebecca hesitated. Did she use this question to practice optimism and objectivity? The ladies of the press club deserved to hear the truth.

"Speaking not as a hotel associate, but as an individual concerned about the future of a Denver icon, I have to tell you that the changes happening under the TITHE management are breaking my heart. History is being squelched there. Physically and strategically, they're doing everything they can to obliterate the Keep's past, eschewing its traditional elegance and refinement in favor of cheap entertainment."

The DWPC audience was one of the few with whom she felt comfortable using words like *eschew*. It was also one she was confident would empathize with her viewpoint. Murmurs of disapproval and concern rippled through the room.

"But isn't the building protected from alteration by its historic landmark designation?"

"That's a common misconception," Rebecca replied. "Landmark status only applies to exterior changes and prohibits demolition of the structure. Inside, the owners can change whatever they want."

"But what about The Keep's legendary service and high standards of excellence? Surely those endure."

232

She knew it was disloyal, even risky, to reveal anything negative about her employers. But the encouragement implicit in this conclave of like-minded women overruled Rebecca's cautionary instincts. She spilled. The lowered housekeeping standards, chronic short staffing, discontinuation of Afternoon Tea and live music, abandonment of all the special little touches that once distinguished the Griffins Keep—all came tumbling out. The reaction was predictable outrage.

"Well, it's obvious we have to do something about this before it goes any further," one outspoken magazine editor declared. The group at large applauded her intention. Everyone had fond memories of The Keep, none of which included bouncy castles.

"No, please, ladies! I couldn't agree with you more. But we really need to think this through before doing anything rash or antagonizing."

"Who's antagonizing?" demanded a prominent local author. "I'd call it challenging. Objecting. Protesting. That's our right— and our responsibility—as concerned citizens when we learn about something we love going to shit."

*Going to shit.* The ember of a subversive idea began to glow in Rebecca's mind.

"Now, we don't want to make things difficult on the job for Becky," another older member said, appealing to the cooler heads among them. Turning to Rebecca, she continued, "Don't you worry, dear. You just think about what we can do to help bring the Keep's plight to the attention of others who care about the hotel's reputation and its future, and then let us know. We're all behind you."

It was just what Rebecca needed to hear. The ghost of Great-Aunt Frankie prodded her to action. *Drive dull care away.* She smiled conspiratorially and began, "Well, if you're up for a little passive-aggressive demonstration, I do have a suggestion."


Afternoon Tea in the Griffins Keep lobby had been discontinued altogether. But groups meeting in the hotel could still request Afternoon Tea as a catering option on Fridays and Sundays. Within the week, the DWPC had booked their event.

"We have reserved the Griffins Keep Silver Spoon Club from 1:00 to 2:00 next Friday for Afternoon Tea," reported the e-newsletter. "Hats are strongly encouraged—the bigger the better.

And bags large enough to conceal our 'ammunition' are a must. Come one, come all, to make your disapproval known. And be sure to get the word out to your media friends that the 2:15 photo opp is not to be missed."

RSVPs were so numerous that the smaller Silver Spoon venue had to be upgraded to the former Grand Salon to accommodate the more than sixty press club ladies and their invited guests. Like every other space in The Keep, the Grand Salon had been "reimagined." It was now the Throne Room. The Victorian-style loomed carpet had been replaced by slate tiles. The imposing center bay window, once framed with damask and lace panels, was now draped in cheap red velveteen. On either side, elevated, exaggerated regal chairs dominated the décor. Gilded with garish gold spray paint and glitter, the "thrones" looked more like old shoeshine chairs than royal perches. Perfect props for selfies and posers.

"I remember when a bunch of us did sit-ins in the old Silver Spoon back in the 70s, before they allowed women in the place," a retired lawyer-turned-writer recalled wistfully. "What a scandal we created!"

Ninety-six-year-old columnist and local legend Polly Patterson, who had known Rebecca's great-aunt well, was less sentimental. "I remember when this city aspired to the aesthetic and the sublime. Looking around downtown and The Keep today, that vision seems tragically absent. I'm just glad Frankie didn't live to see this place settle for tacky mediocrity."

Rebecca distanced herself from the DWPC Tea for plausible deniability. She was scheduled to do a site tour for some important potential clients at 2:00. The press club had intentionally timed their own agenda to coincide. It also just so happened that the Governor typically wrapped- up his usual Friday lunch at the Pirates Pub right around 2:00.

"Thank you so much for a lovely Tea," the ladies made a point to tell the staff as they trickled out of the Throne Room, resisting the urge to add how much the ambiance left to be desired.

Some went to the mezzanine Powder Room; others made their way directly to the elevators. Within fifteen minutes, all sixty-plus saboteurs had made their way to the seventh-floor. They positioned themselves around the balcony to completely surround the atrium. Frankie's old colleague, Polly, had been given the honor of signaling the commencement.

With drill team precision, the ladies of the press—and a few gentleman friends—prepared for the assault. From bags and briefcases they withdrew rolls of toilet paper. Each grasped the sheet at the end of the roll. When Polly raised her hand and snapped her fingers, they tossed the rolls out into the open atrium space.

The simultaneous unfurling of so many streamers of tissue was magical. By the time they reached the lobby ninety feet below, all that remained of most of the rolls was the cardboard tubes. Confused and curious onlookers, including many members of the media, picked up the tubes and found them pre-stuffed with propaganda.

"Don't Crap Out the Keep"

"Stop the History Wipe"

"Chic is Shit"

"Don't Piss on the Past"

"Join the T.P. Party—Boycott Griffins Keep!"

Bemused visitors and staff shuffled through drifts of unspooled tissue. Many of them looked up and waved at the unrepentant vandals or gave thumbs-up salutes. The spectacle was captured by at least two local TV news crews and several media photographers. Within minutes, it was all over Facebook and YouTube.

The Governor retrieved a cardboard tube from the floor and chuckled as he read the message inside. "'Bout time somebody said it," he commented to his entourage.

TITHE management was not amused.

"That group is *never* allowed in the Griffins Keep again," Ms. Jordan declared in concluding the weekly sales team meeting the next Monday morning.

"But how exactly will that work?" Dawn asked innocently. "Of course we'll never book another event for the women's press club, but how can you keep them out, really? The building is open to the public, day and night. Is Security going to make everyone show their club membership cards? Search every bag for rolls of T.P.?"

"All any of you need to know is that we're working on a procedure for dealing with this kind of publicity stunt," Ms. Jordan snapped. "Now that's all for this morning. Back to work, everybody."

Having been seated on the far side of the room, Rebecca was the last to leave Ms. Jordan's office. As the manager shuffled

235

papers and stuffed them in a file folder, she said, "These Denver people seem to think they have some personal stake in what happens with the hotel. An absurd proprietary sense, like it's any of their business. You'd think we were defacing the place with obscene graffiti or something. I just don't get it."

"No," the former hotel historian agreed quietly, "You don't."


For the time being, at least, TITHE was keeping its hands off the Spa. Remodeling disruptions aside, business there continued as usual, luxurious and lucrative. Their overpriced line of haircare products was the only one that Rebecca's thinning hair seemed to benefit from. Heading across the lobby to replenish her supplies that morning, she had to give a wide berth to the workmen ripping up chunks of the floor for the installation of some new TITHE feature, the specifics of which were being kept secret.

Approaching the Spa entrance, Rebecca marveled again at the craftsmanship of the polished onyx which once framed the Keep's Grand Fireplace. She envisioned the only historic photograph which showed the griffin originally mounted above the mantel. For the first time, it occurred to the historian that, of all the griffins depicted around The Keep, the fireplace guardian was the only one with its sword pointing downward, rather than held upright.

*Pointing..... Pointing to what?*

Mentally recreating the mythological creature's position, her mind's eye plotted an invisible line from its sword tip to the right hand side of the Spa entrance—and to the enigmatic darker pattern in the semi-precious stone, reverently identified by the old Hispanic woman months ago.

It had been right there, in plain sight all along. The secret posed by Edward Brooking's riddle.

> *The stone Madonna's heart of gold,*
> *O'rsees a cache of wealth untold.*

The magnitude of the epiphany staggered her. The legendary treasure buried beneath the Griffins Keep and guarded by Knights Templar for more than a century—It had to be here, somewhere below the sacred image revealed and deliberately placed by master stone masons—Freemasons.

236

Rebecca glanced with trepidation at the workmen tearing up the floor. Did they know how close they were? Was that the explanation for their mysterious project? No. TITHE couldn't know. They didn't have the clue. They didn't have the vision to put the pieces together. Rebecca did. At last she understood. And she believed.

Contractors and hotel engineers could be heard toiling on the mezzanine above her. Bursting with revelation, Rebecca went in search of Manuel and Lochlan, the two men whose knowledge of hidden history had engendered her insight and who would know—hopefully—what should be done about it.

Manuel's eyes widened as Rebecca revealed the potential hiding place of the Keep's golden treasure. The contractor shook his head and smiled at his own blindness.

"A good Christian all my life," he said at last, "Yet I have walked by this image of the Virgin Mary a hundred times over the past few months and never seen it."

"Why would you?" Rebecca said. "It's just a discoloration in the stone. The pattern used to be partially obscured by a band of onyx about seven-feet high. All the columns in the atrium were banded at that same height. As best I can make out from old photographs, the bands were removed sometime in the 1930s. Probably part of R.J. Kuhrsfeld's attempts to strip The Keep of its mystical powers."

Lochlan studied the image, marveling. "It fits with the Knights Templars history," he said. "It was religious faith that inspired the true 'Soldiers of the Cross' in their quest to regain the Holy Land for Christianity. They served the Church and pledged allegiance to the Pope—and the Holy Mother. They invoked her strength and prayed to her for victory. The crusading knights sought the Virgin's favor with their valor in battling the Arab infidels."

"So Mary's likeness would be the perfect marker for what the Knights Templar held sacred and precious."

"The Keep's buried treasure."

"Wow," the construction boss and the engineer murmured simultaneously, trying to appear nonchalant as the threesome strolled away from the spa entryway stone.

237

"Now what?" Rebecca asked when they'd found a quiet corner away from others' earshot.

"Now we delve," Lochlan said. "Manuel, you have a friend with a metal detector, right?"

"The newest best imaging ground scanner," Manuel confirmed.

"We're lucky they're doing all this work in the lobby, tearing up the floor. Shouldn't be too hard to convince Security that scanning the area is all part of the job. How soon can you arrange for your friend and his equipment?"

"For this? Tonight. How can we wait? My friend, he is an expert with the device. He has located many valuable objects in the ground. He is also a Masonic brother. He can be trusted."


"I still can't believe they didn't let you go along," Maureen said as she and Rebecca sat nursing drinks and killing time at Baby Doe's Irish Pub, a block away from the Griffins Keep, "especially since it was you who told them where to look."

Rebecca drummed impatient fingers on the bar. "It's killing me," she admitted. "But they were right to do this without me. Lochlan and Manuel and his friend Gregorio are all well known to the hotel security staff. Their poking around the current lobby construction won't arouse suspicion. My presence there at 9:00 at night, on the other hand, would be difficult to explain."

"I suppose."

"Lucky thing there aren't any big events planned in the hotel this evening. Fewer potential witnesses to worry about."

"Corporeal witnesses, at any rate," Mo half-teased. "You can bet The Keep spirits—especially the Templar knights overseeing the place—will be paying rapt attention to the gentlemen with the mysterious underground scanning device."

"What if they actually discover something? What would it mean?"

"Well, for one thing, it would confirm all those treasure rumors that have floated around since before the hotel opened. For another, it would prove that there are secrets in The Keep's past we can only guess at. Always good to pull the rug out from under complacent historians, if you ask me. They're such know-it-alls. Need their perceptions of the past rocked every now and then. And, by extension, their perceptions of the present."

238

Rebecca smiled at her roommate's jibe and clinked her raised glass to Mo's. "Here's to totally rocked historians, among whom I count myself foremost at this moment. And to unexpected paradigm shifts that allow us to see in the dark.

"What's taking those guys so long?"


The Surf's Up security guard on duty in the basement glanced up from his PC just long enough to acknowledge the three familiar workmen heading for the service stairs.

"Hold on a minute, guys," he ordered just before Gregorio ducked out of sight. "Is that a metal detector you've got there?"

Gregorio paused but did not falter. "Yes, it is," he said. "Do you know something of them, my friend?"

The guard smiled broadly. "Hell yeah, I know something of 'em," he said. "My crazy brother-in-law's like an amateur treasure hunter. Lemme see that thing."

Gregorio had no choice but to oblige. Lochlan and Manuel backtracked to flank him.

"Whoa! State-of-the-art 3D deep-scan imager. Oscilloscope, value bar. real-time analysis of target depth, shape, size and type. These mutha's cost a shitload," he said, checking out the instrument. "Lookin' for buried treasure yourselves?"

The three chuckled jovially.

"If only," Lochlan said. "Much more exciting than scoping out plumbing. No, we're just supposed to pinpoint the location of buried pipes so the new lobby feature installation doesn't puncture any of them. Pretty routine. Pretty boring, I'm afraid."

The guard frowned. "I'd think you'd have schematics for that sort of thing."

"Schematics, sure. But there've been so many alterations to The Keep over time, this is the only way to be sure exactly what's where, you know?"

"Yeah, OK," the guard said. "Seems pretty late for you guys to be working, though."

Manuel shrugged. "Tell us about it," he said. "Just when we thought we were done for the day, we are told we must have this completed by morning."

"Work's a bitch, all right," the guard empathized. "You guys'll let me know if you find any golden stash, right?"

The workmen laughed at the idea.

239

"You'll be the first to know, amigo," Manuel assured him as they turned again to climb the stairs to the lobby level.

As they made their way toward the right-hand side of the former Grand Fireplace, Lochlan and his two co-conspirators cast wary glances about the atrium lobby.

Gregorio set right to work, sweeping the floor beside the Madonna pattern in the onyx with the detector head. The oscilloscope automatically compensated for the magnetic and electrical effect s of the soil and mineral strata at various depths. The LCD screen displayed images of the layers beneath the surface. "This depth analysis feature can detect underground cavities and chambers," he explained as they watched the display intently.

Nothing unusual. Was Rebecca's hunch wrong? Gregorio pushed the detector right up to the base of the stone entrance below the Virgin Mary. She seemed to gaze down at it serenely.

"Look! There's something here. A shaft, much too regular and squared for a natural feature. This was made by man."

"How deep is that?" Lochlan asked.

"About fiften meters. As deep as this head can probe."

"The shaft obviously goes deeper," Manuel said.

Gregorio reached into a canvas bag of accessories. "This large head can see even farther down," he said, attaching it to the probe. "Generally, the longer the target has been buried, the more it will have oxidized and the greater the depth at which it can be detected."

"The value bar identifies targets as one of four categories," Manuel explained. "Gold, Valuable, Steel, or Iron. It can also detect non-metallic containers."

Their eyes never left the screen as Gregorio methodically moved the larger head around the stone column. The squared shaft appeared to continue. Down and down. At 21 meters, it opened out into a large cavity, made visible by a red line on the screen.

"Now we're getting somewhere." Manuel could scarcely contain the excitement they all felt.

Within the chamber, the imager detected a non-metallic object, a box or a trunk, 4.8 meters long by 2.6 meters wide by 3.3 meters high, buried beneath the lobby floor.

"Damn! That's gotta be as big as a dumpster." Before Lochlan could ask what it was, the value bar displayed the answer in large red letters.

"GOLD"

The engineer quickly computed the mental math. "Nearly 40 cubic meters of gold!" he calculated, astonished. "How many solid ingots would that equate to?"

His compatriots stared at the display, momentarily too stunned to move or to think.

"Turn off the screen." Manuel ordered Gregorio, quietly but urgently. "There are surveillance cameras in the lobby. They must not see."

His friend complied instantly. "There is a treasure here," he whispered breathlessly. "The largest treasure I have ever found, by far."

# CHAPTER 24

The pleased pirate expression on Lochlan's face as he approached the bar telegraphed his announcement.

"It's real."

Rebecca and Mo leapt from their stools and embraced him simultaneously. Other Baby Doe's patrons looked over, wondering at their public display of elation.

"I can't believe it," the historian exclaimed in a whisper.

"Believe it. It's real. And it's huge. But we can't talk here." He grabbed Mo's drink, downed the last of it, and tossed a fifty-dollar bill on the table. "My place is nearby. Let's go."

"Where are Manuel and Gregorio?" Rebecca asked as they hurried from the pub.

"Still at The Keep, pretending to do a little work in the lobby, trying to take it all in, no doubt. You were right about the hiding place," he said, embracing her impulsively. "That beautiful Madonna kept her secret from all but you. Gawd damn, this is exciting! Wait'll you hear just *how* exciting. It exceeds even the most farfetched of my crazy expectations. They weren't crazy! I'm not crazy! The Freemasons' secret treasure exists."

Lochlan's Capitol Hill apartment occupied one side of a turn-of-last-century stone duplex. Floor-to-ceiling bookshelves covered two walls of the front room. Through an arched doorway, Rebecca glimpsed part of a piano and a music stand. A polished brass magnifying glass on a stand flashed in the lamplight on a rolltop desk by the bay windows.

"Please, sit ladies." Lochlan motioned to the worn leather sofa with an antique steamer trunk as its coffee table. The beautifully polished hardwood floor shone between large Turkish rugs. The vintage light fixture had been rescued from the trash heap after a Keep remodel several decades earlier. The stained glass window in the transom above the front door was one of many that had once graced the hotel's original ballroom. The place smelled subtly of wood and incense and book bindings. Rebecca felt instantly at home.

Too excited to sit, she loosed her volley of treasure trove questions. "How deep? How big? How much do you think it's worth?"

No less impatient than his visitors, Lochlan hastily related the 3D ground scanner's revelations. "Staggering, really, when you think about that much gold, what it would be valued at, what it could buy...."

"We can buy The Keep! We can wrest it from TITHE and undo all the awful changes they've made, take it back to its original glory. The Freemasons would approve, don't you think?" Rebecca ventured hopefully.

Lochlan shook his head. "The treasure may technically belong to TITHE, since it's buried under hotel property. Ownership in this case would be a very interesting question. It certainly doesn't belong to us."

"No Finders-Keepers law? Are you sure? What if we could recover it in secret and no one else would ever know the source of our sudden windfall? Couldn't you claim to have inherited some castle estate in Scotland from a long-lost relative or something? We can't just leave it there, now that we know. How could you dangle the golden carrot and snatch it away so quickly?"

Lochlan put a finger to his lips, signaling her to hush. He leaned back against the desk, hands braced on both sides, and glowered at Rebecca from beneath graying brows.

"We *can* just leave it there," he said, "And we must."

Maureen understood. "The Freemasons buried the gold for a reason, Beck," she said. "It's empowered the Griffins Keep for more than a century. It's crucial to its function as a spiritual portal and sanctuary, as much as the alignment and the sunlight and the underground aquifer."

"Not just the Keep, but the prosperity and success of the whole city may be derived from the Freemasons' buried gold,"

Lochlan explained. "Remember, the entire hotel is a cornerstone, the cornerstone of Denver. The oscilloscope showed the treasure chamber in a sandstone stratum, sandstone comprised of billions of tiny quartz crystals."

Mo extrapolated. "The sandstone transmits the fabled elemental properties of the gold—its aura of power and immortality—not only throughout The Keep, but throughout the entire area."

"I don't care about the entire area," Rebecca said, aware of how petulant she sounded. "Denver's big enough to fend for itself now. I only care about the Griffins Keep. And if finding this treasure isn't a godsend enabling us to save it from indignity and degradation, then...well, then I don't know what."

Her fervor fizzled. She knew Lochlan and Maureen were right. Leaving the treasure *in situ* and perpetuating the secret were imperative. They dared not undo all that the Freemasons had brought into being with secret rituals and personal sacrifices about which they knew nothing.

"What about Manuel and Gregorio? What if they have different ideas about the treasure? What if one or both of them can't resist bragging about what they've found?"

"After considering all the tantalizing possibilities, they will come to the same conclusion," Lochlan was confident. "They themselves are Freemasons. Even if they share the news with their brother Masons, it will go no farther. Brookings knew that when he left the Lodge the clue to the gold's whereabouts. These guys have been keeping secrets for centuries, don't forget."

Rebecca blew out her breath, relenting. "The earth revolves around the sun," she said, citing what was once a much bigger secret.

"And we're not the center of the universe." Lochlan smiled and planted a soft kiss on the top of her head.

A heartbeat later, animating with an impromptu Highland Fling, he declared in his best Scottish brogue, "Doesna mean we canna celebrate the hell outta this momentous discovery! Will ye bonnie lasses join me for a wee dram o' my finest whiskey? I've been savin' it for just such a fateful occasion."

That night after Maureen went home, in his mahogany four-posted bed, Rebecca and Lochlan made love, rapturous and transcendent.

"Oh, Pete, no!" Rebecca reacted to the assistant manager's news, remembering the inspiration he'd taken away from his visit to the archives months ago. "You can't leave. You love The Keep. I was counting on you to move into upper management and advocate for the hotel's history."

"I do love The Keep, you're right," Pete conceded after divulging the news that he'd given notice. "That's exactly why I have to go. We've talked about this, Rebecca. You understand. The Keep is losing its heart and soul, incrementally, day by day. Everyone who knows the hotel feels it. I thought I could make a difference, thought I could stop it, but I can't. The new owners don't give a damn about anything but profit and exploitation. I can't stand to watch them bleeding her to death anymore."

Rebecca hugged him, unreasonably hoping to hold him in place forever. Of course he had to go. He cared too much, just as she did. Recent developments were wearing him down, demanding more compromise than he was willing to make. The instincts for integrity and self-preservation would serve him well, wherever his future path led him.

She wanted so much to tell Pete about the Masonic treasure beneath the entrance to the Spa. Wanted to restore his faith in The Keep magic. But the secret was not hers to reveal.

"Before I go, I have something to share with you," he said. "I got this a couple weeks ago on etsy.com. I check that site and eBay periodically for Keep memorabilia up for auction. Got it for $19. You're gonna drool with envy."

From his inside jacket pocket, Pete produced a tarnished silver teaspoon.

"Where did it come from?"

"An antiques dealer in San Diego. I contacted her, told her I worked at The Keep. But she had no memory of how it came to her. Knew nothing about its origins."

In the bowl of the spoon, a bas relief showing two sides of the Griffins Keep. Atop its handle, a number of symbols. "Don't know if they're Masonic or Templar or what," he confided. "But look here, on the back of the handle: '100% Colorado silver.' How rare is that?"

Rebecca took historical stock. "This has to be from the earliest years of the hotel. I've never seen or heard of anything like it. May I?" she asked, holding out her hand.

"Obviously some of these symbols, like the unfinished pyramid on the top of the handle, are Masonic. But the crossed miners' pick and sledge, the three snowcapped mountain peaks, the rods bundled together with the ax head—these are all elements of the Colorado State Seal. The 'G' in the center of the triangle is definitely Masonic, like the G for Geometry inside their square-and-compass symbol."

"Or it could just be a 'G' for Griffin," Pete pointed out.

Rebecca had to smile at herself. "Guess my imagination could be making me see Masonic secrets where there are none."

"See here on the back of the handle," Pete directed, taking it back. "Green: Smith Co.—Denver.' I did some research in old city directories at the History Colorado library and found out there was a silversmithing company owned by a Mr. Elias Green in Denver around 1890, on Blake Street. His advertisement said that he specialized in custom pieces."

"So this may be the only piece of its kind produced?"

"Seems likely."

"Wow. You're right. I'm drooling."

"You can have it for a couple days to study more carefully. I trust you. Plus I know where you work," Pete teased.

"Thank you, Pete. I'll guard it with my life."

He grinned at her extreme assurance before turning serious. "You know, a few minutes before you came down, I was standing here in the lobby, just holding it and thinking. *How long has it been since this spoon has been in this place?* Probably more than a hundred years. How much the Griffins Keep has changed since this piece was crafted! It's such a tangible link to the hotel's past, you know? I could almost feel the power of the reconnection. Crazy, huh?"


"Hannah came by for a nice visit yesterday," Rebecca's mother said about five minutes into their weekly phone call. "I know a grandmother isn't supposed to have favorites, but she's such a delight, practically bursting with idealism and romantic notions. She reminds much more of you than of Ruthie at her age," she declared. "Your sister was always so down-to-earth. Hannah is as free-spirited and light-hearted as you used to be."

247

*Used to be.* Rebecca prayed silently that her niece would be spared having that spirit and heart snuffed by life's disillusionments.

"And how are things at work, sweetie?" her mother never failed to ask.

Rebecca sighed. "More of the same. Don't get me started. One of my favorite people—who happens to be one of The Keep's best managers—is leaving. And he's just one in a long line."

Since TITHE's takeover, The Keep had lost its executive chef, its executive housekeeper, the banquets manager, all of the Pirates' Pub senior staff, several engineers, countless housekeepers and kitchen staff.

"He was too conscientious, took too much pride in the hotel's reputation to watch her go downhill. Nearly every day I hear from one of my fellow associates about some guest or other complaining about the TITHE changes, declaring they'll never come back to the hotel they've patronized and loved, sometimes for decades. It's grim."

"Oh, I hate to hear that," her mother said. "It's such a shame. What if you and the other employees who are concerned about what you see happening write it all down, everybody sign it, and present it to the general manager? Wouldn't that be worth a try?"

"Branson doesn't care about employee opinions. Input has never been solicited and, when offered, is invariably ignored or shut down. What do the worker bees know? We're not business people. We're just the ones in direct contact with our guests every day."

"Now, Becky, be careful. Bitterness is not only unattractive but also ineffective. I'm surprised to hear you sound as if you've given up. It's not like you."

"I know, Mom. I know. And I haven't given up completely. But lately I have to wonder why I'm sticking around The Keep. With the historian position eliminated, I'm just an unusually knowledgeable sales receptionist."

"So why *are* you sticking around? You're obviously frustrated there."

"Not sure," Rebecca realized as she said it. "Partly to see what happens next, I guess. But more than that, I feel like there's something important left for me to do at the Griffins Keep. Something only I can do. I don't know what it is—yet. I only know it's not time for me to leave. I have to figure it out."

248

*Everyone at the Keep is here for a reason,* Lochlan had said when she was new on the job, *especially you.* She'd failed as guardian of the hotel's historical treasures. Except for the few things they'd managed to stash in the secret sub-basement room, the artifacts were gone. Surely there was another role for her in The Keep's story.

"Well, I don't care what you say about the place going downhill. It will always be special to me. With our wedding anniversary stay just before your father passed and my 80th birthday brunch, the hotel will hold a place in my heart forever. And I know a lot of others who say the same whenever I proudly mention that my daughter works at the Griffins Keep. No matter what those TITHE people do to its surface, they can never wipe away the deep layers of happy memories The Keep holds for so many people."

It sparked.

Rebecca had thought Maureen's idea crazy, but there was no mistaking the intriguing result of their experiment.

"It should have struck me as soon as Pete said he got this little spoon from a seller in San Diego. That's where Harrison Griffin passed away in 1904. Pete's research indicated that the spoon may be one of a kind, created for the hotel's opening. What if it were made specifically for founder Harrison Griffin himself? And what if Griffin sold it later when he fell on hard times? Poor guy was almost destitute in his final years, having built and lost at least three fortunes over his lifetime."

Mo held the silver object and closed her eyes. "That would explain the vibes I'm getting from it," she said. "Really powerful. If this were his spoon, it would have been a prized possession."

"A possession into which he would have invested something of himself," Rebecca ventured, half-joking. "What if it still holds a residual trace of his spirit?"

"One way to find out," Mo declared, popping up from the kitchen table where they'd both been examining the small artifact. "You keep that prehistoric horn thingy in your jewelry box now, right?" she called as she headed up the stairs to Rebecca's room. She was back to the table in no time, with Rebecca's *myotragus Balearicus* talisman in hand.

249

"I think you've come to realize as well as I do that this mysterious little trinket of yours somehow repels negative spirits and attracts positive ones. Let's see if it interacts with Mr. Teaspoon here." Mo laid the horn beside the silver spoon and watched expectantly, as if awaiting the two to strike up a conversation. Nothing happened.

"Maybe they need time to get acquainted," Rebecca suggested with a bemused smile, "or a little privacy."

"Very funny. What if they actually touch...."

And that's when it happened. The silver spoon sparked. Startled, the two women instinctively drew back. Willoughby erupted in his home-invader bark.

"What the ....! Did you see that spark come off the handle?"

Mo flashed Rebecca a told-you-so look. "Hush, Willoughby," she said.

"But horn is organic and porous. It doesn't create—let alone conduct—electricity. There's that little twist of wire I ran through the hole to suspend it from a chain, but that couldn't have caused it. Do it again."

Her roommate held the talisman and gingerly touched the tip of the horn to the hotel representation in the bowl of the spoon. The silver piece began to vibrate, like a tuning fork.

"How are you doing that?" Rebecca demanded.

"I'm not. I swear!"

A mild electrical shock shot through Mo's hand and up her arm. The top of the spoon handle sparked again. Unmistakable. Inexplicable. Thrill bumps ran up across the back of Rebecca's neck. "What on earth is going on here?!"

Mo laid the horn gently on the table. She laced her fingers together and pressed conjoined fists to her lips as she leaned on her elbows and studied the two potent artifacts before her. At length, she looked up and said, "I have to conclude that what we've just witnessed has much more to do with the metaphysical realm than the physical."

"Ya think?" Rebecca tried and failed to make light of it.

"This is weird, Beck. I'm not sure what to make of it. But I think we can safely say there's some bizarre sympathetic energy generated by both of these objects. It's good energy, I'm pretty sure. But the combination produces a really intense dynamic."

"Maybe Pete will let me keep the spoon so we can touch the two together to start a fire on our next camping trip."

"Yeah, don't think so. How about instead you give it back to him ASAP, and keep it as far away from the horn as possible until it's out of this house. We have no idea what we're messing with here. But it's sure as hell paranormal."

"You'll get no argument from me on that point."

"Oh, and by the way," Mo called after her as Rebecca started upstairs to return the horn to her jewelry box, "The teaspoon wasn't made for Harrison Griffith, as you thought. He had it commissioned as a gift for his wife Jenny upon the opening of the hotel."

"How could you know that?"

Mo walked over to the foot of the staircase to look her roommate in the eye. "Jenny Griffin's spirit told me. She wanted to be sure we got the story straight."

# CHAPTER 25

**Teen Plunges to Death in Griffins Keep Atrium**

Denver — A local teen celebrating his seventeenth
birthday at the Griffins Keep hotel fell to his death at
5:23 PM yesterday when a bungee cord anchored on the
seventh-floor balcony somehow detached and sent him
plunging to the lobby floor. Conner Royal died instantly
of a broken neck as horrified Happy Hour revelers
looked on. Miraculously, no one in the hotel atrium was
injured.

"It was horrible," said a tearful Caitlin Royal, twin
sister of the victim, who was in line to leap next.
"like the part holding that end of the cord to the balcony
post just dissolved all of a sudden. I was taking a picture
with my phone, and something weird flashed through
it. It was so quick, it was over before we got what had
happened."

The TITHE corporation, which    acquired    the
Griffins  Keep  eight  months  ago, recently  began
offering atrium bungee jumping as part of their efforts
to  make  the hotel  more  entertainment focused. The
teens chose to hold their joint birthday party there
because they thought leaping from the seventh floor
and bouncing back up again would be fun.

"No expense will be spared in our efforts to determine the cause of this tragic accident," said TITHE spokesperson LaTishia Jordan. "The bungee jumping attraction was closed immediately and will not reopen until the investigation is concluded and we are satisfied that the activity can be resumed with complete safety assurances. Our heartfelt sympathy goes out to the young man's family."

Rebecca's boss stepped up to the PR challenge like the seasoned pro she was. Privately, Ms. Jordan was badly stricken by the incident.

"We've got to pull any mention of bungee jumping from the website, all social and print media—stat," she told the hotel's PR team in their emergency damage control meeting at 6:30 the next morning. "The so-called experts who rigged up that damned thing certified the cords as safe and secure. The official line from the top is that this tragedy was a freak accident that no amount of precaution on TITHE's part could have averted. Let's erase this nightmare fast and furiously, people."

A moment later, her tone transformed from authoritative to vulnerable. "I have a 17-year-old son myself," she said softly. "That poor kid probably didn't even weigh 150 pounds." LaTishia's voice broke. She paused to pull herself together before concluding with steely resolve, "If they even *consider* reinstating that deathtrap, I swear to god I'll walk.

"Now get busy, all of you. We've got a reputation to salvage."


Chad Tagawa himself appeared on property the next day. The amusement resort industry giant could ill-afford a public stain on his safety record. Chad was pissed. As he watched morbidly curious visitors in the atrium gaze upward and point to the section of the seventh-floor balcony cordoned off by crime-scene tape, he made his executive decision.

"This frickin' atrium is no good to us," he decreed. "It's not only a liability, it's wasted space. It's gone. I want it closed off at the third floor and a 25-story—no, 17-story—tower erected right in the center of the building. We'll call it the Conner Royal Tower in memory of the dead kid. One floor for every year of his young life—

254

so tragically cut short," he added with mock drama. "The Royal Tower in the Griffins Keep. How perfect is that? A goddam gift,"

"Dude, it's like brilliant," gushed the sycophantic Mickey Branson.

"Hell, yeah," Chad said, actually breaking into a grin. "PR gold, bro! Might even keep his family from suing us. Imagine the revenue from all those new rooms."

Tagawa high-fived his managing director. "You can buy me a brewski in the Kipling to celebrate."

The Denver Landmark Preservation Commission presented an obstacle Tagawa and Branson had not anticipated. Any change to the exterior of a historically designated structure required the DLPC's sign off. TITHE attorneys argued that the proposed tower was an interior addition and thus beyond the commission's purview. The battle was on.

Longtime Keep associates and patrons were appalled by Chad Tagawa's atrium infill idea. It went without saying that the stained glass skylight, too, was slated for obliteration. The developer's sword dangled over The Keep's heart. The hotel's magic and majesty hung in the balance. Only the laughing children in the lobby bouncy castle seemed oblivious to the gathering clouds.

"What do you make of all the recent disturbing developments?" Rebecca asked Lochlan one afternoon as they waited for the service elevator.

"Seems Rosslyn was right about drastic changes unfolding this year when she charted The Keep's horoscope," he said. "With this new proposal of Tagawa's, for the first time, I actually fear for The Keep's continuation."

"What do you mean? Do you think it will go out of business?"

Lochlan shook his head sadly. "I think it may lose its soul— and its souls. This building was designed by a Master Mason to be spiritually significant, with incorporated elemental and geometrical powers we can only guess at. There's no way of telling how major structural alterations will impact or pervert those mystical elements."

*Has the transformation already begun?* Rebecca wondered, Was the bungee death evidence of an ominous shift in The Keep's nature, somehow tied to the changes TITHE had undertaken and the occultist practices the Tagawas might be engaging in? What

255

would closing off the atrium mean to the building's role as a waystation for transmigrating spirits?

Griffins Keep GM Mickey Branson did not hold "All Hands" meetings, as had his predecessor Mr. Beaumont, to inform staff of developments that affected hotel operations. That sort of forum invited questions and opinions, neither of which Branson cared to deal with. Instead, he sent down what Rebecca characterized as decrees, email blasts announcing executive decisions handed down by himself or TITHE. The latest proclamation was an unprecedented two-in-one:

> Due to the recent tragic accident in the hotel's lobby, the atrium space is slated to be permanently closed off at the third-story level. Additional guest rooms and meeting spaces will be added in the proposed 17-story tower addition as soon as the TITHE legal team can conclude ongoing negotiations with the Denver Landmark Commission.
>
> In the meantime, we plan to wean the Griffins Keep from its artesian well and connect to Denver Water as our sole source henceforth. This process will entail at least one temporary complete shut-off of the system, a minor inconvenience to hotel operations of which you will be apprised in advance.
>
> We appreciate your cooperation as we implement these changes over the course of the coming weeks.

"'Our cooperation'—like we have a choice," longtime houseman Marty muttered when he read the printed version posted above the timeclock. "Just when I think they can't screw up this place any more than they already have, they prove me wrong."

Lochlan clocked out for lunch right behind the houseman. "I'm afraid these latest proposed changes may do much more than just screw up The Keep. They have the potential to kill it altogether."

"Whadja mean about killing The Keep?" Marty asked when they'd filled their trays and found seats in a corner of the employee dining room. "You make it sound like a living thing."

256

Lochlan stabbed a garbanzo rolling off his plate. "Not so much living as functioning," he clarified. "This building was constructed with a purpose more important than sheltering wealthy visitors. Alter its key structural elements, and you jeopardize that higher function."

"A function for spirits, right?" Marty had chatted with the engineer often enough to know that his focus extended beyond the physical maintenance of The Keep.

"Aye, for spirits," Lochlan confirmed. "They need this place to help them on their way to the next plane of existence—into The Light, some might say."

"And without the open atrium and the well, their way will be closed?"

"Without its special sunlight and subterranean water source, I fear that it will."

"And...what will the spirits do if they can't move on?"

Lochlan said nothing, but noting the veteran employee's grave expression, Marty concluded, "So this is WAY worse than bad redecoration."

"Way. These changes are so serious that it wouldn't surprise me if the spirits themselves find a way to stop them."

Monty considered the possibility. "But ghosts can't affect the real world, can they?"

"Which real?" Lochlan countered. "You make a good point, though. Spirits can produce minor phenomena, like electrical anomalies, cold spots, sensations of contact, sometimes even kinetic movement. But to effect major developments, undertake significant action, they need a physical host."

"Like you?" Marty ventured.

Lochlan gulped his iced tea and shook his head. "Not me. No. But someone we both know. Selected long ago, snatched untimely from her own continuum to serve the spirits of the Griffins Keep when the need arose in the future. Someone whose destiny is about to be realized."


Rosslyn had not yet seen the new décor in The Keep's lower-floor guestrooms. Rebecca invited her and her daughter Miranda for lunch in the Pirates Pub in order to get their take on all the changes the hotel was undergoing.

"Would you mind terribly if we visited Room 864 before we see the redecorated rooms?" Rosslyn asked. "I know it has weird vibes for you, but I'm keen to know what's going on with the nasty spirit in there. Wonder if we can get her to move on."

Reluctantly, Rebecca agreed. *Please don't let me see anything, please don't let me see anything* she prayed silently as they entered the now notorious suite.

"This is strange," Rosslyn said, moving slowly through the bedroom toward the dressing room. "She's gone. Completely gone. I no longer sense any trace of her."

Miranda perched on the upholstered bench at the foot of the bed and said simply, "She was getting too ugly. We sent her to visit The Monster—Hennie and me. Hennie knew how to lure her down to the Club. We found the spot and summoned it." Her smile of satisfaction was chilling. "And no one who goes down with The Monster ever comes back."

The two older women exchanged astonished glances. After an uneasy pause, Rosslyn declared, "Good riddance, then," appraising her daughter with a new sort of worry. "I think it's time that we, too, moved on."

Rebecca had been able to get keys to two of the newly decorated rooms. The first was one of the smaller rooms on the fourth floor. The space which had appeared cozy with Victorian appointments seemed overwhelmed by the large-scale furnishings and lamps that now crowded it.

"Someone should have told this designer that big does not equate to elegant," Rosslyn said, trying to take it in.

"Wait till you see a corner suite, with all the same elements, plus." Rebecca took them next to 732.

"Oh dear....." The psychic sounded almost fearful as she proceeded slowly through the entry hallway into the sitting room, taking in the vinyl-framed flatscreen TV, the button-tufted vinyl sofa and chairs. "I feel as if I'm in a padded cell."

After walking through the bedroom, the mother and daughter rejoined Rebecca with stricken looks on their faces. "I'm hearing that we should sit for a while," Rosslyn said.

"Do so carefully," Rebecca warned. "This furniture isn't very sturdy—or comfortable."

For several moments, the three sat in silence, listening to the rhythmic clicking of the ceiling fan's stainless steel blades. A workman chipping away at the exterior sandstone outside one wall sounded like something was trying to claw its way in.

"It's all so cheap looking, like a Super 8 Motel or something," Miranda said quietly. "None of this fits here."

Rosslyn agreed. "And it feels terribly empty. Not physically, but spiritually."

She tried adjusting the oversized pillow at her back before tossing it on the floor in disgust. "These changes are more than superficial. This cold décor reflects a deeper, callous disrespect by the new owners for the hotel's character. It's very disturbing. I'm hearing the spirits crying No No No No, over and over again." She stood and began to pace the room.

"Mom, what's 'pablum'?" Miranda asked, seemingly out of nowhere.

"I'm sorry...What?"

"Pablum. What does it mean?"

Unsure, Rosslyn looked to Rebecca.

"I think pablum used to mean a sort of baby food," the historian offered. "But over the years, it's come to mean anything bland or tasteless."

"Oh," Miranda said. "That makes sense then. Harrison Griffin himself is right over there, by the window, looking around the room and shaking his head. He's saying, 'Pablum. Unworthy pablum.'"

Rebecca looked in the direction Miranda indicated and was taken aback to actually see the hotel founder—insubstantial, indistinct, but unmistakably Harrison Griffin. For a split second only, his gaze met hers and he doffed his bowler hat, bowing his head. Then the apparition winked out, leaving Rebecca to wonder if she'd actually seen anything at all. Automatically, her hand went to her chest and felt the horn talisman, hidden beneath her blouse. She wore it all the time now.

Rosslyn stood completely still, attending to the disembodied voices only she could hear. "Something worse is coming. Much worse. What else is going to change?"

Rebecca told them about the plans for closing off the atrium and capping the artesian well. Rosslyn's eyes rolled up and she stiffened.

"This cannot happen." The ferocity in her voice was subdued only with great effort. "The spirits—the Knights—they're telling me 'We will bring down vengeance before we let you take away the

259

Sunlight and the Living Water, the elements that empower this place.'"

The psychic trembled as she repeated the awful message. "'We will bring it down—and the city with it.'"

The weather was all wrong for a mid-June morning in Denver. Dark clouds smudged the sun. Lighting darted across the eastern horizon, frenetic but silent. Late afternoon thunderstorms were common in the summer. But not storms at 9:00 a.m..

Strangest of all was the wind. It gusted cold out of the northeast. As Rebecca made her way from Sixteenth Street to the Griffins Keep, skyscraper canyons funneled and twisted the blasts, whipping her hair and her skirt around her.

From beneath the streets, there arose a surreal sound. Wind whooshing through the sewers. Breath sucked into, then blew out of the drain vents, producing an eerie polyphony that ranged from deep, guttural moans to banshee howls, like tortured minotaurs lost in a subterranean labyrinth.

"Have you ever heard anything like this?" Rebecca shouted over the noise to Fredrick, the veteran doorman.

He reached up to hold onto his hat. "Never in my 23 years at this entrance," he said uneasily. "But then again, the wind never comes out of the northeast. Must be creating some sort of weird air currents in the sewers. Great sound effects for a horror film."

Things were as unsettled within The Keep as without. Business as usual was impossible.

"Time clock's out of order," Rebecca told Dawn as she sat down at her desk in the sales office.

"The whole computer network is down," Dawn reported. "The reservations system, the switchboard, the cash registers. Nobody can even get their cellphones to work in the hotel. The tech support guys are doing what they can, but they're overwhelmed and can't identify the source of the malfunctions. All the businesses they support in this part of the city are experiencing the same facility-wide failures."

"Electro-magnetic disturbance," Lochlan said when Rebecca found him in the paint shop, "It's the energy of spirits, their interface with the physical world. This is a warning shot across the bow, a small taste of the havoc they will wreak when closing The Keep portal disrupts their afterlife journeys. Disabling computers

260

and cellphones is only the beginning. Transformers will blow. Security systems will fail. Banking and communications and navigation systems will fry. The spirits will make sure the whole city feels their anguish and pays for their entrapment."

"Surely you exaggerate. These are momentary glitches..."

"Up to this point, yes," Lochlan said. "But when pacemakers fail, cars stop in their tracks, and planes fall from the skies over Denver, it will be too late to avert the catastrophe."

# CHAPTER 26

Everything was apparently back to normal the morning after the mysterious electro-magnetic disruptions. Rebecca did not recognize the young man in cook's white who approached her as she was clocking in. But he obviously knew who she was.

"You used to be the hotel historian, right?" he began. "I remember you from that 'Ten Things You Should Know about Griffins Keep History' video they made us watch at new employee orientation. I'm Will Whitby. Hi."

"Hi, Bradley. Nice to meet you. Is there something I can help you with?"

"Well, yeah. Maybe. I hope so. I know the old hotel guest registers got auctioned off a few months ago, right? But didn't I hear they went to the History Colorado Library?"

"Most did. And to be honest, it's a far better place for them. Once they're processed, they'll be available to researchers who request them."

"Any idea how long that will take?"

"I know they've got a huge backlog of materials to inventory and catalog. And they count on part-time volunteers to do a lot of it. Could be quite some time before anyone can get to them."

"Well, I need to get to them—really just one of them—soon. My mom's 50th birthday is coming up next month, and I want to give her something really unusual. Her grandparents—my great-grandparents—spent their honeymoon at the Griffins Keep in

1917. So I thought, wouldn't it be great if I could get a photocopy of the page with her grandpa's signature from back then?"

"It would be a very unique gift, but I don't see how..."

"I was thinking, maybe if you explained my request to the History Colorado guys and asked to see just that one register, they might grant you some kinda special permission. Or maybe you could volunteer to work on the Griffins Keep stuff, and while you're there, you could snap a picture of his signature without anybody minding."

"I suppose it's possible. I've known the registrar for years. And I'm sure he'd understand my interest in the things from The Keep. Do you have the exact date or dates that your relatives stayed at the hotel?"

"Oh, sure! It was June 21. Mom says they used to always talk about how they were here on the only day the Griffins Keep ever closed. You probably know all about it. I guess they were drilling down for the well, and there was some kind of freak explosion that blew out a corner of the building or something."

"Something like that, yes."

"So anyway, do you think you can help me?"

Rebecca had actually been thinking about volunteering to process The Keep materials for HC ever since she'd learned they acquired them at the auction. Who better? Doing a favor for a fellow hotel employee was just the impetus she needed to offer her services.

"We don't even know if the register for that date is among those that History Colorado acquired," she cautioned. "But I'll see what I can do."

The Hart Library at History Colorado Center was thrilled to have Rebecca's help with processing the Griffins Keep items. It did her historian heart good to see the guest registers, banquet menus, and other ephemera being properly preserved at last. The registers were currently stored in six large acid-free boxes.

She crossed her fingers that the guest book including June 21, 1917, was among HC's recent Keep acquisitions. She'd already checked for that date in the few rescued registers she and Lochlan had hidden in the secret sub-basement storage room. If June 21, 1917, was not in the Hart collection, she would have to conclude it had never been recovered by Charlotte when she first scavenged

264

the building to create the hotel archives, way back in the 70s. Regrettably, the series had significant gaps.

Understanding the challenges of late middle-age, a staff member had offered Rebecca the loan of a magnifying glass. Carefully opening one volume after another, the historian wondered why she had never sought out the register from that notorious day in June 1917 before this. Charlotte had, of course, scanned every page of every book in search of famous signatures years ago. But many of the 10" x 16" fabric-and-cardboard-bound historic registers were so damaged and deteriorated that Rebecca had dared not touch them unless she had a very compelling reason. With peeling covers and shredded spines, it was miraculous that some of them held together at all. A few of them didn't.

Gingerly, she lifted a fragile register from the bottom of the third box. The first page was stamped "May 3, 1917;" the last date, "July 16, 1917." *Bingo!* She held the elusive register in her cotton-gloved hands.

She turned the fragile yellowed pages a few at a time, delighting anew in the distinctive handwriting, narrowing in on the date Bradley's great-grandparents had honeymooned at the Griffins Keep, all those years ago.

There it was, stamped in red at the top of the page. Rebecca ran her finger down the columns, searching for the newlywed Nathaniel R. Williams' signature.

What she found instead would change her reality forever.

"Are you all right, ma'am?" the library staff member at the reference desk asked as an unsteady Rebecca walked toward the exit ten minutes later. "Did you find what you were looking for?"

The historian blinked at the young woman, as if awaking from a dream. She shook her head but answered in the affirmative. "Yes, thank you," she said. "I found more than I ever could have imagined."


For the next two days, Rebecca was uncharacteristically withdrawn and introspective. When she was finally ready to share her epiphany with Maureen, her longtime friend struggled to wrap her head around it.

"I don't know what to say to that," Mo stated honestly.

"I'm not surprised."

Silent for some time, Mo tried to fit the bizarre new peg into differently shaped holes.

"On the one hand, it explains so much," she finally said. "But on the other, it presents a whole new set of mysteries."

"You're telling me."

"I thought the discovery of the golden treasure was big. But this...this totally trumps anything."

"The overriding questions at this point, as I see it, are How? And Why?"

"Wish I had answers, Beck. But this is way beyond me, beyond any psychic insights I might have. My advice is to seek out those mediums who seem to be so attuned to the spirits of The Keep's past. Especially the one who's tapped into the Masonic and Knights Templar stuff."

"Margaret," Rebecca said. "She'll be almost as blown away as I am."

"I think you should confide in Lochlan, too. He knows so much about the building, its secrets and its powers. Plus, he cares about you. I suspect you're going to need all the support you can get in the very near future."

The ancient talisman around Rebecca's neck seemed to grow warmer. She was going to need some magic, as well.


Margaret and Molly arrived in the Keep lobby early the next morning. "The spirits told us we needed to come to you even before you called," Molly explained. "They're very worked up over some new development. Do tell!"

"Could be the fact that this atrium is about to be closed off from the sunlight and that the Keep's artesian well will soon be capped," Rebecca said.

"Oh no!" Margaret exclaimed. "Those changes are bound to disrupt—if not completely block—the spiritual flow of The Keep. But that's not what the spirits brought us here to learn. It's not just about the hotel. It's about you. What's changed with you, Rebecca? You seem somehow distant, distracted. We're here to help."

When the historian told the sensitives about her experience in the library a few days earlier, their reactions mingled shock and awe. They knew about the notorious day of the hotel's only shut down. And they understood the implications and the gravitas of Rebecca's disclosure.

"I think we both sensed something remarkable about your connection to The Keep the first time we met you," Molly said. "Of course I can't speak for Margaret, but I confess I'm a little envious. As far as I know, this is unprecedented."

Her fellow medium stood and walked carefully around the construction disarray still littering the lobby. She paused near the Madonna image in the onyx, unaware of how close she was to the golden treasure, and scanned the open balconies encircling the atrium. She closed her eyes and concentrated.

"The Keep spirits are telling me the time is nigh," she said. "But they seem to be blocking me out for the first time. I'm sensing they plan to communicate their intentions directly to you, Rebecca—and only to you. They won't tell me what they need. I keep getting something about 'back to the bones.' I'm hearing that phrase over and over again, more voices joining in with each repetition. They're not referring to the same bones the Freemasons hinted at around Halloween. I'm sorry. I can't tell you what it means."

Molly, in the meantime, had made her way just beyond the far side of the front desk. She cast her gaze to the space below the skylight in the corner above the concierge desk, the place where she'd sensed The Keep's driving force—its essence—on her initial visit back in October. It seemed to Rebecca a long time ago.

"The hotel guardians have a mission for you," Molly told the historian, without taking her eyes from the seventh-story corner. "May the angels grant you strength."

Rebecca nodded solemnly. "I await their instructions."

*Back to the bones.* What was Rebecca to make of that? Stripping bare, returning to basics. If only that could happen with the Griffins Keep! Slash away decades of alterations forced upon the structure so brilliantly conceived and aesthetically wrought. Purge the physical and philosophical perversions that daily dragged the beloved beauty further from its higher purpose.

But how, without destroying the hotel all together?


Rebecca's latest assignment from Ms. Jordan was to "revisit" the recorded self-guided tour script.

"People like it, but it has *way* too much elaboration and *way* too many stories," she explained. "Who wants to hear that much about the history of an old building that doesn't even look like it

267

used to? Don't waste their time with stuff that's not here anymore. I need it cut by half, just a few factoids for each stop."

*Aye, aye, Cap'n!* Rebecca thought. *Stuff that's gone, waste of time. Got it. Out of sight, out of relevance.* Rebecca gnashed her historian teeth. *Tell that to our ghosts.*

Feeling more obsolete than ever, Rebecca stared at the script hardcopy. She missed the days of regularly delivering the information live and in-person, missed the challenge of tweaking it to speak to the interests of each distinctive tour audience. No room for the personal touch in a TITHE universe.

After whittling Harrison Griffins backstory to almost nothing, she proceeded to condense the hotel's special features to bullet points:

- Italian Renaissance architecture.
- Golden onyx wainscoting.
- Electrical-generating dynamos.
- Artesian well water source.
- Fireproof construction.

*Hold the phone.*

"Absolutely fireproof building.,.. Iron, steel, and concrete framework...terra-cotta floors and interior walls. In the event of fire, room contents would be destroyed. But the super-structure itself... "

The former historian was not at her Sales receptionist desk when Lochlan stopped by a few minutes later to talk. To the right of Rebecca's keyboard lay the tour script, one section circled repeatedly with orange highlighter. From that moment, he understood.

The Griffins Keep, the Great Lady of Denver hotels, was about to experience one helluva hot flash.


"How long have you known?" Rebecca asked when Lochlan expressed no surprise at her History Colorado library revelation.

"Since our first conversation about your divorce and your maiden name."

"Were you ever going to tell me?"

"I had faith that all would be revealed when the time was right."

"But if that prep cook hadn't asked me to look in the guest register...."

"Ah, but he did."

"How can it be? What does it mean?"

"It means that everything is unfolding as it was destined to. There's something about your spirit that the Knights valued and banked, if you will, for a future withdrawal. It means payout time is now, and only you can sign for it."

"They've communicated with me directly," Rebecca told him, "The Knights Templar who have guarded the Griffins Keep from the first, they touched me when I hung the *myotrageous* horn around my neck and opened myself to their message."

Lochlan knew about her mysterious talisman and its strange response to the hotel silver teaspoon artifact.

"They didn't tell, but rather showed me in a sort of vision what I was to do," Rebecca explained.

"You're not afraid?"

"Terrified." Her voice broke. "What the Knights require is tantamount to murder. How can I comply?"

"The death of a few to save millions of souls. How often has that been the rationale for havoc throughout history? The elimination of heretics is justified in defense of the Temple. The spiritual portal must be maintained. You can no longer doubt that you are The Keep's defender, designated long ago."

The truth of his words was unassailable. Reminded of her role, Rebecca drew a deep breath, straightened her spine, steeled her resolve. "I'll need the sword of the Third Griffin. Will you retrieve it for me?"

"We'll fetch it together," Lochlan said. "Right now."


Surrounded by tangible reminders of the Griffins Keep's glorious past in the hidden sub-basement repository, Rebecca drew strength. She was not the first to take risks in the name of the Keep's legacy. Artifacts rescued over the decades by gallant employees and collected in this secret space bore witness to the hotel's respectful stewards. All of them—past and present—looked now to her to defend the mystique and the majesty of the place they loved. She felt their expectation and honored their trust.

269

The historian and the engineer who served The Keep above all said little. Their communication went beyond words. Rebecca collapsed onto a pile of embroidered table linens.

"I'm so tired," she said. "So very tired suddenly. I'm not sure I can go through with this. You could do it, Lochlan. You're a much better choice than I for the task ahead. Surely the Knights would welcome your help."

Lochlan sank down beside her and took her hand. "I'll help. Of course, I will. In any way I can. But I haven't your special magic or connection. You know you can't cheat fate at this stage of the game. You won't be alone."

Rebecca knew that to be true. She could already feel the presence of The Keep's countless spiritual sojourners, as well as the Knight guardians.

"You'll do everything you can to get innocent people out of harm's way, won't you? Mo will help you, and Margaret and Molly and Rosslyn. I've told no one else about what lies ahead."

Lochlan put an arm around Rebecca's slight shoulders. "Don't you worry. With all of us working together, we'll lead everyone to safety. You just follow the Knights' instructions."

She leaned against him and quietly began to sob. "I'm so afraid this will be the last thing I ever do."

His heart caught in his throat.

"I won't lie to you," he said at last. "At our age, we feel our mortality in subtle ways almost every day. Little by little or in one grand stroke, death moves closer. The body is temporary, a perishable vessel for the essence of a person. But surely by now you know. The greatest secret the Freemasons built into The Keep is that death is not the end, that this is only one plane of existence among many. This building, this temple, is where travelers take stock, turn a corner on their journey to The Light. You believe that now, don't you?"

Rebecca sighed. "'I believe in God the Father Almighty, Creator of Heaven and Earth,'" she began, reciting the Apostles Creed she'd memorized in childhood. "'...and in the life everlasting.' For real, with all my heart." She squeezed his hand tightly.

Lochlan brushed back her hair with the long fingers of his other hand and tenderly kissed her forehead, her ear, her neck.

"Mmmm, goosebumps," she murmured, turning to look into his eyes. "Thank you for showing me how glorious the communion of bodies—even aging bodies—can be. I'm going to miss this. I'm going to miss you."

"I'll be along presently," he assured her. "For now, concentrate on what the Knights need you to do. It's not every historian who gets to actually make history."

"Promise me that when it's over, no matter what happens, you'll retrieve this sword and keep it from outsiders," Rebecca beseeched him. "Return it to its proper place above the fireplace as soon as you're able."

Lochlan stood and bowed deeply, as he had done once before in this same secret room. "I do so promise," he said, "upon my honor as a knight of the Griffins Keep and your obedient servant." He extended his hand and helped her to her feet.

"Time to go," he said.

# CHAPTER 27

In the center of the former Grand Salon, directly beneath the painted-over archangel fresco, five mature women gathered for a rite of sanction. The fresco's central orb survived, incorporated into a scepter held by one of several court jesters that now frolicked across the ceiling of the so-called Throne Room. The women stood in a circle, linked by arms around each other's shoulders, heads bowed. Margaret led the invocation.

"Glorious goddess, Divine Mother of all Nature, protect and guide our sister through the challenges which lie ahead, and grant her the courage to accomplish the mission which has been pre-ordained. Empower her through your grace to defend this place so vital to spirits and their transmigration. Give her the strength and the resolve she seeks to enable their afterlife journeys and our own, in the name of Your Love and Light."

"Amen," they said in unison.

In the ensuing moment of silence, the historian thought back to the morning of the vernal equinox in the very room where they now stood, the rays of the rising sun shining directly upon the Grand Entrance, the liquid light emanating from the glowing headpiece of the Dominion's scepter and coalescing around her. She marveled again at all that had been set into motion by men with a secret knowledge of the cosmos and an ancient respect for phenomena beyond explanation. She knew without question that the Griffins Keep truly was a sacred place, created to bridge the straits between planes of reality. The elements in play for more than a century were now seriously threatened, and, for reasons she might never understand, it fell to her to preserve the sanctuary.

This was right.

She was ready.

Breaking the physical connection to the others, she raised an arm above her head, open palm outward.

"Crone power!" she cried with a new bravado.

"Crone power!" the others echoed. Maureen and Molly and Rosslyn each grinned and slapped her palm with their own, high-five style. Margaret followed suite, though she couldn't quite manage a smile.

"You got it, girl," she said. "Show these bastards what they're messing with when they mess with the Griffins Keep."


"Protest the Prostitution of Denver's Great Lady" read the placards carried by members of the Denver Women's Press Club, the Past Timers, and like-minded compatriots as they paraded back and forth outside the Carson Street entrance. "Boycott the Griffins Keep!"

The adamant protesters hindered but could not block representatives of city government, the Chamber of Commerce, Downtown Denver Partnership, and sundry media reps arriving to cover the unveiling of the much anticipated new hotel lobby feature. Press releases had promised: "Moments after the artesian well water supply to the old Griffins Fountain is shut off forever, TITHE leadership will unveil a specially commissioned sculpture and wave pool in the atrium lobby. The life-sized statue honors Chad Tagawa's spirit of adventure and entrepreneurial innovation."

The new wave pool, a bit nearer the front desk than the Griffin Fountain, had taken three weeks to install. The sculpture had been kept under wraps—literally—since its arrival and installation just a few days earlier. Rumor had it that the piece depicted the TITHE founder on a surfboard. It had, of course, nothing to do with the medieval castle theme the new Keep was going for. It had everything to do with Chad's ego.

A popular Beach Boys tribute band was on hand for the high-profile occasion. AV crews installed large screens in two corners of the lobby at third-floor level to provide enhanced views of the proceedings to all. They checked the sound. The pseudo-Beach

274

Boys kicked in. And the local power brokers and boosters streamed inside.

On the seventh-floor balcony, Rebecca Bridger prepared to play the role predestined for her decades before. She was dressed in all vintage black, as if for a ghost tour. The *myotragus Balearicus* horn, suspended on a golden chain, dangled between her breasts. Thrust into the back elastic waistband of her skirt and concealed beneath her taffeta peplum jacket, the bronze sword of the third griffin awaited its call to action.

When the band took a break about twenty minutes later, the podium microphone crackled to life.

"Welcome, everyone, to a historic day at the Griffins Keep. I'm Stan Tagawa, CEO of Tagawa International Theatres, Hotels, and Entertainment. And it is my great pleasure to introduce my nephew, the founder of TITHE, Chad Tagawa."

"Hey, everybody!" Chad shouted out. "Make sure you help yourselves to beer and mojitos at the bar here by the Grand Staircase. And we've got awesome munchies being passed by some of our Keepettes. How great are they in their serving wench outfits? This is just a taste of how fun and accessible the stuffy old Griffins Keep is becoming as the newest TITHE property. We're really proud of the transformation we've already accomplished, and we promise there're more big changes on the way. Be sure to scope out these architects' renderings of the new Royal Tower, coming soon."

Flashes flashed. TV cameras panned the scene. Chad returned the mic to his uncle.

"Of all the TITHE properties Chad has acquired throughout the world over the past fifteen years, the Griffins Keep is without a doubt the most impressive. That's why we've chosen it as the spot for this statue, fittingly honoring Chad, his free-spirited lifestyle, and his mega-success. We've chosen today—June 21, the summer solstice—because, as a surfer, Chad has always followed the sun. But before we unveil the sculpture, it's time to say good-bye to a remnant of The Keep's old glory days, the Griffin Fountain."

Unexpectedly, several attendees booed.

"Now, now," Stan said, raising his hand to silence objections. "I know the crusty old relic was beloved by generations of Keep visitors. Many of you may have even tossed a wishing coin or two into it. But it's an archaic reminder of a former time, a time when

275

the Griffins Keep was off-limits to all but the privileged elite. TITHE properties are family friendly properties, affordable accommodations and entertainment for average travelers. Our new branding calls for a new focus. I'm going to turn it over now to The Keep's general manager, Mickey Branson."

Branson stepped up and took the mic. "Let me just add my own welcome to all of you who've taken the time out of your busy day to help us usher in a new era for a Denver icon. As you may know, the Griffin Fountain has been fed since the hotel opened by The Keep's own artesian well, more than 700 feet beneath us. Great bit of trivia. But maintaining our own water company in this day and age makes no sense, practically or economically. We're proud to partner with Denver Water from this day forward to supply all the hotel's water needs. Denver Water reps, where are you? John, Bill—great to have you guys here today. And to symbolize this historic shift, we're kicking off the unveiling by shutting off this fossil of a fountain."

In the hotel basement, Lochlan answered his radio page. "OK, MacKenzie. Close 'er off in ten."

"Copy that." Lochlan counted backwards. *5, 4, 3, 2...1.* With effort, he cranked the steel wheel that sealed off the flow of water from the artesian well to the fountain. The last remaining channel from the spiritual portal was blocked. None could enter or depart.

Lochlan drew a deep breath and blew it out, "It's up to you now, Rebecca," he said.

Above him in the lobby, Mickey Branson declared, "Out with the old!" The Griffin Fountain spluttered and burbled its last. If he expected applause, he was disappointed.

"And in with the new!" Yanking the cord that held the sculpture drape, Branson revealed the bronze statue of a surfer on his board, knees bent, arms outstretched for balance, long hair blown back. It probably resembled Chad twenty years and fifty pounds ago. A mechanism below the turquoise-tinted pool at the base began to undulate, creating waves that splashed against one side before disappearing to be recirculated.

The crowd politely golf-clapped.

"An awesome monument to an awesome dude," Branson proclaimed, draping an arm around Chad's shoulders. "May it inspire visitors to the Griffins Keep for the next century."

"Thank you, Mickey. I've gotta say it's pretty cool," Chad said, beaming. "And thank you all again for coming. We hope you'll

276

stick around for more brews and snacks on the house. Be sure to pick up your souvenir miniature of my statue from the kiosk by the bar—Just $19.95!"

"Mr. Branson!" a reporter from *Westword* called out. "Can you tell us what's going to happen to the old fountain?"

The GM hadn't invited questions. Wasn't prepared. "Well now, we haven't really thought about that. I suppose we could auction it off, like we did with the other artifacts a few months ago. Why, do you want it?" He laughed. The reporter didn't.

"Can you make wishes in the wave pool?" another reporter inquired.

"No need!" Branson replied cheerily. "Here at the new Griffins Keep, we make all your wishes come true! And right now, I'll bet I'm not the only one wishing to hear more tune-age from the Beach Boyz. How 'bout it, guys?"

With that, the band kicked in, effectively shutting down any more questions from the media.

High above it all, Rebecca closed her eyes and began the Kabbalah chant Rosslyn had taught her to summon the spirits of the Templar Knights. The horn talisman grew warm against her skin. She felt their presence. Electrifying. Empowering. The Good Sir Knights could not physically act to preserve the place they protected. But she could.

She was the conduit, the conductor, channeling their powers in defense of The Keep. Rebecca opened her eyes, clutched the balcony railing in the center of the triangular building's hypotenuse, and cast her gaze upward to the skylight, where midday solstice sunrays were endlessly refracted by the stained-glass patterns. She set her sight on the center of the ceiling and focused fiercely.

Like Pete's silver teaspoon, the supportive steel framework below the skylight began to vibrate. Almost imperceptible at first, it quickly increased in modulation, creating a harmonic resonance that would have been heard by those below had the band been less amplified.

A few who felt the disturbing vibrations looked up. Rebecca couldn't think about potential collateral damage in the lobby below. She concentrated completely on the support beams. The vibrations intensified. The supports shuddered. Within moments, they would give way.

*Now.* The command emanated from ancient voices inside her head. Rebecca pulled the third Griffin's sword from her waistband and pointed it dead center.

She did not imagine the stream of sparks that shot from the sword tip. The shock of it knocked her backwards into the wall and off her feet. She dropped the sword and watched as what happened next seemed to unfold in slow motion.

The heavy winch detached. It plummeted 100 feet to the lobby below. The statue of Chad Tagawa was decapitated. Chad himself and the uncle who stood beside him in self-congratulatory satisfaction were crushed beneath the huge iron hoist.

Pandemonium ensued, as shards of broken skylight showered down upon the panicked guests. In the blind rush for the two lobby exits, a woman with a walker fell and was nearly trampled.

The fire alarms sounded. Lochlan, Maureen, Rosslyn, Margaret and Molly herded people to safety, making sure everyone got out before the next stage of the retribution.

Rebecca struggled to stand as the Knights' spirits surged within her. The horn suspended over her heart grew almost too hot to bear. Their collective energy was astonishing, intoxicating. She imagined for a moment she could fly were she to leap from the railing. She looked down upon the lobby chaos with detached curiosity and surreal calm.

"Ladies and gentlemen!" Mickey Branson's voice came over the rarely used hotel-wide public address system. "Don't panic," he said, barely managing to suppress the panic in his own breast. "We seem to be experiencing some sort of earth tremor. Please make your way to the nearest exit quickly and calmly. Do not attempt to use the elevators. Take the Grand Staircase or the service stairs inside the walls opposite the public elevators. Emergency personnel are on their way."

Guestroom doors flew open to the hallways. Frightened people, visitors and staff, hurried to obey Branson's directions and evacuate the premises. No one on the seventh floor stopped to question the small woman in black, making her way not toward the stairs, but rather toward a predesignated spot on the balcony. Ten panels right of one corner post. Thirteen panels left of the other. She positioned herself deliberately behind the inverted balcony panel and turned toward the corner high above the concierge desk.

278

For the first time she saw what the mediums had described. Incredibly bright, constantly swirling, and pulsing with the same harmonic resonance as the building's steel frame. Numberless entities. Shining power. Elemental and ethereal. The Keep's essence. Given form with stone and iron, consecrated by bone and blood. Empowered by sacred geometry, golden treasure, solstice sunlight, and—until minutes ago—subterranean waters.

*This sanctuary shall not be defiled.* She fell to her knees before the blazing phenomena, grasped the handle of the third Griffin's sword with both hands and thrust it aloft.

"Make of me your instrument!" The strange phrasing came naturally form somewhere deep in her subconscious.

A bolt of blinding light flashed from the guardian multitude and set the sword ablaze with heatless flame. Emboldened, Rebecca stood and aimed the blade at the mezzanine balcony far below. Lightning burst from its tip, and the sigil-smattered carpet caught fire. Within seconds, the black lacquered walls were consumed. Spectral spiritual sparks within the flames evinced the complicity of the hotel's ghosts. Their purge was begun.

Still clutching the handle with both hands, Rebecca swung the blazing sword in a wide arc around the atrium mezzanine, then up to the third floor, continuing the broad sweeps, level by level, to the sixth floor.

Two papier mache griffins suspended in midair combusted phoenix-like, ashes in an instant. Huge sections of the skylight directly above had given way with the winch, exposing glimpses of the glass-bricked top floor through shard-rimmed gaps. Directing her weapon first below, then through the openings, she sparked the devastation of the executive suites on eight and nine, until the only floor not ablaze was the one on which she stood.

Continuing vibrations of the metal framework spawned an unearthly symphony that swelled throughout the structure, resonating beyond the sirens and the screams. The steel skeleton sang as flames danced from room to room, obliterating all contents. In an instant, Rebecca saw them feeding the blaze, the spirits of the Griffins Keep. They morphed and melded, focused and faded, flashed and flickered out, reclaiming their sanctuary.

What seemed like forever was essentially over in less than nine minutes.

The flames that had engulfed the sword suddenly spluttered out. The vibrations stopped. The Knights' spirits abandoned their

279

temporary vessel and returned to their rounds. Rebecca collapsed, exhausted, on the balcony floor.

Suffocating smoke billowed throughout the Griffins Keep atrium. The door of the guestroom directly behind Rebecca burst open and a fresh breeze blew through its broken windows to clear the air. With impressive efficiency, the Keep's thirteen ventilation shafts worked to remove the smoke not sucked through the broken skylight, which acted as a central chimney. A shaft of sunlight beamed through a space in the remaining stained glass and fell directly onto the silenced Griffin Fountain.

EMTs loaded the Tagawas' bodies onto stretchers and hustled them out of the building, kicking the severed statue head out of the way. Other than Rebecca, only a handful of firefighters remained to witness the finale.

The fountain gushed back to life, shooting water six stories into the air. Glorious sprays and droplets glittered like diamonds in the sunbeam.

From the fountain's center urn, something other than water began to bubble.

Glowing globes.

Shimmering energies.

Orbs.

*Are they visible to anyone else?*

The bright, translucent baubles began to spin around the Griffin geyser in a mesmerizing double-helix pattern, rising upward. Like flocks of birds, they reeled in perfect synchronization, the first of them rising to make room for more emerging from the fountain's depths. And more. And more.

Below the fragmented skylight, the initial wave of orbs spread out at the seventh-floor level. Soon a second wave hovered below that. The orbs drifted in shifting planes like the mass ascension of hot air balloons in a box formation. Hundreds of them. Layer upon layer. A few darted about the atrium like ecstatic fireflies. The joy, the relief, and the gratitude emanating from the entities washed through her.

Rebecca understood somehow that they were all there— Harrison Griffin, Edward Brookings, Sybil Thorne, Collier Hendricks, Marjory Crispin, Charlotte Woods, Max Barnes, and numberless other spirits—some tied to The Keep, some just passing through.

280

The fountain's eruption suddenly dropped to a burble. The orbs throughout the atrium wavered in anticipation.

Time hit Pause.

Weakened but strangely euphoric, Rebecca dragged herself across the balcony floor to grasp a filigreed iron panel and peer down upon the scene below. A new wave of orbs began to arise from the point where the copper griffins' wingtips touched above the urn. These moved more deliberately, shone more brilliantly than the others. Indigo. Iridescent. She watched in wonder as they rotated faster and faster.

*They're coming for me.* The breeze that had dispersed the smoke had no effect on their trajectory. *I know them. I've always known them.*

Lochlan rushed into the now deserted lobby with Maureen and frantically scanned the topmost open floor.

"Can you see her? What's happening?" he demanded of the psychic.

Mo found she was incapable of answering as she watched the whirling orbs ascend to the seventh floor where they lifted a small, limp figure dressed in black from the balcony. Surrounding the form like a swirling funnel, they enveloped it in light.

A cry of elation. A flash of transmutation. The dark garment bundle dropped back to the floor beside a charred bronze sword. Riding the ray of solstice sunlight through the fractured glass ceiling, the deep blue orbs vanished, their host increased by one.

# CHAPTER 28

"We had four engines on the scene in under six minutes, and of course our priority was getting everyone out," the fire chief told reporters in the aftermath of the Griffins Keep incident. "It is a testament to the courage and skill of our firefighters that practically every guest and employee was evacuated to safety. The few who were trapped in the service stairwell all survived with minor complications from smoke inhalations."

The chief shook his head, still struggling to process it all himself.

"The fire moved so fast. It didn't behave like any fire I've ever seen. Our preliminary investigation seems to indicate that the flames in some cases went right through doors to the guestrooms without burning them. As you may know, the superstructure of the hotel is all metal and concrete, so it's essentially fireproof. But every floor except one and seven was gutted. Furniture, carpets, window coverings—all destroyed. And I understand TITHE had just invested millions in major redecoration.

"The top two floors fared even worse than the lower levels, since many of the interior walls and the floor between them were constructed later, with wooden supports rather than the older fire-resistant terra cotta. The ninth floor in the 45-degree corners was completely destroyed."

"What about casualties from the falling glass?"

"Surprisingly few and surprisingly minor," the department spokesman was pleased to report. "It's almost as if everyone in the lobby was shielded by some sort of invisible umbrella—except, of course, the unfortunate Tagawas."

"Chief, you said 'practically' every guest and employee got out," a reporter sought to clarify. "Any fatalities?"

The fire official hesitated before answering. "Well, yes and no. Two of the firefighters discovered an older woman collapsed by the balcony railing on the seventh floor. Of course they administered CPR, did everything they could to revive her, got her down to an ambulance immediately. Tragically, it was too late."

"Was she a guest of the Griffins Keep?"

"No. We're told she worked here. We're withholding her identity pending notification of kin, of course. I should add that her death doesn't appear to have been related to the fire."

"Are you saying she died of natural causes?"

"That's correct. I understand she was in her early 60s. Heart attack or stroke, we think. Probably happened right before the incident."

"What about the two men crushed in the lobby by something that fell from the skylight, just before the fire started? Do you think their deaths and the fire were related?"

Denver's chief of police stepped in to answer this one. "It seems likely the freak accident and the subsequent fire were both caused by the same phenomenon. Several witnesses have reported feeling some sort of earth tremor right before the winch came loose from its moorings and took the lives of Stan and Chad Tagawa, the uncle-and-nephew team that helmed TITHE, Inc., owners and operators of the Griffins Keep since last October. We have no reason to suspect foul play at this point. Let's just say the tremors—or whatever they were—could certainly have also ruptured a gas line, disconnected wires, created a spark. It's much too soon to draw any conclusions."

The Griffins Keep manuscript collection at History Colorado's Hart Library was so popular with researchers that they had to make reservations weeks in advance to view the materials.

"No special consideration for relatives of past employees?" the 40-ish woman had asked hopefully. "My aunt was the hotel historian twenty years ago."

284

The librarian had politely ignored her attempt to jump the queue. "Sorry, no exceptions. We'll contact you in April to confirm your viewing date."

Hannah Spencer waited patiently. It wasn't like she needed access right away for an assignment or anything, although it might lead to a great story for her cyber-mag. This was personal.

"I remember your aunt," the librarian confided when she confirmed the research appointment with Hannah three weeks later. "Took one of her 'ghost' tours of The Keep when I was about twelve. I'll never forget it. She tried to tell us she was wearing the bewitched hair of the dead former historian and that it gave her all of that woman's knowledge by sinking its roots into her brain. Creeped me out like you wouldn't believe."

Hannah smiled. "Sounds like Aunt Becky," she'd said, shaking her head. "Probably a good thing she had no kids of her own. But my sibs and I always loved her imaginative storytelling."

When the day arrived, Hannah was escorted to the research room and given a pair of special gloves for handling the artifacts. Over the years, she had gone through many different boxes of Keep files, broadly sampling ephemera of the hotel's early years. In this age of virtual realities, tangible objects were still unmatched in their power to evoke the past. Old banquet menus, photographs, correspondence, advertisements. They all fascinated her with their glimpse into a more elegant, more discerning era. But her mission today was focused. She had requested one of the old guest registers. Specifically, the volume which included June 21, 1917—the day the hotel had closed due to a mysterious "explosion" apparently related to tapping a deeper aquifer for the artesian well. Hannah had a theory she was ready to test.

Carefully, she turned the fragile pages covered with distinctive fountain-penned guest signatures until she came to the one stamped with the date in question. Unconsciously holding her breath, she scanned down the columns for any entry that was not like the others.

There.

Hannah rubbed her eyes to be sure she was seeing it right. In the column desk clerks had used to tick off guests when they checked out, one entry was not followed by a checkmark.

Her scrutiny shifted to the signature itself.

She sat back in her chair. After a long moment, she pulled her personal electronic device from a pocket and navigated to the photos.

Hannah had inherited her Aunt Becky's Bancroft Booklets, the inexpensive little paperbacks that had romanticized and popularized Colorado history for mid-twentieth-century readers. Young Becky had carefully inscribed each booklet at the top of the title page, and Hannah had photographed one of them: "Property of Miss Rebecca Holcomb."

In retrospect, Hannah would not remember what had prompted her speculation. But she would never forget the moment it was confirmed. The book inscription, the signature of the guest who never checked out on the day of that unexplained phenomenon—The very same.

Rebecca's name. Rebecca's handwriting.

Rebecca's destiny.


"As you can see, the main entrance on the Grand Avenue side of the building has been reopened, easily accessed via elevator from a tunnel under Grand, connected to the parking structure across the street."

"Capital! The overdue restoration of Mr. Brooking's masterful vision."

"Thank goodness arriving guests have a clear view to the Front Desk again."

"A tunnel, you say? I seem to recall something like that running under Carson to the Silken Rose. Not that I had any personal knowledge of it...."

"That old tunnel has been restored, as has the tunnel running from The Keep sub-basement to the Capitol, for those who enjoy that sort of thing," the hotel tour guide explained.

"Always liked that third griffin with his sword above the Grand Fireplace."

"So lovely to see all the velvet sofas and potted palms back in the atrium. Afternoon Tea should be served in the eighth-floor Ladies Ordinary, not the middle of the hotel lobby."

"The eighth floor has been returned to its original grandeur," the guide assured them. "The two-story Ordinary, as well as the Ballroom and Banquet Hall, feature all the elegant appointments that graced those spaces when the Griffins Keep opened."

"I confess I'm disappointed," a guest groused. "Art Deco was the Bees' Knees. Much more streamlined than this pretentious Italian Renaissance and fussy Victorian décor. A step backwards, if you ask me."

"Well, of course, everyone has different tastes, and you can't please them all," their hostess granted. "When the hotel was gutted by fire—witnessed by many of you, I believe - Mrs. Kuhrsfeld-Tagawa seized the opportunity to recreate the interior as it had been in the beginning. With the deaths of her husband and nephew, she became the major stockholder in TITHE and the guiding force in The Keep's renaissance. Her choices held sway, and most people have applauded the hotel's return to gracious hospitality and the charm of a bygone era."

"'Bygone era,' you say? What balderdash! Classic elegance is timeless."

"I still think it's appalling that the help are better dressed than the clientele. Do the guest chambers no longer include mirrors?"

The patient guide tried to rein-in her flighty tour guests. "Now I really must ask those of you who keep drifting off to kindly stay with the group," she admonished. First-time visitors and those long associated with the Griffins Keep were generally courteous and attentive. It was the guests from more recently who always seemed to make a fuss, fretting about what they no longer recognized. The historian understood their disorientation and tried her best to gently acquaint them with the hotel's renovated context.

"Here on the mezzanine we'll see one major alteration to the original layout." She guided them into the 45-degree corner which once housed the Silver Spoon Club. "Good evening, Curtis," she said to the entryway greeter. "Just bringing a tour through." He doffed his railroad conductor's cap to the guests as they passed.

"This new hotel museum showcases historical Griffins Keep items collected, retrieved, or donated by past employees and friends of the hotel. Many of them were preserved only through the efforts of dedicated associates who understood their importance to future appreciation of The Keep's character. You are, of course, most welcome to return and linger here longer after our tour concludes." Her guests bounced from one artifact to another around the room, lighting up with personal memories.

287

"I can't tell you how many times I polished that silver coffee urn."

"Look, dear! Here's the postcard we sent Fanny in 1903!"

"It is the cigarette holder I found on the room service tray that night."

"I helped carry that barber chair into the sub-basement hiding place."

"Oh, these marvelous military bandsmen! All fifteen of them on display together again. And they look as good as new."

"Mrs. Kuhrsfeld-Tagawa herself secretly rescued the bandsmen when they were slated for auction," the docent explained. "She remembered them from her childhood and invested a great deal of money in their painstaking conservation out of personal love for the figures."

Exiting the museum space, their guide cautioned, "As we move around the hotel, those of you with special sensitivity may encounter some of The Keep's corporeans. There's no reason to fear them. They're probably just as leery of contact as you are, and they're easily spooked. Please bear in mind that the cameras they use are very fast. Take care not to get caught in one of their photographs if you can avoid it. It seems to excite them, and then they argue about what—if anything—they've captured. It can be very disruptive to hotel business."

In low murmurs, all agreed to move about with discretion. "We certainly don't want to interfere with the daily commerce."

"The Griffins Keep must continue as the premiere meeting place and waystation for discerning sojourners like ourselves— from everywhere."

"And everywhen."

"'Best Rest in the West.' Still a damned good motto, I reckon."

The perennial tour guide glowed. "As it was purposed, may it ever be," she concurred in benediction.

# ABOUT THE AUTHOR

Claryn Vaile is a Colorado native with a passion for local history and historical architecture. She has served on the faculty of Metropolitan State University and is a member of History Colorado, Historic Denver, Inc. and the Denver Woman's Press Club. She is fascinated by the paranormal and loves to stay in historic hotels, purportedly haunted or otherwise

# ACKNOWLEDGEMENTS

This book would not have been possible without the extraordinary insights of some very special people. I am sincerely grateful to Stephanie, Mary, Marilyn, Laura, and Douglas for nudging me gently toward new ways of perceiving the lingering traces of history and those who preceded us.

## Other Exquisite Fiction from D. X. Varos, Ltd.

*Therese Doucet:*    THE PRISONER OF THE CASTLE OF ENLIGHTENMENT

*Samuel Ebeid:*    THE HEIRESS OF EGYPT
THE QUEEN OF EGYPT

*G. P. Gottlieb:*    BATTERED

*Phillip Otts:*    A STORM BEFORE THE WAR
THE SOUL OF A STRANGER
*(Oct. 2020)*

*Erika Rummel:*    THE INQUISITOR'S NIECE
THE ROAD TO GESUALDO

*J. M. Stephen:*    NOD
INTO THE FAIRY FOREST
RISE OF THE HIDDEN PRICE
*(Nov. 2020)*

*Felicia Watson:*    WHERE THE ALLEGHENY MEETS THE MONONGAHELA
WE HAVE MET THE ENEMY
SPOOKY ACTION AT A DISTANCE

*Daniel A. Willis:*    IMMORTAL BETRAYAL
IMMORTAL DUPLICITY
IMMORTAL REVELATION
PROPHECY OF THE AWAKENING
FARHI AND THE CRYSTAL DOME

CPSIA information can be obtained
at www.ICGtesting.com
Printed in the USA
LVHW041231040522
717765LV00001B/1

9 781941 072769